Born in Normandy in 1850, Guy de Maupassant showed little initial inclination for literature. He led an outdoor life as a child, and at twenty he went to Paris to study law. It was only after his discharge from the army at the end of the Franco-Prussian War that he began to write in earnest, submitting his efforts to Gustave Flaubert, who assumed the role of Maupassant's mentor and refused to allow him to publish his still-imperfect work. By 1880, Maupassant had completed his apprenticeship; his first published story, *"Boule de Suif,"* was acclaimed a masterpiece. Thus commenced a decade of extraordinary literary productivity and popular success, during which he was to write six novels and over three hundred stories, as well as essays, articles, and travel books. His personal life, however, was less fortunate. He was plagued increasingly by headaches, fits of blindness, and melancholia, a deterioration attributable in great part to the growing ravages of a disease contracted as a youth. By 1890, he had entered a mental darkne from which he was never to emerge. He was com to an asylum in 1892; the following year

SELECTED STORIES

by

Guy de Maupassant

TRANSLATED BY
Andrew R. MacAndrew

WITH A FOREWORD BY
Edward D. Sullivan

A MERIDIAN CLASSIC

NEW AMERICAN LIBRARY

A DIVISION OF PENGUIN BOOKS USA INC., NEW YOR
PUBLISHED IN CANADA BY
PENGUIN BOOKS CANADA LIMITED, MARKHAM, ONTA

NAL BOOKS ARE AVAILABLE AT QUANTITY DISCOUNTS WHEN USED TO PROMOTE PRODUCTS OR SERVICES. FOR INFORMATION PLEASE WRITE TO PREMIUM MARKETING DIVISION, NEW AMERICAN LIBRARY, 1633 BROADWAY, NEW YORK, NEW YORK, 10019.

Library of Congress Catalog Card Number: 83-62756

This collection previously appeared in a Signet Classic edition.

MERIDIAN CLASSIC TRADEMARK REG. U.S. PAT. OFF. AND FOREIGN COUNTRIES
REGISTERED TRADEMARK–MARCA REGISTRADA
HECHO EN WINNIPEG, CANADA

SIGNET, SIGNET CLASSIC, MENTOR, ONYX, PLUME, MERIDIAN AND NAL BOOKS are published *in the United States* by New American Library, a division of Penguin Books USA Inc., 1633 Broadway, New York, New York 10019, and *in Canada* by Penguin Books Canada Limited, 2801 John Street, Markham, Ontario L3R 1B4

First Meridian Classic Printing, May, 1984

4 5 6 7 8 9 10 11 12

PRINTED IN CANADA

CONTENTS

FOREWORD

Maupassant has always been a problem to literary critics because he provides so few peculiarities or eccentricities for them to deal with. The elegant economy of his narrative line, so admired and imitated by other writers of stories, caused him to be devalued by the critics, especially in France, where, although widely read, he has never been highly esteemed. For many Frenchmen his popular success was reason enough to deny him a solid literary reputation, while others believed he simply had nothing to say to them. His highly perfected talent for compression, together with the apparent simplicity of his style, have given rise to a certain number of misconceptions about him.

Maupassant obviously set great store by keenness of observation, and his training under Flaubert perfected his natural gifts. It has therefore been easy to claim that he was nothing but an observer who saw only the surface of life, who was interested merely in the visible and superficial aspects of things, or in the exact way—as he himself noted—in which one cab-horse differs from all other cab-horses. Actually, as one reads his stories, it becomes clear that he was obsessively concerned not with what can be observed, but with what is hidden from view: with precisely those aspects of life and character that can only be inferred or that even elude our grasp entirely. Deeply rooted in the mind of this most realistic of writers was the sense that reality escapes him, that not everything meets the eye.

Basic to his art is the belief that appearances deceive: our senses register inaccurately the phenomena of the world, we fool ourselves even as we try to fool others, and we live our lives surrounded by ignorance, hypocrisy, and subterfuge. We dimly sense realms that lie beyond the visible—realms which, though closed to us, fascinate us. Maupassant must be included among those who were haunted by the need to plunge into the unknown—but at the same time he was fearful of what might be disclosed. His thirst for knowledge of the way the mind works led him to an interest in the psychological investigations carried on by his scientific contemporaries, like Charcot; and to a preoccupation, expressed in a substantial number of stories, with the themes of the fearful, the unknown, and the supernatural. In these stories we find him intent upon probing far beneath the surface of what is conventionally called reality. His dread of being deluded drove him to depict the world as it is and not as it purports to be. He was driven to the depths because the surface deceives: People protect themselves with masks; society screens itself by hypocrisy. The task of a writer, as he saw it, was to lift those masks and remove that screen by using the highly perfected brief narrative as an instrument with which to reveal, for a fleeting instant, the real basis on which human society operates.

As we look at Maupassant's career, we are conscious of a strange and terrible drama that underlies it, for his life and works drive inexorably to a dramatic conclusion. The chief element in this drama is not, however, the fact that Maupassant died in an insane asylum of general paralysis presumably caused by syphilis contracted in his youth, nor is it the fact that a young man of great talent achieved rapid success, wrote a large number of very remarkable works, many of them enduring masterpieces, but was cut down at the very height of his career. The real drama of his decline lies in the fact that he was aware of it as he neared the end. He thrashed about, struggling against violent headaches and fits of blindness, hallucinations and despair, still writing stories and novels —all of which bear in various ways the marks of the struggle he was waging. We can see in them his agonizing sense of bewilderment—a sense of having lost the road—and a nostalgic desire to return to the beginning, to start over again. This is why in the last years of his life, though he was only forty-three when he died, he evoked and imitated the abundant and fruitful years of his early career; this is why his last works echo his earliest achievement in such a haunting way.

Maupassant's literary debut was closely bound to a particularly painful moment in the history of France: the French defeat of 1870. The first sentences of his first great success, "*Boule de Suif,*" evoke a precise historical moment—the entrance of the Prussian troops into Rouen. The military defeat provided the material for a literary triumph: "*Boule de Suif,*" written in 1880, ten years after the disastrous events it describes, was immediately recognized as a masterpiece, and its author was launched on his meteoric career, which had but ten years to run. In 1890, Maupassant's last coherent written words before madness closed in evoked that defeat of 1870 as if he felt that the same magic words could ward off catastrophe and turn it into victory.

His early years gave no hint of his talent. Born in Normandy in 1850, he spent his youth there, happy and exuberant, much fonder of sea and countryside than of school. He was never a bookish person and there was nothing unusual about his youth and background except for the fact that Gustave Flaubert, author of *Madame Bovary*, was a close friend of the family—which turned out to be a matter of some consequence.

When he was twenty, he was sent to Paris to study law—studies that were soon interrupted by the outbreak of the Franco-Prussian War. He enlisted, spent a dull winter as a private in a badly equipped company in the forest of Les Andelys, and was involved in the general retreat and disaster. His letters, written just before the collapse, express his utmost confidence in a French victory. The defeat came as a profound shock to him, and these memories of humiliation remained with him to the end, and were recalled again and again to be transformed into stories.

After his demobilization, he returned to Paris, where his father had found him a poorly paid job as a government clerk in the Naval Ministry. Then began a pattern of existence which furnished the substance of many later stories: weekdays given over to routine clerical work and all the problems of surviving on his meager salary; Saturdays spent boating on the river Seine, for he loved the river and was immensely proud of his skill as an oarsman; Sundays spent lunching at Flaubert's, hearing the latter's criticism of his first literary efforts, and attending the gathering of writers and artists who regularly assembled there on Sunday afternoons—writers like Taine, Zola, Daudet, Turgenev, and once or twice, Henry James.

This was the period—the ten years before *"Boule de Suif"*—during which he absorbed the material for his stories and sharpened his technical proficiency. He published very little at this time, but was content to live, to observe, and to undergo a thorough apprenticeship under the master Flaubert. Out of this period came the material for most of his best stories, even those written toward the end of his life. They can be grouped, as they are in this edition, in categories which correspond to the different aspects of his own experiences. He had known Normandy and the Norman peasant from his childhood, and he recreated the landscape and the attitudes in such stories as "The Story of a Farm Girl," "Big Tony," and "A Piece of String." He had experienced the war of 1870, and he drew on these memories for *"Boule de Suif,"* "The Adventure of Walter Schnaffs," "The Two Friends," "The Little Soldier," and others. To these experiences he could add his knowledge of civil servants and the oddities of bureaucracy, and of the carefully measured world of the bourgeois, the inner workings of which are revealed in such stories as "The Necklace" and "Uncle Jules," grouped here under "Town Folk." From somewhere in his own private world he drew those stories of hallucinations and madness—"The Horla," "A Madman," "Who Knows?"—stories written by a sane man and an artist, but by one who had some intimate knowledge of such matters. In sharp contrast, he could draw on the most happy and carefree experiences of all—the hours spent boating on the Seine. In his passion for the Seine, he found a sense of life and joy, what he called "an instinctive visual love," and from this life he drew such charming and scandalous stories as *"Mouche."*

It is characteristic of Maupassant that, when he describes life on the river in *"Mouche,"* he is not only aware of the beauty of the scene but also of the darker and more unpleasant undercurrents. He recalls delicate sunrises, when the morning mist changes from dead white to a brilliant rose, and he evokes nights on the river under a silvery moon which invites the most magnificent dreams. Then he adds: "And all of that, symbol of our eternal illusion, was created for me on this foul water which ferried to the sea all the filth of Paris."

For Maupassant life on the river was not a static contemplation of beauty, but a rowdy, lusty existence with gay companions. Renoir's magnificent "Luncheon of the Boating Party" (which may be seen at the Phillips Gallery in Washington) captures some aspect of this world. Maupassant himself appears in Renoir's painting, along with Zola and others, and the canvas could easily serve as an illustration for some of Maupassant's stories.

The serious part of his life in these early years was his literary activity, his apprenticeship to Flaubert. Although Maupassant was a genuine disciple, and received a lengthy and thorough training at the feet of the master, he wrote works very different from Flaubert's in almost every way—precisely because the great lesson Flaubert taught was that one had to discover one's own originality. The best description of this relationship is in Maupassant's essay on the novel which is a preface to *Pierre et Jean:*

> For seven years I wrote verse, short stories, longer stories, and even a wretched play. Nothing survived. The master read everything, then, the following Sunday at lunch, developed his criticisms and inculcated into me gradually two or three principles which are the essence of his long and patient teaching. . . . It is necessary to examine long and carefully anything you wish to express in order to discover an aspect of it which has never been seen or noted by anyone. There is, in everything, an unexplored area, because we are accustomed to use eyes clouded by what others before us have seen. The slightest thing has something unknown about it. We must find it.

The emphasis from the beginning, the great lesson of the master, was to seek out what lay behind appearances, and this was a precept that Maupassant followed assiduously all his life and that is the basis of his art.

All of this activity and training produced results. By 1880 Maupassant was ready, and *"Boule de Suif"* was written quite independently of Flaubert, who did not see it until it was set up in proof, but who hailed it immediately as a masterpiece. There is a brief drama in the timing of all this, for Flaubert died only a few weeks after his disciple had set forth on his own independent career. *"Boule de Suif"* was written as one of a group of anti-militaristic stories by six different authors and published in one volume, *Les Soirées de Médan,* under the auspices of Émile Zola, whose story, "The Attack on the Mill," opened the collection. Maupassant's story marked him as a brilliant new writer and he was launched. Henceforth, he had no difficulty finding publishers for the steady stream of stories and articles that flowed from his pen. He wrote novels as well, because a writer has to show his skill in the longer form if he wants full recognition.

For ten years he produced abundantly, and during the period between 1880 and 1890 he wrote over three hundred short stories, six novels, and some two hundred articles and essays, as well as several travel books. As if this were not enough, an American publisher of Maupassant at the beginning of this century, Mr. Walter Dunne, tranquilly added to his edition some sixty-five stories not written by Maupassant at all, as Francis Steegmuller revealed in his biography, *Maupassant: a Lion in the Path*. These passed, in America, as genuine Maupassant stories for nearly fifty years and some were reprinted in various editions and anthologies, so that a large part of Maupassant's popular reputation in America rested until recently on a number of not very good and rather salacious stories that he never wrote.

Underlying the stories he actually did write is a set of basic assumptions about the way of the world from which derive the peculiar qualities and limitations of his art. These assumptions can be traced to the philosophers who, he claimed, were his favorites—Herbert Spencer and Schopenhauer. But it is doubtful that—interested in literary questions from the point of view of the practitioner and tolerating theory only when it could lead to a practical solution—he ever read extensively in either. His outlook on life was shaped to a large degree by the prevailing philosophical concepts as they circulated in conversation and was colored by his own peculiar brand of pessimism.

According to Maupassant, knowledge could be acquired only through the senses, which may distort more than they reveal. Unable to imagine something we have not already perceived, our imaginative power is restricted by the range of our experience, and thus we are, in his view, prisoners of our own senses, each living walled up in a world of his own, dependent for contact with others on these defective instruments of perception. From time to time, each person may well feel overwhelmed by a sense of solitude and futility, as Maupassant did; and it is precisely this loneliness which, as an artist, he expressed scrupulously and powerfully.

Such a view of life affected both the form and subject of

Maupassant's work. He was convinced that most men fail to use their senses properly and to take full advantage of even their admittedly limited possibilities; they remain blind and deaf to much that goes on about them. They are like a character in one of his stories, "one of those men who go through life without ever understanding what is below the surface, the nuances, the subtleties, who guess nothing, suspect nothing and cannot conceive that anyone might think, believe, judge, or act differently from themselves." Since ordinary people are imperceptive, it is the task of the writer, of the artist, to be a more penetrating observer than other men. He visualizes the world in accordance with the dictates of his own temperament, observes sharply, and then re-creates his own particular illusion of things; the great artist is one who imposes on humanity his own illusion or vision and makes men accept his illusion as truth.

Another consequence of this view of life is that psychological analysis in fiction becomes an absurdity. Since we are isolated from each other, no one can possibly know or imagine what goes on in the mind of anyone else; we cannot penetrate another's being. For Maupassant, the only valid technique consisted of observing the character from without, but observing him so sharply that one can deduce what goes on inside. He revealed the inner man by his external actions, holding any direct revelation to be false because it does not correspond to any conceivable action in life. This is the so-called objective method, derived from Flaubert, in which the writer refuses to play God but remains on the level of his characters, using only the observations that are normally available in life.

Although there is a certain gain in vitality in thus dealing with life on its own terms, it is clear that this technique imposes limitations. While the system is adequate, and even appropriate, to the simple and primitive minds of the people in many of Maupassant's short stories, it breaks down when called upon to deal with more complicated, more self-conscious, more introspective minds. Henry James, as might be expected, was acutely conscious of the loss when he wrote: "M. de Maupassant has simply skipped the whole reflective part of his men and women—that reflective part which governs conduct and produces character." Observer and artist though he was, Maupassant lacked the moral insight with which to probe very deeply into the uncharted regions of man's mind. What he lacked above all was faith in man; not content to observe merely the skin of life, he zealously set about stripping off the outer layer, but he did not believe that he would find anything but hypocrisy, dishonesty, and guile underneath. And his deepest obsession was his strong sense that there might be nothing at all beneath that surface: only hollowness—or horror. Eventually, for Maupassant, this vision of emptiness, this surfeit of sensation and the meaninglessness of matter were too shattering for him to endure. His personal life was a pursuit of pleasure, and in his stories he revealed his awareness of the hopelessness of the pursuit. Betrayed by what now might be considered naïve materialism, unable to conceive of salvation, attacked by disease, he fell into artistic sterility—a strong theme in his last works—and then into madness. "Maupassant's short story," wrote Theophil Spoerri, "is the perfected expression of an age which has lost itself amid things."

Whatever his limitations, his great merit, of course, is that the stories he tells are good. Even apart from the art of narration as developed by Maupassant, the events themselves will compel your attention. "However halting your words and insipid your rendering," observed Somerset Maugham, "you could not fail to interest your listeners if you told them the bare story of '*Boule de Suif*.'" His preoccupation with narrative distinguishes him sharply from Chekhov, who represents the opposite pole: the short story as atmosphere or feeling. Many of Chekhov's stories cannot be summed up or retold at all; their merits lie elsewhere.

Maupassant's stories are, of course, a good deal more than anecdotes, and there is a high degree of rather subtle art involved in their elaboration. The great principle of this art, which lacks those flamboyant peculiarities that inspire some critics, is its economy. There is hardly a word wasted as a scene is set, and people are brought to life with the utmost brevity.

Maupassant's particular view of life, with all its limitations and its consequences for his technique, is reflected in certain obsessive themes, all related to the idea of looking behind the mask. Masks and disguises abound in his stories in unnumerable forms: there is the direct use of an actual mask in a story that tells of an old man who wears one to costume balls, out of regret for his vanished youth; there are disguises that are discovered dramatically, as in "Uncle Jules," or used merely for trivial titillation, as in a story of the lady's maid who turns out to be a man wanted for criminal assault; and there is the fundamental exposure of society and its conventions in "*Boule de Suif*," the glimpse beneath the surface of the morals, the religion, and the patriotism of bourgeois and aristocrats alike. Cornudet, that wry commentator in *"Boule de Suif,"* goes on, in a sense, whistling the "Marseillaise" through the rest of Maupassant's work, a sardonic fanfare that marks the collapse of the walls of hypocritical convention. And yet, while Maupassant was obsessed by a passionate desire to penetrate the mask, he was also torn by a deep distress at the brutishness, the emptiness that lie behind it; in his own heart of darkness, like Conrad's Kurtz, he found only "the horror."

Beginning with his brilliant success in 1880, Maupassant flashed like a meteor across the literary horizon; but, after a few years of intense production, a decline set in as his eyes began to trouble him and as his headaches increased. Success had made of him a social lion and the diversions of Parisian society now claimed much of his energy. These activities, unlike the rowdy diversions of his youth, rarely enriched his work; his creativity diminished; he knew it and this increased his distress. His last two completed novels, *Strong as Death* and *Our Heart,* directly reflect the social circles in which he now moved and his own preoccupation, as a successful man of forty, with failure, sterility, and old age—an anguished portrait of the artist as an old man.

His career ended with one last burst of creative effort, which produced some first-rate short stories and the first chapter of a pathetic but powerful novel, *L'Angélus.* Taken together, the stories written in 1890 are a kind of summing-up of his whole career, each a symbolic representation of a facet of the author's life. *"Mouche,"* quoted earlier, is a brilliantly written poetic evocation of the old days of boating on the Seine, full of nostalgia for a vigorous, rowdy, uncomplicated life. *"Mouche"* looks backward, but another story, "Who Knows?," seems to look ahead, for it describes the hallucinations of a man who has voluntarily entered an insane asylum. "The Olive Grove," one of his best stories, picks up again the favorite theme of paternity tardily revealed, which was to Maupassant another form of the deceptiveness of appearances and the need to remove the masks. "Useless Beauty" is another attempt, this one successful, to deal with aristocratic society, a subject that he had failed to manage adequately in his novels.

In his last work, *L'Angélus,* he apparently felt the need to sweep away the present, to break with what he had been doing, to make a fresh start. What is most striking about this urge is the fact that the action of this last novel is set at *precisely* the same moment in history as his first and most famous story, the moment when the Prussians entered Rouen; even the sentences which evoke it echo closely the opening lines of "*Boule de Suif.*" Maupassant was thrusting back toward the beginning of his glory in a vain desire to retrace the route with a surer knowledge of where the pitfalls lay. He had gone back to the beginning; the circle was complete.

EDWARD D. SULLIVAN
Princeton University

BOULE DE SUIF
AND OTHER STORIES

I

PEASANTS

The Story of a Farm Girl

I

The weather was very good and so the farm people hurried through their meal and went back to the fields.

Rose, the maid, remained all alone in the large kitchen where the fire was dying in the stove under a cauldron full of hot water. Now and then she dipped into the cauldron for some hot water with which to wash the dishes. She washed them unhurriedly, often stopping to look at the two squares of light which the sun cast through the window onto the long kitchen table, revealing the defects in the glass.

Three venturesome hens were looking for crumbs under the chairs. The smells of the poultry yard and the warm fermented odors of the farm sheds poured in through the half-open door and cockcrows resounded in the silence of the scorching noon.

When the maid had washed the dishes, wiped the table, cleaned the stove, and put the plates away in a tall dresser next to the loudly ticking wooden clock, she drew a deep breath, feeling a little dizzy and oppressed without knowing why. She glanced at the blackened plaster of the walls, at the soot-covered rafters of the ceiling from which hung spider webs, smoked herrings, and strings of onions, and then sat down, a bit sickened by the smell that the day's heat brought out from the earthen floor on which so many things had spilled and dried throughout the years. In addition to that ancient odor, there was also the sour smell of the pans of milk set out to raise the cream in the next room. This was the time when she usually did some sewing, but she didn't feel up to it and instead went out to get a breath of fresh air.

Outside, in the bright warmth of the sun, a gentle languor came over her, and a feeling of well-being spread through her limbs.

Before the doorstep, the dunghill constantly exhaled a glimmering vapor. Hens wallowed in the dung, lying on their sides, some scratching with one claw in search of worms. A magnificent rooster strutted in their midst. Every now and then, he would pick one of them out and circle round her with a clucking call. The hen would rise nonchalantly and receive him with calm detachment, bending her legs and supporting him with her wings. Then she would shake her feathers, from which the dust flew out, and stretch herself out again on the dung, while the rooster crowed to register his triumph. And from all the neighboring poultry yards other roosters replied, as if they were all flinging amorous challenges at one another.

For a while the girl stared blankly at these maneuvers; then she lifted her eyes and was dazzled by the beauty of the apple trees, which were in bloom and completely white, like powdered wigs. At that moment an exuberant young colt galloped past her; it went twice around the field, along the tree-lined ditches, and then stopped dead and looked around as though surprised to be there all by itself.

She too felt like running and jumping, but also like stretching herself out and resting in the hot, motionless air. She took a few steps, hesitating, closing her eyes, gripped by an animal well-being. But then she went slowly to the henhouse to look for eggs. She found thirteen, picked them up, and took them to the house. As she was lining them up in the larder, the smells of the kitchen made her feel sick again, so she went out and sat in the grass.

The farmyard, surrounded by trees, seemed asleep. The tall grass, in which yellow dandelions stood out like bright lights, was a vivid green, the new green of the very young spring. The shadows of the apple trees contracted into small circles and lay at their feet; over the roofs of the farm sheds with saber-leaved irises growing out of their thatches, a slight haze floated, as though the moisture of the stables and storerooms was escaping through the straw.

The girl walked toward the shed where carts and buggies were kept. Nearby was a green gully with a large, fragrant patch of violets in it, and beyond it there was an open view of the countryside—wheat fields with clumps of trees here and there, and scattered groups of fieldworkers with their little white horses pulling plows guided by inch-high peasants, looking like tiny puppets in the distance.

The servant girl got herself a bundle of hay from the barn and threw it into the gully to use as a seat. But as she was still not feeling very well, she undid it, spread the hay, and stretched herself out on her back, her hands under her head.

Gradually her eyes closed and a delightful torpor descended upon her. She was about to fall fast asleep when she felt two hands creeping gently over her bosom. Abruptly, she sat up. It was Jacques, a big, strapping farmhand from Picardy who had long been pursuing her with his attentions. He had been working in the sheepfold when he saw her lie down in the shade, and he had come up stealthily, holding his breath, his eyes shining, bits of straw sticking in his hair.

He tried to kiss her but she was as strong as he, and she slapped him. Slyly, he begged her pardon. They sat down then, side by side, and talked like two friends. They spoke of the weather and how good it was for the crops, of the signs that showed they were going to have a good year, of their master who, they agreed, was a nice man, and then of their neighbors, of everyone in the district, of themselves, of their native village, of their childhood, of their parents whom they had left behind—maybe for good. All these memories moved her, and he, with his one-track mind, drew closer to her and rubbed himself against her side, trembling, seized by a wild desire. She said:

"It's a long time since I seen my ma. It ain't no fun to be away from her so long."

And her eye wandered off into the distance, toward the deserted village that could be seen to the north.

Suddenly he seized her by the neck and kissed her once more. She hit him full in the face with clenched fist. It was a powerful blow and his nose bled. He got up and leaned his head against a tree. Then she felt sorry for him. She got up, walked over to him, and asked:

"Does it hurt bad?"

But he just laughed. It was nothing, except that she'd managed to land her blow right in the middle of his face. He kept murmuring:

"Ah, you sure got some punch there. . . ."

And he looked at her with admiration and respect. His feeling for her was quite different now; it was the beginning of true love—he had now really fallen for this big, powerful girl.

When the bleeding had stopped, he suggested they go for a little walk, as he was now afraid of her heavy hand if they were to stay at too close quarters. But it was she who took his arm, the way engaged couples do when going for an evening stroll along the main street, and said:

"That wasn't right of you, Jacques, to show me such disrespect."

He protested, assuring her that he did respect her, but that he was in love with her. Nothing could be simpler than that.

"Then," she said, "you want to marry me?"

He hesitated, casting a sidelong glance at her as she looked away into the distance. Her cheeks were full and red and her large breasts bulged under her cotton frock. Her thick, fresh lips and her bare neck were sown with tiny droplets of sweat. He felt his desire return, brought his mouth close to her ear, and whispered:

"Yes, I want to. . . ."

Then she flung her arms around his neck and kissed him so lengthily that it took the breath away from both of them.

From that moment, they began the ever-recurring game of love. They fooled around in corners, they had dates in the moonlight, in the shadow of a haystack, and they bruised each other's legs under the table with their big, hobnailed boots.

Then, little by little, Jacques seemed to tire of her; he avoided her, hardly ever addressed her, never insisted on seeing her alone. This worried her and made her very sad. And then she realized she was pregnant.

It drove her to despair at first, but soon the despair changed to rage, a rage that grew with every day, especially as she could never meet with Jacques, who now carefully avoided her.

Then, one night, while everyone in the farm was asleep, she got up, slipped on her skirt, and went outside. Barefoot, she crossed the yard and pushed open the door of the stable where Jacques lay in a large box of straw above his horses. Hearing her come in, he pretended to snore, but she hoisted herself up to him and, squatting down next to him, shook him until he sat up. Then he asked her:

"What do you want from me?"

Shaking with fury, she hissed through clenched teeth:

"What I want is for you to marry me, since you promised to."

He laughed and answered:

"Well, if you had to marry every girl you have a bit of fun with, that'd be the end of everything."

She caught him by the throat, threw him on his back so that he couldn't get away from her fierce stranglehold, and shouted in his face:

"I'm pregnant! Do you hear, I'm pregnant!"

He was gasping for breath and they remained immobile for a moment, the two of them, silent in the black silence of the night that was only broken by the sound of a horse's jaws as it pulled hay out of the manger and slowly chewed it.

When Jacques realized that she was the stronger, he murmured:

"All right . . . if it's like that, I'll marry you."

But she no longer believed in his promises. She said:

"I want the banns put up right away."

"Right away," he said, "right away."

"Swear by God then."

For a few seconds he hesitated, then resigned himself and swore:

"I swear by God."

She loosened the grip of her fingers and silently left.

During the next few days she had no opportunity to speak to him. At night the stable was always locked, and she was afraid to make too much noise lest it cause a public scandal.

Then one morning she saw a new farmhand come into the kitchen for his breakfast. She asked:

"Has Jacques left?"

"Yes," the man said, "and I've been hired in his place."

She was trembling so much that she couldn't take the saucepan off the fire, and when everyone was at work, she went up to her room and cried with her face buried in the bolster so as not to be heard.

During the day she tried to obtain some information without making anyone suspicious about her state. But she was so obsessed by her misfortune that she imagined everyone she asked about Jacques sniggered maliciously. She couldn't find out anything except that he had left the neighborhood altogether.

II

After that her life was a continuous torment. She worked like a machine, without noticing what she was doing, and with only one thought in her head: "What'll happen if they find out?"

This constant preoccupation made her quite incapable of normal reasoning, and she never considered any means of avoiding the impending disaster that was coming closer every day, relentlessly as death.

She'd get up every morning long before all the others and stare long and hard at herself in a broken mirror, which she'd use when she brushed her hair, to see whether her belly had gotten so big that everyone would notice it.

During the day, she'd often interrupt her work and look downward to see whether the vastness of her midriff wasn't making too conspicuous a bulge under her apron.

Months passed. She hardly spoke to anyone anymore. When she was asked something, she failed to understand, became frightened, and looked blank, her hands trembling.

And all that caused the farmer to say to her:

"I don't know what's come over you, my poor girl, you've been sort of silly for some time now."

At church, she hid behind a pillar and refused to go to confession, afraid to meet the priest who, she thought, possessed some superhuman power that enabled him to divine people's secrets.

At table during meals, she suffered terrible anguish when her companions happened to look at her, and she imagined that the sparkling eye of the cowherd, a sly, precocious boy, was constantly fixed on her.

One morning the mailman handed her a letter. She had never received one before, and was so upset that she was forced to sit down. What if it was from him? But since she couldn't read, she just sat there trembling with anxiety and holding the ink-covered piece of paper in her hand. She slipped it into her pocket, unable to trust anyone. Afterward, she often interrupted whatever she was doing to glance at those evenly spaced lines ending in a signature, hoping vaguely that she'd somehow end by discovering the meaning of the message. Finally, driven desperate by impatience and anxiety, she went to see the schoolteacher. He made her sit down and read the letter to her:

> My dear Daughter,
> This is to let you know that I am very sick. I have asked our neighbor, Monsieur Dentu, to take his pen and beg you to come home if you can.
> For your loving mother,
> César Dentu, Deputy Mayor.

She left the schoolteacher's without saying a word, but as soon as she was alone, her legs gave way under her and she let herself fall by the roadside. She lay there until nighttime.

When she got back, she told the farmer about the letter and he gave her permission to leave for as long as was necessary, promising that he'd get some temporary help to do her chores while she was away and take her back whenever she returned.

Her mother was in a coma and died on the very day her daughter arrived. On the following day, Rose gave birth to a seventh-month baby, a horrible-looking little skeleton, so thin it made her shudder. From the way it clenched its bony little hands that looked like a crab's claws, it seemed to be suffering terribly.

Nevertheless, it lived.

She told everyone she was married but that she couldn't take care of the baby, and she left it with some neighbors, who promised to take good care of it.

Then she went back to the farm.

And then, in her heart that had suffered for so long, there arose like the dawn a feeling quite new to her—love for the puny little creature she had left behind. But this new love was yet another agony, an agony that made her suffer every hour, every minute, since she was separated from the being she loved.

What tormented her more than anything else was a mad desire to kiss it, to hug it, to hold it in her arms, to feel the warmth of the little creature against her own flesh. She could no longer sleep at night, and during the day she never thought of anything else. When she was through with her work in the evening, she would sit down by the fire and stare into it, as people do who are thinking about something far away.

The people around her began to talk and they teased her

about her lover, inquired whether he was handsome, tall, and rich, asked her when the marriage would be and when the christening. She would run away then, usually to hide and cry by herself, for those questions stung her like so many needles.

To take her mind off these hurts, she worked with a wild frenzy, and since she was constantly concerned about her child, she kept thinking of ways to amass as much money for it as possible.

She resolved to work so hard that her master would decide to increase her wages. So, little by little, she took over all the work there was to do around the house. A maid who had become useless was dismissed—there was no longer anything for her to do because Rose did the work of both. She also saved on bread and on candles, on the corn that had been thrown too lavishly to the chickens, on the fodder for the cattle that had been previously wasted.

She was as stingy with the farmer's money as she was with her own, and as she drove shrewd bargains for him—selling at the top price everything that left the farm and thwarting the cunning tricks of peasants who tried to get too much for their products—she alone was entrusted with the marketing operations, with supervising the farmhands, and with keeping the accounts. In no time she became indispensable.

She watched everything so closely that, under her direction, the farm prospered as never before. For miles around they spoke of "that maid on Monsieur Vallin's farm" and Farmer Vallin himself repeated wherever he went:

"Ah, that girl! I'm telling you, she's worth her weight in gold!"

But time went by and her wages remained the same. Her efforts were accepted as something any loyal servant owed his employer, nothing but a sign of good will. Rather bitterly, she began to realize that while the farmer was making, thanks to her, an extra hundred and fifty to three hundred francs a month, she still received only the same two hundred and forty francs a year.

She then resolved to demand an increase. Three times she went to see the farmer but each time, once in his presence, she spoke of something else. She somehow felt that it was shameful to ask for money, that there was something degrading about it.

At last, one day when the farmer was having his midday meal all by himself in the kitchen, she told him in an embarrassed tone that she would like to speak to him on a private matter. He raised his head and looked at her with considerable surprise. He put both hands on the table: in one he held a knife pointing toward the ceiling and in the other a big piece of bread. He looked closely at the girl and she became flustered. She told him that she wanted to go to her village for a week because she didn't feel well.

He immediately granted her request and then, looking quite embarrassed himself, added:

"And when you come back, I'd like to ask you something."

III

Her baby was nearly eight months old now. She didn't recognize it. It had become pink, round-cheeked, chubby all over, a roll of living fat. Its fingers, kept spread fan-wise by fleshy little cushions, wiggled with visible satisfaction. She pounced on it like a beast of prey and kissed it so violently that it became frightened and started to scream. She cried too, aggrieved that the baby didn't recognize her and that it stretched its hands toward its wet nurse as soon as it saw her.

Within a day, however, it got accustomed to her face and laughed when it saw her. She took it and walked around with it, ran about excitedly, holding it in her outstretched arms, and sat with it in the shade of the trees. Then, for the first time in her life, she opened her heart to a human being and told the child, who couldn't understand her, all about her sorrows, her work, her hopes, and her worries. And she tired it with the violence and insistence of her caresses.

She took an infinite delight in holding it in her hands, in washing and dressing it, even in cleaning up the mess it made, as if this intimate care she took of it was an affirmation of her maternity. She examined it, was surprised that she could ever have produced it, and chanted under her breath, tossing it up and down in the air:

"This is my little baby, this is my little baby. . . ."

She cried all the way home and, once she got there, the farmer called her to his room. She went, very surprised and rather nervous without knowing why.

"Sit down," the farmer said.

She did so and for some moments they remained sitting side by side, both embarrassed, their arms limp and cumbersome, and like the peasants that they were, not looking into each other's faces.

The farmer—a big man of forty-five, twice a widower, jovial and headstrong—was obviously embarrassed, a state which was unusual for him. Finally he decided to talk, and he spoke in a vague, hesitant tone, looking somewhere into the distance.

"Rose," he said, "have you ever given a thought to settling down some day?"

She turned deathly pale. As she didn't answer, he went on:

"You're a good girl, Rose. You're quiet, hard-working, thrifty. A wife like you, Rose, would sure make a man's fortune."

She remained motionless; her eyes filled with horror and she did not even try to understand what was going on; her thoughts whirled inside her head as if she were threatened by a deadly peril. He paused for a second and then went on:

"You see, Rose, a farm without a mistress is no good. . . . Even with a servant like you around."

He fell silent, not knowing what else to say, and Rose stared at him with the air of a person facing a murderer and ready to flee at the first gesture he makes.

Five minutes went by like that. At last he asked:

"So what do you say? Does it suit you?"

With a sad face she said:

"What's that, master?"

Impatiently, he replied:

"What? But to marry me, what else!"

She got up, but then fell back in her chair, as if broken in two. She remained there without budging, like a person struck by a terrible piece of news. Finally the farmer became impatient.

"Come on, think," he said. "What more do you want me to say?"

She was staring at him, bewildered and then, suddenly, tearfully, she repeated twice, quite out of breath:

"I can't, I can't."

"And why can't you?" the farmer said. "Come on now, don't be stupid. I'll give you until tomorrow to think it over."

And he hurriedly left the room, relieved that this step, which he found so embarrassing, had been taken and quite satisfied that his offer would be accepted the next day; it was a quite unhoped-for boon for her. For him, of course, it was an excellent bargain too: He would bind to him for good a woman who would in the long run bring him more money than the biggest available dowry in the district.

There could be no question of unequal status between them, for in the country everyone is the equal of everyone else. The farmer works as hard as the farmhand, who some day may become a farmer himself, and a maid can become mistress of the place at any moment without its bringing about any drastic changes in her life or habits.

Rose didn't undress that night. She just sat on her bed. She was so annihilated that she didn't even have strength left to cry. She remained in a state of inertia, not aware of her body, her mind distraught, as if someone had raked through it with one of those tools which carders use to tear apart wool for mattresses.

Only at odd moments did she manage to gather her thoughts, and then she shuddered at the idea of what was going to happen.

Her terror increased and each time the big kitchen clock struck in the sleepy silence, she broke into a cold sweat. Her head was swimming, nightmare succeeded nightmare; the candle went out; she became delirious, delirious the way peasants do when they imagine the evil eye is on them and they feel an unconquerable urge to flee, to escape, to run before misfortune like a sailboat scudding before the gale.

An owl hooted. She shuddered, sat up, passed her hand through her hair and then all over her body, like a madwoman. Then she got up and went downstairs, moving like a sleepwalker. When she found herself in the courtyard, she bent low so as not to be seen by some roaming farmhand, for the moon, about to sink below the horizon, was throwing a bright sheet of light over the fields. Instead of opening the gate, she climbed over the fence and was soon in the open countryside. She went straight ahead in a fast, springy stride and, without realizing it, would occasionally utter a piercing yell. Her colossal shadow was stretched out on the ground near her, gliding along with her; and at times some night bird came and circled over her head. Dogs in the farmyards barked as she passed by and one of them leaped over a ditch and pursued her, trying to bite her. But she turned on it, howling like a beast herself, and the frightened dog fled back to his kennel where he cowered in silence.

Now and then she came across a young family of hares jumping and playing in the field. But as the furiously racing figure came toward them, looking like a delirious Diana, the timorous creatures scattered, the mother and the little ones hiding behind some hillock while the father zigzagged away at great speed. From time to time his bouncing shadow, with long ears sticking up, stood out against the setting disk of the moon that was about to dive from the edge of the world and was casting its slanting rays around like a vast lantern put down on the ground.

The stars grew dim and some birds twittered—day was approaching. Rose, exhausted, was breathing hard. When the sun finally pierced the purple sky of dawn, she stopped.

Her feet were swollen and refused to carry her any longer. She caught sight of a pond whose stagnant water looked like blood under the red reflection of the new day, and she went toward it, her heart pounding hard in her chest, to dip her feet in the water.

She sat down on a tuft of grass, removed her heavy, dusty boots, pulled off her stockings, and dipped her bluish legs into the still water from which now and then some bubbles rose to burst on the surface.

A wonderful freshness rose from the soles of her feet to her throat and suddenly, as she gazed into the deep pond, her head began to spin and she felt an overwhelming desire to throw her whole body into it. All the pains, all the worries and torments would be ended once and for all. She no longer thought of her child; all she wanted was peace, complete rest, to go to sleep and to sleep forever. She stood up, raised her arms, and took two steps forward. The water was up to her thighs and she was about to plunge in when a painful stinging around her ankles made her jump back. She let out a shrill cry. From her knees to the soles of her feet, hung long black leeches, sucking her blood. She could actually see them swelling up. She didn't dare touch them, but just shrieked with pain. Her desperate screams were heard by a peasant driving by in his cart. He came over to her, tore the leeches off her flesh, shrank the wounds with herbs, and drove her back to her master's farm.

She stayed in bed for two weeks. On the morning when she got up and went to sit in front of the door, the farmer suddenly appeared before her.

"Well then," he said, "it's all settled now, ain't it?"

At first she didn't answer. But as he stood there waiting, probing her with his obstinate eye, she said with a painful effort:

"No, master, I can't."

He lost his temper then.

"You can't, my girl? How's that?"

She began to cry and repeated:

"I just can't."

He glared at her, then shouted in her face:

"You must have a lover then!"

Trembling and ashamed she mumbled:

"Perhaps that's it."

The man, red as a poppy, stammered out in his rage:

"Ah, so you admit it, you slut! And who the hell is the bird? Some barefoot tramp, some penniless, homeless starveling, I bet! Who is he? Tell me!" And as she didn't answer, he shouted: "All right, let *me* tell you who he is. It's Jean Baudu, isn't it?"

"No," she cried, "it ain't him."

"Then it must be Pierre Martin?"

"No, no, it ain't, Master."

He went on, naming every man in the vicinity, while she kept saying no and wiping her eyes with a corner of her blue apron. He continued to search for his rival with the persistence of an animal, scratching at her heart to uncover its secret like a hound scratching at a hole to get at the game it smells inside. Suddenly the farmer exclaimed:

"Well then, I'm sure it's Jacques, that farmhand who was here last year. I heard that you were going around together and that you'd decided to get married."

Rose was breathless. The blood rushed to her face and set it aglow. Suddenly her tears stopped and dried on her hot cheeks like drops of water on a red-hot iron.

"No," she shouted, "not him, not him!"

"Are you sure?" the sly farmer asked, giving her a close look and sensing that he had stumbled upon the truth.

She answered hurriedly:

"It's not him, I swear, I swear—"

She tried to think of something by which to swear, not daring to invoke sacred things, but he interrupted her:

"He followed you everywhere, didn't he? And he all but ate you up with his eyes during meals. So it's him you've promised to stay faithful to, is it?"

This time she looked the farmer straight in the face.

"No," she said, "no, never, never. And I swear by God that if he came today and asked me to marry him, I wouldn't have him for nothing in the world."

She sounded so sincere that the farmer hesitated. Then he said, as if he were talking to himself:

"What is it then? We would've heard if something had happened to you. Well, since there was no damage, there's no reason why a girl should reject a good match because of something like that. So I say there must be something more to it."

She didn't answer. She was choking with agitation. He asked again:

"So you don't want to?"

She sighed: "I can't, master."

He turned on his heels and walked away from her.

She thought she was rid of the matter and spent the rest of the day in a more or less peaceful state of mind. But she felt tired, exhausted, as though she, and not the old white horse, had been turning the threshing machine from dawn to dusk.

She went to bed as early as possible and fell asleep right away.

Toward the middle of the night, two hands groping in the dark landed on her bed and woke her up. She jumped up in fright but then recognized the farmer's voice.

"Don't be frightened, Rose," the farmer said, "it's me. I must talk to you."

At first she was greatly surprised. Then, as he tried to slip under her sheets, she realized what it was that he really wanted, and began to tremble. She trembled violently, feeling quite helpless in the darkness, still heavy with sleep and entirely naked in her bed next to this man who wanted her. She didn't consent, but she resisted lackadaisically, having to struggle against her own instinctive drive—always stronger among primitive natures and ineffectively held in check by the vacillating will power of their pliable, deadened minds. She turned her head now toward the wall, now toward the room, to avoid the farmer's mouth as it pursued hers, and her body twisted slightly under the blanket, unnerved by the weariness of the struggle. He became brutal, intoxicated by desire. With a violent jerk, he pulled the blanket off her, and she knew she couldn't go on resisting. Taking refuge in an ostrichlike coyness, she hid her face in her hands and gave him free rein.

The farmer spent the rest of the night with her. He returned the next night and every night after that.

They lived together like man and wife.

One morning he announced:

"I've had the banns put up. We're getting married next month."

She said nothing, for what could she say? She did nothing, for what could she do?

IV

She married him. She felt she had fallen into a hole with sides so steep that she could never scramble out, and that terrible disasters in the form of big rocks were suspended over her head, threatening to crush her at the first provocation. She felt that she had cheated her husband and that he was bound to find out about it at any time.

And then she thought of her baby—the source of all her unhappiness but also of all her happiness on earth. She went to see him twice a year, and each time returned feeling sadder than before.

As time went by, however, she grew accustomed to the situation, her apprehensions subsided somewhat, and she became more cheerful, only feeling a vague anguish somewhere at the edge of her conscious mind.

Years passed. The child was going on six. She was almost happy now. But suddenly the farmer's mood darkened. For two or three years, there had seemed to be something worrying him, and this worry weighed more and more heavily on his mind. After dinner, he would remain seated at the table, his head in his hands, looking infinitely sad, eaten by some secret sorrow. His words became sharp and brutal at times; it seemed as if he had a grudge against his wife somewhere in the back of his head, for he would often answer her harshly and sometimes even furiously.

Once, a small boy from the neighborhood came to fetch some eggs and, being very busy, she was a bit rough with him. Her husband walked up to her and said in a nasty tone:

"If that kid was your son, I bet you wouldn't treat him like that."

She gaped at him, unable to find an answer. He had stirred up all her slumbering anguish.

During dinner, he didn't address her, didn't even look in

her direction. He seemed to hate and despise her and she thought he must have found out everything about her.

She lost her head. Not daring to remain alone with him, she ran off to the church.

Night was falling. The narrow nave was in total darkness. She heard someone walking toward the choir. It was the sacristan preparing the tabernacle lamp for the night. That spot of quivering light, lost in the darkness of the arches, seemed to Rose to be the last hope remaining to her. Her eyes fixed on it, she fell to her knees.

The slender lamp rose into the air to the rattling of a chain. Then she heard the regular thuds of wooden clogs on the flagstones, as though someone were jumping up and down, and a shrill bell rang out the Angelus through the thickening shadows.

As the sacristan was leaving, she went up to him.

"Is M'sieu le Curé at home?" she asked.

"I guess so," the sacristan said. "He always has his dinner at Angelus time."

She pushed open the door of the rectory. The priest was about to start eating his dinner. He asked her to sit down.

"Yes, yes, I know; your husband has already spoken to me of the matter that brings you here."

The poor woman nearly fainted. The priest went on:

"What can I do for you, my child?"

He was quickly swallowing spoonfuls of soup and dripping it onto the greasy cassock bulging over his stomach.

But Rose couldn't make herself say anything. She could neither plead nor implore. She stood up. The priest said:

"Be brave."

And she walked out.

She returned to the farm without knowing what she was doing. The farmer was waiting for her. The farmhands had gone while she had been away. She fell down heavily at his feet. With tears streaming from her eyes, she moaned:

"What is it you have against me?"

He began to shout and to swear.

"Why haven't I got any children, damn it! When a man gets married he doesn't want to be childless for the rest of his days. So that's what I have against you, see! You know that a cow that has no calf is worth nothing, and let me tell you something—a woman who has no children is also worth nothing, understand!"

She cried, muttering again and again:

"It ain't none of my fault, it ain't none of my fault. . . ."

He relented a bit and said:

"I don't say it's any of your fault but you must understand that it can get a man down."

V

From that day on, she had only one thought—to have a child. And she confided in everyone around her.

A woman from the neighborhood advised her to make her husband drink a glass of water with a pinch of ashes dissolved in it every night. The farmer was willing. But it didn't work.

"Still, there must be some secret way," they decided, and they kept looking for one. Someone told them about a shepherd who lived ten miles away from them and the farmer harnessed his buggy and went to consult the man.

The shepherd gave him a loaf of bread stuffed with certain herbs over which he had made some signs. They were told to eat some of the bread at night, just before and after. . . .

The whole loaf was eaten without any result.

A teacher then initiated them into the mysteries of some secret ways of love unknown in the villages, ways that never failed, he assured them. But, this time, they failed.

The priest advised them to make a pilgrimage to the shrine at Fécamp. Rose went with a crowd of others and prostrated herself in the abbey, adding her plea that she be made pregnant once more to all the other coarse pleas these peasants addressed to the Almighty. That also proved futile.

She began to imagine that she was expiating her earlier sin and an immense despair came over her. She wasted away in her grief and her husband, too, seemed to be visibly aging. It was "eating his blood away," they said of him, as he wore himself out in vain hope.

Then there was war between them. He insulted her, struck her, nagged her all day long, and at night, in their bed, breathless with hatred, he abused her in the foulest language.

One night, not knowing what new torment he could inflict upon her, he told her to get up and wait for morning outside the house in the driving rain. As she didn't comply, he caught her by the throat and started pummeling her face with his fist. She didn't resist, didn't say a word. Driven to a frenzy, he jumped with both his knees on her belly and with clenched teeth, completely mad, flailed at her with his fists.

She suddenly had a movement of revolt. With a powerful jerk, she threw him off her and he tumbled against the wall. She sat up, and in a changed, strident voice, screeched:

"Me, at least, I know I can have a child! I know because I had one with Jacques. He promised to marry me, but he ran away."

The man was stunned. He remained there, lying against the wall, just as haggard as she. He stuttered:

"What did you say? What did you say?"

She began to weep then and mumbled through her flowing tears:

"That was the reason why I didn't want to marry you in the first place, that was it. I couldn't tell you the truth or you'd have kicked me out penniless and with my kid to look after. You don't have no child yourself so you can't have no idea what it feels like—"

With growing surprise, he kept repeating:

"So you have a child . . . so you have a child. . . ."

Amid hiccoughs she managed to say:

"You forced me into it, you know you did. I didn't want to marry you."

He got up, lit a candle, and with his hands behind his back, started pacing up and down the room. She was still in bed, crying. Abruptly he stopped in front of her and said:

"So it's my fault, it's me who couldn't make you a child, is it?"

She didn't answer. He resumed his walk and then, stopping again, asked:

"How old is he now, your kid?"

She whispered:

"Going on six."

He asked again:

"How come you didn't tell me before?"

She moaned:

"How could I tell you?"

He was still standing facing her.

"Get up," he said.

She rose painfully. But when she was standing on her feet, leaning heavily against the wall, he suddenly burst into a huge laugh, the loud laughter of their happier days. And as she stared at him, perplexed, he said:

"Well, let's bring the kid here, since we can't manage to make one together."

She was so frightened that, if she hadn't been in such a weakened state, she would have taken to her heels. But the farmer was rubbing his hands together.

"And me who wanted to adopt one," he said. "I even asked the priest to get me one of them little orphans. . . . But now we've found one, we've found one. . . ."

Then, still roaring with laughter, he kissed his astonished, weeping wife on both cheeks, shouting as though she couldn't hear him:

"Come on, Mother, let's go and see whether there ain't some soup left in the pot. I sure wouldn't mind a plateful right now."

She slipped into her skirt and they went downstairs. As she knelt to relight the fire under the pot, he, all smiles, paced up and down the kitchen, repeating again and again:

"Well, I must say, here's something that makes me feel good. And I'm not just saying that. It makes me feel good, real good!"

[*Histoire d'une fille de ferme,* March 26, 1881]

Big Tony

I

For ten miles around, everyone knew Papa Tony, Big Tony, Tony-My-Brandy, Anthony Mâcheblé, the innkeeper of Tournevent.

He had made famous the small village in the fold of the valley that descended toward the sea, a poor little hamlet consisting of ten Normandy peasant houses, each surrounded by ditches and trees. The houses were huddled together in this ravine covered with grass and shrubs, around a bend that gave the hamlet its name, Tournevent. They seemed to have sought shelter in the hollow, like birds sheltering in the furrows during storms, looking for protection from the wind which blew across the wide expanses of the sea, the cruel and salty wind that burned like a flame and destroyed life like the winter frosts.

The whole hamlet seemed to belong to Anthony Mâcheblé, who was most often called Tony or Tony-My-Brandy because of the phrase he constantly used:

"My brandy is the finest in France."

He referred, of course, to his homemade cognac.

For twenty years he had been feeding his brandy to the local population and each time a peasant asked him:

"What d'you have for me today, Big Tony?" he would invariably reply:

"My brandy, son-in-law, because my brandy, it warms your

gut and clears your head for you. There ain't nothing better than that for the health."

For he was also in the habit of calling people "son-in-law," although he'd never had a daughter, married or otherwise.

Yes, indeed, they all knew Big Tony, the fattest man in the district and probably in the entire province too. His house seemed much too small and narrow to hold him, and when they saw him standing in front of his door, as he did for a great part of the day, they wondered how he ever managed to get through it. But manage he did each time a customer presented himself, for Tony-My-Brandy was automatically allowed to levy a small glass for himself on whatever was consumed in his place.

His inn bore the sign "The Meeting Place of Friends" and Big Tony was certainly the friend of everyone around. People even came from Fécamp and Montivilliers to see him and to have a good laugh listening to him, for that fat fellow could have made a gravestone laugh. He had a way of teasing people without making them angry, of winking to express what he left unsaid, and of slapping his thigh in his fits of merriment, that could draw a belly laugh every time, whether one wanted to laugh or not. And then, it was really a curious sight to see him drink. He would drink whatever was offered him, anything, and drink it with a spark of delight shining in his sly eyes, a delight that came from the double joy of drinking and of being paid big shiny coins for the drink he was filling himself with.

The local jokers would ask him:

"Why don't you drink up the sea, Big Tony?"

He'd answer:

"There're two things that stop me from doing that: number one, it's salty, the sea; and number two, someone would have to bottle it first, because I can't lap it up in its present container."

There were also, of course, his quarrels with his wife. That was a comedy people enjoyed watching. They had bickered every day of the thirty years they had been married. But while Tony took it good-naturedly, his wife raged. She was a big peasant woman who walked with long stiltlike strides and whose face resembled an angry screech owl's. She spent her time breeding chickens in the tavern's small backyard and she was famous for the way she had of fattening her poultry.

When the gentry of Fécamp threw a big dinner party, they had to serve one of Mother Mâcheblés former boarders to make it a first-class meal.

But the woman herself had been born in a vicious mood and she always seemed displeased with things. Angry with the world at large, she had a special grudge against her husband. She resented his cheerfulness, his fame, his health, his fatness. She treated him like a good-for-nothing because he earned his living without working for it; she considered him a hog because he drank and ate enough for ten men. A day never went by without her announcing in despair:

"He really ought to be in a pigsty, that fat oaf! It makes me sick to my stomach to see all that fat!" And she'd shout right into his face: "Just wait a bit and you'll see what'll happen! You'll burst like a bag of grain, you fat lump."

Tony would laugh heartily and answer, slapping his stomach:

"Ha-ha, you mother hen, you plank! Just try and fatten your chicks to my size. I'd like to see you do it!' And pulling back the sleeve on his huge arm, he'd add: "What would you say to a chicken wing that size, woman? Something, ain't it?"

Furiously, the old woman would answer:

"You just wait, just wait a bit . . . . We shall see what we shall see—you'll burst like a bag of grain." And resentfully, she'd walk off, accompanied by the laughter of the drinkers.

As a matter of fact, Tony was an extraordinary sight, so immense, heavy, red, and hard-breathing had he become. He was one of those colossal creatures with whom Death seems to be having fun by playing all kinds of sly tricks, inventing all sorts of treacherous games, making its slow work of destruction irresistibly comic. Death didn't operate with him as it does with others: showing its true sinister nature by turning people's hair white, making its victims thin and wrinkled, continually working on their deterioration so that those who meet them exclaim:

"Well, well, that's really something! Look how he's changed!"

With Big Tony, Death amused itself by fattening him, turning him into a ridiculous freak, painting him red and blue, making him huff and puff, and giving him an overall air of great health and vigor. The transformation it inflicts upon every living creature seemed funny and amusing in Tony, instead of sinister and pitiful.

"Fat lump," Big Tony's wife kept saying, "wait a bit and we shall see what we shall see!"

II

It so happened that Big Tony had a stroke that left him paralyzed. The huge innkeeper was installed in the small partitioned-off room behind the counter. From there, he could hear what was said in the café and talk with his friends, for while his monstrous body was immobilized and helpless, his brain remained clear and unaffected. At first it was hoped that he would recover some use of his big fat legs, but soon that hope vanished and Tony-My-Brandy remained night and day in his bed that was made once a week. Four of his friends, each holding him by a limb, lifted him while his mattress was turned.

Nevertheless, he remained cheerful, although his gaiety was no longer quite the same. He had become rather shy, rather humble, and seemed to be frightened of his wife, who nagged at him all day long as if he were a small child.

"Look at that big lazy hog! Ah, the useless, good-for-nothing drunkard! Ah, what a sight, what a sight!"

He didn't answer back. He just winked slyly behind her back and turned over on his couch. Turning over was the only movement he could manage and he called that exercise "southward-ho" or "northward-ho" as the case might be.

His main pastime was listening to the conversations in the café, and when he recognized the voices of his special friends, he liked to take part in them through his partition. He would then shout:

"Is that you, Célestin, son-in-law?"

And Célestin Maloisel would answer:

"It's me all right, Big Tony. And how's life treating you these days? Are you going to be skipping around like a fat rabbit again soon, my friend?"

"It ain't a question of skipping around as yet," Big Tony would say, "but you'll be glad to know I haven't lost any weight—there's plenty of strength left in my belly still."

Soon he began to invite his closest cronies into his room.

He was delighted to have company, although it hurt him to see them drink without him.

"What hurts me most, son-in-law, is that I can't have my brandy no more. For the rest, well, I don't give a damn, but to have to do without brandy, that sure gets me!"

Now and then the screech-owl's head of Tony's wife would appear in the window, as she shouted:

"Look at him, look at him, that big good-for-nothing! And here I have to feed him and wash him and clean him like a pig!"

When the woman was gone, a red-feathered rooster would sometimes jump up on the windowsill, look into the room with his round, curious eyes, and then let out his resounding cock-a-doodle-doo. Occasionally, too, a couple of hens would fly into the room and search for bread crumbs on the floor around the bed.

Big Tony's friends soon deserted the café room and crowded around the bed of the immobilized colossus. They thought he was great fun, Tony-My-Brandy, even prostrate. He would've made the devil himself laugh, that sly, fat man. Three of his chums came regularly every day: Célestin Maloisel, a tall, thin man slightly twisted like the trunk of an apple tree; Prosper Horslaville, a small, dry fellow with a long ferret-like nose, cunning and inventive as a fox; and Césaire Paumelle, who never said a word but who had great fun nevertheless.

They brought in a board from the backyard, placed it by the bed, and played games of dominoes. And what games they were! They went on from two till six o'clock.

Then Tony's wife became unbearable. She just couldn't stand the thought that her big good-for-nothing lump of a husband should have such a good time while in bed; and so, whenever she saw that they had started a game, she'd make a furious dash for the board, grab the dominoes, and take them back to the café, declaring that it was quite bad enough that she should have to feed that tub of fat, without having to see him mock her and everybody else who had to work hard all day.

Célestin and Césaire just bent their heads under the storm, but the foxy Prosper kept egging the old woman on, for her rages seemed to greatly amuse him.

Once, when she was even more enraged than usual, he said to her:

"You know what I'd do if I were in your shoes, Mother Mâcheblé?"

With her owl's eyes fixed on him, she waited for him to explain himself. So he went on:

"He's hot as an oven, your man, and since he don't ever leave his bed, if I were you, I'd make him hatch eggs for you."

She looked at him with amazement, thinking that he was laughing at her, examining his sharp, cunning peasant's features; then he continued:

"I'd put five eggs under one arm and five under the other, and on the same day I'd start a hen setting. That way all the chicks will be hatched on the same day and as they come out of their shells, you'll take them from your man and give them to the hen, so she can bring them up. That will sure give you plenty of fowls, Mother Mâcheblé!"

The old woman, surprised and hesitant, asked:

"You sure it will work?"

The man replied:

"Will it work? How could it not work? Since eggs even hatch out in those hot boxes, why shouldn't they hatch in a bed?"

That argument impressed her and she left, calmed and thoughtful.

A week later, she entered Tony's room with her apron full of eggs. She said:

"I've set the yellow hen on ten eggs and here are ten more for you. And you'd better see you don't break them."

Bewildered, he asked:

"What d'you mean?"

She said:

"I mean you're going to hatch 'em for me, you good-for-nothing."

At first that made him laugh. But as she persisted, he became angry. He refused to allow her to place those poultry eggs under his arms.

But the old woman warned him furiously:

"You'll get no grub as long as you won't take these eggs. We'll see what happens!"

Tony said nothing, but he was extremely worried.

When he heard the clock strike twelve noon, he called out.

"Hey!" he shouted, "what about my soup? Is it ready?"

From her kitchen his wife replied:

"No soup for you, you lazy, fat lump."

He thought that she was joking and waited. Then he prayed, begged, beseeched, cursed, made desperate "southward-ho's" and "northward-ho's" and pounded on the wall with his fists; but finally he had to give in and allow her to put the ten eggs into his bed—five against his right side and five against his left.

Only after that was he given his soup.

When his friends came to see him they thought his health was much worse, so terribly queer and constrained did he look. And when they started their usual game, Tony didn't seem to enjoy it at all, and he moved his arm with infinite precaution when it was his turn to play.

"What is it—you got a stiff arm now?" Prosper inquired.

"It's a kind of a load under my shoulder," Tony said.

Suddenly they heard someone come into the café and all fell silent. It was the mayor and his deputy. They ordered some cognac and started to talk about local business. As they were speaking softly, Tony wanted to press his ear against the wall; he forgot about the eggs, made a brisk "northward-ho," and landed on top of an omelet.

He swore loudly and that brought his wife rushing in. She'd guessed at the catastrophe and, with one jerk, pulled his blanket off him. At first she stood there motionless in her indignation, her breath taken away by the sight of the yellow mess plastered on her husband's flank. Then she shuddered from sheer fury, flung herself on the paralyzed man, and in her rage, pounded his belly with heavy blows just as she pounded the dirty linen when she washed it at the pond. One after the other, her fists fell on his body with dull thuds, as if she were beating out a tattoo on a huge drum.

Tony's three friends laughed like crazy—choking, coughing, sneezing, shrieking—while the big, prostrate man tried carefully to ward off his wife's attack without breaking the remaining five eggs on his other side.

III

Big Tony was subdued. He was made to hatch eggs. He had to give up the games of dominoes and renounce all the movements he was still capable of making, for his wife deprived him of food every time he happened to break an egg.

He remained flat on his back, staring fixedly at the ceiling and not daring to move, with his arms spread slightly, like the wings of a hen, warming the seeds of the birds sealed in their white shells.

He spoke only in subdued tones, as if he were as much afraid of sounds as of brisk movements, and he kept inquiring about the yellow hen who was performing the same job in the chicken coop as he was in his bed.

He'd ask his wife:

"The yellow hen, did she eat anything during the night?"

And the old woman kept going from her man to her hen and from her hen back to her man, obsessed by the thought of the little chicks that were hatching in the nest and in the bed.

The local inhabitants, who had heard all about it, arrived full of curiosity and inquired quite seriously about how Big Tony was making out. They would come in as though walking into a very sick person's room, trying not to make any noise, and ask with curiosity:

"Well, how's it going?"

And Tony would answer:

"It's going fine, I guess, but I'm almost boiling with the heat. It's just like there are ants galloping all over my body."

Then one morning Tony's wife came into his room in a very agitated state and announced:

"She hatched seven chicks, the yellow hen. Three of them eggs was no good."

Big Tony's heart began to pound with worry: how many chicks would he get out of his ten eggs? He asked:

"Think it'll be today?"

He spoke in the anguished tone of a woman about to become a mother.

His wife replied in an angry voice, tormented by fear of failure:

"I sure hope so!"

They waited. His friends soon came in, knowing that it was about time, and they also looked worried. It became the talk of the village. People at their doorsteps inquired of one another about it.

About three o'clock, Big Tony dozed off. He often slept through half the day. Suddenly a persistent tickling under his right arm woke him up. His left hand shot across there and caught a small animal.

His emotion was such that he started emitting shrill cries, releasing the chick, which ran across his chest.

The inn was full of people. The customers flooded into his room and crowded around his bed like people crowding around a circus performer. Then his wife came in and cautiously picked up the little chick which was trying to hide under her husband's bearded chin.

No one spoke. It was a warm April day. The window of Tony's room was open and through it they could hear the yellow hen summoning her newly hatched brood in the backyard.

Big Tony, who was sweating with anguish and greatly agitated, muttered:

"I can feel another one under my left arm now."

His wife plunged her hard, calloused hand under the sheets and brought out a second chick which she held with the dextrous efficiency of a midwife.

The neighbors wanted to have a look at it, and so it went from hand to hand and was scrutinized as though it were a freak.

For the next twenty minutes no chicks materialized, but then all at the same time, four of them broke out of their shells. There was a great murmur among the audience and Big Tony smiled broadly, happy over this achievement. He was becoming proud of this peculiar fatherhood. His friends hadn't often come across the likes of him, after all. He was really a remarkable fellow.

He announced:

"That makes six. Ah, what a christening that would make, dammit!"

A loud laugh rose among his audience. More people crowded into the inn, and still others had to wait outside in the street. Everyone kept asking:

"How many of 'em did he have?"

"He's had six."

Tony's wife carried the additional family to the hen. The hen clucked desperately, fluffed out her feathers, opened her wings wider to receive her additional batch of fledglings.

"Here's one more!" Big Tony hollered.

He was wrong. There were three more. It was turning into a real triumph! At seven in the evening the last chick broke its shell. So all the eggs had been good! Big Tony, radiant and happy, free again and covered with glory, kissed the back of the fragile creature, almost smothering it with his lips. He wanted to keep this last one in his bed until the next day, so overwhelmed was he with motherly tenderness for the tiny thing to which he had given life. But his wife took it away from him despite his supplications.

The delighted onlookers began to leave, commenting on the event, and Prosper, who had remained behind, asked Big Tony:

"Well, Tony-My-Brandy, I'll be the first to be invited to your chicken fricassee, right?"

At the thought of a fricassee, Big Tony's face lit up and he said:

"I sure will invite you, son-in-law!"

[*Toine*, January 6, 1885]

Pierrot

Madame Lefèvre was a rural lady, a widow, one of those semi-peasant women who go in for ribbons and hats with all sorts of trimmings, who choose their words carefully and put on grand airs, who try to conceal their coarse, primitive natures under ridiculously pretentious exteriors, just as they hide their big red hands in silk gloves.

She had as a servant a very simple peasant woman named Rose.

The two women lived in the center of the Caux district of Normandy, in a little green-shuttered house by the roadside. In front of the house, they had a narrow strip of land on which they grew vegetables.

And one night, a dozen onions were stolen from it.

As soon as Rose realized the onions were missing, she rushed to warn her mistress and Madame Lefèvre hurried down in her woolen petticoat. It was a day of great despondency and serious apprehensions. Someone had stolen—stolen from Madame Lefèvre! Therefore there were thieves around, and hence they might very well come back.

The two frightened women examined the footprints left behind, debated the matter, and made all sorts of assumptions:

"Look, they must've come this way, climbed over the fence here, and jumped down onto that flower bed. . . ."

They trembled for the future. How could they ever sleep soundly again?

The news spread. Neighbors came, looked at the footprints, and discussed the matter, after the two women had explained their findings and assumptions to each new arrival.

A neighboring farmer offered them a piece of advice:

"You ought to get yourselves a watchdog."

That was a good idea. They really ought to have a dog, if only to warn them of an unwelcome presence. Ah, certainly not a big dog, good Lord! What would they do with a big beast? Just feeding it would ruin them. All they needed was a little wisp of a dog that could yap.

When at last they were alone again, Madame Lefèvre expounded lengthily on the pros and cons of having a dog. Having weighed the matter, she found thousands of objections; the thought of the dog devouring a whole bowl of food filled her with icy horror, for she belonged to that thrifty breed of rustic ladies who only have a few coppers to give ostentatiously and publicly to beggars or to throw into the collection plate in church on Sundays.

Rose, who loved animals, advanced her own arguments in favor of a dog and adroitly defended them. Finally it was decided that they would have a dog—a very small one, to be sure.

They began to look for one, but there were none around except big ones, the kind that would gulp down enough food to send shivers down one's spine.

There was, of course, the grocer at Rolleville who had a very small pooch, but he insisted on being paid two francs for it, to cover the expenses of rearing it. Madame Lefèvre wouldn't hear of that. She was willing to feed a small dog but she certainly wasn't going to pay for it.

One morning, the baker, who had followed the story closely, brought along in his delivery van a strange little animal, entirely yellow, almost limbless, with the body of a crocodile, the head of a fox, and a turned-up tail—a big plume nearly as large as the rest of the beast. A customer, the baker said, was trying to get rid of it.

Madame Lefèvre found this freak beautiful, since it cost nothing. Rose kissed it and asked what its name was, to which the baker replied: "Pierrot."

Pierrot was installed in an old soapbox and, to start with, they offered him some water to drink. He drank. Then he was presented with a piece of bread. He ate it. That worried

Madame Lefèvre a bit, but then she had an idea: "Once he is accustomed to the place, Pierrot can be let loose and he can roam around and find himself enough to eat."

They let him roam around but that didn't prevent him from being hungry. To tell the truth, the only time he ever yapped was to ask for his pittance of food, but then he yapped with remarkable zest. Otherwise, anyone could walk into the vegetable garden unmolested. Indeed, Pierrot rushed to greet all comers and never let out a sound on those occasions.

Nevertheless, Madame Lefèvre became accustomed to the little animal. She even felt a certain affection for it and occasionally fed it bits of bread dipped in the gravy of her own stew.

But she had never thought of the dog license and when they came and asked her to pay eight francs—"It will be eight francs, madame"—just like that, and for that wisp of a dog that wouldn't even yap, she almost fainted from the shock.

It was at once decided that they must get rid of Pierrot. But how? There wasn't anyone within ten miles in any direction who had any use for him, so they would have to do it the hard way: Pierrot would have to dive into the pit, the fate of all dogs people wanted to get rid of.

In the middle of a vast plain, there stood a small hut, or rather something that looked more like a thatched roof rising straight up from the ground. This was the entrance to a marlpit. Under that roof, a great perpendicular shaft descended to the underground galleries of the mine sixty feet below. Once a year, when it was time to fertilize the land, someone went down into the marlpit. The rest of the time it was used as a death house for unwanted dogs, and so around the mine entrance, plaintive howls, fierce barking, or desperate yapping sounds were sometimes heard rising to the surface.

Shepherds' and hunters' dogs rushed from the neighborhood of this moaning hole in panic, and when anyone leaned over the shaft, a putrid stench hit him in the face.

Horrible tragedies took place down below in the darkness. When, for instance, an animal had been in agony for ten or twelve days, feeding on the dreadful remains of its predecessors, another beast, perhaps bigger and certainly more vigorous, might be thrown in. They would be alone, hungry, their eyes gleaming in the dim galleries. They would stalk each other, move around stealthily, hesitant and afraid. Finally, goaded by hunger, they would fly at each other's throats; they would fight furiously, desperately; and the stronger would eat the weaker—devour him alive.

When it was decided that Pierrot should be made to "take the dive," they looked about for an executioner. A laborer who was mending the road asked half a franc for the job, which seemed exorbitant to Madame Lefèvre. The farmhand next door was willing to content himself with twenty-five centimes, but Madame Lefèvre felt even that was too much. Then Rose remarked that it would be better if they carried Pierrot there themselves, thinking that at least the mutt wouldn't be ill-treated on the way to the hole and, as it were, warned of the fate reserved for him. So the two women resolved to take Pierrot there at nightfall.

That evening, they gave him a plateful of nice soup, with even a small sliver of butter in it. He swallowed it down to the last drop, and as he wagged his tail with joy, Rose picked him up and wrapped him in her apron.

They set off, with long, rapid strides, looking like a couple of female marauders hurrying across the fields. Soon the thatched roof came in sight and then they reached the pit. Madame Lefèvre bent over the shaft and listened to find out if there were some groaning animal in there. There wasn't. Pierrot would have the place to himself. Tears pouring down her cheeks, Rose kissed Pierrot and tossed him down the shaft. Then the two women leaned over the hole and listened intently.

They heard a thud followed by the shrill, heartbroken scream of a wounded beast and then a succession of pained little cries and squeals and imploring appeals. The little dog stood there, looking up toward the opening, and yapped and yapped and yapped.

The women were gripped by remorse, by horror, by a mad, unreasoning fear, and before they knew what they were doing, they found themselves running away from there. Since Rose was the faster on her feet, Madame Lefèvre kept calling out to her:

"Wait for me, Rose, wait, I tell you!"

The night was filled with all sorts of horrible nightmares. Madame Lefèvre dreamt that she was sitting at the table about to eat her soup. But when she removed the lid of the tureen, there was Pierrot, and the next thing, he was leaping out and biting her nose.

She woke up, but still thought she could hear him yapping. She listened—nothing; she must have been mistaken.

So she went to sleep again and found herself walking along an endless, winding road. Suddenly, she caught sight of a basket in the middle of the road, one of those large farmer's baskets, and somehow it filled her with fear. Nevertheless, she finally opened it and Pierrot, who had been concealed inside, caught her hand in his teeth and wouldn't let go. She began to run like a madwoman, with the dog hanging at the end of her arm, his teeth sunk into her hand.

She jumped out of bed at daybreak and, almost out of her senses, hurried to the marlpit.

Yes, he was still yapping, just as he had yapped throughout the night. She cried then and called him all sorts of tender names and he answered her, using all the affectionate inflexions there are in a dog's vocabulary.

She wanted him back and promised to make him happy till the day he should die a natural death.

She hurried to the well-digger, the man whose job it also was to go down into the pit when fertilizer was needed. She told him her troubles. He listened in silence and when she had finished said:

"So you want 'im back, your mutt? That'll be four francs."

She almost leaped into the air. All her sorrow was gone.

"Four francs! Four francs! . . . What are you talking about? . . ."

"Mebbe you think, lady, I'm going to haul my ropes and tackles over there, rig 'em, and go down that shaft just to please you? Besides, he might bite me into the bargain, your lousy cur. You didn't have to throw him in there in the first place."

She walked away full of indignation. Four francs indeed!

She went home, called Rose, and told her about the well-digger's exorbitant demand. Rose, a person full of resignation, repeated:

"Four francs! That's a lot of money, madame." But then she added: "But what about throwing some food down to poor Pierrot, so he won't die down there just like that?"

Madame Lefèvre consented with joy and within seconds they were on their way to the pit again, carrying a large piece of buttered bread.

There they cut it into small portions which they dropped down in turns, all the time talking to Pierrot. And no sooner had he swallowed one piece that he started demanding the next.

They returned that very evening, then the next day and every day after that, but making only one trip a day.

Then one morning, just as they were about to drop in the first morsel, a formidable bark came from the pit. There were two of them down there! Another dog had been thrown in, a big one this time.

Rose called: "Pierrot, Pierrot!" and Pierrot yapped and yapped. They began to toss in their bits of bread, but each time they did so, there was a brief and violent tussle in the darkness, followed by Pierrot's whimpering from the pain inflicted upon him by the teeth of his companion. The other, being the stronger, ate everything.

It was in vain that the women specified with each offering: "This is for you, Pierrot, for you!"

It was obvious that Pierrot was getting nothing.

At a loss, mistress and servant looked at each other, and then Madame Lefèvre said in an irritated voice:

"Well, I'm certainly not going to feed all the dogs people decide to toss into this hole. We'll just have to give up."

And outraged at the thought of all the condemned dogs scrounging on her, she walked away, taking with her what was left of the bread and butter she had brought for Pierrot; as she walked, she ate it herself.

Rose walked behind, wiping her eyes with a corner of her blue apron.

[*Pierrot,* October 9, 1882]

Coco

Lucas' farm was known in the district as The Farm, although no one could explain exactly why. Probably the peasants associated the phrase with the idea of wealth and prosperity, and there was no doubt that the farm was the largest, the richest, and the most efficiently run in the vicinity.

In the huge farmyard, encircled by five rows of magnificent trees that had been planted to protect the short, delicate apple trees from the violent winds off the plain, stood long buildings with tiled roofs in which grain and fodder were stored, beautiful stone cowsheds, stables that held thirty horses, and a red-brick dwelling house that looked like a little château.

The manure heaps were well kept, the watchdogs lived in kennels, and a crowd of chickens ran about in the high grass.

Each day at noon fifteen persons, the farmer and his wife, the farmhands, the dairymaids and the servants, sat down at a long table in the kitchen on which a pot of soup steamed in a big earthenware tureen with blue flowers painted on it.

The farm animals—the horses, the cows, the pigs, and the sheep—were well fed and well looked after, and Monsieur Lucas, a tall man getting rather potbellied, made his rounds of the farm three times a day, seeing to it that everything went right.

A very old white horse lived in a corner of the stables. They kept him out of pity. The farmer's wife had decided that he should be fed until his natural death, for she had reared him and remained attached to him, and he reminded her of many things from the past.

A fifteen-year-old stableboy named Isidore Duval, who was called more simply Zidore, took care of the old pensioner. In winter, he gave the animal his ration of oats and hay, and in summer he was supposed to go four times a day to change the grazing spot where the horse was tethered, so the oldster might have plenty of fresh grass to eat.

The animal was almost paralyzed and lifted painfully his heavy legs, which were swollen at the knees and just above the hoofs. His coat, which was no longer groomed, looked like an old man's hair and his very long white eyelashes gave his eyes a sad look.

When Zidore led him out to graze he had to pull very hard on the rope, for otherwise the animal dragged itself along too slowly, and the boy, leaning forward and breathing hard, would swear at the horse and feel sorry for himself because he had to look after such an old nag.

The farmhands noticed the boy's resentment against Coco and made fun of him, constantly teasing him about the horse. In the village the boys nicknamed him Coco-Zidore.

The boy was furious and his desire to avenge himself on the old horse grew. He was a thin, long-legged boy, always very dirty, with a thatch of thick, bristling, coarse red hair on his head. He looked rather stupid and stuttered badly when he tried to explain something, as though ideas had great difficulty in taking shape in his brutish mind.

For a long time he had wondered why they kept Coco and was very indignant to see good things wasted on a useless animal. Since Coco didn't do any work, Zidore felt it was unfair to feed him; he was revolted at wasting oats, which were so expensive, on a paralyzed nag. Often, against the express orders of Monsieur Lucas, he saved on Coco's food by giving him only half his ration of oats and also economized on his hay and straw. And all the time hatred for the animal grew in the boy's confused brain: the hatred of a peasant—a stingy, greedy, underhand, ruthless, brutal, and cowardly peasant.

~

When summer came round again, Zidore had to keep moving the old horse around the field. It was quite far from the house, and the stableboy would set out, more furious each morning, walking heavily across the wheat fields. The men working there called out to him jokingly:

"Hey, Zidore, give my best to Coco!"

He never answered. But as he passed by, he'd break a twig from the hedge, and when he had moved the stake to which the horse was tied, he would wait for him to resume his grazing and then come up treacherously from behind and switch at his legs. The old nag would try to run away, to kick, to dodge the blows; he would run round and round his post as though on an indoor track, and the boy would pursue him, striking him doggedly, his teeth clenched in fury.

Then the boy would walk off slowly, without turning back, while the horse, with his old eyes following him and his flanks heaving after having been made to trot, watched him leave. He wouldn't lower his bony white head to the grass until the blue blouse of the young peasant was out of sight.

When the nights were hot, Coco was left out to sleep by the edge of the ravine, beyond the wood, and Zidore was the only one to see him.

The boy would then amuse himself by throwing stones at him. He would sit down on a bank ten steps away and stay there for as long as half an hour at a time, occasionally tossing a stinging stone at the nag which remained standing tethered in front of his enemy, keeping his eyes on him all the time, and not daring to start grazing as long as he was there.

But the stableboy continued to be tormented by the thought of feeding a horse which no longer worked. He felt that the miserable jade was stealing the food of others, robbing men of what was theirs, squandering the good Lord's bounty, and harming him, Zidore, directly as well, because he had to work for his living while that miserable beast—

So, gradually, each day, when the boy moved the stake to which the animal was tied, he reduced the strip of pasture on which the animal could graze.

The horse went without food, grew thin, weakened. Too weak to break the rope, he would stretch his head helplessly toward the vast expanse of green, shiny grass that was so close by and that he could smell so distinctly although it was out of reach.

Then one morning Zidore decided not to move Coco at all. He had really had enough, he thought, of walking all that distance just for the sake of that ugly carcass.

Nevertheless, he did walk all that way—to savor his vengeance. The frightened animal was waiting for him, but that day he didn't hit the horse. He just strolled around him with his hands in his pockets. He even pretended he was about to move the stake, but then banged it deeper into the ground instead and left, delighted with this new idea.

The horse, seeing the boy leave, neighed to call him back; but the boy started to run, leaving the old white nag all alone in the small ravine, without a blade of grass within reach of his jaws.

Famished, he tried desperately to reach the succulent grass that he could almost touch with his nostrils. He went down on his knees and stretched out his neck, extending to the utmost his long, foaming lips, but all to no avail.

The old animal spent the whole day trying to reach the grass and his vain and frantic efforts exhausted him completely. He was tormented by hunger and exasperated even further by the sight of food stretching out as far as he could see.

The stableboy didn't return that day. He wandered off to the woods to look for birds' nests.

When he came on the following day, Coco, now very weak, was lying on the ground. The horse got up when he saw the boy, expecting to be moved at last. But the young peasant didn't even touch the mallet that lay in the grass by the stake. He went up close to the animal, glared at him, and tossed a clod of earth in his face. Then he walked off whistling.

The nag remained standing as long as he could see the boy.

Then, having apparently realized the futility of his attempts to reach the nearby grass, he lay down again on his flank and closed his eyes.

On the next day Zidore didn't show up.

The day after that, he found the old white nag dead.

He stood there, looking at the carcass, proud of his achievement and at the same time a bit surprised that all was over so soon. He poked Coco with the toe of his boot, picked up one of his legs, let it go, and sat down on the dead nag; he remained sitting there for a while, his eyes fixed on the grass, thinking of nothing.

He returned to the farm but said nothing about what had happened, for he wanted to have a pretext to go wandering at the hours when he was supposed to move the old horse's stake.

He went to see it on the following day. Crows took off at

his approach. Innumerable flies were crawling on the corpse and buzzing around it.

Back at the farm, he announced the death. The animal was so old that no one was surprised. The farmer told two farmhands:

"Grab your spades, boys, and dig a hole wherever he is."

So the men buried the horse on the exact spot where it had died of starvation.

And grass—lush, green, vigorous grass—grew up, nourished by the poor corpse.

[*Coco,* January 21, 1884]

The Avowal

The midday sun rains down on the undulating fields lying between the clumps of trees around the farmhouses. A variety of crops—ripe rye, yellowing wheat, light green oats, and dark green clover—spread a great cloak, striped, soft, and rippling, over the naked belly of the earth.

Over there, on the crest of a rolling field, stretches an endless row of cows, like soldiers manning a line; some lying down, others standing, they blink their big round eyes in the brutal light as they ruminate and graze in a field of clover vast as a lake.

Two women, mother and daughter, follow a narrow path between the fields, walking rhythmically, one behind the other, toward that army of cows.

Both carry two tin pails held away from their bodies by barrel hoops, and with every step they take, the metal casts a white and dazzling flame under the beating sun.

They don't say a word. They are on their way to milk the cows. When they reach them, they put down their pails, go up to the two nearest beasts, and kick them in the ribs with their clogs to make them stand up. The beasts rise slowly —first straightening their forelegs, then, more painfully, raising their massive hindquarters that seem weighed down by the huge udders of pink, pendant flesh.

The two Malivoires, mother and daughter, kneeling beneath

the cows' bellies, pull with swiftly moving hands at the beasts' swollen teats which release at each squeeze a slender thread of milk into the pail. As the women go from beast to beast, to the end of the long row, yellowish froth rises to the brim of their pails.

As soon as they have finished with a cow, they send it off to graze a fresh patch of meadow.

Then they retrace their steps, more slowly this time with their load of milk, the mother walking ahead, the daughter following behind.

But the daughter suddenly stops, puts down her load, lets herself slide to the ground, and starts to cry.

The mother, no longer hearing footsteps behind her, turns and stands there gaping.

"What's the matter?"

The daughter, Céleste, a big redhead with flaming hair and flaming cheeks flecked with freckles as if droplets of fire had fallen on her face one day as she worked in the sun, murmured in the soft whine of a child that has been spanked:

"I can't carry the milk no more."

The mother looked at her suspiciously, then said again:

"What's the matter?"

Crumpled on the ground between her two pails and hiding her eyes in her apron, Céleste replied:

"There's something pulling inside me. I just can't."

For the third time, the mother repeated:

"What's the matter then?"

The daughter moaned:

"Looks like I'm in a family way."

And she sobbed.

The old woman then put down her load, so taken aback that she couldn't say a word. Finally she managed to mumble:

"So . . . so . . . so you're in a family way, you tramp? How could that be?"

They were rich farmers, the Malivoires: solid, well established, respected, shrewd, and influential.

Céleste stammered:

"I think I am, just the same."

The shocked mother looked at her tearful daughter prostrate before her. A few seconds passed and then she shouted:

"You in a family way! You in a family way! And where'd you get yourself into that mess, you slut?"

Céleste, shaken by emotion, muttered:

"Think it must have been in Polyte's coach."

Mother Malivoire tried to understand, to find out who could have possibly brought this misfortune on her Céleste. If the boy was well off and well considered, things could always be arranged; it wouldn't really be half so bad. Céleste wasn't by any means the first to whom such a thing had happened. But still, considering the gossip that could start and their position in the village, she was annoyed.

"And who was it," she said, "did that to you, you little bitch?"

Céleste, resolved to make a clean breast of it all, mumbled:

"Think it must have been Polyte."

Then Mother Malivoire, in a mad rage, pounced on her daughter and beat her with such frenzy that she lost her bonnet.

She hammered hard with her fists on her daughter's head, on her back, everywhere; and Céleste, prostrate between the two pails which gave her some protection, simply covered her face with her hands.

The cows, surprised, had stopped grazing and were watching them with their big round eyes. The nearest of them mooed, stretching its nose toward the women.

When she was breathless from beating her daughter, Mother Malivoire stopped. Panting, she regained control of herself a bit and decided to get to the bottom of the matter:

"Polyte! My God, can it be? How could you—with a coach driver? Were you out of your mind? He must've put a spell on you, the good-for-nothing!"

And Céleste, still lying on the ground, whispered into the dust:

"I didn't have to pay my fare."

Then the old Norman peasant woman understood.

~

Every week, on Wednesdays and Saturdays, Céleste went to town with the farm produce—poultry, cream, and eggs.

She left the house at seven in the morning with two big baskets—one with dairy produce, the other with chickens—and walked to the highway to wait for the coach to Yvetot.

She set down her goods and sat in the ditch by the wayside. The chickens with their short, sharp beaks and the ducks with their wide, flat bills thrust their heads between the wicker bars and stared at her with their round, stupid, and bewildered eyes.

Soon the public coach, a kind of yellow trunk with a black

leather cap on top of it, came along, its rear jouncing from the jerky trot of a white nag.

Polyte, the driver—a big, jolly fellow, already potbellied despite his youth, baked by the sun, burned by the wind, tempered by the rain, reddened by liquor until his face and neck were the color of brick—cracked his whip and called out to her from afar:

"Morning, Miss Céleste, and how are you feeling today?"

She handed her baskets up to him and he stowed them on the roof, after which she climbed into the coach, raising her leg high to reach the step and uncovering a strong, rounded calf encased in a blue stocking.

Each time, Polyte came out with the same joke:

"My, my, haven't lost no weight, have you!"

And each time she found it funny and laughed.

Then he let out a "Hup, Cocotte" to his skinny nag to get it moving again. Céleste dug into her pocket for her purse, cautiously drawing out of it fifty centimes—thirty for herself and twenty for the baskets—and reached over Polyte's shoulder to give them to him. He took the money, saying:

"So we still won't be having it today, our little bit of fun?"

And he laughed heartily, turning around to have a leisurely look at her.

It always hurt her to have to pay out that half-franc for the two-mile ride. And it was even worse when she didn't have any coppers and had to part with a whole silver coin.

So one day, when the time had come to pay, she said:

"For a steady fare like me, you could make it just thirty centimes."

He laughed.

"Thirty centimes, my beauty, you're worth more than that, for sure!"

She pressed him further:

"You'd still make more than two francs a month out of me."

Flicking the nag with his whip, he cried:

"Know what? I'd like to be accommodating, so I'll forget the fare for a bit of fun."

She asked him with a stupid look:

"What's that you say?"

That made him laugh so much that he wound up coughing.

"A bit of fun is a bit of fun, by God. A girl and a boy can go ahead and play a game for two and they don't need no music for that."

She understood, blushed, and said:

"I don't go in for that sort of game, M'sieu Polyte."

But that didn't discourage him and, enjoying himself more and more, he repeated:

"You'll get to it, my beauty, to the bit of fun a girl and boy can have together."

After that, he got into the habit of asking every time she paid:

"And what about our little bit of fun—still not today?"

She joked about it too and answered:

"Not today, M'sieu Polyte, but Saturday for sure."

And still roaring with laughter, he shouted:

"It's a date then, my beauty—Saturday!"

But she kept calculating that during the two years that this had been going on, she had paid Polyte a good forty-eight francs, and in the country you don't find forty-eight francs in a wheel rut. And she also reckoned that in another two years she'd have paid out close to a hundred francs.

So one day, a spring day when they were alone in the coach and he asked as usual:

"What about our bit of fun—still not today?"

She answered:

"Whatever you say, M'sieu Polyte."

He wasn't in the least surprised. He stepped over the seat, mumbling happily:

"So let's get going. I knew we'd get to it in the end."

And the old white nag trotted along so smoothly that it seemed to be joggling up and down on one spot, ignoring the occasional shouts which rose from the depths of the coach:

"Hup, Cocotte! Hup, Cocotte, get a move on!"

Three months later, Céleste realized she was pregnant.

⁂

She told her mother the whole story in a tearful voice. The old woman, pale with fury, asked her:

"So how much did it come to?"

"Four months," Céleste said, "that makes eight francs for sure."

At that, the peasant woman gave unbridled vent to her rage, and pouncing on her daughter once more, she again beat her until her breath gave out. Then she straightened herself up and said:

"Did you tell him?"

"I sure didn't."

"Why didn't you?"

"Because then maybe he'd have made me start paying again."

The mother thought for a while, then picking up her pails again, she said:

"C'mon, get up and try to walk."

After a pause, she added:

"Well, don't say nothing to him as long as he don't notice himself. That way we'll have saved at least six or eight months of fares."

Céleste, back on her feet but still crying, bonnetless and puffy-faced, set off again, walking heavily and muttering under her breath:

"Of course I won't tell him."

[*L'Aveu*, July 22, 1884]

The Piece of String

All along the roads around Goderville, peasants and their womenfolk were moving toward the town, this being market day. The men walked unhurriedly, their whole bodies swaying forward at each stride of their long, bandy legs, deformed by hard labor—by the weight of the plow, which jerks the left shoulder up at the same time as it twists the waist; by mowing the wheat, for which, to get a firm footing, they must spread their knees wide apart; by all the endless, painful chores of farming. Their blue peasant smocks—starched and shiny as if varnished, with small patterns embroidered in white on the collars and cuffs—ballooned around their bony bodies, making them look as if they were about to take off into the air. And from each of these smocks emerged a head, two hands, and two feet.

Some led a cow or a calf by a rope, while their wives, walking behind the animal, flicked its haunches with a leafy branch to make it move faster. The women carried large baskets out of which stuck here a chicken's head, there a duck's. They walked with shorter, quicker steps than their men, their dry, erect figures wrapped in scanty little shawls pinned over their flat bosoms, and with white cloths tied tightly over their hair and topped by bonnets.

Sometimes a wagon drawn by a jerkily-trotting nag would pass by, incongruously jouncing the two men sitting next to each other in front, while a woman in the depths of the vehicle would hang on tightly to the sides to soften the jolts.

The central square of Goderville was astir with a teeming throng of men and beasts. The cattle's horns, the tall, long-napped hats of the prosperous peasants, and their women's bonnets all floated on the surface of the crowd. Shrill, screeching cries merged into a continuous wild din which occasionally was dominated by some great roar exhaled from the robust chest of a joyous peasant, or by the drawn-out mooing of a cow tied to the wall of a house.

It all reeked of stables—of milk and dung, hay and sweat—and gave off that frightful, sour, human and animal smell that is characteristic of those who labor in the fields.

Old M. Hauchecorne from the village of Bréauté had just arrived in Goderville and was on his way to the central square when he noticed a small piece of string on the ground. M. Hauchecorne, thrifty as any true, self-respecting Norman peasant, felt that one ought to pick up anything one could use. He bent down painfully, because he suffered from rheumatism, and took hold of the thin string and was about to roll it up neatly when he noticed the harness-maker, M. Malandain, standing on his doorstep and watching him. They had once quarreled about a halter and since then had remained on bad terms, both of them being inclined to hold a grudge. M. Hauchecorne was rather embarrassed at his enemy seeing him pick a piece of string out of the dirt, so he hurriedly concealed his find under his smock, from there slipped it into his trouser pocket, and then pretended to be still looking on the ground for something that he couldn't find. After which, his head thrust forward and his body bent in two with pain, he went on to the market.

There he was soon lost in the noisy, slow-moving crowd bubbling with the endless bargaining. The peasants poked at the animals, walked away, came back—always hesitant, always afraid of having something put over on them, not daring to decide one way or the other, watching the seller's eyes, forever trying to unmask the trickiness of the man and the hidden defect of the beast.

The women had deposited their vast baskets and pulled out their chickens, which now lay on the ground with their legs tied, their eyes terrified under the scarlet combs. They listened to the offers made them; stuck stubbornly to their own prices, their faces remaining expressionless; or suddenly decided to accept the reduction demanded and called after the customer who was already walking slowly away:

"Fine, agreed, M. Anthime. Have it your way."

Gradually the crowd thinned out and, as the Angelus rang at midday, those who lived too far away to get home dispersed to the inns of the town.

At Jourdain's, the large room was full of people eating and its vast courtyard was full of all sorts of vehicles—carts, gigs, wagons, tilburys, and innumerable dumpcarts splattered with yellow dirt, shapeless and patched up, some with their shafts pointing upward like arms raised to the sky, others with their noses to the ground and their rears in the air.

Close by the dining tables, the immense fireplace, full of limpid flames, cast a lively warmth onto the backs of a row of customers. Three spits were turning, loaded with chickens, pigeons, and legs of mutton. A delicious aroma of roast meat, of juices seeping through nicely browned skin, rose from the hearth, kindling cheerfulness and making mouths water.

The entire aristocracy of the plow was eating at M. Jourdain's—a restaurant owner and horse-dealer, a smart man who had made good money.

Dishes of food and jugs of golden cider were brought in and taken away empty. Everyone talked about his business—about what he had bought and sold. They discussed crops—the damp weather was fine for the green vegetables but not so good for the wheat.

Suddenly a drum sounded outside in the courtyard. Except for a few phlegmatic individuals, they were all on their feet at once and rushing toward a door or a window, their mouths still full and chewing and their napkins in their hands.

When he was through rolling his drum, the town crier intoned in a jerky voice, breaking off his phrases in the wrong places:

"It is hereby—announced to the—inhabitants of Goderville and in general to all—persons present at the market, that there was lost, between nine and ten o'clock this—morning on the Beuzeville Road, a black leather—wallet containing five hundred francs and business documents. The finder is requested to take same to—the town hall or directly to M. Fortuné Houlbrèque in the village of Manneville. The reward is twenty francs."

The town crier left and the muted drumrolls followed by the crier's voice, weakened by distance, were heard again from afar.

Then they all discussed the incident, debating what chances M. Houlbrèque had of recovering his wallet.

The meal was coming to an end.

They were finishing their coffee when the police sergeant appeared in the doorway.

He asked:

"Is M. Hauchecorne from Bréauté here?"

And M. Hauchecorne, who was sitting at the end of the table, said:

"Yes, I'm here."

"M. Hauchecorne," the police sergeant said, "would you be kind enough to come with me to the mayor's office. He would like to have a word with you."

The old peasant was surprised and disturbed. He hurriedly emptied his small glass of brandy, got up, and even more bent than in the morning—because the first steps after sitting down were particularly painful—followed the police sergeant, repeating:

"Here I am, here I am."

The mayor, who was also the town's notary, was sitting in an armchair, waiting for him. He was a big, heavy man, solemn and fond of turning a pompous phrase.

"M. Hauchecorne," he said, "you were seen this morning picking up the wallet lost by M. Houlbrèque from Manneville on the Beuzeville Road."

The bewildered peasant stared at the mayor, frightened by the suspicion directed at him for a reason he did not know.

"Me. . . me . . . I picked up that wallet? Me?"

"Yes, you."

"But—I swear—I don't even know anything about it."

"You were seen, though."

"I was seen? Who saw me?"

"M. Malandain, the harness-maker."

Then the old man remembered, understood, and turning red with anger, said:

"Ah, so it was him saw me, that good-for-nothing! What he saw me do was pick up this here piece of string. Here, have a look, M'sieu le Maire."

He rummaged in his pocket and pulled out the bit of string.

But the mayor, not believing him, shook his head.

"You're not going to try and make me believe, M. Hauchecorne, that M. Malandain, who is a most respectable man, could have mistaken that piece of string for a wallet?"

Furious, the peasant solemnly raised his hand and spat to one side, to protest his innocence:

"Yes it's God's holy truth, M'sieu le Maire. Here, I swear it on my soul and my salvation."

The mayor went on:

"Even after you picked up the item in question, you kept looking around in the mud for a long time, in case some piece of change had rolled out."

The old peasant gasped with fear and indignation.

"How can anyone say that! How can people tell lies like that and ruin an honest man! How can anyone—!"

In vain he protested. No one believed him.

He was confronted with M. Malandain who repeated his accusation and stuck to it. For a whole hour, they abused each other. M. Hauchecorne demanded that he be searched—he was. They found nothing on him.

Finally the mayor, baffled, allowed him to leave, warning him that he would advise the public prosecutor's office of what had happened and await further instructions on the subject.

The news had spread. When he emerged from the Town Hall, a crowd of the curious surrounded the old man and questioned him, some seriously, others banteringly, but none with indignation. So he told them the story about the string. They didn't believe him. They laughed.

He walked off, was stopped again by everyone he met, himself stopped people he knew, re-telling his story again and again, repeating his protestations, showing his turned-out pocket to prove he had nothing there.

They said:

"Go on, you old rogue!"

He lost his temper, became exasperated, feverish, and distressed at being unable to make them believe him. And not knowing what else to do, he kept repeating his story again and again.

Night came and he had to go home. He started out with three neighbors to whom he showed the spot where he had picked up the piece of string, and during the whole trip, he talked about his misadventure.

In the evening, he went around his village, Bréauté, telling it to everyone there, and there too he met with nothing but incredulity.

That made him feel ill during the night.

Around one in the afternoon of the following day, Marius

Paumelle, a farm laborer working on M. Breton's farm in Ymauville, returned the wallet and its contents to M. Houlbrèque in Manneville. The hired hand claimed that he had found it on the road but, being illiterate, had taken it home and handed it over to his employer.

The news spread rapidly throughout the countryside. M. Hauchecorne was advised of it. Immediately, he started going his rounds, re-telling the story, now complete with the happy ending. He felt triumphant.

"What hurt me most, let me tell you, wasn't the thing itself—I want you to understand me—it was the lie. There's nothing hurts a man like being blamed for something on account of a lie."

All day long he talked about the incident. He recounted it to people he met on the road, to drinkers in the taverns, to the people leaving church on Sunday. He even stopped complete strangers to tell it to them. He felt quite safe and yet something kept bothering him, something he couldn't put his finger on. People somehow seemed amused as they listened to him. They didn't seem convinced. He felt they were making remarks about him behind his back.

On Tuesday of the following week, he again went to market at Goderville, prompted solely by his need to explain his case further.

Malandain, standing on his doorstep, began to laugh when he saw Hauchecorne pass by. Why?

He buttonholed a farmer from Criquetot who never gave him a chance to finish, poked him playfully in the hollow of his belly, and shouted in his face: "Ah, you sly old rogue!" and turned his back on him.

M. Hauchecorne was bewildered. Why had the man called him a "sly old rogue"?

When he was installed at Jourdain's, he started explaining his case again.

A horse-dealer from Montivilliers shouted at him:

"Come, come, you old rascal, I know all about that string of yours!"

Hauchecorne stammered:

"But . . . but since they found the wallet?"

But the horse-dealer said:

"Ah, come off it, old man. One fellow finds it, another takes it back. One hand don't know what the other is doing and everything's clear as mud."

He was left speechless. At last he understood. They were

accusing him now of having had the wallet returned by an accomplice.

He tried to protest. The whole table roared with laughter.

He couldn't finish his dinner and left to the accompaniment of jeers.

He returned home, ashamed and indignant, breathless with fury and embarrassment—the more dejected because, with his Norman cunning, he was quite capable of having done what he was accused of and even of bragging about it and viewing it as a smart trick to have played on a person. Vaguely, he felt that he could never prove his innocence because of his reputation for slyness. The unjust suspicion hurt him like a stab in the heart.

So he started telling the story again, each day making it longer and longer, adding new arguments all the time to establish his innocence, protesting more and more violently, making his oaths more and more solemn. He thought up all his arguments in solitude, his mind entirely preoccupied with the story of that piece of string. And he was less and less believed as his defense became more and more complicated and his arguments more and more subtle.

"Those reasons he gives are the reasons of a liar," people said behind his back.

He felt it and it kept gnawing at him. He wore himself out in his vain efforts. He wasted away before their eyes.

Those who wanted a laugh made him tell about the string, just as one makes a decrepit old soldier recount once more the story of a campaign in which he took part. His badly wounded mind began to give way.

By the end of December he had taken to his bed.

He died in the first days of January, and in the delirium of his death-agony, he was still reaffirming his innocence:

"A lil' piece of string. . . . Just a lil' bit o' string. . . . Here, your Honor, have a look. . . ."

[*La Ficelle,* November 25, 1883]

The Little Cask

M. Chicot, the innkeeper of Épreville, pulled up his tilbury in front of Mother Magloire's farmhouse. He was forty, tall, ruddy-faced and potbellied, and he had a reputation as a sly one in the neighborhood.

He hitched his horse to a fencepost and entered the farmyard. He owned some land adjoining the old woman's farm and had long coveted her plot. He had offered to buy it from her perhaps twenty times, but Mother Magloire obstinately refused.

"I was born here and I'll die here," was all she would say.

He found her peeling potatoes on her doorstep. She was seventy-two, thin, wrinkled and stooped, but tireless as a young girl. Chicot gave her an affectionate pat on the back and sat down beside her on a stool.

"So what d'you say, Mother Magloire? Feeling fine as usual, I see?"

"Can't complain, Monsieur Chicot, and what about you?"

"Well, I've a few pains here and there but otherwise no complaints."

"I'm glad to hear that."

And she said no more. Chicot watched her working. Her hard, crooked, knotty fingers looked like a crab's pincers the way they gripped the grayish potatoes in the pail and then, turning them quickly against the blade of an old knife that she held in her other hand, stripped the long peels off them. When a potato was left naked and yellow, she tossed it into a pail of water. Three daring hens came each in turn right up to her skirts, picked up some peels, and scurried off, carrying them in their beaks.

Chicot looked ill at ease, hesitant, and anxious—he had something on the tip of his tongue but couldn't get it out. At last he said:

"Tell me, Mother Magloire—"

"What can I do for you, my good man?"

"You still won't sell me this farm of yours?"

"Ah no, that I won't! Nothing doing. I've told you once and for all and you can just forget it."

"But I've found a way, Mother Magloire, that would suit us both."

"And what's that?"

"Here's what: you sell me your farm and you still keep it. Don't you see how it would be? Listen—and follow me real careful now."

The old crone stopped peeling her potatoes and her light eyes under their wrinkled lids were fixed on the innkeeper.

"Let me explain. Every month I'll give you a hundred and fifty francs. I want you to understand now: each month I'll drive over in this here tilbury and pay you that amount. And for the rest, nothing'll be changed from the way it is now—everything will be just the same. You'll stay in your house, you won't have to bother about me, you'll owe me nothing. All you'll do is take my cash. Well, does that suit you?"

He looked at her cheerfully, with a pleased air.

The old woman eyed him suspiciously, trying to discover where the trap lay. She asked:

"That's for me, but what do you get out of it? I still won't let you have the farm, you know."

"Don't worry about me," he said. "You'll hold onto your farm as long as the good Lord keeps you alive. You're in your own house. All you'll have to do is sign a small piece of paper for me at the notary's; that'll give me the farm after you're gone. You have no children of your own, just nephews, and you don't really care a hoot about them. . . . Well, what do you say? You keep what's yours as long as you live and I give you one hundred and fifty francs every month. Can't you see it's all to your advantage?"

The old woman was still surprised and apprehensive but she was also rather tempted. She answered:

"I don't say no, but I must think it over. Come back sometime next week and we'll talk about it some more. I'll tell you what I think then."

And M. Chicot departed as happy as a king who has conquered an empire.

Mother Magloire thought hard about the deal offered her and she couldn't go to sleep that night. For four days she was in a fever of hesitation. She thought she smelled a rat buried somewhere but the idea of the hundred and fifty francs every month, of that beautiful ringing money that would pour into her apron as if from the sky without her having to do anything for it, dangled before her covetous eyes.

So she went to see the village notary and told him about the offer. The notary advised her to accept it but to demand that Chicot pay her two hundred and fifty rather than one hundred and fifty a month, since at the lowest estimate the Magloire farm was worth sixty thousand francs.

"Even if you were to live another fifteen years," the notary told her, "you would still only get forty-five thousand out of him, even at that rate."

The old woman's spine fairly tingled at the thought of two hundred and fifty francs every month, but she was still wary of possible traps being set for her, and of all sorts of unforeseen things; she stayed in the notary's office until evening, asking him all sorts of questions and unable to make up her mind to leave. Finally she instructed him to draw up the agreement, and when she got home her head was buzzing as though she had downed four mugs of new hard cider.

When Chicot came for his answer, she let him talk and persuade her for a while, telling him that she wasn't really interested—and a little afraid that he would refuse to agree to pay her the extra hundred francs a month. Finally, as he insisted, she announced the sum she was willing to accept from him.

He leaped up in disappointment and refused.

Then, to convince him, she started to reason with him about how long she was likely to live.

"I don't expect to last more than five or six years, I'm sure. I'm going on seventy-three, remember, and I'm none too strong at that. The other day I was pretty sure I was going to pass away. It seemed like there was nothing left inside me, and they had to carry me to my bed."

But Chicot didn't fall for that.

"Come, come, you old trickster, you're as sturdy as the churchtower! I'm sure you'll live to be at least a hundred and ten. I'm sure, quite sure, you'll bury me in the end."

The whole day was wasted on arguing. But finally seeing that the old crone wouldn't budge, the innkeeper agreed to pay her the two hundred and fifty francs per month.

They signed the agreement the next day and Mother Magloire even managed to get an extra fifty francs out of the innkeeper for signing.

Three years passed. The old woman felt wonderful. She didn't look one day older and Chicot was in despair. He felt that he had been handing her the monthly payments for half a century, that he had been cheated, made a fool of, ruined. From time to time he'd go to see Mother Magloire as a farmer goes to the fields in July to see whether the corn is ripe enough for harvesting. She would receive him with a sly twinkle in her eye and look as if she were enjoying the trick she had played on him. He would hastily climb back into his tilbury, muttering:

"Will you ever croak, you old carcass?"

He was at a loss to know what to do. He felt like strangling her when he saw her. He watched her with a fierce, scheming hatred, the hatred of a peasant toward someone who had stolen his goods.

So he began to look for a way out of his predicament.

One day he came to see her. He was rubbing his hands just as he had the first time he had proposed their present deal to her. Then after a few minutes of the usual conversation, he said: "Say, Mother Magloire, why don't you drop into my restaurant and have dinner when you come to Épreville? People are going around saying we're no longer friends, you and me, and that sort of hurts me, you know. And then, you won't have to pay—one dinner, that won't make too much difference one way or another. So whenever you feel like it, don't hesitate. I'd be real pleased to have you at my place."

He didn't have to insist. Two days later, when she came to market, she drove up in front of his place in her gig, driven by her farmhand Célestin—whom she ordered, without the slightest compunction, to put her horse in Monsieur Chicot's stable; then she went in to claim the dinner he had promised she could have on the house.

The innkeeper, delighted, treated her like a great lady, served her chicken, blood sausage, leg of lamb, cabbage and bacon. But she ate very little because she had been frugal in her habits since childhood and lived mostly on soup with a crust of buttered bread to go with it.

Chicot, disappointed, insisted in vain. Nor did she drink. She even refused coffee. Then he asked her:

"But surely, you'll accept a nice little glass of brandy?"

"Ah, now that, yes. I couldn't say no to that."

And he called out at the top of his lungs, so that the whole restaurant could hear him:

"Hey, Rosalie, bring us some brandy here, and I mean the very best!"

The servant brought a tall bottle with a label shaped like a vine leaf and Chicot filled two small glasses.

"Taste this, Mother Magloire. I guarantee you'll find it out of this world!"

The old woman drank it in tiny sips, so as to make her pleasure last. She drained her glass to the last drop and declared:

"Yes, that's a real nice brandy."

Before she'd even finished speaking, Chicot had refilled her glass. She wanted to refuse but it was too late and she proceeded to sip it as she had done the first.

He offered her a third, but she resisted. He reasoned:

"But it's just the same as milk, don't you see? Me, I drink ten glasses like this without any harm. It melts in your mouth like sugar. It does no harm to your stomach or to your head—it's just like it evaporates when it touches your tongue. I'm told there's nothing better for one's health."

Since she was longing to have some more, she yielded to his pleas but accepted only half a glass. Then Chicot, in a burst of generosity, cried:

"Know what? Since you seem to like this brandy, I'll make you a present of a little cask of it just to prove that you and me are still good friends!"

The old woman didn't say no and she left slightly tipsy.

The following day the innkeeper showed up at her farmyard, bringing with him in his tilbury a little iron-hooped cask. He insisted that they should taste the stuff it contained to prove to her that it was exactly the same brandy they had drunk at his place.

When they had had three little glasses each and he was taking his leave of her, he suddenly announced:

"And you know, when you're through with this, there's more where it came from. You don't have to be shy—I never grudge a thing to my friends. In fact, the sooner you finish this cask the better I'll like it." And he climbed into his tilbury.

Four days later he was back. The old woman was at her doorstep, cutting up stale bread to put into her soup. He came up close and spoke to her nose to nose, trying to smell her breath. When he caught a whiff of liquor, his face lit up and he said to her:

"Won't you stand a glass of brandy to your old friend?"

So they had three glasses each.

And soon a rumor spread over the countryside that Mother Magloire was getting drunk all by herself. People would discover her, sometimes in her kitchen, sometimes in her yard, sometimes along some road outside her place, and they would have to carry her home like a corpse.

Chicot didn't go to see her anymore, and when they spoke of the old peasant woman to him, he'd say with a sad expression:

"It's a real shame to start drinking at her age! There's no way out when it gets hold of an old person. I'm sure it'll get her into trouble in the end!"

And it did get her into trouble. She died the following winter, around Christmas time, when she passed out drunk in the snow.

When Monsieur Chicot inherited the farm he commented:

"Ah, if she hadn't taken to drink, the old crone, she might easily have lasted another ten years!"

[*Le Petit Fût,* April 7, 1884]

At Sea

The following item recently appeared in the papers under the dateline "Boulogne-sur-Mer, January 22":

> A frightful disaster has caused consternation among our coastal population, which has already been so hard-hit during the last two years. A fishing trawler commanded by Captain Javel was carried westward off its course as it was entering port and thrown against the breakwater.
>
> Despite the efforts of the lifeboat and the life lines thrown to them, four men and a boy were lost.
>
> The bad weather continues and fresh disasters are feared.

Who was Captain Javel? Could it be the brother of one-armed Javel?

Was the poor man swept away by the waves, or perhaps dead under the debris of his wrecked ship, the Javel I'm thinking of? If so, he had once before witnessed a tragedy at sea, terrible and simple as are all great tragedies of the deep.

It happened eighteen years ago. The elder Javel was then master of a smack, which is an ideal fishing boat. Sturdy, fearing no weather, round-bellied, constantly bobbing on the waves like a cork, always out at sea, forever whipped by the biting, salty winds of the Channel, it plows the billows tirelessly—its sails ballooning, trailing at its side a great net that sweeps over the ocean bottom, grabbing and tearing loose all the sleeping creatures of the rocks: the flat fish that hug the sands, the heavy crabs with their hooked claws, and the lobsters with their pointed whiskers. When the breeze is fresh and the waves are short and choppy, the smack begins to trawl. The net is tied to a long, iron-sheathed wooden bar that is lowered by means of two cables running through two blocks rigged one at each end of the boat. And so the smack, drifting with the wind and the current, drags along this rig which ravages and robs the sea floor.

Javel's crew consisted of his younger brother, four other men, and a boy. They set out from Boulogne on a clear day, hoping to trawl. But when they were out, the wind rose and a squall chased the smack. They reached the English coast, but the stormy seas smashing against the cliffs made it impossible to enter a port. The smack then turned back to sea and returned toward the coast of France. The storm was still so violent that the breakwaters could not be negotiated, and the harbor entrances were wrapped in froth, din, and danger. The little smack turned away once more. The waves tossed it around, shook it, and battered it; but it took all this pluckily, accustomed as it was to rough weather that had sometimes forced it to wander for five or six days between the two neighboring countries without being able to put into a port on either side.

Finally, while the craft was out in the open sea, the storm subsided somewhat, and although the waves were still quite big, the skipper ordered the trawl lowered.

The heavy net was passed overboard and two men forward and two aft began to pay out the cables that held it through the blocks. But when the trawl touched the bottom, a large wave tipped the boat; and the younger Javel, who was on the forward block directing the maneuver, slipped and got his arm caught between the ship's side and the rope that had been slackened for a second when the net had reached the bottom and then had tightened again when the boat was lifted by the waves. He made a desperate effort to loosen the rope with his free hand, but by now it was taut and wouldn't budge.

Shaken by pain, he called for help. They all rushed to him. His brother abandoned the wheel and also joined them. They all took hold of the rope and pulled, trying to slacken it and free the arm that it was crushing. It was all in vain.

"Must be cut," a seaman said, and he produced a big, sharp jackknife that in two slashes could have saved the younger Javel's arm.

But of course, cutting the rope meant losing the trawl net and that meant losing money, a great deal of money—fifteen hundred francs—and it was the property of the elder Javel who hated to let go of what he had. So, his heart filled with agony, he shouted:

"Wait, don't cut it! I'll try to luff. . . ." And he rushed to the wheel and tried to bring the boat closer to the wind. But the smack hardly responded because the net made it unmaneuverable; in addition, it was drifting with the wind and current.

The younger Javel slipped down to his knees, his teeth clenched, his eyes haggard. He said nothing. His brother came back, still worried about the jackknife.

"Wait, wait, don't cut it yet. We'll anchor. . . ."

The anchor was dropped, the chain paid out. Then they tried to wind the cables around the capstan to slacken the ropes that held the trawl. Finally they got enough slack and released the lifeless arm in its blood-stained, woolen sleeve.

The younger Javel's face was blank. They removed his jacket and saw a horrible mass of flesh with blood gushing from it in many streams, as if someone were pumping it out. The man looked at his arm and said:

"I've had it!"

As the blood formed a river on the deck, a seaman shouted:

"Why, he'll empty himself like that. We must tie it off."

So they got a rope, a dark, tarred piece of rope, turned it around the arm above the wound, and tied it as tight as they could. The jets of blood diminished gradually and finally the bleeding stopped completely.

The younger Javel got up, his arm hanging at his side. He took it in his other hand, lifted it, turned it, and shook it. It was quite loose. The bones were broken and only the tendons held it to the rest of his body. He looked at it gloomily, thinking something over. Then he sat down on a folded sail and the others advised him to keep wetting his injured arm with brine to prevent the "black rot."

They placed a bucket of water next to him and every minute or so, he would dip a glass into it and pour a thin, transparent stream over his horrible wound.

"You'd be better off down below," his brother said, and he went down. But within an hour he was back on deck, for he hadn't felt too good down there all by himself. Besides, he preferred to be out in the fresh air. So he sat down on the folded sail and started bathing his arm again.

The fishing was good. Big, white-bellied fish lay next to him, jerking in their death agony, and he watched them as he poured the seawater on his wounded limb.

When they were about to return to Boulogne, a new squall came up and the little fishing boat resumed its mad rush back and forth between the French and English coasts, jouncing, shaking, and rolling the gloomy wounded man.

Night came and the sea remained rough until dawn. As the sun rose, the English coast was once more in sight. But then the weather improved a bit, and they turned back toward France, beating into the wind.

Toward evening the wounded man called his shipmates and showed them some black stains on his arm—the sinister marks of rot on the loose part of the limb.

The sailors examined it and voiced their opinions.

"It could very well be the Black One," one man mused.

"You must keep it in the brine," another seaman advised.

They brought a bucket of seawater and poured it on the arm. The injured man turned livid, his teeth gnashed, his body twisted slightly. But he didn't cry out. And when the scorching pain caused by the salt water had subsided a bit, he said to his brother:

"Give me your knife," and when the other handed it to him, he said: "Hold my arm up straight. That's right, now pull."

His brother did as he was told.

Then the younger Javel began to cut off his own arm. He cut it slowly, thoughtfully, snapping off the remaining tendons with the razor-sharp blade of the jackknife, and soon he had nothing but a stump left. He gave a deep sigh and said: "Had to do it. I'd had it, otherwise."

He seemed relieved, took a deep breath, then began again to pour water on what was left of his arm.

The night that followed was again too rough to enter port.

When it was day again, the younger Javel picked up his severed arm and examined it at length. The rot was now easily visible. His shipmates came and looked at it too, and it passed from hand to hand, all of them poking and smelling it.

The older brother said:

"Seeing the state it's in, it's best to throw it overboard."

But now the younger brother lost his temper.

"Oh no! No, sir! I don't want it tossed overboard and it's not going to be, since it's my arm!" And he took it back and put it between his knees.

"Still, you can't stop it from rotting," his brother said.

Then the wounded man got an idea: when they stayed at sea for a long time, they preserved their fish in barrels of brine. So he said:

"I guess it'd keep in brine, though?"

"It ought to," the others agreed.

They emptied a barrel which was already full of fish they had caught on an earlier day and put the arm at the bottom of it. They poured brine in over it and then replaced the fish, one by one.

One of the seamen cracked a joke on this occasion: "Hope we don't sell it in the market by mistake!"

And all except the two Javels laughed.

The wind was still blowing and they had to beat to windward again; they didn't come within sight of Boulogne until ten o'clock. The wounded man kept tirelessly throwing water over his wound. From time to time he would get up and walk from one end of the boat to the other. His brother, who was at the wheel, followed him with his eyes, shaking his head.

Finally they put into Boulogne.

A doctor examined the wound and declared it to be in good shape. He dressed it and prescribed rest for the patient. But Javel wouldn't lie down until he had recovered his arm. He rushed back to port, went on board his brother's smack, and found the barrel that he had marked with a cross in chalk. They emptied it while he watched, then he picked up his limb, which had been very nicely preserved in the brine. It looked rather fresher than before, although it was strangely wrinkled. He wrapped it in a napkin that he had brought with him for the purpose and returned home.

His wife and children examined this piece of their father at length, touching the fingers and removing the traces of salt from under the nails. Then they called the carpenter and asked him to make a little coffin.

The following day, the full crew of the smack followed the funeral of their shipmate's severed limb. The two brothers, side by side, led the procession. The parish sexton carried the little corpse under his arm.

The younger Javel didn't go back to sea. He got a job in the port; and later, when he would speak of the incident, he would confide to his listener in a low voice:

"If my brother had been willing to cut loose his trawl, I'd still have my arm, no doubt about that. . . . But he sure didn't like to part with his goods, my brother."

[*En Mer,* February 12, 1883]

II
TOWN FOLK

A Country Outing

For five months they had been talking of having lunch outside Paris on the saint's day of Madame Dufour, whose first name was Pétronille. And since they had been waiting impatiently for this outing for a long time, they got up very early that morning.

Monsieur Dufour had borrowed the milkman's cart, which he drove himself. The two-wheeled cart was quite presentable; its top was supported by four iron rods with curtains attached to them—curtains that were rolled up now, the better to admire the landscape. Only the curtain in the rear had been left loose, and it was flapping like a flag.

The wife, sitting next to her husband, had blossomed forth in an extraordinary, cherry-colored silk dress. Behind them, on two chairs, sat the old grandmother and a young girl, and one could also see the yellow thatch of a young fellow who, since there was nothing for him to sit on, had sprawled out in the bottom of the cart so that only his head showed.

When they had driven down the Champs Elysées and passed the fortifications at the Porte Maillot, the party began to admire the countryside.

When they reached the Neuilly Bridge, Monsieur Dufour announced; "Here we are, in the country at last," and at this signal, his wife became very emotional about nature.

When they reached the traffic circle of Courbevoie, they

were filled with admiration at the vast expanse of the horizon. To the right, at a distance, lay Argenteuil with its church tower standing out; above it appeared the Sannois hills and the Orgemont mill. To the left, the aqueduct of Marly was outlined against the pale morning sky and, farther away, one could also see the high ground of Saint Germain; directly ahead of them, at the end of a chain of hills, the upturned earth indicated the site of the new fort of Cormeilles. And very, very far away, at an impressive distance, they caught a glimpse of the dark green line of the forest.

The sun began to scorch their faces and the dust kept getting into their eyes as, on either side of the road, a barren, dirty, stinking countryside unfolded. One would have thought it had been ravaged by a leprosy that had attacked even the houses, for the skeletons of gutted and abandoned dwellings and of huts that hadn't been finished because the builders couldn't be paid showed nothing to the world but four roofless walls.

Here and there, tall factory chimneys sprang out of the barren soil, the only vegetation in those putrid fields across which the light spring breezes spread the aroma of kerosene and soot mixed with another smell, even less alluring.

Finally they crossed the Seine for a second time, giving rein to their delight as they rolled over the bridge. The river was bursting with light—a haze rose from it, drawn up by the sun. A sweet feeling of peace came over them and they felt refreshed as they breathed a cleaner air that was no longer filled with the black smoke of the factories and stenches from the refuse dumps.

A man who passed by told them the name of the place: Bezons.

The carriage stopped and Monsieur Dufour started to read an inviting sign posted over an eating-place: "Restaurant Poulin, Fish Stews and Fish Fries, Dining Rooms for Private Parties, Garden and Swings."

"Well, what do you say, Madame Dufour—does this suit you? Will you finally make up your mind?"

Madame Dufour read the sign in her turn, after which she examined the house at length.

It was a white country inn, standing by the side of the road. Through the open door one could see the shining zinc of the counter at which two workers dressed in their Sunday best were standing.

Finally Madame Dufour decided:

"Yes, it looks all right," she said; "besides, there's the view."

The cart rolled onto the spacious grounds planted with large trees that extended behind the inn and that were only separated from the Seine by the towpath.

They got out. The husband jumped down first and opened his arms to receive his wife. The footboard, supported by two iron brackets, was very low, so that to reach it, Madame Dufour had to uncover a leg whose erstwhile slenderness was vanishing under the invasion of flesh coming down from her thighs.

Monsieur Dufour, already aroused by the countryside, quickly pinched her calf and then, catching her under the arms, deposited her heavily on the ground as if she were a huge package.

She patted her silk dress with the palms of her hands to shake the dust off it, and began to examine the place she had come to.

She was a woman of thirty-six or so, well fleshed, blooming, and pleasant to look at. She breathed painfully, held in the stranglehold of her corset, and the pressure of that contraption squeezed the quivering mass of her over-abundant bosom right up to her double chin.

Then came the young girl who, placing her hand on her father's shoulder, jumped down lightly without any further help. The yellow-haired boy had climbed down by himself, using the spokes of the wheel, and now helped Monsieur Dufour to unload the grandmother.

After that they unharnessed the horse and tied it to a tree, letting the cart fall on its nose with the two shafts on the ground. The men removed their coats, washed their hands in a bucket of water, and then joined the ladies who were already installed on the swings.

Mademoiselle Dufour was trying to swing herself by standing up on the board, but couldn't manage to give herself a sufficiently vigorous send-off. She was a handsome girl between eighteen and twenty, one of those women who, met in the street, fill a man with a sudden, whipping desire and leave that vague disturbance and agitation of the senses with him until he goes to sleep. Tall, slender at the waist, broad at the hip, she had a very dark complexion and very black hair. Her dress clearly revealed the full curves of her flesh, further accentuated by the movement of her hips as she tried to set the swing going. Her arms were stretched upward as she held on to the ropes above her head so that her breast bulged smoothly at each push she gave. Her hat, carried away by a gust of wind, had fallen behind her. Finally the swing set into motion, revealing her legs, which were quite slender, up to the knee with each swing; and throwing into the faces of the two men who were laughingly watching her the gossamer of her skirts, headier than wine vapors.

Sitting on the other swing, Madame Dufour kept moaning constantly and monotonously:

"Come over here and push me, Cyprien; come, Cyprien, give me a push."

Finally he went over to her. Rolling up the sleeves of his shirt as though he were going to start on a heavy job, he made a tremendous effort and set his wife into motion.

Grasping the ropes tightly, she held her legs out straight to avoid the ground and was delighted by the feeling of dizziness the rhythmic motion of the swing gave her. Her shaken body quivered like a jelly in a dish. But as the motion of the swing increased, she became dizzy and frightened. At each descent she let out a piercing scream that attracted the urchins of the neighborhood, so that she vaguely saw in front of her a row of mischievous faces peering over the garden hedge and distorted in a variety of ways by their laughter.

A maidservant came out from the inn and they ordered lunch.

"A fish fry from the Seine, a sautéed rabbit, a salad, and dessert," Madame Dufour spelled out with an important air.

"Bring two liters of ordinary wine and a bottle of Bordeaux," her husband said.

And their daughter added:

"We'll have our meal on the grass."

The grandmother had been seized by a feeling of tenderness at the sight of the inn's cat and had been chasing it for ten minutes, showering it in vain with affectionate pet names. The animal, although probably secretly flattered by these attentions, remained constantly close at hand without ever allowing her to get hold of it; it walked quietly around the trees, rubbing itself against them with its tail in the air and emitting little purrs of satisfaction.

"Look at that!" the blond young man cried suddenly. He had been ferreting around the grounds. "What swell boats!"

They went to have a look. Two splendid skiffs, fine and worked like costly pieces of furniture, hung in a little wooden boathouse. The boats rested side by side like two tall young maidens, stretched out in all their slender length, evoking a desire to glide over the water on gentle evenings or on bright summer mornings, to slip along past the flower-covered banks where the trees dip their branches in the water, where the eternally shivering reeds tremble and from which the lively kingfishers take off like blue streaks of lightning.

The entire family admired them reverently.

"They sure are beautiful," Monsieur Dufour repeated, examining them like a connoisseur. He had done his share of rowing when he was young, he told the others. Indeed, when he was pulling on those things—and he pretended to be pulling on oars—he didn't care a hoot for the rest of the world. He had, in his time, outraced many of those Englishmen at Joinville. . . . Then he made a few puns about the word *dames,* as oarsmen call oarlocks, saying that rowing men never went out without their *dames,* and for good reason. He got all excited as he spoke and insisted on betting that, with a boat like one of these, he could easily go fifteen miles in an hour, and without even hurrying.

"It's ready," the servant announced, appearing in the doorway.

They hurried off to eat, but they found that the spot Madame Dufour had mentally picked out as the best for their lunch was already occupied. Two young men were having their lunch there. They were obviously the owners of the boats, for they were dressed as oarsmen.

They were reclining—almost stretched out—in their chairs. Their faces were blackened by the sun and their chests were covered by the thin, white cotton jerseys from which their bare arms, as powerful as blacksmiths', emerged. They were two solid fellows, very powerfully muscled, but displaying in all their movements that graceful looseness of limb which is acquired through exercise and which is so different from the deformation produced in the worker by the repetition of the same painful effort again and again.

They exchanged a quick smile when they saw the mother and a look when they saw the daughter.

"Let's give them our place," one of the young men said; "that way we'll make their acquaintance."

The other immediately got up and, holding his half-black, half-red cap in his hand, gallantly offered the ladies the only spot in the garden unreached by the sun. His offer was accepted after a chorus of protestations and then, so that they would feel more as if they were in the country, the family installed themselves on the grass, scorning table and chairs.

The young men carried their plates a few steps away and resumed their lunch. Their bare arms, which they showed off constantly, disturbed the girl somewhat and she even turned her head away and pretended not to notice them, while Madame Dufour, bolder and impelled by a feminine curiosity that was perhaps really desire, kept looking at them constantly, probably comparing them to the concealed ugliness of her husband.

She was sitting on the grass with her legs bent and crossed tailor-fashion, and she kept wriggling constantly on the pretext that ants had got under her clothes somewhere. Monsieur Dufour, soured by the presence of the two strangers and by their amiability, was looking for a comfortable position, which he couldn't find. As to the young man with yellow hair, he was silently tucking away food like an ogre.

"What wonderful weather, monsieur," big Madame Dufour said to one of the oarsmen, trying to be amiable because they had so gallantly yielded their place.

"Oh yes, ma'am," the man replied. "Do you often come out of town?"

"Well, only once or twice a year, to breathe some fresh air. And what about you, monsieur?"

"I come out here every evening and spend the night."

"Oh, that must be ever so nice!"

"It certainly is, ma'am."

And he expanded poetically on his daily life in a way that awakened in the hearts of these shopkeepers, deprived of grass and hungry for a walk across the fields, that silly love of nature which haunts such people throughout the year as they stand behind the counters of their shops.

Moved, the girl raised her eyes and glanced at the oarsman. Then Monsieur Dufour spoke for the first time.

"That's the real life," he said, and turning to his wife: "Could you eat a bit more of this rabbit, dearie?"

"No thank you, my dear," she said and again turned toward the two young men. She indicated their bare arms and asked: "Aren't you ever cold like that?"

They laughed and proceeded to shock the family with tales of their prodigious feats of endurance, of going swimming while they were in a sweat, of long rows through night and fog. And as they spoke, they kept thumping their chests to emphasize each word with the sound it made.

"Ah, you sure look sturdy!" Monsieur Dufour said.

He no longer held forth about the times he had inflicted those wallopings on the English oarsmen.

The girl examined them out of the corner of her eye. The yellow-haired young clerk, whose wine had gone down the wrong way, started to choke and cough, splattering the cherry-colored dress of his lady employer, who angrily demanded some water with which to wash off the stains.

In the meantime, it was growing terribly hot. The sparkling river seemed to radiate waves of heat and the wine fumes mounted to their heads.

Monsieur Dufour, shaken by violent hiccoughs, had unbuttoned his waistcoat and the top button of his trousers. His wife, feeling suffocated, was gradually unhooking her dress. Their clerk was gaily shaking his shock of yellow hair and kept filling his glass. The grandmother, feeling a little tipsy, sat stiffly, looking very dignified.

As to the young girl, she remained impassive, except that a faint sparkle appeared in her eyes and the dark skin of her cheeks turned rather pink.

The coffee finished them off completely. They decided to sing, each singing his own couplet while the others applauded frantically. Then, with some difficulty, they got up. While the two women, rather dizzy, stood there getting their breath, the two men, who were quite drunk, tried to perform some acrobatic exercises.

Heavy, flabby, their faces congested, they hung limply on the rings, quite unable to pull themselves up, while their shirts constantly threatened to escape from their trousers and wave in the wind like flags.

The oarsmen, who had put their boats into the water, now came up and politely offered to take the ladies for a row on the river.

"May I, dear? Please!" Madame Dufour cried.

Her husband stared at her drunkenly, without understanding.

Then one of the oarsmen, holding two fishing rods in his hand, walked over to him. The hope of catching a gudgeon flashed through his head. That shopkeeper's dream lit up his mournful stare. He gave his sanction to everything and installed himself in the shade under the bridge, his feet hanging over the water. The yellow-haired clerk sat down beside him and immediately fell asleep.

One of the oarsmen sacrificed himself and took the mother.

"To the little wood on the Île-aux-Anglais!" he called out, rowing away.

The other skiff proceeded at a slower pace. The man at the oars was staring so hard at his companion that he couldn't concentrate on anything else. A certain emotion had taken hold of him and was sapping his strength.

The girl, sitting in the coxswain's seat, abandoned herself to the gentle sensation of gliding over the water. She felt the ability to think deserting her; her limbs felt supremely relaxed; she was as free of herself as if permeated by total intoxication. She had turned very red and her breath came short. Dizziness caused by the wine and amplified by the heat waves shimmering around her made all the trees along the bank seem to bow to her in salutation. A vague need for sensuous pleasure, a fermentation of the blood, ran through her flesh which was excited by the ardors of the day; she was also stirred by this tête-à-tête on the water in the midst of a countryside emptied by the blazing sky, with this young man who thought her beautiful—whose eye caressed her skin and whose desire was as penetrating as the sun.

Their inability to speak further increased their emotion and they kept looking at the water around them. Then making an effort, he asked her name.

"Henriette," she said.

"Ah, really? Mine's Henri."

The sound of their own voices had a calming effect upon them and they became interested in the river bank. The other skiff had stopped there and seemed to be waiting for them. The other oarsman called out to them:

"We'll join you in the woods. We're going to Robinson's now because Madame is thirsty."

He leaned heavily on his oars and moved off so quickly that in no time he was out of sight.

In the meantime a continuous roar that they had vaguely discerned before was rapidly growing nearer to them. The river itself seemed to tremble as if the deadened sound was emerging from its depths.

"What's that noise?" she inquired.

It was the water falling from the dam that cut the river in two at the tip of the island. He was becoming entangled in this explanation when, through the roar of the cascade, they were struck by a bird's song that seemed to come from very far off.

"Imagine that!" he said. "The nightingales are singing during the day now. The hens must be hatching."

A nightingale! She had never heard nightingales sing. The thought of hearing one now aroused tender, poetic notions in her heart.

A nightingale! That invisible witness of love-trysts invoked by Juliet on her balcony; that heavenly music bestowed upon humans to accompany their kisses; that eternal inspiration of all the languorous romances that open up an azure ideal to the poor little hearts of young girls trembling with emotion!

So she was going to hear a nightingale.

"Don't let's make any noise," her companion said. "We could go ashore by the wood and sit down quite close to it."

The skiff seemed to be gliding on ice. The tree-lined bank was so low that their eyes seemed to plunge into the depth of the wood. They stopped. The skiff was tied up. Henriette leaned on Henri's arm and they made their way among the branches.

"Bend down," he said.

She did so and they made their way through an inextricable tangle of creepers, leaves, and reeds, into a shelter that had to be known to be found and that the young man laughingly called his "private study."

Immediately above their heads the bird was singing full-throatedly. It emitted trills and warbles, then let out great vibrating sounds that filled the air and seemed to fade somewhere beyond the horizon, rolling off along the river and flying away over the meadows, through the blazing silence that weighed on the countryside.

They didn't speak for fear of frightening the bird and making it fly away. They sat next to each other and slowly Henri's arm slipped round Henriette's waist, exerting a gentle pressure. Without anger, she took that bold hand and pushed it farther away from her. And she did so whenever he brought his hand closer. She felt no embarrassment whatever at his caress, as if it were quite natural. And she pushed it off most naturally too.

Lost in a sort of ecstasy, she listened to the bird. She was filled with infinite desires, with sudden tender impulses, with revelations of superhuman poetry, and with such a softening of the nerves and heart that she began to cry without knowing why.

The young man pressed her against him, but now she didn't push him away, didn't even think of doing so.

Suddenly the nightingale fell silent. A distant voice called:

"Henriette!"

"Don't answer," her companion whispered, "or you'll scare away the bird."

She hadn't even thought of answering.

For some time they remained sitting there like that. Madame Dufour must also have been sitting somewhere, for from time to time, they would hear the shrill little cries of the big lady whom the other oarsman must have been fondling.

The girl, still crying, was filled with delightful sensations, her skin hot and prickled all over by an unfamiliar tingling. Henri's head was on her shoulder.

Suddenly he kissed her on the lips. She drew back, furious, and to avoid him, threw herself down on her back. But he threw himself on top of her, covering her with his entire body. He had to pursue that fleeting mouth for a long time before he caught it and welded it to his. Then maddened by a formidable desire, she responded to his kiss, pressing him against her breast. All her resistance collapsed as if crushed by a weight too heavy for it.

Everything around them was quiet. The bird resumed his song. It burst out at first in three strident notes that seemed an appeal for love, then after a moment's silence, it again sang in a weakened tone, in very slow trills.

A soft breeze slipped by, causing the leaves to murmur, and from beneath the tangle of branches came two ardent sighs which blended with the song of the nightingale and the gentle breath of the wood.

Drunkenness seemed to overcome the bird, and its voice, gradually gaining in momentum like a fire flaring up or like a mounting passion, seemed to accompany the crackling of kisses under the tree. Then, the delirium in its throat was let loose in complete abandon. It went through long, drawn-out swoons, great melodious spasms.

Now and then it would stop to rest, threading out only two or three light sounds that ended suddenly on a strident note. Or else it would go off at a mad pace, with gushing scales, with shudders and jerks—a sort of fierce, furious hymn of love followed by cries of triumph.

But then the bird fell silent, hearing below it a moan so deep that one might have taken it for a soul taking leave of this world. The sound lasted for a while and then culminated in a sob.

They were both quite pale as they left their green bed. The sky seemed to them to have become overcast; to their eyes, the glowing sun had been extinguished; they were aware of their loneliness and of the silence around them. They walked quickly, side by side, without touching each other, without talking, for they seemed to have become irreconcilable enemies—as if disgust had sprung up between their bodies and hatred between their spirits.

Occasionally Henriette would call: "Mamma!"

There was a stir beneath a bush. Henri thought he saw a white underskirt quickly pulled over a thick calf. Then the huge lady emerged, a bit embarrassed and even redder than before, her eyes aglow and her stormy bosom perhaps a bit too close to her companion. As for him, he must have witnessed some rather funny things, for his face was furrowed by an irrepressible hilarity that kept bursting out despite all his efforts.

Madame Dufour took his arm affectionately and they returned to the boats. Henri, who was walking in front next to the girl, thought at one point that he heard a hard kiss that was intended to be noiseless.

Finally they returned to Bezons.

Monsieur Dufour, now sober, was impatient. The blond clerk was having a bite to eat before leaving the inn. The cart, already harnessed, was waiting for them in the courtyard. The grandmother was already in her seat, very worried that they might be overtaken by darkness before reaching Paris, for the countryside was none too safe.

Hands were shaken and the Dufour family left.

"So long!" the oarsmen shouted, and received a sigh and a tear in reply.

⁂

Two months later, passing along the Rue des Martyrs, Henri saw a sign over a door which read: "Dufour—Hardware Merchant." He went in.

The big lady was displaying her rotundity across the counter. They recognized each other right away. After a thousand polite remarks, he inquired:

"And how's Mademoiselle Henriette?"

"She's fine, thank you. In fact, she got married."

"Ah . . ." he said, seized by emotion. "And whom did she marry?"

"The young man who was with us then, you know. . . . He'll be the one to take over the business."

"Yes, yes, I remember very well. . . ."

He started to leave, feeling very sad without knowing why. Madame Dufour called him back.

"And how is your friend?" she asked shyly.

"He's fine."

"Please give him our best and tell him to drop in on us whenever he comes by." She turned very red and added: "Tell him I'd like him to do that very much."

"I certainly will tell him. Good-bye."

"No. . . . See you very soon!"

A year later, on a very sultry summer Sunday, every detail of the adventure he had always remembered came back to Henri; the recollection was so vivid and he felt such nostalgia that he returned all alone to his "private study" in the little wood.

As he crept in, he received a shock. She was there. She was sitting on the grass looking very sad, while next to her, still in his shirt sleeves, the yellow-haired young man was stretched out asleep. He had given himself entirely to his sleep, like an animal.

She turned very pale when she saw Henri and he thought she was about to faint. But then they started to talk quite naturally, as if nothing had ever happened between them.

As he was telling her that he often came to this place on Sundays to rest and to relive many past memories, she looked lengthily into his eyes.

"Me," she said, "I think of it every night."

"Well, dear," her husband mumbled, yawning, "I guess it's time we were on our way back."

[*Une partie de campagne,* April 2 and 9, 1881]

A Family Matter

The Neuilly steam tram had passed the Porte Maillot and was speeding down the broad avenue that ends at the Seine. The small engine that pulled the car kept blowing its whistle to warn anything that was in its way, spitting puffs of steam and breathing hard like someone running, its pistons sounding like galloping iron legs. The oppressive heat of a late summer afternoon weighed on the avenue from which, although not a breath of air stirred, rose a white, chalky, opaque, stifling hot dust that stuck to moist skin, got into eyes, penetrated lungs. All along the way, people stood in their doorways trying to snatch a breath of cooler air.

The windows of the tram were lowered, and its speedy motion made the drawn curtains flutter. Since most people preferred to travel on the open top platform on such a warm day, there were only a few passengers inside—mostly hefty, absurdly dressed suburban housewives who make up for their lack of distinction by an aggressive respectability, and some tired office employees, yellow-faced, stooping, with one shoulder higher than the other from days and days of sitting at their desks. The sad, worried faces of all these people also suggested domestic troubles, a chronic shortage of money, the final renunciation of all the hopes they had had early in life; they all belonged to that threadbare army of unfortunates who vegetate in those flimsy plastered cottages bordered by tiny gardens, strewn amidst rubbish dumps in the countryside surrounding Paris.

By the door sat a short, fat man with a puffy face and a big belly resting on the seat between his widespread legs. He wore a black suit with a decoration in the lapel and was talking to a tall, thin, untidy-looking fellow in a dirty white linen suit and a battered old Panama hat. The little fat man spoke slowly, with hesitations that almost made him sound as if he had a stammer. His name was Monsieur Caravan and he was a chief clerk in the Ministry of the Navy. The other man, a former health officer of the merchant marine, was now practicing in Courbevoie, testing on the impoverished local population the remnants of medical knowledge left to him after his adventurous life. His name was Chenet and he insisted on being called Doctor. There were all sorts of rumors about his morality.

Monsieur Caravan had always led the regular life of a bureaucrat. For thirty years he had gone to his office every morning by the same route, meeting at the same spots the same human forms going to their offices, and he had returned every evening by the same route, seeing again the faces that he had watched growing older.

Every morning, after picking up his newspaper at the corner of Faubourg Saint-Honoré, he'd buy a couple of rolls and enter the Ministry, feeling like a man giving himself up to the prison authorities. Once inside, he'd hurry to his desk, his heart filled with worry in the eternal expectation of a reprimand for some negligence he might have been guilty of.

Nothing had ever happened to disturb the humdrum monotony of his existence. Nothing touched him outside the business of his department, his promotions, and his bonuses. Whether he happened to be in the Ministry or at home with his family—for he had married the dowry-less daughter of a colleague—he never spoke of anything but his office. By now his mind, atrophied as it was by his stupefying daily routine, never had any thoughts, hopes, or dreams other than those connected with the Ministry of the Navy. But his professional satisfaction was always spoiled by an underlying bitterness: he had a permanent grudge against the naval paymasters who were always given the appointments as department and assistant department heads in the Ministry—the "tin-brass" as they were called, because they wore the same uniform as other officers, except that instead of gold braid, their rank was indicated by silver. And so every night at dinner, he'd prove again and again to his wife, who already shared all his grudges and resentments, how incredibly unfair it was to give jobs in Paris to these people who should really have been serving at sea.

He was quite old now, but he had never noticed how the years had passed, for he had entered the Ministry straight from school, without any transition; and the teachers before whom he used to tremble had simply been replaced by superiors, the sight of whom terrorized him equally. When he had to enter the room of one of these bureaucratic despots, shivers passed through his entire body, and this constant fear left him with an awkward manner, a humble air, and a sort of nervous stutter.

He knew no more of Paris than a blind man led by his seeing-eye dog. When he read about events and scandals in his cheap newspaper, they struck him as fairy tales invented especially to distract minor employees like himself. A man of order, a reactionary without any definite party allegiance, but automatically an opponent of every innovation, he always skipped the political news in his paper, feeling that it was paid to distort such news on behalf of one cause or another anyway. And when he walked up the Champs Elysées every evening, he'd look at the noisy crowd of pedestrians and at the rows of moving carriages like some traveler who has lost his way in an far-off land.

This year he had completed thirty years of service and they had decorated him with the Légion d'honneur—the method used by martial administrations to reward their pen-pushing slaves for years of miserable servitude, which they officially describe as "loyal devotion to duty." Still, the sudden increase in dignity had caused Caravan to revise his ideas about his talents and had brought about a drastic change in his daily habits. Since then, he had discarded light trousers and fancy jackets and now wore only black pants and black frock coats against which his red ribbon of the Légion d'honneur stood out better. He gave himself a close shave every morning, trimmed his nails with greater care, and changed his shirt every second day—all out of a legitimate respect for the national Order of the Légion d'honneur. From the very day he had been admitted to it, he had become a different Monsieur Caravan, clean, magnificent, and condescending.

At home he mentioned "my decoration" on every possible occasion. In fact, he became so vain about it that he could no longer bear to see any kind of ribbon in another man's buttonhole. He was particularly irritated by the foreign decorations that, he said, "should never be allowed to be worn on French soil." He particularly resented Doctor Chenet, whom he met every evening on the tram, because he always wore some sort of ribbon in his buttonhole—white, blue, orange, green, or whatever it might be.

The topic of the conversation the two men held between the Arc de Triomphe and Neuilly never varied much, and that day, like any other, they first examined examples of local misgovernment which made them both indignant—the mayor of Neuilly catching a generous share of the blame. Then, as unfailingly happens when one is talking to a medical man, Monsieur Caravan passed on to the subject of ailments, hoping thus to pick up a little unpaid advice or even a free consultation by maneuvering with great dexterity so that the other would not see his purpose. As a matter of fact, he had been worried for some time about his mother. She was having frequent fainting spells that lasted quite a long time, and although she was already ninety years old, she wouldn't let him call in a doctor to examine her.

Her great age made Caravan sentimental and he kept saying to Chenet:

"How many people do you see who reach that age?" And he rubbed his hands happily.

Perhaps it wasn't really so much because he was eager to see the old woman remain forever on this earth as because his mother's longevity seemed to hold a certain promise for himself.

"Oh," he went on, "we're long-lived in my family. Take me, for instance—well, I can tell you that, barring an accident, I'll die very, very old."

The health officer gave him a look full of pity. For one second he surveyed his neighbor's congested face, his fat neck, his big belly sagging between his flabby legs, all the apoplectic rotundity of the flaccid, old, white-collar employee. Then briskly pushing back his grayish Panama hat, he said with a snigger:

"I'm not at all sure about that, old man. Your mother's a regular bean-pole, but you, you're just a tub of lard."

Caravan, upset, fell silent.

But the tram had reached their stop and the two men got out. Chenet offered Caravan a vermouth in the Café du Globe where they both often went for a drink. The owner, whom they knew, extended two fingers to them over the bottle on the counter and they each pressed them in turn. Then they joined a table where three domino players had been at the game since noon. After exchanging the friendly and inevitable "What's new?" the players resumed their game. Later, "Good nights" were exchanged and hands touched without the players taking their eyes off their dominoes. Whereupon Caravan and Chenet went home to dinner.

Caravan lived near the Rond-Point de Courbevoie in a small three-story house whose lower floor was occupied by a barber shop. He had two bedrooms, a dining room, and a kitchen, all of which Madame Caravan spent her life keeping clean, while her daughter, Marie-Louise, aged twelve, and her son, Philippe-Auguste, aged nine, ran around outside with the neighborhood children.

Caravan's mother lived on the top floor, above the family. She was notorious throughout the neighborhood for her stinginess, and her striking thinness made people say that the good Lord had applied her own principle of economy to her. She was always in a foul mood and a day seldom went by without her having fits of anger and starting a quarrel with someone. From her window she abused the neighbors standing on their doorsteps, the street vendors, the street sweepers, and also the children who, to get back at her, would follow her in the street, calling out:

"Pears are green, cherries are red,
See the old hag who wets her bed!"

A little Norman maid, incredibly scatterbrained, worked in the house and slept on the top floor next to the old woman, for fear something might happen to her during the night.

When Caravan got home, his wife, who suffered from a chronic mania for housecleaning, was polishing with a piece of flannel the mahogany chairs scattered through the gloom of the rooms. She always wore cotton gloves and a beribboned bonnet which sat aslant on her head, and each time someone surprised her dusting, brushing, polishing, or washing clothes, she would repeat:

"I'm not rich, everything is very ordinary here. My only luxury is cleanliness but to me it's worth every other luxury."

She was endowed with shrewdness and horse sense, and her husband let her guide him in everything. Every evening at the dinner table and later in their bed, they would speak of the goings-on in his office, and although she was his junior by twenty years, he confided in her as to a confessor and scrupulously followed all her advice.

She had never been pretty, and now she was ugly, small, and skinny. Her inept way of dressing completely erased what few feminine attributes she had, instead of making the most of them. Her skirt always seemed askew, and moreover, she often scratched herself quite unabashedly, even in public—a habit that had turned into a true nervous tic. The only adornment she indulged in was a profusion of silk ribbons on the caps she wore inside the house.

As soon as she saw her husband, she got up, kissed him on his side whiskers, and asked:

"Did you get what I asked you to at Potin's, dear?"

He had promised to buy something for her at the Felix Potin store.

He let himself slip into a chair in consternation—he had forgotten all about it for the fourth time in a row.

"It's a jinx," he muttered, "a real jinx. I keep reminding myself all day but when I get out in the evening, it slips my mind altogether."

But as he seemed so sorry about having failed to remember, she consoled him:

"I'm sure you'll think of it tomorrow, dear. And I suppose there's nothing new at the Ministry?"

"Oh yes, there is: one of those tin-brass fellows has been appointed deputy-chief."

"What department?" she asked, becoming very serious.

"Purchasing department."

Her anger was growing.

"You mean in place of Ramon? That was just the spot I'd hoped you'd get. And what about Ramon? He's retiring, I suppose?"

"Yes," he said, "he's retiring."

She was furious now and her bonnet slipped down onto her shoulder:

"That's the limit! Now there's nothing more to hope for from that miserable outfit. What's that new paymaster's name?"

"Bonassot."

She picked up the French Naval Directory that she always kept handy and searched for "Bonassot." She read out:

"Bonassot—Toulon. Born 1851; graduated from Naval

Paymasters' College 1871; promoted Paymaster Lieutenant 1875." Then she looked up at her husband and asked: "Has he seen any sea duty, that one?"

The question had a relaxing effect upon Caravan, and the next minute, his belly was shaking with merriment:

"Well, I guess he's just like Balin . . . his chief, Balin. . . ." And laughing even louder, he added an old joke that the Ministry employees found delightful: "Just let them be sent to inspect the Paris naval station at the Point-du-Jour and they'll get seasick going there on the Seine steamboat."

But she remained unsmiling, as though she hadn't heard him, and said, slowly scratching her chin:

"If only we had a good contact with some elected representative! Because if the legislature found out what's going on in the Navy Ministry, they'd kick the Minister sky-high. . . ."

There were shouts on the staircase and she fell silent. Marie-Louise and Philippe-Auguste, coming in from the street, were exchanging slaps and kicks as they climbed upstairs. Their mother rushed furiously over to them, grabbed each by an arm, and shaking them vigorously, pulled them into the room.

When the children saw their father, they ran toward him, and he kissed them tenderly and at great length. Then he sat down, took them one on each knee, and chatted with them.

Philippe-Auguste was an ugly urchin, disheveled, dirty from head to foot, with the long face of an imbecile. Marie-Louise looked like her mother and already spoke like her, imitating her gestures and words. She also asked him: "Nothing new at the Ministry?" and he replied smilingly:

"Your friend Ramon, who comes and has dinner with us once a month, is leaving us, dear. They've appointed a new deputy-chief in his place."

She lifted her eyes to her father and said with precocious commiseration:

"So they passed you by again and put someone else in over your head."

He stopped smiling but didn't answer. Then, to change the subject, he addressed his wife, who was now cleaning the window panes:

"And how is *maman* feeling up there?"

Madame Caravan stopped wiping the pane, turned around,

straightened her bonnet that had almost slipped down her back, and with her lips trembling, said:

"Ah, yes, speaking of *maman,* she certainly knows how to make life difficult around here. Imagine—this afternoon Madame Lebaudin, the barber's wife, came up to borrow a packet of starch from me. I was out and your mother chased her away and called her a tramp. Ah, you can be sure I made her pay for that, the old crone! She pretended she couldn't hear a word, of course—she always does when she's told the truth about herself—but I know she's no more deaf than I am. I'm sure it's all fake and the proof is that she went straight back to her room without answering a word."

Embarrassed, Caravan didn't know what to say. Then the little maid rushed in and announced that dinner was served. To pass this information on to his mother, he picked up a broomstick that always stood handy in a corner and knocked three times on the ceiling. After that they went into the dining room and the younger Madame Caravan served the soup while they were waiting for the old woman. She didn't come and the soup was getting cold, so they ate very slowly and when the plates were empty they waited some more. Furious, Madame Caravan took it out on her husband:

"She does it on purpose, I tell you! Why shouldn't she? You're always taking her part."

Not knowing what to do caught between the two women, he sent Marie-Louise to fetch her grandmother and, in the meantime, kept looking down into his plate, while his wife angrily tapped the stem of her wineglass with her knife.

The door opened and the girl reappeared. She was alone, out of breath, pale. Speaking very quickly she said:

"Grandma fell down. She's lying on the floor."

Caravan leaped to his feet, threw his napkin on the table, and rushed upstairs. As his footfalls resounded heavily on the stairs, his wife, who felt sure that the old woman was up to one of her tricks, shrugged scornfully, got up, and followed her husband at a much less hurried pace.

The old woman lay full length on her face in the middle of her room, and when her son turned her over she looked strangely still and dry: her yellowed, leathery skin in folds, her eyes closed, her teeth clenched, and her whole thin body rigid.

Caravan went down on his knees next to her and started moaning:

"Mother, poor dear mother. . . ."

But the younger Madame Caravan took a quick look at the old woman and delared:

"Poof! That's nothing, just another fainting spell for sure. She mostly does it to prevent us from having our dinner in peace."

They picked her up, undressed her, and put her to bed. Then Caravan, his wife, and the maid started rubbing her with alcohol. Despite their efforts, however, the old woman did not regain her senses. So they sent Rosalie to get Doctor Chenet. He lived on the river front toward Suresnes. It was rather far and they had to wait a long time. At last he arrived and after having looked at, poked, and examined the old woman, said:

"That's that."

Caravan flung himself on the body, convulsively kissing his mother's rigid face, crying with such profusion that tears as large as raindrops kept falling on the dead woman's face.

The younger Madame Caravan gave a decent display of desolation by letting out sad, weak moans and insistently rubbing her eyes with a handkerchief as she stood behind her husband.

Caravan, his face puffy, his thin hair in disorder, very ugly in his genuine sorrow, suddenly stood up:

"But . . . but are you certain, Doctor, are you absolutely certain?"

The health officer quickly stepped forward and, handling the corpse with the dexterity of a merchant displaying his merchandise, said:

"Here, look at this eye."

He pulled up the lid and the old woman's look reappeared under his finger without having in the least changed, except perhaps that the pupil was now slightly enlarged. This look was like a stab in Caravan's heart, and shudders of terror went through his bones.

Chenet then took the woman's twisted hand, forced the fingers open and, looking as irritated as if faced with a heckler, said:

"Now look at this hand, for heaven's sake! I couldn't possibly be mistaken, please rest assured."

Caravan threw himself on the bed almost bellowing, while his wife, still whimpering, did the necessary things. She brought in a night table on which she put a napkin and four candles that she lit, took a sprig of boxwood that hung over the mantelpiece, and put it on a plate which she placed between the candles after filling it with ordinary water since she didn't have any holy water. Then, after a moment's hesitation, she threw a pinch of salt in the water, probably imagining that she had thus performed some sort of consecration.

When she had completed the setting that must accompany death, she just stood still and waited. Then the health officer, who had helped her to arrange the various items, whispered to her:

"You must get your husband out of here."

She nodded her head, went over to her husband, who was still kneeling by the bed and sobbing, and took one of his arms while Chenet took the other.

They sat him in a chair. Madame Caravan kissed him on the forehead and started lecturing him. Chenet backed her arguments and spoke of firmness, courage, and resignation—the very things that desert one when disaster strikes so suddenly. Then his wife and Chenet took hold of his arms once more and led him away.

He was whimpering like a fat little boy, with hiccoughing sobs, his mind blank, his arms limp, his legs flabby, and he was led downstairs like that, not knowing what he was doing and moving his feet mechanically.

They put him in the armchair at his usual place at the table, in front of his almost empty plate with the spoon dipped in what was left of the soup. He remained there without moving, his eyes fixed on his glass, so shocked that his brain could not resume the process of thought.

In a corner, Madame Caravan was talking to the doctor, asking him all sorts of practical advice, inquiring about various formalities. Finally Chenet, who seemed to be waiting for something, picked up his hat, declared that he hadn't had his dinner yet, said good-bye, and made as though he were going to leave. She exclaimed:

"What? You haven't had your dinner yet! But, please, Doctor, stay and have it here with us! The maid will serve the rest of our dinner, and you can well understand that we won't be able to eat much of it."

He said that he was sorry but he couldn't accept. She insisted:

"Come, please do stay. It's always so nice to have friends at one's side at such moments. And perhaps you'll be able to persuade my husband to take some food—he badly needs to restore his strength a bit."

The doctor put down his hat, bowed, and said:

"In that case, I accept, madame."

She gave the necessary orders to Rosalie, who was completely bewildered, and then sat down to the table herself in order, as she put it: "to pretend to eat, but really just to keep the doctor company."

The soup was brought in again and the doctor ate two helpings of it. Then there came a dish of tripe à la Lyonnaise that spread an aroma of onions, which perhaps decided Madame Caravan to have a little taste.

"It's excellent," the doctor said.

"Do you really think so?" she said smiling and then, turning toward her husband: "Do have some of it, my poor dear Alfred. You simply must make yourself eat something. Remember, you'll have to stay up all night!"

Docilely he handed her his plate. If she had told him to go and put himself to bed he would have done that just as unquestioningly. He obeyed in everything without protest or even thought. And he ate.

The doctor helped himself three times from the dish, while Madame Caravan occasionally picked up a large morsel of tripe on her fork and swallowed it with studied absent-mindedness.

When a bowl of macaroni made its appearance, the doctor greeted it with "Ha! My, my! Another nice dish!" and this time it was Madame Caravan who filled everyone's plate. She even put some into the small plates of her children, who, taking advantage of their parents' lack of attention, had been drinking wine without cutting it with water as they were supposed to, and were now engaged in a kicking contest under the table.

It suddenly flashed into Chenet's mind that Rossini the composer was very fond of the dish they were eating and he blurted out:

"Why, it rhymes! One could begin a poem like this:

> The great Maestro Rossini
> Loved nothing better than macaroni. . . ."

But no one was listening to him. Madame Caravan had grown thoughtful, examining all the consequences that the death of the old woman was going to have, while her husband rolled little bread pellets, lining them up around him on the tablecloth and staring at them like an idiot. Being very thirsty, he kept constantly bringing his glass of wine to his lips; and as a consequence, his head, already shaken by shock and grief, was beginning to swim and everything around him was beginning to dance to the rhythm of the painful process of digestion that had begun in him.

Meanwhile the doctor kept soaking up wine like a sponge and was getting visibly drunk. Madame Caravan herself was going through the reaction that follows all nervous shock and was growing troubled and agitated; and although she drank nothing but water, her head also began to spin a little.

Chenet began to tell stories of death that he thought amusing. In this Parisian suburb, whose inhabitants mostly came from the provinces, one often found that indifference to death—even the death of a father or mother—that irreverence and toughness which is common among peasants but rather rare in Paris.

"Last week, for instance," Chenet was saying, "they called me to Rue de Puteaux. . . . I rushed there and found the patient had passed away, and next to the bed, his family was quietly finishing off the bottle of absinthe that had been bought on the previous day to satisfy a whim of the dying man."

But Madame Caravan wasn't listening. She was busy thinking of the inheritance. As to Caravan, his brain was blank and he couldn't take in a thing.

Coffee was served and it was very strong coffee indeed, to keep their spirits up. Each cup, with a good dose of cognac to go with it, brought color to their faces and completely befuddled their heads, which were already quite shaky.

Chenet seized the brandy bottle and poured some out for everyone "to rinse everything down." After that, without speaking anymore, plunged in the pleasant warmth of digestion, seized by the well-being alcohol provides after a good dinner, they slowly gorged themselves with the sugary cognac that formed a yellowish syrup at the bottom of their coffee cups.

The children dropped off to sleep and Rosalie put them to bed. Then Caravan, unthinkingly obeying the need to escape into stupor that governs those who feel miserable, helped himself several times to the brandy and a gleam came into his bovine eyes.

Finally the doctor got up to leave. He took his friend's arm and said:

"Come with me, old man, a bit of fresh air will do you good. It's very bad to remain immobile when you've suffered a bad blow like this."

Caravan obeyed meekly, put on his hat and took his cane, and the two of them left arm in arm. Under the starlit sky, they walked down toward the Seine.

Fragrant breezes wafted through the night air, for in that season the surrounding gardens were full of flowers which, dormant during the day, seemed to awake at the approach of evening and exhale fragrances that rode through the shadows on light air currents.

The broad avenue with its double row of street lights stretching all the way to the Arc de Triomphe was deserted and silent. But a low rumble came from far away, from the center of Paris which was shrouded in a reddish glow. It was a sort of uninterrupted roll emphasized now and then by the whistling of a train either rushing at full steam across the plain toward the city or fleeing from it through the countryside toward the ocean.

The feel of the fresh air on their faces affected the two men—it impaired Chenet's balance and increased the fits of dizziness that had kept coming over Caravan since dinner. Caravan walked as if in a daze, his brain asleep and paralyzed, feeling no acute sorrow thanks to that state of mental torpor. He even had a vague sense of relief, brought on by the warm, fragrant currents wafting through the night.

When they reached the bridge, they turned right and felt the cool breath of the river. The Seine flowed sadly and quietly before a screen of tall poplars, and the stars seemed to be bobbing in the current. A fine, whitish mist that hung over the bank filled their lungs with damp, moist-smelling air. Caravan stopped abruptly. That smell of the river stirred some very old memories in him.

An old scene from his boyhood came back to him: his mother, kneeling outside their house in Picardy where they came from and washing the family clothes piled at her side, in a slender rivulet that passed through their garden. He almost fancied he could hear the sound of the wooden paddle with which she beat the linen resounding in the quiet of the countryside and her voice calling out to him: "Hey, Alfred, get me another piece of soap!" And he experienced the same smell of flowing water, the same mist rising over the damp river bank—that marshy exhalation whose smell and taste he would never forget and that had come back to him now on the night his mother had died.

He stopped, stiffened by a violent return of despair. It was like a blinding flash suddenly lighting up the whole immensity of his bereavement. This chance whiff of moist river air was enough to hurl him into a hopeless abyss of torment.

His heart was torn at the thought of that separation without end. His life had been lopped off in the middle, his youth was vanishing, swallowed up by that death. The entire past was gone; all the memories of youth were finished—there was no one left who could talk to him of bygone things, of the people he had once known, of the place he had come from, of himself, of the intimate details of his past life. It was as though one half of his being had ceased to exist. Well, all he had to do now was to wait for the other half to die.

And the procession of memories continued. He saw his *maman* when she was much younger, in old dresses she had worn so long that, in his memory, they had become inseparable from her; he remembered her in many scenes he thought he had forgotten, seeing again her facial expressions that had been blurred in his mind, gestures and intonations that had become beclouded in his memory, her habits, her manias, her fits of anger, the frowns on her face, and the movements of her thin fingers—all those familiar ways of hers that were gone forever.

He clutched at the doctor and moaned. His flabby legs trembled and his whole fat body was shaken by sobs as he muttered:

"My mother . . . my poor mother . . . my poor mother. . . ."

But his companion, who was still under the effect of the brandy and was longing to finish off the evening in one of the places he secretly patronized, became impatient over this acute fit of sorrow. He made Caravan sit down on the grassy river bank and almost immediately left him, under the pretext that he still had to see one of his patients.

Caravan stayed there crying for a long time, and when at last he had no tears left, the feeling of rest and relief suddenly came over him again.

The moon had risen and was spreading its placid light

over the land. The tall poplars were adorned with silvery sparks and the mist floating over the plain looked like drifting snowflakes. The stars were no longer bobbing in the river, which now seemed to be covered with mother-of-pearl and flowed on, wrinkled by shiny ripples. The air was gentle and the breeze fragrant. Languor emanated from the sleepy earth and Caravan inhaled the sweetness of the night; breathing in deeply, he felt a freshness, a calm, a superhuman consolation fill him to the tips of his limbs.

He tried, however, to resist the well-being that was pervading him.

"Mother, my poor dear mother," he kept repeating, trying to exasperate himself, to make himself cry from some sort of scruple. But he couldn't. He was not even the least sad at the thought of things that only a short while earlier had made him weep so disconsolately.

He got up, thinking he ought to go home. He walked slowly, taking short steps, wrapped in the calm detachment of the summer night, feeling at rest despite himself.

When he reached the bridge, he saw the lights of the last tram as it was about to leave, and beyond it the lighted windows of the Café du Globe. The sight made him suddenly feel an urgent need to tell someone about his bereavement, to make someone sympathize with him, to make himself interesting. He put on a dejected expression, pushed open the café door, and walked over to the counter where the proprietor was still enthroned. He had somehow reckoned that his appearance would produce a great effect, that everyone in the establishment would rush toward him with their hands thrust out and inquire: "What is it? What's happened?" But no one paid any attention to his woebegone expression. Then he put his elbows on the bar, held his forehead in his hands, and muttered:

"Ah, my God, dear God. . . ."

The café owner gave him a surprised look:

"Are you sick, Monsieur Caravan?"

He answered:

"Oh no, my friend, it's my mother—she just died."

The owner then produced an absent-minded "Ah?" and, as a customer called out from the back of the room: "Another beer, please!" he answered in a thunderous voice: "Just a minute, coming!" and rushed to attend to it, leaving a bewildered Caravan to himself.

The three domino players were still absorbed in their

game, sitting at the same table they had occupied before dinner. Caravan, in his search for sympathy, made his way toward them. When after a while he found that none of them looked up from the game, he decided to speak first:

"Since I saw you last," he said, "I have suffered an awful misfortune."

They raised their heads slightly, the three of them together, but each still had his eyes riveted on the game.

"Why, what's happened?"

"My mother has just died."

One of the men mumbled: "Ah, that's terrible," with that artificial inflection of sympathy used by those who don't care. Another player, finding nothing to say, shook his head, letting out a brief mournful little whistle. The third man just resumed the game as though thinking: "Is that all?"

Caravan had been hoping for a "heartfelt" expression of sympathy, and meeting such a cool reception, he moved away, offended by the indifference of these men in the face of the bereavement that had struck a friend of theirs; in actual fact, at that moment he was in such a state of emotional torpor that he no longer felt any sorrow.

He left the café and went home. His wife was waiting for him in her nightdress. She was sitting on a low chair by the open window and was still musing about the inheritance.

"Undress now," she told him. "We'll talk when you're in bed."

He lifted his head, indicating the ceiling with a look, and said:

"But up there. . . . There's no one there, is there?"

"Ah, but certainly someone's there. Rosalie is there now and you'll go and relieve her at three in the morning, after you've had some sleep."

But he insisted on keeping his underpants on, so as to be ready for any eventuality. Then he wrapped his head in a scarf and joined his wife, who had already slipped under the sheets. For some time they remained sitting next to each other, she still immersed in her thoughts.

Even at this hour, her bonnet was adorned with a rose-colored knot and was slightly tipped over one ear, as if adhering to the irresistible habit of all the headdresses she wore.

Suddenly, turning her head toward him, she blurted out:

"Do you know whether your mother made a will?"

He hesitated:

"I . . . I don't think she did. . . . No, I'm almost sure she didn't."

Madame Caravan looked straight into her husband's eyes and said furiously:

"But that's outrageous! After all, it's a good ten years now that we've been breaking our backs looking after her, feeding her, keeping her under our roof. Your sister certainly would never have done all that for her. And let me tell you, I wouldn't have either if I'd known how she would reward my services. Yes, it's a real stain on her memory! Now you may say that she always paid for her board, but you can't pay for the care your children take of you with money—the only way of showing one's appreciation is by leaving a proper will. That's the way honorable people act. But no, what do I get for all my troubles and worries? Ah, that's really something! It's shocking and quite unbelievable!"

Caravan, not knowing what to do, begged her:

"Darling, please, darling, don't, for my sake. . . ."

At last she calmed down, and speaking in her normal tone again, she said:

"Tomorrow morning we must let your sister know."

He started and said:

"You're right. I never thought of it. I'll send a wire first thing in the morning."

But she interrupted him. No, she had it all planned.

"You won't send it until between ten and eleven so that we'll have enough time to arrange everything before she arrives. It'll take her two hours at the most to get here from Charenton. We'll say that you were completely out of your head. If we let her know late in the morning, we won't have to rush through everything like mad."

Caravan suddenly slapped his forehead and spoke in a timid tone of voice, the way he always did when he spoke of his chief, the very thought of whom was sufficient to set him trembling.

"We must also let the Ministry know."

"Why bother?" she said. "On an occasion like this they're bound to excuse you if you forget to do it. Don't tell them anything, believe me. Your chief won't be able to say a thing, and in fact, he'll look pretty silly if he tries."

"Ah, that's for sure," Caravan said. "Yes, and he'll be furious when he finds I haven't turned up. You're right—

that's a marvelous idea. And when I tell him my mother is dead, he'll just have to stay quiet."

And the employee of the Ministry rubbed his hands with delight, imagining the face his chief would make on hearing Caravan's excuse for having been absent, while above his head lay the body of his dead mother, next to the sleeping maid.

Then Madame Caravan looked worried, like a person preoccupied with something very grave and very hard to tell to others. Finally she made up her mind:

"I understand your mother gave you the clock, didn't she? You know, the one with the little girl playing cup and ball on it."

He searched his memory.

"Ah yes, yes," he said at last, "but it was very long ago. In fact, it was when she came here to live with us. She told me: 'This clock will be yours if you take good care of me.' "

Madame Caravan seemed cheered and reassured. She said:

"Well, so you see, you must go and get it and bring it down here, for if your sister comes, she'll prevent you from keeping it."

"Do you really think so?"

She became angry:

"Certainly I think so! But once it's here, no one will be any the wiser, and it'll be ours once and for all. And the same thing goes for the chest of drawers with the marble top—she gave it to me one day when she was in a good mood. We'll bring it downstairs at the same time."

Caravan seemed rather unconvinced:

"But my dear, don't you think it's rather a big responsibility to take?"

Full of rage, she turned on him:

"Ah, is that so! It looks as if you'll never change. You'd rather let your children die of starvation than do something about it. Since she gave it to us, that chest of drawers, it's ours, isn't it? And if your sister doesn't like it, let her tell me so personally. Much I care about that sister of yours, anyway. So get up and let's bring everything that your mother left us down here right away."

Trembling and subdued, he got out of bed and was on the point of pulling on his trousers when she stopped him:

"No need for you to get dressed. Just go in your underpants. They'll do. I'm going just as I am."

So the two of them, half-dressed as they were, climbed noiselessly upstairs, quietly opened the door, and entered the room where the four lighted candles standing around the plate with the sprig of boxwood in it seemed to be the only ones keeping a vigil over the old woman in her rigid repose. As for Rosalie, she was sprawled in the armchair, her legs stretched out, her hands clutched over her skirt, her head falling on her shoulder, her mouth open, and snoring slightly.

Caravan took the clock. It was one of those preposterous products of the art of the Second Empire. A young woman in gilt bronze with all sorts of flowers in her hair was holding in her hand a cup and ball, and the ball formed the clock's pendulum.

"Give me the clock," Madame Caravan said, "and take the marble top of the chest of drawers."

He obeyed; with great effort and breathing heavily, he got the marble slab onto his shoulder and, trembling, started to go downstairs; while his wife, walking backwards, held up a candle with one hand, carrying the clock under her other arm.

When they were back in their bedroom, she gave a sigh of relief:

"That's the main thing done," she said. "But let's go and get the rest now."

There was a difficulty though: the drawers of the chest were full of the old woman's clothes, which would have to be hidden somewhere. Then Madame Caravan had a bright idea.

"Go and get the large pine box from the entrance hall. It can't be worth more than two francs, so we can put it in here, after all."

When he had brought the wooden box upstairs, they began the transfer.

One by one, while she lay there behind their backs, she took out the collars, the cuffs, the blouses, the bonnets, and all the poor rags belonging to the old woman, and stowed them neatly into the box in order to cheat Madame Braux, the deceased's other child, who was to arrive the following day.

When they were through with the transfer, they first carried the drawers downstairs, then the empty frame of the chest, each holding it by an end; then they looked around their room to pick the best spot for it. They finally decided to put it between the two windows in front of the bed.

Once the chest was in its new place, Madame Caravan proceeded to fill it with her own linen. The clock went on the living room mantelpiece. They tried to gauge the general effect these innovations produced, and they were both delighted.

"It looks very nice," she said.

"Yes," he said, "it looks very good."

So they went to bed. She blew out the candle and soon everyone, on each floor of the house, was asleep.

It was broad daylight when Caravan opened his eyes. His head was all mixed up on awakening and it took him several minutes to remember what had happened. When he did, it gave him a big blow in the chest, and he jumped out of bed feeling very sad and once again ready to burst into tears.

He hurried to the room upstairs where Rosalie was still asleep in the same position, not having awakened once throughout the night. He sent her off to her chores, replaced the burnt-out candles, and then looked at his mother, rolling through his brain those sham profound thoughts, those religious and philosophical commonplaces that haunt mediocre intelligences in the face of death.

But his wife called him and he went down. She had made up a list of things they had to do that morning and now she handed it to him. He drew back in awe when he saw it.

1. Declare the death at the Town Hall.
2. Call the coroner.
3. Order a coffin.
4. Give notice to the church.
5. Contact an undertaker.
6. See a printer for the death notices.
7. See the lawyer.
8. Go to the telegraph office and wire the family.

There were many other little errands for him to do, so he took his hat and left.

In the meantime the news had spread and neighbors started to arrive, expressing their wish to see the dead woman.

In the barber shop on the ground floor of the house there was even a scene about it between the wife and the husband, who at that moment was busy shaving a customer.

The barber's wife, who was knitting a stocking, muttered:

"There's one stingy old woman less in the world now, and there aren't many as mean as that one was. Still, I guess I ought to go up and see her."

The husband grunted as he soaped the customer's chin:

"Only a woman would have such a cockeyed idea! It's not enough for them to have poisoned one another while alive—one can't even leave the other in peace now she's dead."

But his wife said quite unabashedly:

"I just can't help myself; I must go and see her. It's been tormenting me all morning. If I don't see her, I feel I won't be able to get her off my mind as long as I live. Once I've had a good look at her, though, I'm sure I'll be satisfied."

The razor-wielding man shrugged and confided to the gentleman whose cheek he was scraping:

"Well, I'll be damned if I can ever understand these crazy women! I sure can't see much fun in looking at a dead body."

But his wife, who had heard his words, said quite unruffled: "Well, that's just the way it is." Then she put her knitting down on the desk and went upstairs.

Two women from the neighborhood were already there and Madame Caravan was relating the incident to them in great detail.

Then the four women went to the dead woman's room together. They entered stealthily in turns, sprinkled the sheets with salty water, knelt, crossed themselves, mumbled a prayer. Then, back on their feet, they stared at the body for a while, round-eyed and open-mouthed; and the deceased's daughter-in-law, pressing a handkerchief to her face, simulated a disconsolate hiccough.

When they were ready to leave, they turned from the body to the door, and Madame Caravan saw Marie-Louise and Philippe-Auguste standing by it. Still in their nightshirts, they were watching the scene with great curiosity. Their mother immediately forgot her grief and shouted at them in a furious voice:

"Will you get out of here, you nasty brats!"

But when, ten minutes later, she returned to the dead woman's room with a new batch of visitors and went through the sprinkling, praying, and tearful hiccoughing over her mother-in-law once more, she again caught sight of her children, who had followed her as before. She slapped them then out of a feeling of duty, but when they were still there the next time, she simply ignored them. And after that, each time she took a group of visitors up the two brats went along, kneeling when their mother knelt and imitating everything they saw the grown-ups do.

By early afternoon, the throng of curious women had dwindled and soon there were no more visitors. Madame Caravan then busied herself with preparing for the funeral ceremony, and the dead woman was left alone in her room upstairs.

The window of the room was open. Torrid heat poured through it in dusty puffs. The flames of the four candles flickered by the motionless body, while on the sheets, on her face, on her closed eyes, and on her outstretched hands, tiny flies walked back and forth, having the field to themselves at this hour.

Marie-Louise and Philippe-Auguste had in the meantime darted down into the street, and in no time they were surrounded by other children—mostly girls, who are more alert than boys and get wind of the mysteries of life first. They asked questions just like grown-ups.

"Is it true that your grandma's dead?"

"Yes, she died last night."

"What's a dead person like?"

Marie-Louise told them about the candles and the sprig of boxwood, described what the face of the dead woman looked like. That made the children terribly curious and they wanted to see the deceased themselves.

Immediately, Marie-Louise organized the first trip. Five girls and two boys were selected, the oldest and the boldest. She made them remove their shoes, so as not to make a noise, and the party slipped quietly into the house like an army of mice.

Once in the room, the girl, imitating her mother, went through the ritual. She solemnly guided her friends, knelt, made the sign of the cross, sprinkled the bed; and while the children, clinging timidly together, frightened, curious, and delighted, approached the bed to have a look at the dead woman's face and hands, she suddenly began to simulate sobs, hiding her eyes in her little handkerchief. Then suddenly forgetting her grief as she remembered those who were waiting outside, she ran out hurriedly, followed by the first group, to come running back with a second and then a third batch of children; for all the neighborhood kids, including some tattered little beggars, were anxious to take part in this new amusement. And each time, Marie-Louise imitated her mother's make-believe with increased perfection.

She grew tired of it in the end, though. The kids got involved in another game and the old grandmother was forgotten by one and all.

Shadows filled the room and the flickering flame of the candles cast dancing gleams on her dry and furrowed face.

Around eight o'clock, Caravan went into his dead mother's room, closed the window, replaced the candles. He entered the room in a calm, detached way, accustomed to the body, feeling as though it had been with them for months. He even noted that there weren't any signs of decomposition yet and he passed this observation on to his wife as they were sitting down to dinner. She replied:

"Poof, she's made of wood. She'd keep for a year. . . ."

They finished their soup without exchanging a word. The children, who had been left to run free during the whole day, were now exhausted and practically falling asleep in their chairs. So the silence was complete.

Suddenly the flame of the lamp started to sputter. Madame Caravan tried to turn the wick up but only a sort of hissing resulted and the next thing, the light went out completely. They had forgotten to buy oil and now it had run out. Sending the maid to the grocery would have delayed dinner, so they began to look for candles. But there were no candles in the house either, except those burning by the bedside of the dead woman.

Madame Caravan, who was a woman of quick decisions, sent Marie-Louise to get two of those candles, and they waited in the darkness for the girl to come back with them.

They distinctly heard the little girl going upstairs. There was a moment of complete quiet, and then they heard the child tearing madly downstairs again. She burst in terrified, more so than on the previous night when she had first announced the catastrophe. She muttered:

"Oh, Papa, Papa . . . grandmother's dressing!"

Caravan leaped up with such violence that his chair was hurled against the wall.

"What . . . what did you say? What was it?" he kept muttering.

Choking with emotion, Marie-Louise repeated:

"Gr . . . grandmother, she's . . . she's getting dressed . . . she's coming down. . . ."

He rushed upstairs, followed by his dumbfounded wife.

But once up there, he stopped before the door. He was shaking with fear. He couldn't bring himself to go in. The thought of what he might find was too much for him.

Madame Caravan, however, was braver than her husband. She turned the doorknob and walked in.

The room seemed to have grown darker and in the middle of it there was a long, thin, moving figure. The old woman was on her feet, all right.

The first thing she had done on snapping out of her lethargic sleep, before she had even fully recovered her senses, was to raise herself on an elbow and blow out the three candles that were burning by her deathbed. After that, as her strength flowed back, she got up and started looking for her clothes. She was rather taken aback at first by the disappearance of her chest of drawers; but as she eventually found her things in the wooden box, she calmly got dressed.

Then, after emptying the salt water in the plate on her night table, replacing the sprig of boxwood behind the mirror where it belonged, and putting back the chairs in their proper places, she was about to go downstairs. That was when her son and daughter-in-law appeared in the doorway.

Caravan rushed toward his mother, took hold of her hands, and kissed her with tears rolling down his face, while his wife kept repeating hypocritically:

"Ah, how marvelous, how wonderful!"

But it didn't seem to move the old woman. She didn't even seem to understand what it was all about. Stiff as a statue, she looked at them icily and said:

"Won't dinner be ready soon?"

Caravan, at the end of his tether, muttered without knowing what he was saying:

"Of course it's ready, *maman,* we were just waiting for you."

And with an alacrity quite unusual in him, he took his mother's arm, while his wife went downstairs backward, lighting the stairs for them just as she had done on the previous night when her husband was carrying the marble slab from the old woman's chest of drawers downstairs.

When they reached the floor below, the backstepping younger Madame Caravan almost butted into someone who was coming upstairs. It was Madame Braux, Caravan's sister, and her husband, who had just arrived from Charenton.

The woman, big and fat with a huge, elephantine stomach that threw her torso backward, was staring goggle-eyed at the apparition and looked ready to take to her heels. Her husband, a socialist shoemaker, small, hairy all over except for his nose, and very monkey-like, commented with considerable detachment:

"Well, looks like she's been resurrected."

As soon as she recognized them, Madame Caravan began to address them in a most desperate sign language and then said aloud:

"Ah, I see you've come to visit us! What a wonderful surprise."

But Madame Braux, still hazy from her shock, didn't understand.

"Why, it was your telegram that brought us. We understood it was all over. . . ."

Her husband was pinching her from behind to make her keep quiet. Then he said, with a sly chuckle into his thick beard:

"It was very nice of you to invite us, and as you can see, we came over right away."

He was hinting at the difficult relations that had prevailed between the two households for a very long time.

As the old woman reached the last steps, he moved quickly toward her and affectionately rubbed his whiskers against her cheek, shouting into her ear, because of her deafness:

"How are you getting along, Mother? I see you're still going strong, as strong as ever!"

Madame Braux, in her stupefaction at seeing her mother alive when she had expected to find her dead and laid out, didn't even dare to give her a kiss. She just stood there, her huge belly blocking the whole landing and preventing the others from passing.

The old woman, worried and suspicious, looked at all these people around her without saying anything. Her small, hard, gray eyes, resting now on this one, now on another, reflected all sorts of thoughts that made her children uneasy. In order to say something, Caravan explained:

"She hasn't been too well, but now she's perfectly all right, aren't you, *maman?*"

Then the old woman resumed her trip toward the dining room, saying in her harsh, remote voice:

"It was just a fainting spell. And I could hear you all the time."

There was an embarrassed silence. They went into the dining room and sat down at the table; an improvised dinner was produced within a few minutes.

Of them all, only Monsieur Braux had retained his self-possession. His wicked monkey's face kept grinning and he kept saying things with a double meaning that obviously made the others uncomfortable.

Every few minutes the doorbell downstairs rang and Rosalie, looking very flustered, would come to fetch her master, who'd throw his napkin on the table and hurriedly follow her out. At one point, his brother-in-law even inquired if this happened to be their day for receiving. Caravan muttered in reply:

"No, no, it's just deliveries, nothing important. . . ."

Then the maid brought in a package that he absent-mindedly opened. Black-rimmed death notices appeared. Caravan turned red to the very eyes, pushed the notices back into their envelope, and stuffed the envelope into his pocket.

His mother hadn't noticed a thing. She kept her eyes obstinately fixed on the clock whose gilded, ball-shaped pendulum swung back and forth on the mantelpiece. And their embarrassment kept growing in the icy silence.

After a while, the old woman, turned her wrinkled old witch's face toward her daughter, said with a sly sparkle in her eye:

"Next Monday I want you to bring your daughter over here to see me."

Madame Braux, her face lighting up, exclaimed, "Yes, *maman*!" while the younger Madame Caravan, who had turned pale, seemed on the verge of collapse.

By and by, however, the two men began to talk and got involved in a political argument. Braux defended revolutionary and communist ideas and soon became extremely agitated. His eyes burning amid the whiskers on his face, he shouted:

"Owning property, my good man, is tantamount to robbing the working classes. The land belongs to everybody, remember, and inheritance is a shame and a disgrace. . . ."

At this point he suddenly stopped, like a man who had made a very stupid blunder, and then he added in a much gentler tone:

"Anyway, this is neither the time nor the place to discuss these things."

The door opened and Doctor Chenet made his entrance. He was obviously taken aback at first, but he immediately regained control over himself and, going over to the old woman, said:

"Ha-ha! I see *maman* is feeling better today! Oh, I suspected something like this, you know, and as I was coming upstairs just now, I said to myself: 'I'd bet anything that the elderly lady is up on her feet!' " He patted her gently on the back and added: "She's as sturdy as the Pont-Neuf, this woman! And mark my words, she'll bury us all yet!"

He sat down, accepted the coffee that he was offered, and got into the political argument between the two men, coming out on the side of Braux, for he himself had been somehow involved in the Paris Commune.

Soon the old woman felt tired and said she wanted to retire. Caravan jumped up to help her. She looked him straight in the eye and said:

"You'll put my chest of drawers and my clock back in my room immediately."

And while he was stammering something that could have been "Yes, *maman,*" she took her daughter's arm and the two of them departed.

Monsieur and Madame Caravan remained crushed, silent, and prostrate in their total rout, while Braux gleefully rubbed his hands.

Suddenly, maddened with rage, Madame Caravan went for her brother-in-law:

"You're a thief!" she yelled. "You're a crook and a cheat! I'd like to spit in your eye and . . . and. . . ."

She stopped, short of words. He was still laughing and went on drinking his coffee.

But when Madame Braux came back, she immediately pounced on Madame Caravan, and then the two women—one huge with her formidable belly protruding threateningly, the other thin and jerky—both trembling with fury, their voices completely changed, hurled long strings of abuse at each other.

Chenet and Braux came between the two furies and Braux, pushing his better half with his shoulder, got her out of the dining room shouting:

"Go on, you big donkey, you're braying too much!"

After that the couple could be heard in the street, still bickering as they walked off.

Chenet also took his leave soon and the two Caravans remained face to face.

Then the man let himself collapse into a chair, and with cold sweat breaking out on his temples, he groaned:

"Oh God, what can I possibly tell my chief at the office now?"

[*En Famille,* February 15, 1881]

Uncle Jules

A white-haired old beggar held out his hand to us and my friend, Joseph Davranche, gave him five francs. I was surprised. He said:

"That poor old wreck made me think of a story I can't get out of my head. Here it is."

~

My family, which came from Le Havre originally, was not too well off. You might say they just managed to make ends meet. My father worked in an office, came home late, and didn't earn much. I had two sisters.

My mother felt the tightness of our budget acutely and often had acid words loaded with veiled and sly reproaches for her husband. The poor man would make a gesture that saddened me on these occasions—without answering her, he would pass his open hand over his brow as though wiping off the sweat that wasn't there. It hurt me and I was unable to do anything about it.

We tried to save on everything. We never accepted an invitation to dinner so that we shouldn't have to return it. We bought our provisions at reduced prices from the left-overs in the stores. My sisters made their own dresses and discussed at length whether they could afford a piece of braid at fifteen centimes the yard. Our regular fare consisted of a beef soup followed by beef served up with all kinds of sauce. I was told it was wholesome and nourishing. I'd have very much preferred something else.

I had to face abominable scenes for lost buttons or torn pants.

Every Sunday, however, we would go for a walk down by the docks, dressed in our best. My father, in a frock-coat, high hat, and gloves, would give his arm to my mother, who was bedecked like an ocean liner on a festive occasion. My sisters, always ready first, would wait for the signal to set out. But usually, at the very last moment, some stain that had to be urgently removed with a benzine-soaked rag would be discovered on the frock coat of the head of the family.

My father, his tall hat still on his head, waited in his shirt sleeves for the operation to be completed, while my mother hurried off to perform it, after putting glasses on her near-sighted eyes and taking off her gloves so as not to damage them.

Then, with great solemnity, we'd set out. My sisters walked in front, arm in arm. They were of marriageable age and had to be shown off in the town. I walked on my mother's left and my father on her right. I can still remember the pompous air of my poor parents on those Sunday strolls; the stiffness of their walk, the sternness of their expressions. They moved with slow deliberation, their bodies held straight, their legs rigid as if something terribly important depended on their appearance.

And every Sunday, watching the big ocean liners from various faraway lands putting into the harbor, my father would repeat the very same words:

"What if Jules were on that one! That would be some surprise, wouldn't it?"

Uncle Jules, my father's brother, was the only hope of the family, after having once been its disgrace. I had heard of him ever since my earliest childhood so that I felt I'd recognize him right away if I saw him. I was quite familiar with everything connected with him and knew all the details of his existence up to his departure for America, although that period of his life was only mentioned in hushed tones.

There was a stain on his reputation. That is, he had

squandered some money, which is the greatest crime in poor families. Among the rich, a man who gives himself a good time is generally said to be sowing his wild oats and smilingly called "naughty." But in families of modest means, the son who forces his parents to dip into their capital becomes a useless and unreliable good-for-nothing. And the distinction is valid for although the misdeeds are the same, it is the consequences that determine the gravity of an act.

In short, Uncle Jules had considerably reduced the inheritance my father had been counting on—after having, it goes without saying, squandered his own share to the last sou. So, as was often done in those days, they put him on board a merchant ship sailing from Le Havre to America.

Once there, Uncle Jules became a merchant of some kind of goods or other. And soon he wrote that he was making a little money and hoped to be able to make up for the harm he had caused my father. This letter caused a great emotional outflow in the family. Jules, whom we had not thought worth the soles of the boots he wore, suddenly became a man of honor, a noble heart, a true Davranche, with the typical Davranche integrity.

Moreover, a sea captain told us that he had rented a large store and that he was engaged in important trade.

Then, two years later, a second letter arrived from him.

> My dear Philippe [he wrote], I am writing to you because I do not wish you to worry about my health, which is excellent. And my business is good too. I am leaving tomorrow on a long trip to South America and it may be several years before you hear from me again. But do not worry if you don't hear from me—I will return to Le Havre when I have made my fortune. I hope it won't take me too long and that then we will live together happily, all of us. . . .

That letter became a sort of family bible. It was read on the slightest provocation and was shown to everybody.

Then for ten years there was no word from Uncle Jules. But my father's hopes only grew as the years rolled by. As for my mother, she often said:

"When that nice Jules is back, our situation will be quite different. There's someone who really knew how to look after himself!"

And so each Sunday, as he watched the fat black ocean liners appear on the horizon, vomiting long black spirals of smoke into the sky, my father would repeat his eternal words:

"What if Jules were on that one! . . ."

And we almost expected him to be standing there, waving his handkerchief and calling out:

"Hey, Philippe!"

Thousands of plans were based on that certain return. We even made up our minds to buy a small country house near Ingouville with Uncle Jules's money. I'm not sure that my father didn't even start negotiations connected with that purchase.

At that time my older sister was twenty-eight and the younger twenty-six. They were neither of them married yet and that was a source of considerable consternation to everybody.

Finally a candidate for the hand of the second sister materialized. He was a minor employee, not well off but honorable. For my part, I'm quite convinced that it was Uncle Jules's letter that ended the young man's hesitations.

He was accepted enthusiastically and it was decided that after the marriage the whole family would go on a little trip to the Isle of Jersey.

A trip to that Channel Island is the ideal journey for the poor of Le Havre. It isn't far away; one travels by passenger boat; one lands on foreign soil, since the island belongs to Britain. Thus a Frenchman can, after a two-hour crossing, indulge in the study of a neighboring people in their own national environment and observe their ways and customs, which, by the way, are quite lamentable on that island flying the British flag, according to those who talk plainly.

That trip to Jersey became our great preoccupation, our impatient expectation, our permanent dream.

Finally the day came and we went. I remember it as clearly as if it had happened only yesterday. The packet boat was getting up steam at the Granville pier. My father, very tense, supervised the loading of our three pieces of luggage; my mother, also looking worried, took the arm of my unmarried sister who seemed completely lost since the marriage of the other one—like the last chicken in a brood, left all by itself. The newlyweds brought up the rear as usual, which made me turn my head often.

The whistle blew and, standing on the deck of the ship, we watched it leave the jetty and move away on a sea as flat as a green marble tabletop. Then we watched the coast slipping away, feeling happy and proud, like all people who haven't traveled much.

My father was sucking in his stomach under the frock coat from which, that morning, all the stains had been removed, and so he spread around him the smell of benzine which had become so closely interwoven with my memory of Sundays.

Suddenly he caught sight of two elegant ladies to whom two gentlemen were offering oysters. A ragged old seaman was opening the oysters with his knife and handing them to the gentlemen who were passing them on to the ladies. The ladies ate them, daintily holding each shell on their fine handkerchiefs and leaning forward so as not to stain their dresses. Then they swallowed with a quick little movement and tossed the shell overboard.

Probably fascinated by the refinement of eating oysters on the moving steamboat, my father decided it was the proper, distinguished, and elegant thing to do and walked over to my mother and my sisters and asked:

"Wouldn't you like me to order a few oysters for you?"

My mother hesitated because of the extra expense it meant, while my sisters accepted immediately. My mother then said in a sad tone:

"I am afraid it would be too much for my stomach. Get a few for the children, but really only a few or it will make them sick."

Then, turning toward me, she added:

"As for Joseph, he doesn't have to have any. I don't believe in spoiling boys."

So I had to remain by my mother's side, rather resentful at this discrimination and following my father with my eyes as he pompously led his two daughters and his son-in-law over to the ragged seaman.

The two ladies had gone and my father was showing my sisters how they were to eat the oysters without spilling the liquid on their dresses. He even wanted to set them an example, and so took hold of an oyster. Trying to imitate the ladies, he immediately proceeded to spill the entire contents of the shell on his frock coat and I heard my mother mutter:

"Ah, I wish he'd just stayed quiet. . . ."

Suddenly a worried look came over my father's face. He walked away a few steps, stared at his daughters and son-in-law, who were crowding around the old seaman opening the oysters, and then suddenly came over to us. His pallor was striking and his eyes looked very strange. In a hushed voice he said to my mother:

"It's really extraordinary how that fellow with the oysters looks like Jules."

My mother, at a loss, said:

"What Jules?"

"Why . . . my brother. . . . And if I didn't know that he was so well off in America, I'd have thought it was him."

Shocked, my mother muttered:

"You must be crazy. . . . And since you know it can't be him, why do you have to say such stupid things?"

But father insisted:

"I wish you'd go and have a look, Clarisse. I'd rather you had a look for yourself."

She got up and went over to join her daughters. I too was looking at the man. He was old, dirty, and very wrinkled, and seemed completely absorbed in opening the oyster shells.

My mother came back to us. I saw she was trembling. She said very quickly:

"I think it's him all right. You ought to find out about him from the captain. But be very careful or we might get that good-for-nothing on our hands."

My father went and I followed him, somehow feeling strangely moved. The captain, a tall, thin man with long side-whiskers, was walking up and down on his bridge with an air of such great importance that one would have thought he was commanding the huge Indies mail-boat.

My father addressed him with great formality, asked him questions connected with his trade, complimented him, wanted to know what the population of Jersey was, what the island produced, what its ways and customs were, the nature of the soil, etc. Listening to him, one would have thought he was inquiring about a country as important as the United States.

Then he spoke of the *Express,* the ship on which we were, and of its crew. Finally my father said in a hesitant voice:

"You have that old fellow opening the oysters. . . . He looks rather interesting. Would you know anything about him by any chance?"

The captain, who was becoming irritated with this conversation, finally said drily:

"He's an old French tramp I picked up last year in the

States and brought back here. I understand he has some relatives in Le Havre but he won't see them because he owes them some money. His name is Jules Darmanche or is it Darvanche? Well, something like that. I heard he made quite a lot of money at one point over there, but you can see for yourself what a state he's in now."

My father, who had turned livid, muttered in a strangled voice, his eyes haggard:

"Ah, I see, I see. . . . Very good. I'm not at all surprised. . . . Thank you very much, Captain, thank you!" And he walked away, leaving the surprised captain staring after him.

When Father rejoined Mother, he looked so upset that she said to him:

"Sit down here or everyone will notice something has happened."

He slipped down onto the seat, stammering:

"Wh-what are we going to do now?"

She replied quickly:

"We must get the girls farther away from him. Now, since Joseph knows everything, he'll go and ask them to come over here. Above all, let's be sure that our son-in-law doesn't find out a thing."

My father, who had still not recovered from the blow, muttered:

"That's awful, terrible. . . ."

Suddenly, turning furious, my mother said:

"I always thought that thief would come to no good and I've always been afraid we'd have him on our hands some day. But then, what can you expect of a Davranche!"

As my father passed his hand over his brow the way he always did when my mother reproached him with things, she added:

"And now, give Joseph some money so he can pay for those oysters. For it would really be the last straw if that beggar recognized you, wouldn't it? That would be a nice scene on board this boat. Let's go as far away from him as possible, and you'd better see to it that that man doesn't come near us again."

She rose, and the two of them walked off, after my father had given me a five-franc piece to pay for the oysters.

My sisters looked a bit surprised, since they were expecting our father to come back. But I explained that Mother didn't feel too well and I asked the old seaman:

"How much do I owe you, monsieur?"

I was almost on the point of saying "Uncle Jules."

"That'll be two-fifty," he said.

I gave him the five-franc piece and he handed me back the change.

I looked at his hand, a pathetic sailor's hand with the skin so wrinkled and cracked, and then I looked at that pitiful old face, so sad and dejected, thinking to myself: He's my uncle, Father's brother! And I gave him a half-franc tip. He thanked me:

"God bless you, young gentleman!"

He said it in the tone of a pauper receiving a handout, and it occurred to me that he must have done some begging over there before.

My sisters were staring at me, taken aback by my reckless generosity.

When I gave the two francs back to my father, my mother asked me suspiciously:

"Why, do you mean to say they've eaten three francs' worth of oysters? It doesn't sound possible!"

I said firmly:

"I gave him a half-franc tip."

My mother all but leaped up from the shock and glaring into my eyes cried:

"You're mad! What do you mean by giving half a franc to that man, to that good-for-nothing!"

Then she stopped, however, as my father was indicating our in-law with his eyes. And then there was silence.

In front of us, a purple shadow seemed to emerge out of the sea. It was Jersey.

As we were coming alongside the pier, I was seized by a great desire to have one more look at my uncle. I longed to get close to him and to say something nice to him, to make him feel better. But since no one was having any oysters now, he had vanished; the wretched fellow had probably gone down to some corner in the dirty hold where he now lived.

We returned from Jersey by the boat to Saint-Malo so as not to stumble upon him again. My mother was very anxious to avoid that.

I never saw my father's brother again. . . .

Well, that's why you may occasionally see me give a five-franc piece to some tramp.

[*Mon Oncle Jules,* August 7, 1883]

A Horseback Ride

The family, living on the husband's small salary, just managed to make both ends meet. Two children born of the marriage had turned their erstwhile modest life into a humiliating, shameful existence which was painful for a noble family that despite everything clung to its ways.

Hector de Gribelin had been brought up in the paternal manor house in the provinces, under the tutorship of an old priest. They were not rich but they managed to get along and to keep up appearances.

When he was twenty, they began to look for a post for him, and he entered the Ministry of the Navy as a clerk with a starting salary of fifteen hundred francs a year. Here he had run aground, as do all those who have not been prepared from their early years for the rough struggle for existence—all those who look at life through a sort of cloud, who know nothing of how to succeed or about the difficulties they are to encounter, who have failed to develop in their childhood whatever special gifts they may have had—all those who lack the fierce energy to fight and who have received no weapon or tool with which to strengthen their hands.

His first three years at the Ministry were a nightmare.

He had found some family friends in Paris, old people with obsolete ways and little money who lived in the sad streets of the aristocratic Faubourg Saint-Germain, and it was among them that he built his circle of acquaintances.

Untouched by modern life, humble and proud at the same time, these hard-up aristocrats lived in the upper stories of sleepy houses in which every inhabitant from the ground floor to the attic bore a noble name, but in which money was a rare commodity.

The eternal prejudices, preoccupation with rank, and fear of slipping down in the social scale haunted these once-celebrated families which had been ruined by the inertia of their men. It was in this world that Hector met a girl just as poor as himself and married her.

They had two children in four years.

For four years the family, oppressed by hardship, knew no other entertainment than the Sunday stroll along the Champs Elysées and one or two visits a year to the theater, thanks to complimentary tickets obtained by one of Hector's colleagues.

But then, toward spring, the department chief gave Hector some extra work to do for which he received the unbelievable bonus of three hundred francs.

When he brought the money home, Hector said to his wife:

"Henriette dear, don't you think we ought to do something special with this money, perhaps an excursion that the children would be sure to enjoy?"

And after a long discussion they decided that they would go to the country on a picnic.

"Well, for once we can be extravagant," Hector declared, "so we'll hire a carriage for you, the children, and the maid and I'll get myself a horse in the riding school. It will look very nice."

For the entire week the forthcoming outing was their only subject of conversation.

Every evening when he'd return from the Ministry, Hector would pick up his older son, install him astride his knee, and bounce him as hard as he could, repeating:

"That's the way your daddy will gallop next Sunday when we go out on our picnic."

And for the rest of the day, the little boy would clamber up and sit astride the chairs, saying each time:

"I'm Daddy riding a horsy."

Even the maid looked at Monsieur with wondering eyes, imagining how he would accompany the carriage on horseback. And during every meal, she'd listen to him talk about various riding styles and tell of his old exploits when he still lived in the family manor. Ah, he'd certainly learned to ride the proper way, and once he had a horse between his legs, there was nothing to touch him, nothing!

He repeated to his wife, rubbing his hands:

"I'll be delighted if they give me a rather difficult horse. I'm very anxious for you to see me ride. And if you want, we could come back by the Champs Elysées at the time when people are returning from the Bois. We'll cut a good figure and I wouldn't mind at all if we met someone from the Ministry. There's no better way than that for gaining the respect of one's superiors."

The long-awaited day came. The carriage and the horse arrived. Hector hurried downstairs to look his mount over. He had had straps sewn to his trousers and was twiddling a riding crop he had bought the day before.

He lifted each of the animal's four legs in turn, felt them, touched the neck, the flanks, and the hocks, poked its sides with his finger, opened its mouth, examined its teeth, determined its age; and when his family joined him downstairs, he delivered himself of a little lecture on horses in general and on that horse in particular, which he pronounced an excellent animal.

When they were all installed in the carriage, he checked the saddle girth; then, slipping his foot into the stirrup, he raised himself into the air and landed on the back of the animal, which reacted to the shock with a brisk dancing leap that almost threw its rider.

A bit flustered, Hector tried to appease it:

"Come, come, my beauty, all right, quiet now!"

Finally, when the horse had regained its calm, the rider regained his poise and asked:

"Are we all ready?"

The voices from the carriage answered all together:

"Yes."

"Then let's go!" he commanded, and they were off.

The eyes of everyone in the carriage were fixed on him. He trotted English style, bouncing up and down exaggeratedly in his saddle: no sooner had he touched the saddle than he bounced up again as if taking off into space. Sometimes it seemed as though he were going to land on the horse's mane. He looked straight ahead of him intently, his face pale and contracted.

His wife, who was holding one child on her knees, and the maid, who was holding the other, kept repeating:

"There, look at Daddy, watch Daddy!"

And the two little boys, excited by the movement and the fresh air, filled with joy, expressed their delight in shrill little exclamations. The horse, frightened by their piercing cries, started off at a gallop, and while he was trying to control it, the rider's hat rolled onto the ground. The driver of the carriage had to get down and pick it up. As he handed it to its owner, Hector called out to his wife:

"Can't you stop the children from shrieking like that? They're driving the horse mad and it'll bolt."

They ate their lunch, which they had brought along in hampers, on the grass in the Vésinet woods. And although the driver took care of all the horses, Hector kept getting up every minute to see whether his mount needed anything, patting him on the neck, feeding him bread, cake, and sugar.

"He's a great trotter," Hector declared. "In fact, he shook me up a bit during the first minutes. But, as you could see, I recovered quickly enough and he won't do it again—he knows who's master now."

As they had decided, they returned by the Champs Elysées.

The vast avenue was teeming with carriages, and on the sidewalks the dense crowd of pedestrians looked like two long black ribbons unrolled between the Arc de Triomphe and the Place de la Concorde.

A blaze of sunshine fell on all these people and made the varnish of the carriages, the steel of the harnesses, and the brass knobs of the carriage doors gleam.

These human beings, these carriages and horses seemed to be seized by some madness of motion, to be drunk on sheer existence. And in the distance, ahead of them, the Obelisk stood out in a golden haze.

Once they had passed the Arc de Triomphe, Hector's horse seemed to be gripped by a new frenzy and it rushed down the avenue at a great pace. It was apparently in a great hurry to be back in its stall and had decided to disregard completely all of Hector's efforts to slow it down.

The carriage was left far behind. Then, as they were passing the Palais de l'Industrie, the animal, seeing a clear space, turned right and set off at a gallop.

An old woman wearing an apron was crossing the street

just at that moment. She walked slowly and leisurely and came right into Hector's path as he advanced at full speed. Unable to control the horse, he began to shout as loud as he could:

"Hey! Over there! Look out! Hey, you!"

Perhaps she was deaf, for she went calmly on her way until she was struck by the chest of the horse, which descended upon her like a railway engine. She rolled for ten yards or so, her skirts flying in the air, and banged her head three times against the cobblestones.

Several voices shouted:

"Stop him, stop him!"

Hector, beyond himself, was pulling desperately at the horse's mane, shouting:

"Help, help!"

Then a frightful jerk sent him flying over his horse's ears and he fell into the arms of a traffic policeman who had rushed toward him.

Within seconds there was an angry, gesticulating crowd gathered around him. An old gentleman with a distinguished decoration in his buttonhole and a long white moustache seemed especially exasperated and kept saying:

"Damn it, my good man, when one is so awkward, one stays at home! When one doesn't know how to handle a horse, one doesn't go riding in the streets and killing people. . . ."

Four men carrying the old woman joined them. She looked dead; her yellow face was immobile and her cap was pushed to one side and quite gray with dust.

"Take this woman to a druggist's," the old gentleman said in a commanding tone, "while we go to the police station."

With a policeman on each side of him, Hector walked toward the station. A third policeman led his horse. A whole crowd of the curious followed behind them. Suddenly the carriage came into sight. His wife rushed toward him, the maid seemed terror-stricken, the children were shrieking. He explained to his wife that he had to go to the police station because he had injured a woman, that it was nothing, that he'd see them all at home very soon. And his baffled family disappeared.

At the police station, things didn't take long at all. He gave his name—Hector de Gribelin, employed at the Ministry of the Navy. After that they just waited for news of the injured woman. A policeman who had been sent to find out about her returned. She had regained consciousness but she was suffering, she said, "terrible pains in my insides." Her name was Madame Simon, she was sixty-five, and a cleaning woman by trade.

When he learned that she wasn't dead, Hector cheered up and promised to pay for the necessary medical care. Then he ran over to the druggist's where she had been taken for first aid.

People were crowding around the door. The old woman, stretched out limply in a chair, was groaning while two doctors examined her. She had no broken bones but they feared some internal damage.

Hector spoke to her:

"Does it hurt very badly?"

"Oh yes, it hurts something terrible."

"Where?"

"It's like a flame inside my stomach, m'sieu."

One of the doctors crossed over to him:

"Was it you, sir, who caused this accident?"

"Yes, sir."

"Well, I'm sure this woman should be sent to a clinic. . . . I know of one where they would charge her only six francs a day. Would you like me to take care of it for you?"

Hector, quite relieved, accepted, thanked the doctor and returned home. His wife was waiting for him with tears in her eyes. He reassured her:

"It's nothing, really. The Simon woman already feels much better and in three days, I'm sure, she'll be fully recovered. .n the meantime, I've sent her to a clinic. There's really nothing to worry about."

Nothing to worry about indeed!

The next day, after leaving the office, he went to the clinic to see how Madame Simon was progressing. He found her eating a meat broth with a perfectly happy expression.

"Well, how's it going?" he asked.

"Ah," she said, "my poor, dear sir, I don't feel no better than when you hit me. I'm like dead. My health ain't coming back."

The doctor said they must wait and see because there was still a possibility of complications.

He let three days go by and then went back. The old woman, fresh and rosy, her eyes sparkling, started groaning as soon as she caught sight of him:

"I can't move none, my poor, dear sir. I can't use my

limbs no more. It looks like I'll stay this way till the end of my days."

An icy shudder rolled down Hector's spine. He went to see her doctor. The doctor threw up his arms in an impotent gesture:

"Well, what can I say to you? I don't really know. She shrieks as soon as we try to pick her up. It's impossible even to move her in her armchair without her letting out heart-rending cries. So I have to believe what she tells me. I can't get inside her, you know. As long as I don't see her walking around I have no right to suspect her of shamming."

The old woman sat motionless and listened, a perfidious spark gleaming in her eyes.

A week passed, then two weeks, then a month. Madame Simon never left her armchair. She spent her time eating from morning to night and put on a lot of weight. She chatted cheerfully with other patients and seemed to take her immobility in stride. Perhaps she even enjoyed it, viewing it as a well-earned rest after fifty years or so of climbing up and down stairs, turning over mattresses, carrying coal from one floor to another, sweeping and dusting.

Hector, growing desperate, went to see her every day. And every day he found her calm and serene as she told him:

"I still can't move, my poor sir, honest I can't."

And every evening Madame de Gribelin inquired in anguish:

"What about Madame Simon?"

To which, every time, he had no choice but to answer dejectedly:

"No change whatsoever."

They had to send the maid away, her wages being too big a burden in their present situation. They cut expenses to the bone. In no time they had gone through all of Hector's bonus.

Then Hector summoned four well-known doctors to the bedside of the old woman. She allowed them to examine her. They felt her and poked her, and she kept watching them with a sly look.

"I want you to try to walk," one of the doctors said.

"But I can't," she cried, horrified. "I can't, my poor sirs, I can't walk no more. . . ."

They picked her up and dragged her along for a few steps. But she managed to wriggle out of their hands and fall heavily to the floor amidst bloodcurdling shrieks. So they helped her back into her armchair, handling her with the utmost care.

They refrained from making a definite diagnosis but agreed that she was no longer capable of working.

When Hector broke the news to his wife, she let herself drop into a chair, mumbling:

"As things stand now, perhaps the best thing would be to bring her here. That would at least cost us less."

He jumped up:

"Live here, with us? Do you realize what you're saying?"

But she seemed to have resigned herself to the whole thing and answered with tears running down her cheeks:

"Well, what else can we do, my dear Hector? It wasn't my fault, after all!"

[*À Cheval,* January 14, 1883]

The Necklace

She was one of those pretty, charming young women who are born, as if by an error of Fate, into a petty official's family. She had no dowry, no hopes, not the slightest chance of being appreciated, understood, loved, and married by a rich and distinguished man; so she slipped into marriage with a minor civil servant at the Ministry of Education.

Unable to afford jewelry, she dressed simply; but she was as wretched as a *déclassée*, for women have neither caste nor breeding—in them beauty, grace, and charm replace pride of birth. Innate refinement, instinctive elegance, and suppleness of wit give them their place on the only scale that counts, and these qualities make humble girls the peers of the grandest ladies.

She suffered constantly, feeling that all the attributes of a gracious life, every luxury, should rightly have been hers. The poverty of her rooms—the shabby walls, the worn furniture, the ugly upholstery—caused her pain. All these things that another woman of her class would not even have noticed, tormented her and made her angry. The very sight of the little Breton girl who cleaned for her awoke rueful thoughts and the wildest dreams in her mind. She dreamt of thick-carpeted reception rooms with Oriental hangings, lighted by tall, bronze torches, and with two huge footmen in knee breeches, made drowsy by the heat from the stove, asleep in the wide armchairs. She dreamt of great drawing rooms upholstered in old silks, with fragile little tables holding priceless knickknacks, and of enchanting little sitting rooms redolent of perfume, designed for tea-time chats with intimate friends—famous, sought-after men whose attentions all women long for.

When she sat down to dinner at her round table with its three-day-old cloth, and watched her husband opposite her lift the lid of the soup tureen and exclaim, delighted: "Ah, a good homemade beef stew! There's nothing better. . ." she would visualize elegant dinners with gleaming silver amid tapestried walls peopled by knights and ladies and exotic birds in a fairy forest; she would think of exquisite dishes served on gorgeous china, and of gallantries whispered and received with sphinx-like smiles while eating the pink flesh of trout or wings of grouse.

She had no proper wardrobe, no jewels, nothing. And those were the only things that she loved—she felt she was made for them. She would have so loved to charm, to be envied, to be admired and sought after.

She had a rich friend, a schoolmate from the convent she had attended, but she didn't like to visit her because it always made her so miserable when she got home again. She would weep for whole days at a time from sorrow, regret, despair, and distress.

~

Then one evening her husband arrived home looking triumphant and waving a large envelope.

"There," he said, "there's something for you."

She tore it open eagerly and took out a printed card which said:

"The Minister of Education and Madame Georges Ramponneau request the pleasure of the company of M. and Mme. Loisel at an evening reception at the Ministry on Monday, January 18th."

Instead of being delighted, as her husband had hoped, she tossed the invitation on the table and muttered, annoyed:

"What do you expect me to do with that?"

"Why, I thought you'd be pleased, dear. You never go out and this would be an occasion for you, a great one! I had a lot of trouble getting it. Everyone wants an invitation; they're in great demand and there are only a few reserved for the employees. All the officials will be there."

She looked at him, irritated, and said impatiently:

"I haven't a thing to wear. How could I go?"

It had never even occurred to him. He stammered:

"But what about the dress you wear to the theater? I think it's lovely. . . ."

He fell silent, amazed and bewildered to see that his wife was crying. Two big tears escaped from the corners of her eyes and rolled slowly toward the corners of her mouth. He mumbled:

"What is it? What is it?"

But, with great effort, she had overcome her misery; and now she answered him calmly, wiping her tear-damp cheeks:

"It's nothing. It's just that I have no evening dress and so I can't go to the party. Give the invitation to one of your colleagues whose wife will be better dressed than I would be."

He was overcome. He said:

"Listen, Mathilde, how much would an evening dress cost —a suitable one that you could wear again on other occasions, something very simple?"

She thought for several seconds, making her calculations and at the same time estimating how much she could ask for without eliciting an immediate refusal and an exclamation of horror from this economical government clerk.

At last, not too sure of herself, she said:

"It's hard to say exactly but I think I could manage with four hundred francs."

He went a little pale, for that was exactly the amount he had put aside to buy a rifle so that he could go hunting the following summer near Nanterre, with a few friends who went shooting larks around there on Sundays.

However, he said:

"Well, all right, then. I'll give you four hundred francs. But try to get something really nice."

~

As the day of the ball drew closer, Madame Loisel seemed depressed, disturbed, worried—despite the fact that her dress was ready. One evening her husband said:

"What's the matter? You've really been very strange these last few days."

And she answered:

"I hate not having a single jewel, not one stone, to wear. I shall look so dowdy. I'd almost rather not go to the party."

He suggested:

"You can wear some fresh flowers. It's considered very chic at this time of year. For ten francs you can get two or three beautiful roses."

That didn't satisfy her at all.

"No . . . there's nothing more humiliating than to look poverty-stricken among a lot of rich women."

Then her husband exclaimed:

"Wait—you silly thing! Why don't you go and see Madame Forestier and ask her to lend you some jewelry. You certainly know her well enough for that, don't you think?"

She let out a joyful cry.

"You're right. It never occurred to me."

The next day she went to see her friend and related her tale of woe.

Madame Forestier went to her mirrored wardrobe, took out a big jewel case, brought it to Madame Loisel, opened it, and said:

"Take your pick, my dear."

Her eyes wandered from some bracelets to a pearl necklace, then to a gold Venetian cross set with stones, of very fine workmanship. She tried on the jewelry before the mirror, hesitating, unable to bring herself to take them off, to give them back. And she kept asking:

"Do you have anything else, by chance?"

"Why yes. Here, look for yourself. I don't know which ones you'll like."

All at once, in a box lined with black satin, she came upon a superb diamond necklace, and her heart started beating with overwhelming desire. Her hands trembled as she picked it up. She fastened it around her neck over her high-necked dress and stood there gazing at herself ecstatically.

Hesitantly, filled with terrible anguish, she asked:

"Could you lend me this one—just this and nothing else?"

"Yes, of course."

She threw her arms around her friend's neck, kissed her ardently, and fled with her treasure.

The day of the party arrived. Madame Loisel was a great success. She was the prettiest woman there—resplendent, graceful, beaming, and deliriously happy. All the men looked at her, asked who she was, tried to get themselves introduced to her. All the minister's aides wanted to waltz with her. The minister himself noticed her.

She danced enraptured—carried away, intoxicated with

pleasure, forgetting everything in this triumph of her beauty and the glory of her success, floating in a cloud of happiness formed by all this homage, all this admiration, all the desires she had stirred up—by this victory so complete and so sweet to the heart of a woman.

When she left the party, it was almost four in the morning. Her husband had been sleeping since midnight in a small, deserted sitting room, with three other gentlemen whose wives were having a wonderful time.

He brought her wraps so that they could leave and put them around her shoulders—the plain wraps from her everyday life whose shabbiness jarred with the elegance of her evening dress. She felt this and wanted to escape quickly so that the other women, who were enveloping themselves in their rich furs, wouldn't see her.

Loisel held her back.

"Wait a minute. You'll catch cold out there. I'm going to call a cab."

But she wouldn't listen to him and went hastily downstairs. Outside in the street, there was no cab to be found; they set out to look for one, calling to the drivers they saw passing in the distance.

They walked toward the Seine, shivering and miserable. Finally, on the embankment, they found one of those ancient nocturnal broughams which are only to be seen in Paris at night, as if they were ashamed to show their shabbiness in daylight.

It took them to their door in the Rue des Martyrs, and they went sadly upstairs to their apartment. For her, it was all over. And he was thinking that he had to be at the Ministry by ten.

She took off her wraps before the mirror so that she could see herself in all her glory once more. Then she cried out. The necklace was gone; there was nothing around her neck.

Her husband, already half undressed, asked:

"What's the matter?"

She turned toward him in a frenzy:

"The . . . the . . . necklace—it's gone."

He got up, thunderstruck.

"What did you say? . . . What! . . . Impossible!"

And they searched the folds of her dress, the folds of her wrap, the pockets, everywhere. They didn't find it.

He asked:

"Are you sure you still had it when we left the ball?"

"Yes. I remember touching it in the hallway of the Ministry."

"But if you had lost it in the street, we would have heard it fall. It must be in the cab."

"Yes, most likely. Do you remember the number?"

"No. What about you—did you notice it?"

"No."

They looked at each other in utter dejection. Finally Loisel got dressed again.

"I'm going to retrace the whole distance we covered on foot," he said, "and see if I can't find it."

And he left the house. She remained in her evening dress, too weak to go to bed, sitting crushed on a chair, lifeless and blank.

Her husband returned at about seven o'clock. He had found nothing.

He went to the police station, to the newspapers to offer a reward, to the offices of the cab companies—in a word, wherever there seemed to be the slightest hope of tracing it.

She spent the whole day waiting, in a state of utter hopelessness before such an appalling catastrophe.

Loisel returned in the evening, his face lined and pale; he had learned nothing.

"You must write to your friend," he said, "and tell her that you've broken the clasp of the necklace and that you're getting it mended. That'll give us time to decide what to do."

She wrote the letter at his dictation.

By the end of the week, they had lost all hope.

Loisel, who had aged five years, declared:

"We'll have to replace the necklace."

The next day they took the case in which it had been kept and went to the jeweler whose name appeared inside it. He looked through his ledgers:

"I didn't sell this necklace, madame. I only supplied the case."

Then they went from one jeweler to the next, trying to find a necklace like the other, racking their memories, both of them sick with worry and distress.

In a fashionable shop near the Palais Royal, they found a diamond necklace which they decided was exactly like the other. It was worth 40,000 francs. They could have it for 36,000 francs.

They asked the jeweler to hold it for them for three days, and they stipulated that he should take it back for 34,000 francs if the other necklace was found before the end of February.

Loisel possessed 18,000 francs left him by his father. He would borrow the rest.

He borrowed, asking a thousand francs from one man, five hundred from another, a hundred here, fifty there. He signed promissory notes, borrowed at exorbitant rates, dealt with usurers and the entire race of moneylenders. He compromised his whole career, gave his signature even when he wasn't sure he would be able to honor it, and horrified by the anxieties with which his future would be filled, by the black misery about to descend upon him, by the prospect of physical privation and moral suffering, went to get the new necklace, placing on the jeweler's counter 36,000 francs.

When Madame Loisel went to return the necklace, Madame Forestier said in a faintly waspish tone:

"You could have brought it back a little sooner! I might have needed it."

She didn't open the case as her friend had feared she might. If she had noticed the substitution, what would she have thought? What would she have said? Mightn't she have taken Madame Loisel for a thief?

Madame Loisel came to know the awful life of the poverty-stricken. However, she resigned herself to it with unexpected fortitude. The crushing debt had to be paid. She would pay it. They dismissed the maid; they moved into an attic under the roof.

She came to know all the heavy household chores, the loathsome work of the kitchen. She washed the dishes, wearing down her pink nails on greasy casseroles and the bottoms of saucepans. She did the laundry, washing shirts and dishcloths which she hung on a line to dry; she took the garbage down to the street every morning, and carried water upstairs, stopping at every floor to get her breath. Dressed like a working-class woman, she went to the fruit store, the grocer, and the butcher with her basket on her arm, bargaining, outraged, contesting each sou of her pitiful funds.

Every month some notes had to be honored and more time requested on others.

Her husband worked in the evenings, putting a shopkeeper's ledgers in order, and often at night as well, doing copying at twenty-five centimes a page.

And it went on like that for ten years.

After ten years, they had made good on everything, including the usurious rates and the compound interest.

Madame Loisel looked old now. She had become the sort of strong woman, hard and coarse, that one finds in poor families. Disheveled, her skirts askew, with reddened hands, she spoke in a loud voice, slopping water over the floors as she washed them. But sometimes, when her husband was at the office, she would sit down by the window and muse over that party long ago when she had been so beautiful, the belle of the ball.

How would things have turned out if she hadn't lost that necklace? Who could tell? How strange and fickle life is! How little it takes to make or break you!

Then one Sunday when she was strolling along the Champs Elysées to forget the week's chores for a while, she suddenly caught sight of a woman taking a child for a walk. It was Madame Forestier, still young, still beautiful, still charming.

Madame Loisel started to tremble. Should she speak to her? Yes, certainly she should. And now that she had paid everything back, why shouldn't she tell her the whole story?

She went up to her.

"Hello, Jeanne."

The other didn't recognize her and was surprised that this plainly dressed woman should speak to her so familiarly. She murmured:

"But . . . madame! . . . I'm sure . . . You must be mistaken."

"No, I'm not. I am Mathilde Loisel."

Her friend gave a little cry.

"Oh! Oh, my poor Mathilde, how you've changed!"

"Yes, I've been through some pretty hard times since I last saw you and I've had plenty of trouble—and all because of you!"

"Because of me? What do you mean?"

"You remember the diamond necklace you lent me to wear to the party at the Ministry?"

"Yes. What about it?"

"Well, I lost it."

"What are you talking about? You returned it to me."

"What I gave back to you was another one just like it. And it took us ten years to pay for it. You can imagine it wasn't easy for us, since we were quite poor. . . . Anyway, I'm glad it's over and done with."

Madame Forestier stopped short.

"You say you bought a diamond necklace to replace that other one?"

"Yes. You didn't even notice then? They really were exactly alike."

And she smiled, full of a proud, simple joy.

Madame Forestier, profoundly moved, took Mathilde's hands in her own.

"Oh, my poor, poor Mathilde! Mine was false. It was worth five hundred francs at the most!"

[*La Parure,* February 17, 1884]

III

HUNTING AND FISHING

The Fishing Hole

The charge that brought Léopold Renard, upholsterer, before the criminal court read: "Causing bodily harm resulting in death."

The principal witnesses were Madame Flamèche, the victim's widow, one Louis Ladureau, cabinetmaker, and one Jean Durdent, plumber.

Next to the accused stood his wife, small, ugly, looking like an ape disguised as "a lady in black."

And here is how the accused, Léopold Renard, described the tragedy:

"Let me tell you that the first victim in this misfortune is myself and that it was all beyond my will. Ah, good God, the facts speak for themselves, Your Honor! I'm an honest, hard-working man, an upholsterer located in the same street for sixteen years—well known, well liked, respected by one and all, highly considered, as was testified by my neighbors and even my concierge, who's not always such good company. I like to work, I like to save money, I like honest folks and honest pleasures. And that's just what brought about my downfall. Well, so much the worse for me, but since my will wasn't involved in it, I, for one, still respect myself.

"Well then, every Sunday for five years now, my wife and myself, we've gone to spend the day at Poissy. That gives us a breath of fresh air, not to mention the fact that we are fond of fishing. In fact, we like fishing even more than we do fried onions. It was my wife Mélie gave me that passion, the nasty thing, and she feels even stronger about it than me, the pest; and it was she who got me into all this mess, as you'll see.

"Me, I'm a gentle fellow and there isn't two sous' worth of wickedness in me. But her, she's something else again! She's small and thin but, *oh-là-là!*, she's meaner than a weasel. Now, don't get me wrong—I'm not trying to deny that she has some good points. Sure she has, and some very important ones for a man with a business like mine. But then, her character! . . . You can ask around where we live. You could even question the concierge who gave me such a nice character reference just now. She'll tell you a few good ones about my wife!

"Every day she'd nag me for the nice way I treat people: 'I sure wouldn't let 'em step on my toes like you do,' she'd say. 'Ah, I most certainly wouldn't allow them to do that to me.' Ah, Your Honor, if I'd listened to her, I'd have got myself involved in at least three fist fights every month."

At this point Madame Renard interrupted him:

"Keep talking, my good man, we'll see who has the last laugh."

He turned toward her and said with great candor:

"Why shouldn't I put it all on you, since you aren't on trial here."

Then, turning back to the presiding magistrate:

"May I go on, Your Honor? So, me and my wife, we went to Poissy every Saturday evening so we could start fishing at daybreak on Sunday. It's a habit that became what they call second nature with us. Three years or so back, I discovered a spot. *Oh-là-là!* What a spot!—well shaded, at least eight feet of water, maybe even ten, well, a regular hole, and with more smaller holes by the bank—a true nook for fish and a paradise for a fisherman. Well, Your Honor, I had the right to consider that hole like my private property in view of the fact I was just like its Christopher Columbus. And everyone around knew it and no one protested. They even called it 'Renard's spot,' that hole, and no one tried to fish there, not even Monsieur Plumeau, who, let me say without the least desire to offend him, is notorious for stealing spots belonging to others.

"So I was certain to have my spot to myself and I went back there every time, like its rightful owner. As soon as we got there on Saturday, me and my wife, we'd get aboard my *Delilah*—that's my boat that I had built at Fournaise's shipyard, a very light and reliable thing—and, as I was saying, we'd get aboard and go baiting and, let me tell you, there's no one around who can touch me for baiting and they all know it, my pals. Now if you asked me what I use for bait, I wouldn't tell you because that has nothing to do with the accident and I wouldn't have to answer, it being my private secret. At least two hundred people have tried to get it out of me and I've been offered innumerable glasses of liquor and fed I don't know how many portions of fried fish and marinated eel to spill it. But just let 'em go and try to make the chub come! Ah, yes, believe me, lots of people have tried to reach me through my belly, to find out what I use. The only person who knows it, besides me, is my wife and she won't tell any more than I would, ain't that so, Mélie?"

The presiding magistrate interrupted him:

"Would you please come to the point as quickly as possible."

The accused went on:

"I'm getting there, I'm getting there, Your Honor. Well then, on that Saturday—July eighth—we left by the five twenty-five train. Then, before we'd even had our dinner, we went baiting just like we did every Saturday. The weather looked promising and I says to Mélie: 'Looks good,' I says; 'looks like we're going to have a great day tomorrow.' And I even remember her answering: 'Yes, it looks like it.' Because we never talked much more than that to each other.

"Then we went back and had dinner. I was pleased and I was thirsty. And that's what caused it all, Your Honor. I says to Mélie: 'Mélie, the weather's fine and I guess I'll be all right if I drink a bottle of *waking potion?*' We'd christened a little local white wine that because if you drink too much of it, it keeps you awake and all that, see what I mean?

"She says: 'Suit yourself, but if you do, you'll be sick again and you'll never get out of bed tomorrow morning.' Well, I must admit she was right there, she was wise and shrewd and all, and I don't mind giving her credit. Nevertheless, I couldn't restrain myself and I drank up my bottle and that brought the whole thing about.

"So I couldn't go to sleep. Ah, good Lord, that *waking potion* kept me awake until two in the morning. But then I did go to sleep and I slept so deep I wouldn't have heard the angel holler at the Last Judgment.

"Well, to make a short story of it, at six o'clock my wife wakes me up. So I jump out of bed, quickly slip into my pants and my sweater, rub a bit of water on my snout, and we're off in our *Delilah*. Too late. When we got to my fishing hole, the spot was taken! That had never happened to me before, Your Honor, never, never, not once in three years! I felt like I was being robbed in plain daylight. I said: 'Ah, damn, damn, damn!' And just then, my wife begins to bawl me out: 'So you see what your *waking potion* does to you? Ah, you're nothing but a drunkard! Well, I suppose you're pleased with yourself now, you big oaf!'

"I didn't say nothing. She was quite right about it all.

"Nevertheless, we disembarked close to our spot, hoping to catch some leftovers at least. And I thought to myself, who knows, perhaps he won't catch a thing, this fellow, and he'll leave to look for another place.

"He was a thin little guy in a white linen jacket and a straw hat. He was there with his wife too—a big dame who was working at her embroidery behind him.

"Now when that woman saw us install ourselves so close, she started to grumble like this:

" 'Looks like there's no room on the river.'

"And my wife, who was just about boiling with rage, said quite loud:

" 'People who have manners inquire about the ways of a place before they come and squat in spots that have been reserved by others.'

"But me, I didn't want no trouble and so I says to Mélie:

" 'Shut up, Mélie,' I says, 'let 'em be and we'll see what'll come of it.'

"So we tied the *Delilah* under the willows, got out on the bank, and started fishing elbow to elbow, Mélie and myself, just like the other pair.

"Now, here, Your Honor, I must go into some technical details.

"We'd hardly been there more than five minutes when the fellow's float starts plunging twice, three times, and the next thing I see, he pulls out a chub thick as my thigh . . . well, not quite really, but almost. Me, my heart began to jump inside my ribs and the sweat broke out on my forehead and, to make things worse, Mélie says to me:

" 'Well, you bum, did you see that one?'

"And while this is going on, Monsieur Bru, the Poissy grocer, passes by in his boat and calls out to me:

" 'I see someone's taken your place, Monsieur Renard?'

" 'Yes, Monsieur Bru,' I says to him, 'there are tactless people in this world who have no idea how to behave.'

"The little guy in the white linen jacket didn't seem to hear a thing and neither did his fat wife—a real cow, that one!"

The presiding magistrate interrupted him again:

"Be careful of what you're saying. You're insulting the widow of the victim, Madame Flamèche, who is here present."

Renard apologized:

"Beg your pardon, Your Honor, my temper got the better of me.

"Well then, not even a quarter of an hour later, the little guy catches another chub, and then another one almost on top of it, and believe it or not, one more, five minutes later. Me, I had tears in my eyes and then I felt Madame Renard boiling too and she was taking digs at me all the time:

" 'Ah, what a miserable sight! Isn't he having himself a wonderful time stealing your fish, you poor slob! And you, you aren't catching a thing! What do you bet you won't even get a frog today, you fool! Ah, it makes my hands itch just to think of it. . . .'

"But me, I says to myself: 'Let's wait till noon. He'll surely leave for lunch and I'll just take my place and that's all. Because, you see, Your Honor, I always take my lunch with me when I'm fishing on Sundays. We bring our food in the *Delilah*, Mélie and me.

"But what do you think happens? Well, let me tell you: at noon the pig gets out his lunch, and to top that, while he's eating it, he catches himself one more chub!

"Well, Mélie and me, we also eat a bite. Oh, nothing much —we didn't have much appetite left, as you can well imagine.

"Then, while I'm digesting, I take the magazine *Gil Blas*. You see, I read it every Sunday because that's the day it has the piece by Colombine in it. I used to make Madame Renard furious by making her believe that I had met that Colombine woman. But there's no truth in it—I don't know her and haven't ever set eyes on her even. Still, I have to admit—she writes well and what she says makes real sense, especially for a woman. She suits me fine, and there really aren't many females like her.

"I started telling all that to my wife and teasing her, but she blew her top right away and so I just shut up.

"Well, at that very moment, I see the two witnesses, Monsieur Ladureau and Monsieur Durdent, appear on the other side of the river. We all knew each other by sight.

"The little fellow in white had gone back to fishing and he was catching so many that I was shaking like a leaf. And his wife, she says to him:

" 'We sure have discovered a good spot, Désiré! We'll come back here all the time.'

"I felt cold shivers up and down my spine when I heard that, and Madame Renard started in on me again.

" 'And you call yourself a man,' she said. 'What kind of a man d'you think you are? You've got nothing but chicken's blood in your veins, you wet hen!'

"All of a sudden I say to her: 'Know what, I'd rather leave now, because otherwise I'm liable to do something stupid.'

"But then she hisses at me as if she's holding a red-hot iron in front of my nose:

" 'Just as I said, you aren't a man, you! So now you want to give up your fishing hole and take to your heels. Well, go on, you coward!'

"That hurt me, hearing her talk about me like that, but still I didn't do a thing.

"Now, it so happens that at that moment the other fellow pulls out a bream. I never saw such a big one before in my life. Never!

"And then my wife starts talking like she's thinking out loud. On purpose, see. 'There's a fish that could easily be described as a stolen fish,' she says, 'in view of the fact that it was us who baited this spot ourselves, personally. The least they could do is to refund us the money we spent on the bait.'

"Then the fat wife of the little guy in white turns on her and says:

" 'Would you be referring to us, by any chance, Madame?'

" 'I'm referring to the ones who are stealing fish and taking advantage of money spent by others.'

" 'So you're accusing us of stealing, are you?'

"And so they argue like that for a while and then they start on some abuse. By God, I must hand it to them, they know plenty of double-barrelled expressions, the sluts. And they shouted them so loud that the two above-mentioned witnesses here could hear them from the opposite bank and, kidding-like, started hollering across the river: 'Hey, ladies, shout a bit quieter if you can. You're making it impossible for us to catch a fish!'

"Now the fact is that the little guy and me, we weren't taking any more part in it than a couple of tree stumps. We stayed there, our noses down, staring into the water, pretending we couldn't hear a thing.

"But by God, I swear we could hear all right. 'You're a damn liar,' 'You're an old bag,' 'You're a filthy fat tramp,' and on and on. A seaman wouldn't do any better.

"Suddenly I hear a noise behind me. I turn my head and I see the big dame attacking mine with her umbrella. Bang-bang! Mélie takes two blows on her head. So she gets mad, my Mélie, and she always swings when she gets mad. So she catches the fat one by her hair and pam-pam-pam—slaps fall all over the place like plums from a plum tree in the wind.

"Me, I'd have let them fight it out between themselves—I believe in women on one side and men on the other. One mustn't ever mix in such things. But the little guy gets up all of a sudden and I see he's about to jump my wife. Ah, no, friend, not that! So I put my fist out and the fellow runs straight into it, and then, poom-poom, one in the nose and one in the belly; and the next thing I see, the little guy raises his arms, then he raises a leg, and he falls backward, straight into the river, into the fishing hole.

"I sure would've pulled him out, Your Honor, if I'd had a chance to do it right away. But to complicate things, in the fight between the two dames, the fat one was definitely getting the upper hand over my Mélie. Now, I realize I shouldn't have gone to my wife's rescue while the fellow was kicking in the drink, but I never thought he'd drown.

"I said to myself: 'It'll cool him off,' and I rushed to separate the ladies. And believe me, I got plenty of bruises and scratches and bites while I was trying to tear them apart, those two leeches!

"What I'm trying to say is that it took me a good five minutes, maybe ten, to pull them off each other. And so when I looked at the river, there was nothing there—nothing—and it was still, just like a lake. But then I heard the two witnesses here shouting from the other side: 'Get him out, get him out!'

"It's easier said than done because me, I can't swim, much less dive—that's for sure.

"It was the man from the dam and those two gentlemen who got him out with their boathooks and I'd say it took them a good quarter of an hour to do it. They found him at the bottom of my hole with at least eight feet of water over him, as I told you before, but when they got to him, he was already dead, the little guy!

"These are the facts and I swear they're correct. On my honor, I'm innocent."

The witnesses having corroborated the story, the accused was acquitted.

[*Le Trou,* November 9, 1886]

VI

MEN AND WOMEN AT WAR

Boule de Suif

For days on end, the tatters of the routed army had been passing through the city. This was no longer a fighting force, but a formless horde. The men, their beards long and dirty, their uniforms ragged, trudged along sluggishly, having lost their regiments and their flags. They all looked dejected and exhausted, with no will or thought left in them, walking just by force of habit and dropping with fatigue as soon as they stopped. Most of them were conscripts—peaceful civilians bent under the weight of their rifles, small, locally mobilized groups, easily frightened and prone to enthusiasm, as prompt in attack as in flight; but there also appeared the red breeches of the regular army—the debris of a division mauled in a great battle—among whom there were somber-looking artillery men mixed up with foot soldiers of every description; and from time to time there appeared the shiny helmet of a dragoon on foot, stepping heavily and having great trouble keeping up with the lighter pace of the infantrymen.

Some sharpshooter detachments, bearing such heroic names as "Avengers of Defeat," "Citizens of the Grave," and "Sharers of Death," passed by in their turn, looking like bands of robbers. Their leaders—former cloth or grain merchants, former dealers in soap and tallow turned warriors by circumstance and named officers by virtue of their well-to-do positions or the length of their moustaches—were draped with arms, woolies, and gold braid and discussed in resounding voices various plans for forthcoming campaigns, sounding as if they alone were supporting France in her agony on their cocky shoulders. But often they were afraid even of their own soldiers, men handy with a bag and a rope, who were often capable of crazy daring, but who could easily turn into a bunch of murderous plunderers.

It was rumored that the Prussians were about to enter Rouen.

The National Guard, who for two months had been patrolling the surrounding countryside very cautiously, occasionally shooting its own sentries and preparing to give battle whenever a tiny rabbit stirred in a thicket, had now returned to their family firesides. Their weapons, their uniforms, all the deadly equipment with which so very recently this National Guard had terrorized the mileposts along the national roads within a three-league radius of Rouen, had suddenly vanished.

Finally, the last French soldiers crossed the Seine, moving toward Pont-Audemer through Saint-Sever and Bourg-Achard. The general in command, in despair, obviously incapable of attempting anything with these shapeless scraps of an army and himself bewildered by this great rout of a people so often victorious and now so badly beaten despite its reputed bravery, brought up the rear, walking on foot between two of his staff officers.

Then a deep silence, a fear-laden waiting descended upon the city. Many potbellied citizens, emasculated by their trade as shopkeepers, awaited the arrival of the victorious invaders with anxiety, trembling lest their roasting spits and kitchen knives should be mistaken for weapons.

All life seemed to be suspended; the shops were closed, the streets silent. Now and then some inhabitant, weighed down by this quiet, darted hurriedly along the walls. The agony of waiting made many wish that the enemy would come quickly.

On the afternoon of the day after the last French troops had left Rouen, some Prussian Uhlans, coming from no one knew where, rode rapidly through the town. Soon afterward, a black mass of men came down Saint Catherine's hill and two more invading streams appeared on the roads leading from Darnetal and Boisguillaume. Then, with perfect timing, the three forces converged on the Town Hall, and all the surrounding streets were flooded with the German army deploying its battalions that made the pavements ring under their heavy, rhythmic step.

Orders shouted in unfamiliar, guttural voices floated up along the walls of the houses that looked dead and deserted, while behind their closed shutters eyes watched these victors who, by the law of war, were now masters of the city and of the lives and belongings of its inhabitants. In their darkened rooms, the people of Rouen felt bewildered, as one feels in the presence of a cataclysm, of the huge, murderous natural catastrophes against which all human wisdom and resourcefulness are completely helpless. For every time the established order of things collapses, security is destroyed and everything that was protected by law, be it man-made or natural, is exposed to ferocious and unreasoning brutality. An earthquake crushing a whole population beneath its collapsing buildings; a river in flood rolling drowned peasants along with the carcasses of their cattle and the beams of their roofs; a triumphant army mowing down all who try to defend themselves, while driving others away as prisoners—looting in the name of the sword, and holding thanksgiving services to God to the accompaniment of cannon salutes—these are all frightful scourges that suspend faith in eternal justice and discredit what we have been taught about the protection of heaven and the reason of man.

~

Small detachments of German soldiers stopped at the door of each house and knocked before going inside. They were taking possession of the captured city. The citizens of the defeated country were now asked to be amiable and cooperative with the victors.

Once the first feeling of terror subsided, a new order soon established itself, and the city was calm again. In many families the Prussian officer ate at the family table. In some cases he was a well-brought-up man who said politely how sorry he was for France and how much he disliked taking part in this war. This attitude was appreciated by his hosts, who in addition felt they might very well need his protection some day. By treating him nicely, they would perhaps manage to avoid being given too many soldiers to feed. Anyway, what was the sense of offending a person upon whose good will they so completely depended? Defiance would have constituted rashness rather than true patriotic courage, and rashness was a foible the citizens of Rouen had overcome since the time of the heroic defenses of old that had made it so famous. Finally, they said—drawing this clinching argument from the French art of living—that it was perfectly all right to be courteous to the invader in one's own home as long as one didn't display undue familiarity toward him in public. So outside they hardly knew him, while at home they chatted very willingly; and each evening the German remained longer and longer, warming himself at the family hearth.

Gradually the town recovered its ordinary aspect almost entirely. The French inhabitants, it is true, didn't leave their houses too often, but the streets teemed with Prussian soldiers. Besides, the German officers of the Blue Hussars, arrogantly trailing their long instruments of death along the sidewalks, didn't seem to have any greater scorn for the civilian population of Rouen than had had the French officers of the Chasseurs, who, the previous year, had drunk in the same cafés.

Nevertheless, there was something in the air, something subtle and indefinable, some faint alien whiff, some smell of invasion. It pervaded private dwellings and public places, changed the taste of foodstuffs, and gave the local people the impression that they were on a very distant journey among barbarous and dangerous tribes.

The victors demanded money, lots of money, and the inhabitants kept paying, luckily being quite rich. But the richer a Norman merchant is, the more acutely he feels the loss of each parcel of his possessions as it passes into someone else's hands.

And so, a couple of miles or so downstream from the city, toward Croisset, Dieppedalle, and Biessart, bargees and fishermen would often dredge up from the bottom the swollen corpse of some German soldier who had been stabbed, kicked to death, or had his head crushed by a stone, and been thrown into the river from a bridge. The river's slimy bottom covered up these dark, savage but legitimate reprisals; these silent, unpublicized heroic actions that were more dangerous than great open battles but that conferred no glory on the performers. Hatred of the foreigner is always bound to mobilize some intrepid men who are ready to risk their lives for an idea.

At last, when the invaders, although subjecting the city to their oppressive discipline, failed to commit any of the horrors for which they had a reputation all along the line of their victorious advance, the inhabitants became less subdued, and the drive for gain stirred once again in the hearts of the local merchants. Some of them had big investments in Le Havre, which was still occupied by the French army; and they hoped to get there by traveling by land to Dieppe, which lay within the German occupation zone, and then taking a boat from there to Le Havre.

German officers they knew used their influence, and finally a permit to leave was obtained from the general in command of the area.

So a large four-horse coach was hired and the ten persons who were to go registered their names with the owner of the coach. They were to leave on Tuesday before daybreak so as not to attract undue attention.

Frost had already been hardening the ground for some days and on Monday, around three in the afternoon, thick black clouds coming from the north swept over the town, bringing snow. It snowed all that evening and throughout the night.

At four-thirty in the morning, the travelers gathered in the courtyard of the Normandy Hotel where they were to take the stagecoach. They were still full of sleep and shivering with cold under their wraps. And as they stowed their belongings aboard in the darkness, they looked, in their heavy winter clothes, like a group of obese priests in cassocks.

Somehow two men recognized each other, then a third went over to them. A conversation started.

"My wife's coming along," one man said.

"So's mine."

"And mine too."

Then the first man announced:

"We're not coming back to Rouen, and if the Prussians move on Le Havre, we'll go across to England."

It turned out that the others had similar plans since they were motivated by similar reasons.

As yet the horses had not been harnessed. A small lantern carried by a stableboy kept emerging from some mysterious door only to vanish through another one. The stamping of the horses, muffled by their droppings, and a voice swearing and talking to the animals came from inside the shed. Then the faint jingle of harness bells announced that harnessing had begun; and soon this jingling turned into a clear, continual ringing to the rhythm of the animals' movements, now stopping, then starting again, accompanied by the dull clanging of a shod hoof against the ground.

Suddenly the door was closed and all noise ceased. The frozen travelers, standing stiff and motionless, stopped talking.

A continuous curtain of snowflakes fell dazzlingly to the ground around them, wiping out the outlines of objects, covering everything with an icy moss; and there was no sound in the great silence of the town buried in winter other than the vague, infinitely repeated whisper of the falling snow, which was rather a sensation than an actual noise, a sort of intermingling of molecules that seemed to fill space and bury the world.

The man with the lantern reappeared at last, and this time he was pulling behind him a sad-looking horse who seemed extremely displeased at being disturbed. He placed him against the shaft, fastened the traces, and fussed about for quite a while, as he had to fix the harness using only one hand since the other held the lantern. As he was going to get the second horse, he noticed the travelers standing there immobile and already covered with snow and said to them:

"Why don't you get on board? You'd at least be sheltered from the snow in there."

It hadn't occurred to them and they hurriedly climbed in. The three men installed their three wives on the back seat, then got in themselves. Other shapes, shadowy and hesitant, then occupied the remaining seats without exchanging a word.

Feet sank into the straw scattered over the floor. The ladies in the back had brought along small copper footwarmers with burning charcoal in them, and for some time they enumerated the advantages of these warmers, repeating to each other things they already knew.

Finally the coach was harnessed with six horses instead of four, because the snow made pulling so much harder, and from outside a voice shouted:

"Is everyone aboard?"

From inside a voice answered "Yes"—and they were on their way.

The stagecoach moved very, very slowly; the wheels sank into the snow; the whole body of the coach groaned and creaked; the horses slipped, huffed, puffed, and steamed; and the driver's gigantic whip cracked and flew relentlessly in all directions, tying itself in knots then untying itself again, like some very thin snake, and suddenly stinging some bouncing crupper that would then become tense for a moment and produce a violent effort.

But the daylight was imperceptibly growing and the light snowflakes that one of the travelers—a true native of the textile region of Rouen—had compared to a rain of cotton, had stopped falling. Dirty light filtered through the thick, dark, heavy clouds that made the countryside, cut by an occasional line of rime-covered trees or a snow-capped hut, seem even whiter and more dazzling in contrast.

Inside the coach, the passengers examined each other with curiosity in the bleak light of the dawn.

At the back, occupying the best places, Monsieur and Madame Loiseau were napping opposite each other. He was a wholesale wine merchant on Rue Grand-Pont, a former clerk who had bought out his bankrupt employer and made a fortune. He sold very bad wine at very low prices to the small retail merchants in the villages around Rouen and had, among his friends and acquaintances, a reputation as a sly and unscrupulous man to deal with, a true Norman, full of tricks and joviality.

Indeed, his reputation as a chiseler was so well established that one evening, at a reception given by the *préfet,* a certain Monsieur Tournel—a subtle and biting wag who was the author of many fables and songs and the pride of the local community—proposed to the ladies, who seemed a bit sleepy, a game called *"Loiseau vole,"* which means either "the bird flies" or "Loiseau steals," depending on how one looks at it. This pun took off from the *préfet's* reception rooms and flew all over town, and for months on end made all the chins in the province shake with merriment.

Besides this, Loiseau was famous for the variety of tricks that he played on people and for his jokes both in good and in bad taste, so that whenever he was mentioned, people felt compelled to remark:

"Ah, that Loiseau, he's really priceless!"

A short man, he had a big, rotund belly above which showed a ruddy face sandwiched between graying side-whiskers.

His wife was a tall, heavy, determined woman with a loud voice and the ability to make quick decisions. She represented order and arithmetic in their family firm, while he brought animation to it with his lively activities.

Next to them and maintaining a rather dignified reserve

since he belonged to a higher caste, sat Monsieur Carré-Lamadon, a gentleman of substance, well established in cotton—the owner of three textile mills, an officer of the Légion d'honneur, and a member of the *Conseil Général.* Under the Third Empire, he had always been a leader of the loyal opposition, in the hope of receiving a higher price for coming over to the side of the cause that he had steadily combated with what he himself described as the "weapons of courtesy." Madame Carré-Lamadon, who was much younger than her husband, had been the consolation of the officers of good family serving in the Rouen garrison. She sat opposite her husband, petite, pretty, and charming, wrapped in her furs and looking sadly around the gloomy interior of the carriage.

Their neighbors, Count and Countess Hubert de Bréville, bore one of the most ancient and noble names of Normandy. The count, an old aristocrat with an air of grandeur, used every available artifice to emphasize his natural resemblance to King Henry IV, who, according to a legend that brought glory to the family, had made a Bréville lady pregnant—an occurrence which made her husband a count and obtained for him the governorship of the province.

Like M. Carré-Lamadon, the count was a member of the *Conseil Général,* representing the Orléanist party in it.

The story of his marriage with the daughter of a small shipowner from Nantes had always remained a mystery, but since the countess looked like a grand lady, knew how to entertain better than anyone else, and was even said to have been loved by a son of Louis-Philippe, the local aristocracy considered her very highly. Her salon was the first in the area, the only one where the gallantry of old was preserved and to which admission was difficult.

It was estimated that the fortune of the Brévilles, consisting entirely of good securities, afforded the count an annual income of half a million francs.

These six persons sitting in the back of the coach represented the serene, wealthy, and powerful mainstay of society—honorable and respected people of religion and principle.

It so happened that all the occupants of the rear seat were women; next to the countess sat two nuns who kept picking at long rosaries and muttering paternosters and Ave Marias. One of them was fairly old, with a smallpox-pitted face that looked as if she had received a broadside of grapeshot full into it. The other nun was very frail, with the chest of a consumptive and a thin, very pretty face tormented by the kind of faith that can turn people into martyrs or drive them insane.

Facing the nuns sat a man and a woman, and it was they who aroused the curiosity of the the others. The man was well known—he was Cornudet the democrat, a staunch advocate of republican government, the terror of respectable people. For twenty years he had been dipping his great red beard into the beer mugs of all the democratic cafés of Rouen. He had managed, with the assistance of his brothers and some friends, to go through the quite considerable fortune left by his father, a confectioner, and had then proceeded to wait for the establishment of the Republic—which, he felt sure, could not fail to reward him for his devoted consumption of so many revolutionary mugs of beer. On the Fourth of September, the day the Third Republic was established, probably the victim of a practical joke, he received the impression that he had been appointed *préfet* of the province and even tried to take over the administration—only to be thwarted by the janitors of the *Préfecture*, who, left the sole masters of the place, refused to recognize him and forced him to retreat.

Otherwise a very nice fellow, harmless and amiable, he had given himself wholeheartedly to the preparation of the city's defenses. He had ditches dug, trees felled across the roads, boobytraps planted all over the countryside; and then satisfied with his efforts, he withdrew hastily into the city. Now he had decided that he would be more useful to France in Le Havre, where further defense work might be needed.

The woman next to him, one of those described as of easy virtue, was locally famous for her tremendous rotundity which had earned her the nickname of Butterball. Short, all curves, with flesh bulging from every part of her, with each finger like three fat little sausages strung together at the joints, with a tight and shiny skin and an immense bosom that overflowed from her dress—she was nevertheless extremely appetizing and very much in demand, so delightful was her freshness to the eye. Her face was like a red apple, like a peony bud about to bloom, and in the middle of it, there opened two superb dark eyes shaded by long thick eyelashes and, below them, a charming mouth, small and moist—a mouth made for kisses and furnished with small, gleaming teeth. She also had a reputation for many other priceless qualities.

As soon as she was recognized, the respectable ladies began to whisper, and words such as "prostitute" and "public disgrace" were whispered loudly enough for her to raise her eyes and sweep her traveling companions with a look so defiant and arrogant that they at once fell silent, and all lowered their eyes, except Loiseau who watched her with an air of great amusement.

After a while however, the three ladies resumed their conversation. And now, the girl's presence made them feel somehow closer to one another. Probably they felt compelled to pool their respectability as married ladies, to emphasize the gap between themselves and this woman who openly sold herself; for sanctioned love always looks down upon its unlicensed counterpart.

The three men too, linked by their conservative instincts in the face of Cornudet, started to talk about business and money matters, and there were certain notes of disdain for the poor in what they said. The count spoke of the losses he had suffered through the fault of the Prussians, of wasted harvests and stolen cattle, with the detachment of a man, a millionaire ten times over, who would hardly feel the constraining effects of those losses after a year or so. Carré-Lamadon, whose textile business had been severely affected, had taken the precaution of sending six hundred thousand francs to England, a tidy little sum that he kept in reserve against any eventuality. As to Loiseau, he had managed to sell the balance of the cheap wines left in his cellars to the French army supply corps, so that by now the government owed him an impressive sum which he reckoned to collect in Le Havre.

And so the three men kept exchanging quick, friendly glances. Although they were of very different backgrounds, they were brothers in money and members of the great brotherhood of the "haves," of those who can make gold ring whenever they put a hand into their trouser pockets.

The stagecoach moved so slowly that by ten in the morning they had only covered ten miles. Three times the men had to get out and climb a slope on foot. They were beginning to worry because they had planned to have lunch at Tôtes and it didn't look as if they could possibly get there before nightfall. They were all watching for some inn on the road, but then the stagecoach sank into a snowdrift and it took two hours to get it out.

Their appetites increased and began to bother them seriously, but they saw no roadside inn, not the smallest tavern; the passage of the hungry, retreating French and the advancing Prussians had thoroughly discouraged the catering industry.

The gentlemen went to every farmhouse along the road and tried to obtain some provisions, but they couldn't even get any bread; the cautious peasants had carefully hidden their reserves fearing looting by the soldiers, who, left without rations, would grab anything they could find to chew on.

At about one in the afternoon Loiseau announced that he really felt a terrible vacuum in his stomach. All the others had been feeling the same way for quite some time, and as the desire to eat became more intense, conversation petered out.

Now and then one of them yawned, then almost immediately someone else yawned too, and in no time, everyone in turn, according to his character, manners, and social position, opened his mouth, loudly or discreetly as the case might be, and hurriedly placed his hand in front of the gaping hole as breath poured from it.

Several times Butterball bent forward as if she were looking for something under her skirts. She seemed to hesitate, looking each time at her companions and then sitting up again. The travelers' faces were pale and drawn. Loiseau claimed that he would pay a thousand francs for a ham. His wife was on the point of protesting this extravagance but gave up. It always hurt her to hear of wasting money, even in jest.

"I must say, I feel rather uncomfortable too," the count said. "I really can't imagine how I could have come on this trip without bringing some provisions for the road."

Every one of them was reproaching himself for the same thing.

Then Cornudet, who had a wineskin full of rum, offered it to the others. His offer was icily declined by everyone except Loiseau, who swallowed a few drops and thanked him, saying:

"That's good; it warms you up and deceives your hunger a bit."

The liquor put him in a better mood and he suggested that they should do the same as the people in the song "The Little Ship," who ate the fattest passenger. This allusion to Butterball, although indirect, shocked the well-brought-up people. They ignored it. Cornudet alone cracked a smile.

The two nuns had stopped muttering over their rosaries and now sat motionless, their hands thrust into their sleeves and their eyes obstinately lowered, probably dedicating to heaven the suffering that it was visiting upon them.

At three in the afternoon they found themselves on an endless plain without a single village in sight. Butterball suddenly bent very quickly and from under her seat produced a large basket covered with a spotless white napkin. Then she took out of it a small china plate, a fine silver goblet, and a large casserole in which lay two whole chickens, cut in pieces and embedded in jelly. In addition, one could see that there were other delicious things in the basket: all kinds of *pâtés*, various fruits and sweetmeats—indeed, enough provisions to last a person three days without her having to rely upon the cooking of the roadside inns. Moreover, the necks of four bottles stuck out from among the food.

Butterball took a chicken wing and proceeded to eat it very daintily, now and then taking a bite of one of those little *Régence* rolls, as they were called in Normandy.

All eyes were drawn to her. The aroma of chicken spread, expanding nostrils, filling mouths with an overabundance of saliva, and making jaws contract with a painful sensation under the ears. The loathing of the ladies for this woman was becoming overwhelming and turning into an itch to kill her, to throw her off the coach into the snow—silver tumbler, basket, provisions, and all.

But Loiseau, who was devouring the tureen full of chicken with his eyes, suddenly said:

"Congratulations! I see that Madame was more provident than the rest of us. Some people think of everything!"

She looked at him and said:

"Wouldn't you like some, monsieur? It must be rather unpleasant to fast from early morning on."

He bowed.

"Well, I won't refuse—I might just as well be frank with you and admit that I can't stand it any longer. And then, it's wartime after all, a time of emergency, isn't it, madame?" And sweeping a glance around him, he added: "At moments such as this, it is such a relief to come across obliging people."

He had a newspaper with him which he spread across his knees so as not to stain his trousers. Then he produced the knife he always carried in his pocket, opened it, planted its point in a chicken thigh shiny with jelly, dismantled it with his teeth, and chewed it with such obvious relish that a general sigh of distress passed through the carriage.

Then Butterball, in a voice that was ever so humble and gentle, invited the two nuns facing her to help themselves to her provisions. Both of them accepted forthwith, muttering their thanks, and proceeded to eat with great speed. Nor did Cornudet refuse his neighbor's invitation, and they formed a sort of table by spreading newspapers between the four of them.

Mouths opened and closed, chewed, swallowed, gulped fiercely. For his part, Loiseau was working hard, and in a low voice, he kept trying to persuade his wife to join him. She held out for a long time but then, as a spasm ran through her entrails, she yielded. So her husband, turning a smooth sentence, asked their "charming traveling companion" if he might be allowed to offer a small piece to Madame Loiseau. She replied: "But certainly, monsieur," smiled amiably, and proffered the casserole.

They went through a brief moment of embarrassment when they had uncorked the first bottle of Bordeaux, because there was only one tumbler. But they passed it from hand to hand, wiping it each time. Cornudet alone, no doubt out of chivalry, placed his lips on the spot still damp from the lips of his neighbor.

Then surrounded by eating people, overcome by appetizing smells, the count, the countess, and the Carré-Lamadon couple went through that odious trial known as the torment of Tantalus. Suddenly the young wife of the industrialist sighed so loudly that all heads turned toward her. She was almost as white as the snow outside and the next moment she closed her eyes, let her head slip forward, and lost consciousness. Her husband, trembling with anxiety, looked to the others for help. No one knew what to do until the elder of the two nuns lifted the sick lady's head, slipped Butterball's tumbler between her lips, and made her swallow a few drops of wine. The beautiful lady stirred, opened her eyes, smiled, and in a dying voice, announced that she felt much better but the nun made her drink a tumbler full of wine so that the fainting should not recur, explaining:

"It's hunger that did it, that's all."

Butterball, embarrassed, her face burning, addressed her four traveling companions who had continued to fast, murmuring:

"Oh dear me, if I only dared offer these ladies and gentlemen—"

She fell silent, apparently fearing a rebuff, but Loiseau took the answer upon himself:

"Well, as far as I'm concerned, I say that in a case like this we're all brothers and it's our duty to help one another. Well then, ladies, don't let's stand on ceremony—better accept, for who knows whether we'll even find a house to spend the night in. At the rate we're progressing, we'll never reach Tôtes before tomorrow noon."

They still hesitated because none of them wanted to take upon himself the responsibility of saying yes.

Then the count settled the matter. He turned toward the big, perplexed-looking girl and, speaking with the utmost aristocratic courtesy, said:

"We accept your offer, madame, and greatly appreciate it."

It was only the first step that was difficult. Once they had crossed the Rubicon, they let themselves go altogether. Soon Butterball's basket was considerably depleted. It still contained some *pâté de foie gras,* some pressed lark, a piece of smoked tongue, some pears, a box of *Pont-l'Evêque* cheese, a few *petits fours,* and a jar of pickles and onions because, like most women, she had a taste for sharp things.

Since it was too awkward to eat this woman's provisions without talking to her, they spoke—with reserve at first and then since she behaved with great dignity, with more abandon. Madame de Bréville and Madame Carré-Lamadon—very much women of the world—were discreetly gracious. The countess, particularly, showed her the amiable condescension of a grand lady who cannot be sullied by any contact, and was charming. However, the big Madame Loiseau, who had the soul of a gendarme, remained sulky, said very little, and ate a lot.

Of course, they came to speak of the war. They told of the atrocities perpetrated by the Prussians and of some French acts of bravery, and all these people who were running away paid homage to other people's courage. Soon personal stories began to be told, and Butterball related with sincere emotion, with the great passion often displayed by women of her sort when they express their natural feelings, the circumstances under which she had left Rouen.

"At first I thought I would be able to stay there and get along with them," she said. "I had plenty of food stored in my house and I preferred to feed a few of their soldiers rather than have to move to some strange place. But when I saw them, those Prussians, it was too much for me; they made my blood boil and I was so furious that I cried for a whole day. Ah, if only I was a man, I'd have shown them something, believe me! When I looked through my window at those fat pigs in their spiked helmets, my maid had to hold on to me to prevent me from hurling my furniture at them. And when a group of them came and said they were going to be billeted in my house, I grabbed the first one by his throat. . . . And let me tell you, they aren't any harder to strangle than the next man—I'd have done in that one if they hadn't pulled me off him by my hair. So after that I had to go into hiding, and as soon as the opportunity arose, I left town and here I am."

She was congratulated. She rose considerably in the esteem of her companions, who had never exhibited any such daring. Cornudet listened to her with the approving smile of a kindly apostle, with the air of a priest hearing a layman praise God; for long-bearded democratic tribunes feel they have a monopoly of patriotism, just as the clergy in their cassocks have a monopoly of religion. He, in his turn, spoke in dogmatic tones, with an eloquence picked up from the proclamations that are stuck on walls every evening, and he finished with a bit of a flourish by giving a great lashing to "that crook Badinguet."

But Butterball grew angry, for she was a Bonapartist. She became redder than a cherry and stammered in her indignation:

"I'd like to see the likes of you in his place! That sure would've been a real mess! I say that it's your people who let that man down and if ever your kind of joker comes to power, there'll be only one thing to do—leave France and settle somewhere else!"

Cornudet, unperturbed, kept smiling with his air of disdainful superiority, but one felt that gross abuse was not very far off when the count interceded and—not without some difficulty—calmed the exasperated woman by proclaiming with great authority that every shade of opinion was entitled to respect. In the meantime the countess and the wife of the manufacturer, who shared the instinctive hatred of the well-bred for the Republic and the unreasoned affection of all women for colorful and despotic regimes, felt drawn despite themselves toward this prostitute who had such great dignity and whose feelings were so close to theirs.

Now the basket was quite empty. Between the ten of them, they had finished everything it contained and they wished it had been even larger. The conversation, nevertheless, continued for a few minutes, but it was much cooler in tone now that they were through eating.

Night was coming on and gradually the darkness became very thick; and the cold, which is always felt more keenly when one is digesting, made even Butterball shiver, despite her protective layer of fat. So the Countess de Bréville offered her her footwarmer, in which the charcoal had been renewed several times since the morning; and Butterball readily accepted, for her feet were awfully cold. On seeing this, Mesdames Carré-Lamadon and Loiseau lent theirs to the two nuns.

The driver lit the lanterns and they shone brightly on the steamy cloud hovering above the sweaty rumps of the off-horses and on both edges of the road; under the moving reflection of the lights, the snow seemed to be rolling along.

Inside the coach, it was now impossible to make out a thing. Suddenly, however, a brief commotion took place between Cornudet and Butterball; and Loiseau, whose eyes were trying hard to pierce the darkness, thought he saw the bearded tribune quickly pull back, as if he had received a well-aimed, silent blow.

At last some tiny lights appeared ahead of them. It was Tôtes. They had been actually traveling for eleven hours, and counting the stops to feed and rest the horses, had been on the way for fourteen hours. They drove into the town and stopped in front of the Commercial Hotel.

As soon as they came to a stop, the coach door opened and a familiar sound sent a cold shudder down the travelers' spines—the noise of a sheathed saber dragged along a pavement. A German voice shouted something.

Although the coach had stopped none of them stirred; it was as though they were afraid to be butchered as they stepped out. Then the driver picked up one of his lanterns and held it up inside the carriage, suddenly lighting up the two rows of faces with their mouths gaping and their eyes popping out with fear and bewilderment.

Next to the driver, with the light shining directly on him, stood a German officer. He was young, very tall, very thin and very blond, and seemed encased in his uniform like a girl in her girdle; and the flat, shiny cap which he wore on one side of his head made him look like a bellboy in an English hotel. His disproportionately long moustache of straight blond hair which tapered off gradually, ending in one single, hardly visible blond hair on each side of his face, seemed to weigh down the corners of his mouth, pulling at his cheeks and giving his lips a downward droop.

Speaking French with an Alsatian accent, he stiffly invited the travelers to alight:

"Veel you come out bleeze, laties and chentlemen!"

The nuns were the first to obey, having the docility of saintly maidens accustomed to humble submission. The count and countess were next, followed by the manufacturer and his wife. Loiseau then pushed his heavy wife out in front of him, and when he himself had put his foot on the ground, he said to the German: "Good evening, sir," prompted by an instinct for self-preservation rather than by natural politeness. The officer, however, with the arrogance of those who have absolute power, stared at him without answering.

Butterball and Cornudet, who, although they sat closest to the door, were the last to come out, looked at the enemy with pride and scorn. The big girl tried to control herself and look composed, while the radical pulled tragically at his long red beard with a slightly shaking hand. They wanted to maintain their dignity, both feeling somehow that in encounters of this sort, each person represented his country a bit, and both feeling revolted at the spinelessness of their companions. She tried to show more dignity than the respectable women; he felt that he had to set an example and continue his mission of resistance to the invaders that he had started by organizing the digging of the ditches.

They entered the vast kitchen of the inn and the German asked for their authorization to travel from the general in command of the area. All their names were listed on it with a description and the profession of each traveler. He examined it at some length, checking the information with the person it pertained to, and then suddenly declared: "All right," and walked off.

Then they breathed a sigh of relief. They were hungry once again and so they ordered supper. It took half an hour to produce, and while two servants were preparing it, the travelers went to have a look at their rooms, which all gave on a long corridor that had a large, frosted-glass door marked in the usual way at the end of it.

When they had come downstairs again and were about to sit down to the table, the innkeeper in person appeared. He was a former horse trader, a big asthmatic fellow with wheezes, rattlings, and warbles of phlegm constantly going on in his throat. From his father he had inherited the name of Follenvie.

The innkeeper asked:

"Mademoiselle Elisabeth Rousset?"

Butterball shuddered, turned toward him, and said:

"That's me."

"The Prussian officer would like to talk to you, mademoiselle, right away, please."

"Talk to me?"

"Yes, if you're Mademoiselle Elisabeth Rousset."

Surprised, she thought a few seconds in silence, then said firmly:

"Maybe I am, but I won't go just the same."

They crowded around her, everyone trying to find the reason behind the German's demand. The count said:

"I don't think you are right, madame. Your refusal to see him could make things quite difficult, not only for you but for us, your traveling companions, as well. It is always pointless to resist those who are in a stronger position. Anyway, his request doesn't seem to be fraught with any danger for you. I'm sure it's just some small red-tape formality, nothing more."

All the others agreed with him, argued with her, begged her, lectured her, and in the end convinced her; for they were all afraid that her stubbornness might complicate the situation. At last she said:

"All right, but I am only doing it for your sakes."

The countess took her hand:

"And we certainly appreciate it."

Butterball went out. They waited for her to return before sitting down to the table. One and all wished that it was he who had been summoned instead of that violent and irascible woman and mentally prepared platitudes to tell the Prussian officer if he was called next.

After ten minutes she reappeared, red, furious, exasperated, breathing heavily, and muttering: "Ah, the swine, the dirty swine!"

They all pressed her to tell them what was the matter,

but she wouldn't talk. And when the count insisted, she answered with an air of great dignity:

"No, I don't wish to talk about it. It's my private concern."

They sat down then around a large tureen from which emanated a cabbagy fragrance. Despite the alarm caused by the incident, supper was rather gay. The cider was good. Monsieur and Madame Loiseau, and the nuns too, had ordered some instead of wine, for the sake of economy. The others took wine, while Cornudet asked for some beer. He had his own special ritual with the beer—opening the bottle, making the liquid froth, examining it, holding his glass at various angles, and then placing the glass between his eye and the light and admiring its color at length. When he drank, his long beard that had kept the tinge of his beloved drink seemed to tremble from sheer ecstasy, and his eyes squinted so as not to lose sight of the mug; it looked as if he were fulfilling the only function for which he had been born. One might say that he had established in his mind a sort of organic link between the two great passions of his life—Pale Ale and the Revolution—at least it is safe to say that he couldn't consume the former without thinking of the latter.

Monsieur and Madame Follenvie ate at the very end of the long table. The man, puffing like a ramshackle locomotive as he ate, had to work too hard at inhaling to be able to talk. But his wife never stopped chattering. She dwelt in detail on the impression the arrival of the Prussians had made on her; reported what they said and what they did; explained that she hated them because, in the first place, they cost her a lot of money and in the second, she had two sons in the army. She mostly addressed the countess, flattered to be talking to a lady of quality.

And when the innkeeper's wife lowered her voice to say certain indiscreet things, her husband would interrupt her from time to time with:

"It'd be better if you kept quiet, Madame Follenvie."

But paying no attention, she went on.

"Yes, ma'am, them people does nothing but eat potatoes and pork and pork and potatoes. And don't go imagining that they're clean either, because they most certainly ain't. And let me tell you, they make filth all over the place, if you'll pardon my saying so. And you should see them going through their drill for hours and hours every single day, out in the field: march forward and march back and turn this way and that way. . . . Wouldn't they be better off if they were working all this time in their own country, on their farms or building their roads? But no, ma'am, those soldiers, they ain't no advantage to no one! And it's poor people like us who must feed them so they can learn better how to kill! I'm nothing but a poor old woman without no education, but when I see them running themselves ragged from morning to evening, stamping around that way, I says to myself: When there are so many folks who make all them useful discoveries, why must there be so many others who are so harmful? Isn't it horrible to go around killing people, whether they're Prussians or Englishmen or Poles or Frenchmen? How come if we take revenge even on someone who's wronged us, it's bad and they put us in prison for it; but when they go out with rifles hunting out boys like they was game or something, it's good and they give medals to the one who's killed the most? No, ma'am, I sure won't ever understand that!"

Cornudet then said in a loud voice:

"War is barbaric when it's an attack on a peaceful neighbor; it is a sacred duty when it is the defense of one's native soil!"

The old woman lowered her head.

"Sure," she said, "it's different when you do all that to defend yourself. But still, I say that maybe it'd be better if we killed all them kings who make war to have a bit of fun."

Cornudet's eye sparkled.

"Hear, hear, citizeness!" he concurred.

Monsieur Carré-Lamadon was deep in thought. Although he was a fanatical admirer of famous military leaders, the peasant woman's common sense made him think of the wealth that so many wasted and therefore expensive hands could bring to a country, of all that unproductive manpower which could be used on the great industrial tasks that otherwise it would take centuries to achieve.

But Loiseau got up from the table and went over to talk in whispers to the innkeeper. The fat man laughed, coughed, and sputtered, his huge belly jouncing merrily at Loiseau's jokes. Then the innkeeper ordered six barrels from the wine merchant, to be delivered in the spring after the Prussians were gone.

They were very tired and retired to their rooms as soon as supper was over.

But Loiseau, who had noticed a few things, let his wife get

into bed and then proceeded to put his eye and ear in turns to the keyhole, trying to penetrate what he called in his mind "the mysteries of the corridor."

After a vigil of an hour or so, he heard a slight rustle and, peeking hurriedly through the keyhole, caught sight of Butterball looking more curvaceous than ever in a blue cashmere negligee with white lace trimmings. With a candlestick in her hand, she was on her way to the frosted-glass door at the end of the corridor. But as soon as she had passed, a door opened in her wake and Cornudet, in shirt sleeves and suspenders, emerged from his room and waited to intercept her on her return. He accosted her, she stopped, and a whispered argument ensued. Butterball seemed to be energetically defending the door to her room. At first, alas, Loiseau couldn't hear what they were saying; but gradually, as the argument grew heated, their voices rose and he could make out phrases. Cornudet was saying:

"Come on, don't be silly, what difference could it make to you?"

She, looking indignant, answered:

"No, my dear man, there are moments when one simply doesn't do that sort of thing; and here, especially, it'd be a real disgrace."

Obviously he didn't understand and he asked her what she meant. Then she became angry and her voice rose even higher.

"What do I mean? You really don't understand what I mean, with the Prussians in the house and perhaps even in the next room!"

He fell silent. The patriotic chastity of this whore who wouldn't allow herself to be touched in the presence of the enemy must have stirred up his faltering dignity, for after merely kissing her, he returned stealthily to his room.

And Loiseau, feeling somewhat on fire too, left the keyhole, made a gleeful little *entrechat,* slipped into his nightclothes, lifted the sheet under which lay his hard and heavy wife, woke her up with a kiss, and inquired:

"Do you still love me, darling?"

After that the whole house was plunged into complete silence until there arose from some undetermined direction —it could just as well have been from the cellar as the attic —a mighty snoring, regular and monotonous, like the dull, protracted rattling of a steam engine under great pressure. Monsieur Follenvie had gone to sleep.

Since they were due to leave at eight the next morning, they all gathered in the kitchen before that hour. But the coach, its hood covered with a thick layer of snow, stood lonely and abandoned in the middle of the courtyard. Neither the horses nor the driver were to be seen. They vainly searched for the driver in the stables, in the hay lofts, in the coach shed. Then all the gentlemen decided to comb the whole of the little town to find him, and they dispersed. They met again in the square before the church, which was surrounded by low houses inside which they could see Prussian soldiers. The first Prussian they saw was peeling potatoes, a second was scrubbing out a barber shop; a third, whose beard covered his whole face except for his eyes, was kissing a crying baby and rocking it on his knees, trying to calm it; and meanwhile the fat peasant women, whose men were in the army, were using sign language to explain to their obedient conquerors the chores they expected them to do: to chop wood, to put the soup on the stove, to grind the coffee, or even, in one case, to do the laundry for the hostess, a feeble old grandmother.

The count, quite surprised, questioned the beadle, who was just coming out of the rectory.

"Oh, they aren't bad at all," the old man told him. "They aren't even Prussians from what we're told. They come from farther away, I don't know where exactly, and they've all left a wife and children somewhere there. They don't enjoy taking part in this war at all, I'm sure, for the women must be crying for their men wherever they come from, and that causes as much misery there as it does here. We in this town can't complain too much for the moment, since they don't do us any harm and they work as hard here as they would in their own homes. You see, sir, poor people are bound to help each other. It's the strong and the mighty that go in for wars."

Cornudet, shocked by this cordial harmony between the conquered and the conquerors, preferred to seclude himself in the inn. Loiseau quipped:

"They're re-populating the land."

Carré-Lamadon said sternly:

"They're repairing the damage they've caused."

But they hadn't found the coach driver.

And when he was discovered at last, it was in a small café in town, drinking in the most brotherly fashion with the Prussian officer's orderly. The count called out to him:

"Didn't we order the horses harnessed for eight in the morning?"

"Well, yes, but since then I've received other instructions."

"What instructions?"

"Not to harness at all."

"Who gave you those instructions?"

"The Prussian major did."

"Why?"

"I don't know why. Go and ask him. I've been ordered not to harness and so I won't harness, and that's that."

"Was it the major who gave the order in person?"

"No, sir. He told the innkeeper to tell me that from him."

"When?"

"Last night, just as I was about to turn in."

The count, Carré-Lamadon, and Loiseau returned to the inn very worried.

They wanted to see Follenvie immediately but the maid told them that the innkeeper never got up before ten because of his asthma, and that he had expressly ordered them not to disturb him before that hour unless the house was on fire.

They would have approached the Prussian officer directly but that couldn't be done, although he lived in that very inn—Monsieur Follenvie was the only one allowed to speak to him on civilian matters. So there was nothing to do but wait. The ladies went back to their rooms and became absorbed in the usual futilities.

Cornudet installed himself in the kitchen by the tall fireplace where a big fire was burning. He had a small round table from the café room brought there, ordered a mug of beer, and sat there puffing at his pipe—that pipe which, among radicals, was almost as respected as its owner, as if it too had rendered outstanding services to France by serving Cornudet. It was a superb meerschaum, well broken in, black to match its master's teeth, but fragrant, curved, shiny, and unbelievably comfortable to his hand; and it put a nice final touch to his appearance. He sat there, hardly moving, his eyes fixed either on the fire or on the frothy head on top of his beer; and after each sip he'd pass his long thin fingers through his long, lank, graying hair with an air of satisfaction and suck in the fringe of froth that had remained caught on his moustache.

Loiseau, on the pretext of stretching his legs, went to make a tour of the local wine retailers, trying to get some orders.

The count and the manufacturer got to talking politics and

discussing France's future. One had faith in the Orléans dynasty, the other in some unknown savior, some hero who would appear from nowhere at the very moment when everything seemed lost, some new du Guesclin or Joan of Arc or, who knows, some new Napoleon the First. Ah, if only the Imperial Prince weren't so young!

Cornudet listened to them, smiling condescendingly like a man who knows very well what the future will actually be, and the kitchen filled with the smoke of his pipe.

As ten o'clock struck, Follenvie appeared. Hurriedly they questioned him, but he could do no more than repeat the same words three or four times, without variation:

"The officer, he just says to me 'Monsieur Follenvie,' he says, 'you'll forbid them to harness that coach tomorrow, see. I,' he says, 'don't want them to leave until I give the say-so myself. D'you understand? All right then, that'll be all.' "

They then wanted to talk to the officer. The count sent in his card, and Monsieur Carré-Lamadon added his name and all his titles. The Prussian sent them an answer—he'd see the two of them when he had finished his lunch, that is, at around one in the afternoon.

The ladies came down and although they were quite worried, they managed to eat something. Butterball looked sick and seemed to be in a state of great agitation.

They were finishing their coffee when the orderly came for the two gentlemen. Loiseau decided to join them, and then they asked Cornudet to come too in order to make the delegation as impressive as possible. But he declared proudly that he would never have any dealings with the German, resumed his place before the fire, and ordered himself another beer.

The three men then followed the orderly and were ushered into the best room in the inn, where the officer—sprawled in an armchair and smoking a long clay pipe, his feet resting on the mantelpiece, draped in a gaudy dressing gown probably appropriated from a bourgeous with bad taste—received them. He didn't stir, didn't greet them or even look in their direction, thus offering a magnificent illustration of the natural arrogance of the victorious soldier.

After a few seconds had elapsed, he said:

"Vat is id you vant?"

"We would like to proceed on our journey, sir," the count said.

"No."

"May I inquire the reason for this refusal?"

"Pecause I ton'd vant."

"May I respectfully observe to you, sir, that your general in charge has given us permission to travel all the way to Dieppe and as far as I know, we haven't done anything to deserve this change."

"I ton'd vant ant zat's all. You can go now."

The three men bowed and withdrew.

The afternoon was a dreary affair. They couldn't understand the German's whimsical behavior at all. The most extraordinary thoughts occurred to them. They were crowded in the kitchen, discussing the matter endlessly and making the most incredible assumptions. Perhaps they were being kept as hostages? But why? For what purpose? Perhaps they were going to be imprisoned? Or could it be that they would be asked for a substantial ransom before they were allowed to proceed? That thought caused a panic among them, and the richest were the most frightened, seeing themselves forced to redeem their lives by handing bagsful of gold to that arrogant soldier. They racked their brains trying to think up acceptable lies, ways of dissimulating their wealth and of convincing the fellow that they were really quite poor, very poor indeed. Loiseau removed his gold watch chain and hid it in his pocket. The approaching darkness increased their apprehensions. The lamp was lit, and since there were still two hours to go till dinner, Madame Loiseau suggested a game of cards to while away the time. They accepted. Even Cornudet took part after having, out of politeness, put out his pipe.

The count shuffled the cards and dealt them, and Butterball was directly dealt a winning hand. Soon the excitement of the game allayed their apprehensions somewhat, and Cornudet even noticed that Loiseau and his wife were using a special code with which to cheat.

As they were about to sit down to dinner, Monsieur Follenvie came in and said in his croaking voice:

"The Prussian officer asked me to find out whether Mademoiselle Elisabeth Rousset hasn't changed her mind yet."

Butterball, who was standing there looking rather pale, suddenly turned crimson and became so furious that it took her breath away and made her unable to speak. After a few moments, she burst out:

"You can tell that rat, that swine, that Prussian beast that I'll never, d'you hear, never do it! Never, never, never!"

The fat innkeeper left and Butterball was immediately surrounded, questioned, begged to tell what the Prussian wanted of her. At first she wouldn't talk, but after a while her fury overcame all else and she blurted out:

"What does he want . . . what does he want? Well, he wants to sleep with me!"

No one was shocked by her outspokenness, so vivid was their indignation over the German's demand. Cornudet put down his mug so violently that it broke. There was a unanimous clamor of disapproval against the uncouth soldier—an angry outburst, a feeling of solidarity in resisting the enemy—as if every one of them had been asked to share personally in the sacrifice. With an air of great disgust, the count declared that "those people" behaved like the barbarians of old, while the ladies expressed their heartfelt and energetic sympathy to Butterball. The two nuns, who only appeared for meals, silently lowered their heads.

When the first wave of indignation was past, they ate their dinner. There wasn't much conversation during the meal. They were thinking.

The ladies retired early. The men remained behind, smoking. Then they organized a game of cards which they invited Monsieur Follenvie to join, in order to question him tactfully about possible ways of overcoming the officer's resistance. But he was entirely absorbed by the cards and, ignoring their questions, just repeated:

"Let's get on with the game, gentlemen, let's get on."

And he concentrated so entirely on the game that he even forgot to expectorate, with the result that organ-sounds would occasionally emanate from his breast. His whistling lungs produced the full asthmatic scale from low, hoarse tones to the shrill quivering notes of a young rooster's first attempts to crow.

He even refused to go upstairs to his room when his wife, who had turned in earlier, came down again for him. So she went to bed all by herself, for she was an early bird, always up with the sun, while her man was of a nocturnal species, always prepared to spend the night in the company of friends. He shouted after her:

"Put my mulled egg by the fire," and plunged back into the game.

But when the others saw that they wouldn't get anything out of him, they declared that it was getting late and was time to call it a night; everyone retired to his room.

The next morning they all got up quite early. They still harbored a vague hope that they would be allowed to leave, wished more ardently than ever that they would be given permission, and were horrified at the thought that they might have to spend another day in that odious little inn.

Alas! The horses were still in the stable and the driver was again out of sight. Having nothing better to do, they just hung around the coach.

Lunch was very gloomy and one could sense a certain coolness toward Butterball. This was because night, which gives one time to think, had changed their opinions somewhat. They almost resented her failure to comply secretly with the Prussian's wish and in that way to present her traveling companions with a nice surprise in the morning. Could anything be simpler? Who'd have ever known? She could've saved face before the officer by telling him that she was going through with it in order to spare the others great hardship. What importance could it have for her, after all? None of them, however, expressed his thoughts aloud.

In the afternoon, as they were bored to distraction, the count suggested that they take a little walk to the outskirts of the small town. They all wrapped themselves up warmly and the company set out—except for Cornudet, who elected to remain by the fire, and the two nuns, who spent their time with the parish priest at the church.

The cold, which grew worse every day, stung their ears and noses cruelly, and their feet became so sore that each step caused them actual suffering. When they reached the countryside, the sight of it under its limitless white cover struck them as so unbearable that they hurriedly turned back, their souls frozen and their hearts oppressed.

The four women walked in front, with the three men following them at a little distance. Loiseau, who had grasped the general mood, suddenly started wondering aloud "how long that bitch" was going to force them to stay in this awful place. The count, always courteous, said that he couldn't demand such a painful sacrifice from any woman and that if she were to make it, it would have to be on her own initiative. Monsieur Carré-Lamadon remarked that if the French were to start a counteroffensive and break through Dieppe—it was very much in the air, he asserted—the two armies would be bound to clash exactly at Tôtes. This remark caused the other two gentlemen to look worried.

"What about trying to make it on foot?" Loiseau suggested.

The count shrugged.

"Just think," he said. "In this snow? With our wives? Besides, they'll set out after us immediately and it won't take them ten minutes to capture us and bring us back here as prisoners. Then we'll *really* be at the mercy of these soldiers."

That made very good sense. The others had no argument with it.

The ladies were talking of fashions, but there was a strain in their voices, as if something unsaid lay between them.

Suddenly the Prussian officer appeared at the end of a street. His tall figure stood out against the backdrop of snow, accentuating his wasplike waist. He walked with his knees bent outward, with the peculiar walk of officers trying not to muddy their shiny boots.

He bowed slightly as he passed the ladies and looked disdainfully at the men, who, it must be said, had the dignity not to raise their hats—although Loiseau did make a gesture as though he intended to remove his.

Butterball turned red to the ears and the three married ladies felt wounded in their pride at being surprised by that soldier in the company of a woman he was treating so cavalierly.

They spoke then of the man, of his figure, of his features. Madame Carré-Lamadon, who had known many officers and who judged them as a connoisseur, found this one "not bad at all," and even regretted that he didn't happen to be French; for then he would have made a very handsome Hussar, who would've turned all the ladies' heads.

Once back in the inn, they didn't know what to do with themselves. They even exchanged rather sharp words about things that didn't really matter. They ate dinner in silence, rose from the table as soon as it was over, and went back to their rooms, hoping to fall asleep very quickly so as to kill time.

In the morning they came down with tired faces, bursting with impatience. The ladies hardly spoke to Butterball at all.

A bell rang. It was ringing for a christening.

Butterball had a child that was being brought up near Yvetot in a peasant family. She saw him once a year at most and hardly ever thought of him, but now the baby about to be baptized suddenly caused her heart to fill with passionate tenderness for her own child and she decided to attend the ceremony.

As soon as she had left, her companions looked at one another and drew their chairs closer together, for they felt the time had come when they had to do something drastic. Loiseau had an inspired idea: what about suggesting to the officer that he keep Butterball with him and allow the others to proceed on their way? Monsieur Follenvie was charged with transmitting this suggestion to the officer but in no time he was back. The German, who knew human nature, had thrown him out, declaring that no one was to leave until his whim had been satisfied.

This was too much for Madame Loiseau's plebeian temper: "Why, we aren't going to die of old age here because of her! After all, it's that slut's trade to do that with men, isn't it? So I don't think she has any right to reject just this one. I ask you! She must've accepted anyone who came along in Rouen, even coachmen! In fact, I know she did. She's been with the *préfet's* coachman—I know it for sure because he buys wine from us. And today, when she can get us out of trouble, she starts turning up her nose and being difficult all of a sudden, the snotty thing! For my part, I say he's behaving very nicely, that officer. He must've been deprived of it for a long time, and I'm quite sure that if it hadn't been indiscreet, he'd have picked any of the three of us first. But no, he was willing to content himself with the one who's for all comers. So that shows he respects married women, doesn't it? Just think—he's the lord and master around here and all he has to say is 'I want,' and he could have any of us delivered to him by his soldiers."

The two other ladies felt a tingling in their spines. The eyes of pretty little Madame Carré-Lamadon sparkled and she turned slightly pale, as if she felt she was already being forcibly taken by the officer.

The men, who had been talking among themselves, came over. Loiseau, furious, wanted to turn that "horrible creature" over to the enemy with her wrists and ankles tied. But the count, who had three generations of ambassadors in his lineage and who looked and behaved like a diplomat himself, was an advocate of tact and maneuver.

"We ought to try to persuade her," he said.

And they held a secret conference.

The women moved closer together, the pitch of their voices was lowered, and each started to contribute her ideas.

It must be said that it was all done quite decently and the ladies, particularly, found very delicate turns of phrase and quite charming and disarming ways of conveying the most inappropriate things. A stranger overhearing them would never have guessed what they were talking about, so well were the conventions of language respected. But the layer of coyness every society lady presents to the world was just paper-thin and the three women blossomed out as they spoke of this tingling adventure, enjoying it tremendously and feeling in their element, poking at love with the sensuousness of a greedy cook poking at the food as he prepares dinner for someone else.

Their good mood came back to them, so amused were they with the intrigue. The count found the jokes a bit risqué but they were told so well that he couldn't help smiling. Then Loiseau in his turn came out with a few even cruder remarks without anyone taking offense at them, since the statement made originally by his wife had expressed the common feeling: It was that slut's trade after all, so why should she reject just this one of all people? Indeed, the pretty Madame Carré-Lamadon seemed to think that if she were in Butterball's shoes, she'd just as soon go with this one as with any other.

They planned their line of conduct at length, as one plans the siege of a fortress. Each of them took upon himself a role to play and chose his line of argument and of behavior. Then the overall plan was drawn up and the ruses, ambushes, and tricks to force this living fortress to open her doors to her enemy were discussed.

Cornudet, however, kept out of it, remaining aloof from the whole business.

They were so bent on their conversation that they didn't notice when Butterball came back from the christening. But then the count made a light "sh-sh-sh" sound and they all looked up. She was standing in front of them. They fell silent, too embarrassed at first to say anything. The countess, more adept than the others at social subtleties, asked Butterball:

"Well, how was the christening? I suppose it was great fun?"

The big girl, still very moved, told them in detail about the ceremony, describing those who had taken part in it and even what the church looked like, and adding at the end:

"It does you such a lot of good to pray a bit now and then."

Until lunch, the ladies contented themselves with chatting with her in an ordinary friendly way, in order to make her more trusting and to weaken her resistance to their advice.

Once at the table though, they got down to business. At first there were some vague remarks about self-sacrifice. Ancient examples were cited: Judith and Holofernes; then, for no reason at all, Lucrece and Sextus; and finally Cleopatra, who made all the captive enemy generals pass by her couch, reducing them there to servile slaves. A fantastic yarn was then spun, generated in the imagination of these ignorant millionaires, in which heroic female citizens of Rome went to Capua to rock to sleep in their arms Hannibal, his lieutenants, and his phalanxes of mercenaries. They cited all the women who had stopped conquerors and turned their own bodies into battlefields, into instruments of domination, into weapons; women who had smothered and vanquished by their heroic caresses horrible, hated men, immolating their chastity on the altar of self-sacrifice and revenge.

They even spoke in subdued tones of that Englishwoman of noble birth who had deliberately contaminated herself with a horrible venereal disease in order to transmit it to Bonaparte, and of how the conqueror had been saved almost miraculously by sudden impotence at the hour of the fateful tryst.

And all these stories were told in a decent and respectable way, with occasional bursts of patriotic fervor such as were likely to produce in their audience a desire to emulate.

Listening to them, one might have thought that woman's sole function on earth was the perpetual sacrifice of her person to the whims of brutal warriors.

The two nuns didn't seem to hear, appearing lost in profound meditation. Butterball was silent too.

They gave her a chance to think it over during the afternoon. But their tone toward her had undergone a certain change and they no longer addressed her as Madame but as Mademoiselle, although none of them could have explained exactly why. It was as if they had brought her down a rung in the standing she had gained since they'd met, as if they wanted her to be aware of her shameful status.

Just as the soup was being served, Monsieur Follenvie

made his appearance and inquired, as he had on the previous day:

"The Prussian officer wishes to know whether Mademoiselle Elisabeth Rousset has still not changed her mind."

Butterball's reply was "No, monsieur," in a very dry tone.

During dinner the coalition against her seemed to disintegrate. Loiseau made several unfortunate remarks. Each one of them racked his brains in an effort to produce more glorious historical precedents, but they didn't come up with anything worthwhile. Then quite by chance, the countess, probably vaguely impelled to pay some respect to religion, suddenly asked the elder of the two nuns to tell them some glorious deeds from the lives of the saints. Of course, many of the saints had committed acts that would be criminal in our eyes, but the Church readily absolved those transgressions when they were performed for the glory of God or for the good of one's neighbor. It was a powerful argument and the countess used it to her advantage. Then whether by tacit agreement or by the sort of veiled support at which those wearing ecclesiastical habit are usually so expert, or simply through a happy misunderstanding brought about by a helpful stupidity, the old nun gave the coalition a formidable bolstering. She, whom they had thought shy and retiring, turned out to be bold, verbose, and violent. This one did not bother with the subtleties of casuistry—her doctrine was forged of steel, her faith never wavered, her conscience was not weighed down by scruples. She found Abraham's sacrifice quite simple, for she herself would have killed her mother and father without hesitation if she had been ordered to do so from on high. Nothing could displease the Lord, she held, as long as the intention behind it was praiseworthy.

The countess reaped great profit from the sacred authority of her unexpected ally and made her hold forth edifyingly on the moral axiom that the end justifies the means. She asked her:

"Tell me, Sister, do you believe that God would approve of any line of conduct and forgive any act, so long as the motive behind it was a pure one?"

"There is not the slightest doubt about it, ma'am: an action that is wrong in itself often becomes praiseworthy by the thought it has sprung from."

And they went on like this, unraveling God's wishes, foreseeing His decisions, involving Him in matters that were really none of His business.

It was all presented in a veiled, clever, discreet form. But each word of the saintly sister made a dent in the indignant resistance of the courtesan. As the conversation took a slightly different turn, the woman with the rosary spoke of the establishments of her order, of her Mother Superior, of herself, and of her pretty neighbor, dear Sister Saint-Nicéphore. They were being sent to a Le Havre hospital to attend hundreds of soldiers stricken there with smallpox. She described the disease and the suffering of those afflicted with it. And, she said, while they were being detained here by the whim of that Prussian, many Frenchmen whom they could perhaps have saved were dying there! Looking after soldiers, she explained, was her special skill, and she had been with them in the Crimea, in Italy, and in Austria; in describing all these campaigns, she turned out to be one of those drum-and-trumpet sisters who seem to be especially made to follow armies and pick up the wounded in the wake of battles, and to be more efficient than sergeants in taming the big unruly warriors—a true bang-bang-boom nun, with a ravaged face, pitted with numberless pockmarks, looking like a picture of war damage.

Her words seemed so devastatingly effective that none of the conspirators bothered to speak after she had finished.

No sooner was the meal over than they all hurried to their rooms, and they didn't come down again until quite late the next morning.

Lunch was quiet. They were giving the seeds time to sprout and to bear fruit. Then the countess suggested they go out for an afternoon walk. The count, as if by a previous plan, took Butterball's arm, and they fell behind the others.

He spoke to her in that familiar, paternal, slightly disdainful tone in which men in a high position speak to venal women, calling her "my dear child," dealing with her from all the height of his social position and of his unquestioned dignity. He went straight for the sore point.

"So I see," he said, "that you prefer to expose us all, as well as yourself, to all the violent reprisals that are bound to follow a Prussian defeat, rather than agree to go through with something that you've done so often before in your life?"

As she didn't answer, he started to gently reason with her, appealing to her emotions. Although he managed to remain distant, he became quite gallant, paying a compliment when necessary and even making a show of friendliness and warmth. He exalted the great service she could render them all and spoke of their gratitude; then suddenly changing his tone, he said to her with cheerful, cocky familiarity:

"And then you know, my dear girl, he will certainly go around boasting later of having had a taste of a beautiful woman! I'm quite certain he couldn't find many women as attractive as you back home in his own country."

Butterball made no answer, and they caught up with the others.

When they got back to the inn, she went upstairs and didn't come down again. They were all extremely worried. What was she going to do? How annoying it would be if she decided to continue her resistance!

It was dinnertime. They waited for her, but she didn't appear. Then Monsieur Follenvie arrived and announced that Mademoiselle Rousset didn't feel well and that they shouldn't wait for her. They all pricked up their ears. The count walked over to the innkeeper and inquired in a whisper:

"All right now?"

"Yes."

Tactfully, he said nothing to his companions, only slightly nodding his head. They all heaved sighs of relief and cheerful expressions appeared on their faces. Loiseau shouted:

"Ah, at last, dammit! Well, the champagne's on me if there is any in this establishment."

There was. The innkeeper returned with four bottles, which gave Madame Loiseau quite a shock. Everyone became talkative and noisy, their hearts filled with shrill gaiety. The count seemed to have discovered that Madame Carré-Lamadon was a charmer and the manufacturer made some elegant compliments to the countess. The conversation was lively, playful, and full of allusions.

All of a sudden Loiseau's face took on an anxious expression and his hands shot into the air.

"Quiet!" he shouted.

Surprised and already frightened, they all fell silent.

Then Loiseau, cupping his hand around his ear, turned that organ of hearing toward the ceiling and, going "sh-sh-sh," turned his eyes upward. He listened a little longer, then said in his ordinary voice:

"You needn't worry, all's going well."

They were slow to understand at first, but then they smiled.

He repeated his act after fifteen minutes and several times more in the course of the evening, pretending also to be heckling someone on the floor above, giving advice with double meanings that he dug up from his traveling salesman's repertoire. Now he would sigh very sadly and say: "Ah, the poor girl"; next he'd mutter between his teeth in pretended anger: "That disgusting Prussian pig!" At times he'd take the others by surprise by repeating several times: "Enough, enough, enough!" and then adding, as though talking to himself:

"Just so long as we see her again some time! Hope he don't kill her with all that, the poor slut. . . ."

Although these jokes were in lamentable taste, they made them laugh; no one was shocked because, like everything else, indignation depends on the environment, and the atmosphere that had formed around them was loaded with suggestive thoughts.

By the time they had reached the dessert, the ladies themselves were indulging in witty and discreet double meanings. Eyes shone, for they had had quite a lot to drink. The count, who kept his air of stern dignity even at such licentious moments, made a highly appreciated comparison between their present situation and that of people who, after being icebound and forced to hibernate somewhere in the polar region, see the southward route opening up for them.

Loiseau, in great form, raised his champagne glass.

"Here's to our regained freedom!" he shouted and they all rose to their feet cheering him. Even the two nuns, on the insistence of the ladies, consented to dip their lips into the yellow, bubbly stuff they had never tasted before. They said that it tasted rather like lemonade, although they found it had a somewhat better taste.

Loiseau summarized the general mood again:

"Isn't it a shame there's no piano around here, otherwise we could organize a little quadrille. . . ."

Cornudet didn't say a word, didn't make a gesture. He seemed to be deep in grave thought, now and then tugging at his long beard as if he wanted to make it even longer. But toward midnight, as they were about to break up, Loiseau, who was not too steady on his feet, slapped the people's tribune on the belly and said, stammering slightly:

"You don't seem to have very much to say tonight, citizen. You're not much fun tonight."

Cornudet then raised his head and glared terrifyingly at the company:

"Let me tell you, the whole bunch of you, that you have perpetrated an infamy!" And walking toward the door, he repeated once again: "An infamy!" and disappeared.

At first, this had the effect of cold water. Loiseau looked bewildered for a moment but soon recovered and, shaking with laughter, cried:

"So the grapes are green, old fellow. So they're green, the grapes!"

As they didn't understand what he meant, he told them about the "mysteries of the corridor" he had observed, and that caused a further loud explosion of merriment. The ladies were having the time of their lives. The count and Monsieur Carré-Lamadon had tears running from their eyes. They couldn't even bring themselves to believe Loiseau.

"Why, are you really sure he was trying to . . ."

"I'm telling you! I saw it with my own eyes."

"And you say she wouldn't, because—"

"Because there was a Prussian in the next room."

"Impossible!"

"I swear it!"

The count was choking. The industrialist was clasping his belly with both hands. Loiseau went on:

"And so, obviously, he doesn't find it so very funny this evening. In fact, he doesn't seem to appreciate it at all."

And all three went into roars of laughter, until they felt sick and out of breath.

On that note they parted. But Madame Loiseau, who belonged to the nettle species of plant, remarked to her husband, just as they were getting into bed:

"That little Carré-Lamadon monkey! There was real disappointment in the way she was laughing all evening, because, you know, when a woman is accustomed to going for a uniform, it makes very little difference to her whether it's French or Prussian. Now, I ask you, isn't that a disgrace! Ah, good Lord!"

And throughout that night, light noises and rustlings were to be heard in the darkness of the corridor, making one think of hard breathing, or bare feet creeping by in the darkness. Certain it is that they didn't go to sleep for a long time, for thin slivers of light were visible under the doors till late. Champagne has that sort of effect, they say—it prevents people from going to sleep.

The next day a bright winter sun turned the snow into a dazzling mass. The coach was there, in front of the inn door, harnessed at long last; and an army of white pigeons wrapped in their thick plumage, with a black point in the middle of their pink eyes, strolled importantly between the legs of the six horses, searching for their livelihood in the smoking droppings that were scattered around.

The driver, wrapped in a sheepskin, was installed on his box, puffing at a pipe, and the smiling travelers were busy loading the provisions they had bought for the rest of their trip.

They had to wait for Butterball. She appeared. She seemed a bit troubled, a bit shamefaced. She came shyly toward her traveling companions who, with one movement, looked away, as if they hadn't seen her. The count, with great dignity, took his wife's arm and moved her farther away from the risk of such an impure contact.

The big girl stopped, flabbergasted. Then, gathering all her courage, she went up to the manufacturer's wife and greeted her with a humbly muttered, "Good morning, madame." The lady replied with an insolent, hardly perceptible nod followed by a look of outraged virtue. They all suddenly became very busy and somehow managed to give her a wide berth, as if they were afraid that she carried some contagious disease in her skirts. Then they climbed hastily into the coach. She got in last and silently took the seat she had occupied during the first part of their journey.

They seemed not to see her, not to know her, although Madame Loiseau examined her from her place with great indignation and remarked in a low voice to her husband:

"Thank God I don't have to sit next to her!"

The heavy carriage stirred and they were on their way once again.

At first there was general silence. Butterball didn't dare raise her eyes. She felt indignant with her neighbors and humiliated at having given in to them and allowed them to push her hypocritically into the arms of that Prussian and be besmirched by him.

At last the countess turned to Madame Carré-Lamadon and broke the painful silence.

"I believe you've met Madame d'Etrelles?"

"Yes, she's a close friend of mine."

"An enchanting person, isn't she? She's so charming and at the same time so cultivated. . . . She's an artist to the tip of her fingers—she sings awfully well and you should see her drawings. . . ."

The manufacturer was talking to the count and occasionally a word could be heard amid the rattle of the glass:

"Bonds . . . discount . . . premium . . . stocks. . . ."

Loiseau had swiped from the inn an old pack of cards, greasy from five years of contact with poorly wiped tables, and he started a little game with his wife. The nuns picked up the rosaries that hung from their belts, made a simultaneous sign of the cross, and suddenly their lips started moving simultaneously. They moved faster and faster, their vague murmuring sounding as if they were racing over the *oremus*. They stopped now and then for a second, kissed their medallions, then hurriedly resumed their rapid muttering. Cornudet sat motionless, absorbed in thought.

After three hours or so, Loiseau put his cards away and declared:

"I'm getting quite hungry."

His wife reached for a package tied with string and produced from it a piece of cold veal. She sliced it carefully into thin, firm slivers and the two of them proceeded to eat.

"I think we ought to follow their example," the countess suggested.

The count and the Carré-Lamadons consented, and provisions prepared jointly by the two couples made their appearance. It was one of those dishes with a china hare on its lid to indicate that inside a hare in the form of *pâté* was buried under a succulent assortment of *charcuterie* with white rivers of lard running through the brown flesh of the game mixed with other finely chopped meats. A beautiful square of Gruyère cheese that had been wrapped in newspaper retained the looking-glass imprint "Various News Items" on its creamy, glossy flank.

The nuns each lopped off a round of garlic-smelling salami. Cornudet plunged both hands at once into the deep pockets of his overcoat, and when they emerged, one hand held four eggs and the other a loaf of bread. He removed the shells, tossed them into the straw under his feet, and took a bite out of an egg—small bits of yolk getting lost in his beard, where they looked like bright little stars.

Butterball, in her hectic rush to get ready to leave and because of her general state of bewilderment, hadn't thought of preparing anything; and now, choking with rage, she watched all these peacefully feeding people. She was seized by a violent access of anger and she opened her mouth to tell them what she thought of them all in a torrent of abuse that rose to her lips. But choking with exasperation, she was unable to speak.

No one paid any attention to her or looked her way. She felt drowned in the scorn of these respectable rats who had first sacrificed her, then discarded her as something unclean and quite useless.

Then she thought of her large basket of food that the others had so greedily devoured at the beginning of the journey, of her two chickens shiny with jelly, of her *pâtés,* her pears, and her four bottles of Bordeaux wine; and her rage fell, like a taut rope suddenly untied; she felt she was about to cry. She made a frantic effort, stiffened herself, and swallowed her sobs—trying to stop her tears as a child does; but they burst out, glistening on the ends of her lashes, and soon two big drops left her eyes and crept slowly down her cheeks. Others followed these two, rolling faster, falling like the drops of moisture that filter down a rock, dropping at regular intervals on her bulging breast. She remained stiff, staring straight ahead, her face pale and rigid, hoping that they wouldn't notice.

But the countess did notice and made a sign to her husband, who shrugged as if to say: "And what am I supposed to do about it? It's really not my fault." Madame Loiseau gave a triumphant soundless chuckle and murmured:

"She's crying from shame."

The two nuns went back to their prayers, after rewrapping the remainder of their salami in a piece of paper.

Then Cornudet, who was busy digesting his eggs, stretched his long legs out under the seat opposite him, leaned back, crossed his arms, smiled like a man who has just thought up something terribly funny, and proceeded to whistle the "Marseillaise."

The faces around him darkened. This song of the masses was obviously not appreciated by his neighbors. They became nervous and irritated; they felt like howling the way dogs do at the sound of a barrel organ. He was aware of this and still went on and on, now and then even mumbling the words:

> The sacred love of our cou-oun-tree
> Guide and support our venging hand

And let freedom and liber-tee-ee
Join those who defend our land. . . .

They were moving faster now that the snow was harder. And all the way to Dieppe, throughout the long dull hours of the journey, through the bumps of the road, in the falling night and then in the profound darkness that filled the coach —fiercely determined—he went on with his avenging and monotonous whistling, forcing their tired and exasperated brains to follow the song again and again, from beginning to end, imposing upon them the words that loomed behind each measure.

Butterball was still crying; and from time to time, a sob she couldn't control would slip out in the darkness between two couplets of the "Marseillaise."

[*Boule de Suif*, April 16, 1880]

The Adventure of Walter Schnaffs

Ever since he had crossed the French border with the invading army, Walter Schnaffs had considered himself the most wretched man on earth. He was pudgy, found the marches hard, huffed and puffed a lot, and suffered torture from his feet which were very flat and very fat. Besides, he was a peaceful, kindly man with nothing fierce or heroic about him. He was the father of four children whom he adored and the husband of a young blond woman whose affection, kisses, and attentions he badly missed each evening. He liked to get up late, to go to bed early, to eat nice things slowly, and to drink beer in the taverns. He also believed that everything that was pleasant in life would vanish with death; and so loathed acutely, both with his reason and with his instinct, such things as cannons, rifles, revolvers, sabers, and, above all, bayonets—probably feeling that he was quite incapable of protecting his big belly in a form of combat which was based on agility.

And when, at night, he had to roll himself in his greatcoat and lie on the hard ground among his snoring comrades, he thought at length of those he had left back home and of all the dangers lurking in his path. What would happen to his little children if he was killed? Who would provide for them and bring them up? As it was, he hadn't left them too well off, although he had gone into debt to leave his wife some money. . . . And, sometimes, Walter Schnaffs wept.

At the beginning of every battle, he felt his legs turn so weak that he would have let himself fall had he not been restrained by the thought that the whole army would pass over his body. The whistling of the bullets made the hair on his skin bristle.

For several months he had lived in constant terror and anguish.

As his army corps moved forward across Normandy, he was sent out one day with a light reconnaissance patrol with instructions to reconnoiter a sector of the countryside and then to fall back and rejoin the main unit. The country around them seemed quiet and there were no indications of any organized resistance.

So the Prussians were going down unconcernedly into a small valley cut by deep ravines when rifle bullets started to whistle all around them, stopping them dead as a score or so among them fell. Then a group of sharpshooters appeared suddenly from a clump of trees and rushed toward them with fixed bayonets.

At first Walter Schnaffs remained standing still, too bewildered and surprised even to run. Then he felt a terrible longing to flee, but it immediately occurred to him that he would be as slow as a tortoise trying to get away from these lean Frenchmen who were bounding along like goats. So, noticing a large gully full of bushes covered with dead leaves only about six yards from him, he jumped in with both feet forward, without even bothering about how deep it was, just as one might jump into a river from a bridge.

He went like a dart through a thick layer of creepers and sharp branches that tore his face and hands, and landed heavily on a bed of stones. He looked up, and through the rent he had left in his fall, he saw a bit of sky. That revealing hole could give him away, so he crawled carefully on all fours farther along the gully, under the cover of entangled branches, moving as fast as he could as far away as possible from the fighting. Then he stopped and sat crouched amid the dry grass, like a hare.

For some time he could hear shots, shouts, and groans; but soon the sounds of battle weakened and then stopped altogether. Everything was silent and quiet.

Suddenly something moved very close to him. He shuddered fearfully. It was a small bird on a branch, shaking the dry leaves. For a whole hour after that, Walter Schnaffs' heart beat fast.

Night was filling the gully with shadows and the soldier began to think. What was he to do now? What would happen next? Should he try to rejoin his army? But how? Which way was he to go? And even if he managed to make it, it would only be to return to the life of anguish, fear, exhaustion, and suffering that he had led since the outbreak of hostilities. No, he couldn't stand it any longer! He didn't have enough energy left to stand the long marches or to face danger at every moment of the day and night.

But what was he to do? After all, he couldn't hide in this ditch until the war was over. No, that was unthinkable. Oh, if he could only have lived without eating, the prospect of staying there wouldn't have depressed him overmuch; but one had to eat, and to eat every day.

And so he was all alone, in uniform and armed, in enemy territory, far from those who could protect him. Shivers ran all over his body.

Then suddenly a thought flashed through his head—Ah, if only he could be made a prisoner of war by the French! And his heart beat violently out of sheer longing to be captured. Ah, to be a prisoner! He'd be safe and fed, have a roof over his head, be sheltered from bullets and sabers, and protected from all lurking dangers by prison walls and prison guards! Ah, what a dream! And without further ado he resolved: "I'll surrender and become a prisoner of war."

He got to his feet with the idea of carrying out his resolution without wasting any time. But he stopped under the sudden impact of unpleasant thoughts and new misgivings: Where was he going to get himself made prisoner? How? Which way was he to go? Grim pictures of death whirled through his head. Ah, the terrible dangers he would have to face, venturing out across the countryside in his spiked Prussian helmet! What if he came across peasants? If those peasants saw a helpless Prussian who had lost his way, they'd kill him like a stray dog; they'd stick him and batter him with their pitchforks, their spades, their picks, their sickles; they'd beat him into a pulp, into a paste, with all the exasperated rage of the vanquished!

What if he came across sharpshooters? Those French sharpshooters were a desperate bunch who recognized no rules of war, submitted to no discipline. They would certainly shoot him just for the fun of it, to while away a few minutes, to see what kind of a face he'd make while being shot. And he already felt as though he were being stood up against a wall, looking into twelve rifle barrels whose twelve black little holes stared back at him.

What if he met the regular French army? The men in the vanguard would mistake him for a scout—for some cunning, seasoned soldier sent alone on a reconnaissance mission—and they'd fire on him. And he immediately thought he could hear the scattered reports of the rifles fired by the soldiers lying in the brushwood while he, standing in the middle of a field, was riddled with their bullets like a sieve—bullets that, in his imagination, he already felt piercing his flesh.

Dejectedly, he sat down again. There seemed to be no way out for him.

Now it was completely dark—a mute, black night. He made no further movement, except for the shudders that ran through him at the slightest unfamiliar noise coming from the shadows. A rabbit burrowing at the edge of its hole almost sent Walter Schnaffs into headlong flight. The hooting of an owl tore at his heart, filling him with sudden fright which stung like a wound. He strained his big eyes open, trying to see in the darkness; and every minute he imagined he heard someone coming toward him.

After endless hours of agony, he noticed through the ceiling of branches that the sky was becoming lighter. He felt tremendously relieved and stretched his limbs, suddenly relaxed; his heart resumed its normal beat, his eyes closed, and he slept.

When he awoke it seemed to him that the sun had reached the middle of the sky and that it must be close to noon. No noise disturbed the gloomy quiet of the fields and Walter Schnaffs realized that he was acutely hungry.

He yawned, his mouth watering at the thought of sausage, delicious army sausage, and he felt a pain in his stomach.

He got up, walked a few steps, realized how weak his legs were, sat down again, and thought. For another two or three hours he kept listing pros and cons, reversing his resolution every few seconds, torn by clashing considerations, feeling miserable and exhausted.

Finally he decided that the most logical thing for him to do would be to wait for some villager to come by—a lone, unarmed villager, and without any dangerous working tools either—and to rush out and make the man understand that he wished to surrender to him.

So Schnaffs removed his helmet, whose spike could betray

him, and ever so carefully stuck his head out and looked around. No solitary figure of a man stood out against the horizon. At a distance to his left, beyond an avenue of trees, there was a great country house flanked by turrets.

He waited until evening, suffering atrociously, with only the crows flying around him and no sound but the plaintive rumblings of his stomach. And another night was creeping up on him.

He stretched himself out at the bottom of his lair and fell into a feverish sleep haunted by nightmares, the sleep of a hungry man.

The dawn broke again over his head and he resumed his lookout. But the countryside remained as empty as on the previous day and a new fear pervaded Walter Schnaffs—he might die of starvation! He visualized himself stretched on his back in his hole with his eyes closed. All sorts of tiny black beasties would creep onto his corpse and proceed to eat him up; they'd devour every part of him at the same time; they'd slip under his clothes and bite into his cold skin. Then a large black raven would land on his face and pick out his eyes with its pointed beak.

That just about drove him frantic. He imagined that he was already too far gone to walk and was about to pass out from weakness. He had just decided to make a rush for the first village, risking whatever dangers there were, when he saw three peasants walking to the fields with their sharp pitchforks over their shoulders, and dived back into his retreat.

However, when evening started darkening the plain, he crawled cautiously out of the ditch and started to walk—crouching and fearful, his heart pounding wildly—toward the remote manor house, preferring it to a village that would be like a cave full of tigers. When he reached the house, he saw that there was light in the lower row of windows. One of these was even open; an aroma of roast meat suddenly broke upon Walter Schnaffs' nostrils and, hitting him straight in the stomach, convulsed him and took his breath away. He stood there, panting, irresistibly attracted, his heart suddenly filled with a desperate audacity. Then all at once, without his giving it any further thought, his silhouette—that of a Prussian soldier, spiked helmet and all—stood out sharply in the frame of the lighted window.

Eight servants, seated around a large table, were having their dinner in the manorial kitchen. But suddenly a maid dropped her glass and remained open-mouthed, her eyes fixed on the window. All the other eyes followed hers. They had caught sight of the enemy!

Good God! The Prussians were attacking the manor!

First there was one scream, one single scream made up of eight screams in eight different tones, a bloodcurdling cry of terror. Then there was a desperate rush, a panicky scramble at the door leading to the rest of the house. Chairs were toppled over, men kicked down women and stepped over them. In two seconds the room was empty, the table with all the food on it, deserted. Walter Schnaffs stared at it all through his window, completely stupefied by surprise.

After a few seconds of hesitation, he climbed onto the windowsill, jumped down into the kitchen, and crossed toward the plates. He was so hungry that he shook as if in a fever, but fear still held him back. He listened. The whole house seemed atremble; running steps thumped across the floor over his head. The Prussian, bewildered, tried to make out what was going on. Then he heard dull thuds, the thuds of things falling onto soft ground; it was, he realized, the sound of human beings jumping from the windows of the first floor.

Then all the noise and agitation died down and the big manor house became quiet as a tomb.

Walter Schnaffs installed himself in front of a plate that looked untouched, and ate. He ate in great mouthfuls, afraid of being interrupted before he could gulp down enough food. He used both hands to throw big pieces into his mouth, which opened like a trap door; and his throat expanded as the food packages descended one after another into his stomach. Now and then he would interrupt himself, feeling he was about to burst like an obstructed pipe. Then he would take a jug of hard cider and flood the obstruction out of the way, as one does with a stuffed-up drain.

He ate everything that had been in the plates and in the dishes, emptied all the bottles, and then—drunk with drink and food, stupefied, red, and shaken by hiccoughs, his brain unclear and his mouth greasy—he unbuttoned his uniform. He was unable to get up. His eyes closed, his thoughts became completely confused, he rested his heavy head on his arms which were crossed on the table before him, and he gently lost all notion of things and events.

~

The final crescent of the waning moon faintly lighted the

horizon above the trees of the manorial park. It was the chilly moment that precedes the dawn. Some shadowy figures sneaked through a thicket and occasionally a point of steel would glitter in the pale moonlight.

The silent manor house loomed like a great black shadow above the park, only two of its windows shining in the darkness.

Suddenly a thunderous voice resounded:

"Forward, dammit! Come on, boys, to the assault!"

Then, within seconds, doors, shutters, windows collapsed under a human onrush that broke, crushed, felled everything in its way as it crashed into the manor. Fifty soldiers, armed to the teeth, bounced into the kitchen where Walter Schnaffs was having his peaceful little rest. Fifty loaded guns were pointed at his chest and he was thrown down, rolled over, and tied hand and foot.

Panting with surprise and still too stupefied to understand what was going on, he was beaten, battered, and filled with terror.

But then a fat man in a uniform covered with a lot of gold braid placed his foot on Schnaffs' belly and shouted fiercely:

"Surrender! You are my prisoner now!"

The Prussian understood the one word "prisoner" and he moaned:

"Ja, ja, ja. . . ."

They picked him up, sat him on a chair, and tied him to it; his conquerors, puffing like whales, stared at him with great curiosity. Several of them had to sit down, both physically and emotionally at the end of their tether.

And he was smiling. At long last he was a prisoner of war!

Another officer walked in and said:

"The Prussians have fled, Colonel, and they seem to have had many wounded. We are now in full control of the place."

The fat colonel wiped his forehead with a handkerchief and shouted fiercely:

"Victory!"

And he wrote down in a small notebook which he drew out of his pocket:

"After a fierce engagement, the enemy was hurled back and forced to retreat, carrying off his dead and wounded. By our estimate, his casualties amounted to fifty men. Several prisoners have been taken."

The younger officer said:

"What are your further orders, Colonel?"

"We shall," the colonel said, "withdraw in good order so as to avoid the enemy's counteroffensive maneuver which will be executed with the backing of heavy artillery and superior forces."

And he ordered the retreat.

The column re-formed under the manorial walls and set out, with Walter Schnaffs surrounded on all sides, his hands tied, and under a special guard of six men with drawn and loaded revolvers.

They sent scouts out to see whether the way was clear and then advanced cautiously, often coming to a full stop.

By the following dawn, they had reached the town of La Roche-Oysel, for it was the National Guard of that town who had performed this feat of arms.

The people of the town were waiting for them, anxious and excited. As soon as they caught sight of the prisoner's spiked helmet, a great clamor arose. Women threw their arms up to heaven; old men shed tears; an ancient grandfather, trying to hurl his crutch at the prisoner, hit one of his guards on the nose.

The colonel roared:

"I demand that the safety of the prisoner be respected!"

They arrived at the Town Hall. The town's prison was opened and Walter Schnaffs was thrown into it after his hands had been untied. Two hundred armed soldiers were deployed around the building to guard him.

Then, despite the symptoms of diarrhea that had been tormenting him for some time, the Prussian, mad with joy, began to dance crazily, throwing his arms and legs in the air and shouting delightedly until, exhausted, he fell down near a wall.

He was a prisoner! He was saved!

And that is how Champignet Manor was recaptured from the enemy within six hours of its occupation.

Colonel Ratier, a wool merchant in civilian life, who had led the assault at the head of La Roche-Oysel's National Guard unit, received a decoration.

[*L'Aventure de Walter Schnaffs,* April 11, 1883]

The Two Friends

Paris was besieged. It was hungry and gasping. There weren't many sparrows chirping on Parisian roofs and the rat population in the sewers was decreasing. People ate anything.

Monsieur Morissot, a clockmaker by trade but a man of leisure by force of circumstance, was walking along one of the outer boulevards on a clear January morning. He was walking gloomily, his stomach empty, his hands in the pockets of his army trousers, when he came face to face with a brother-in-arms. He stopped short. It was Monsieur Sauvage, a fishing acquaintance.

Every Sunday before the war, Morissot would leave his house at daybreak with a bamboo rod in his hand and a tin box on his back. He'd take the Argenteuil train, get off at Colombes, then walk the rest of the way to Marante Island. As soon as he reached that land of his dreams he'd begin to fish, and he fished until nightfall.

Every Sunday, he would meet there a short, rotund, jovial fellow named Monsieur Sauvage—a haberdasher from Rue Notre Dame de Lorette, and another fishing fanatic. They'd often spend half a day side by side, their fishing rods in their hands, their feet hanging over the water, and they became friends.

There were days when they didn't say a word to each

other and other days when they talked. Anyway, they got along wonderfully without need of words since they had similar tastes and the same ideas about most things.

In the spring, at around ten in the morning, when the rejuvenated sun sent floating over the peaceful river a light vapor that moved with the current, and the warmth of the new season reached the backs of these two rabid fishermen, Morissot would occasionally say to his companion:

"Isn't it great here!"

And Sauvage would answer:

"There's nothing I enjoy more."

And that was enough for them to understand and appreciate each other.

In the fall, toward the end of the day—when the sky, turned blood-red by the setting sun, cast on the water the outlines of the scarlet clouds, then dyed the whole river purple, set the horizon aflame, made the space between the two friends fiery red, and turned to gold the leaves that were already turning brown and shuddering at the foretaste of winter—Sauvage would look smilingly at Morissot and say:

"What a sight!"

And Morissot would answer delightedly, without taking his eyes off his float:

"It's better than the boulevards, isn't it?"

Now, they pressed each other's hands hard, greatly moved on seeing each other under such different circumstances. Monsieur Sauvage sighed and muttered:

"Ah, all the things that have happened since we last met!"

Morissot groaned mournfully:

"And on top of it all, what rotten weather! This is the first nice day we've had this year!"

And, indeed, the sky was completely cloudless and flooded with light.

They walked side by side, both feeling dreamy and sad. Morissot said:

"And the fishing? Remember? What pleasant memories!"

Sauvage said musingly:

"Will we ever go back there?"

They entered a small café and each drank a glass of absinthe. Then they set out to walk along the streets again. Suddenly Morissot stopped:

"What about another glass of absinthe?"

Sauvage accepted:

"I'm your man."

They entered another café.

When they emerged their heads were spinning quite badly, as happens to people who drink on empty stomachs. The weather was unseasonably warm and a gentle breeze tickled their faces. The mildness of the day was making Monsieur Sauvage feel completely drunk; he stopped:

"What about going there right now?"

"Where?"

"Fishing."

"But where could we go?"

"Why, to our island, of course. The French advance posts are near Colombes. Now, I happen to know Colonel Dumoulin and we'd have no difficulty getting past."

The longing to go fishing sent a shiver through Morissot. "All right then, let's do it."

And each went to his home to pick up his fishing tackle. An hour later they were walking side by side along the highway. Then they reached the town where the colonel was stationed. He smiled when he heard their request and granted it, and they continued on their way, now carrying an official pass.

Soon they had passed beyond the French advance posts, crossed the deserted town of Colombes, and reached the small vineyards that descended toward the Seine. It was about eleven o'clock.

Across the river, the village of Argenteuil seemed dead. The heights of Orgemont and Sannois dominated the countryside. The great flatland that stretches all the way to Nanterre was completely deserted, its cherry trees bare and its soil gray.

Monsieur Sauvage pointed to the heights and murmured: "The Prussians are up there. . . ."

A feeling of uneasiness came over the two men in face of that deserted countryside.

The Prussians! They had never yet set eyes on them, although they had been aware of their presence around Paris for many months—strange, invisible, and all-powerful creatures, ruining, starving, and devastating France. A sort of superstitious terror was mingled with the hatred they felt for that unknown and victorious people.

Morissot said between his teeth:

"And what if we happen to meet some?"

Sauvage replied with the Parisian banter he had retained despite everything:

"Well, if we did, we'd offer them some fried fish."

Still they hesitated to go on, intimidated by the silence weighing on the entire countryside.

Finally Sauvage made up his mind:

"Let's go ahead, but carefully."

So with a great deal of caution they made their way down toward the river through a sloping vineyard—bent in two, crawling, keeping to the cover of the bushes as much as they could, their eyes anxious and their ears perked up. When they reached a strip of bare ground which separated them from the river bank, they ran across it, and once by the water, hid in the dry reeds.

Morissot put his cheek against the ground to listen, in case someone was walking close by. He heard nothing. They were alone, quite alone.

Reassured, they started to fish.

Across the water, in front of them, deserted Marante Island shielded them from the sight of the opposite bank. The small restaurant on the island was closed and looked as though it had been abandoned for years.

Sauvage caught the first gudgeon. Morissot caught the second. And after that, every minute or so, one of them would pull out his line with a small silvery creature hooked on the end of it. It was incredible fishing. As they slipped their catch into a fine-meshed net immersed in the river at their feet, a feeling of joy came over them, the sort of joy one feels in being able to do something one loves after long deprivation.

The kindly sun was pouring some of its gentle warmth between their shoulder blades and they no longer listened to anything except the splashes of fish, or thought of anything except fishing. The rest of the world had ceased to exist for them.

But suddenly there was a dull thud that seemed to come from underground and that made the bank quiver under their feet. It was the cannon.

Morissot turned his head and saw—at a distance above the river bank—the tall outline of Mont-Valérien and, at the top of it, a white crest of smoke from the cannon that had just fired. At that moment, a second jet of smoke rose from the summit of the stronghold, followed in a few seconds by the rumble of another explosion. Then a succession of explosions followed as the mountain exhaled its deadly breath, pouring out milky fumes that rose slowly into the sky and formed a little cloud above it.

Sauvage shrugged and said:

"There they go again."

Morissot, anxiously watching his float plunge twice in a row, was suddenly seized by the anger of a peaceful man against these lunatics who could think of nothing better than their war, and he grunted:

"They must all be real idiots to go on killing one another like this!"

"Worse than wild animals," Sauvage concurred.

And Morissot, who had hooked a small carp, declared:

"And to think that it'll always be like this as long as countries are run by governments."

"The Republic," Sauvage dissented now, "would never have gone to war. . . ."

"Under kings," Morissot interrupted him, "we have wars against foreigners; under the Republic we have wars among ourselves."

And they started a quiet argument, analyzing problems of high policy with the sound reasoning of gentle, limited men and agreeing in the final analysis on one thing—men would never be left alone to do as they really pleased. And all that time, Mont-Valérien kept thundering, destroying French homes with its shells, mangling lives, crushing human beings, cutting short dreams and aspirations, and inflicting wounds that would never heal on the hearts of mothers, wives, and daughters in faraway towns and villages.

"Well, I suppose that's life," Monsieur Sauvage declared.

"I'd say that's death rather," Monsieur Morissot said with a snort.

But then they shuddered. They had felt unmistakably that someone had walked by behind them. They turned their heads and saw, standing behind them, four men: four big, armed men, bearded and dressed like lackeys—livery, flat visorless caps, and all—but pointing their guns at them.

Their fishing rods fell out of their hands and drifted downstream.

Within the next few seconds, the two Frenchmen were grabbed, dragged into a boat, and taken over to Marante Island, which they had imagined was deserted. Behind the restaurant that had looked so abandoned to them, they saw a score of German soldiers; and sitting astride a chair and smoking a clay pipe, there was a sort of hairy giant who addressed them in excellent French:

"Well, gentlemen, was your fishing successful?"

A soldier then deposited at the giant's feet the net full of fish that he had been careful to bring along. The Prussian smiled:

"I see you didn't do badly at all! But I wish to entertain you on another subject now. Listen to me and don't get excited. As far as I am concerned you are a couple of spies sent here to watch over me. So, since I've caught you, I'd be quite justified in having you shot. You were pretending to fish in order to conceal your real intentions, and now that you've fallen into my hands, so much the worse for you—we're at war, after all.

"On the other hand I am sure, since you managed to pass the French outposts, that you must know the password to re-enter the city. So, if you'll give me that password, I'll let you live."

The two friends stood side by side, their faces livid, their hands shaking slightly under the nervous strain. They remained silent. The officer went on:

"No one would be the wiser. You'll go back peacefully and it will all remain a secret, as long as you yourselves keep it. Now, if you refuse to co-operate, you'll have to die. Make your choice."

They remained immobile, without opening their mouths.

The Prussian pointed calmly at the river:

"Just think—perhaps within five minutes you'll be at the bottom of this river. Yes, in five minutes! I suppose you have families?"

Mont-Valérien was still spitting fire.

The two fishermen stood there and said nothing. The German issued some orders in his own tongue. Then he moved his chair a bit farther away, so as not to be so close to the prisoners. Twelve men with rifles at the ready came and formed a line twenty yards from the two friends. The officer announced:

"I'll give you one more minute. And not two seconds more."

Then he got up briskly, went over to the Frenchmen, took Morissot by the arm, led him aside, and whispered:

"Hurry up, your friend won't know a thing. Give me the password. I'll pretend I've taken pity on you."

Morissot didn't answer.

The Prussian then tried this on Sauvage, and Sauvage too remained silent.

And they stood side by side once more.

The officer then issued another order and the soldiers raised their rifles. Then, by chance, Morissot's eyes fell upon the net full of their catch, lying in the grass a few steps away. A ray of sunlight gleamed in the knot of fish, some of which were still writhing. Try as he might to control himself, tears filled Monsieur Morissot's eyes. He whispered:

"Good-bye, Monsieur Sauvage."

And Sauvage replied:

"Good-bye, Monsieur Morissot."

They shook hands, shaken from head to toe by an insurmountable trembling. The officer shouted:

"Fire!"

Twelve shots merged into a single explosion.

Monsieur Sauvage fell in one piece, landing on his nose. Monsieur Morissot—who was much taller—swayed, pivoted, and collapsed across his friend's body, his face turned toward the sky while streams of blood poured from his tunic which had burst open across his chest.

The German officer said something again and his men dispersed. They returned with ropes and stones which they tied to the two bodies. Then they carried the two dead friends to the bank.

Mont-Valérien never stopped rumbling and now it was topped by another mountain, a mountain of smoke.

Two soldiers picked up Monsieur Morissot—one by the head, the other by the feet; two other soldiers picked up Monsieur Sauvage in the same way. The bodies were swung a few times and then hurled into the river. They curved through the air and plunged into the water. They sank almost immediately, the stones dragging them down feet first. Water spouted, frothed, rippled, and then became calm again, and tiny wavelets came to die on the bank. There was only a little blood left floating on the surface for a while.

The officer, still calm and serene, said in a low voice: "It's the fishes' turn now," and walked toward the house.

Suddenly he caught sight of the net of gudgeon lying in the grass and called:

"Wilhelm!"

A soldier in a white apron came running. The officer, tossing the catch of the two executed men to him, commanded:

"Fry up these little fish for me while they're still alive. They'll be delicious."

Then he went back to smoking his pipe.

[*Deux Amis*, March 24, 1883]

The Little Soldier

Each Sunday, as soon as they were free, the two little soldiers set out.

Leaving the barracks, they turned right and crossed Courbevoie in long rapid strides, as if marching in formation. Then as soon as they were past the houses, they went at a more leisurely pace, following the bare, dusty highway that leads to Bezons.

They were small and thin, lost in their too ample, too long army coats whose sleeves hid their hands, and hampered in their movements by their huge, floppy red breeches that forced them to spread out their legs when they wanted to walk fast. And under their tall, stiff *shako* caps one could only see the smallest bit of their faces—too hollow-cheeked Breton faces, simple with an almost animal simplicity, with calm, gentle blue eyes in them.

They never talked on the way but forged ahead with one single idea in mind which to them replaced the need for chatting—they had found a spot at the edge of Champioux Wood which reminded them of home, and it was the only place where they felt good.

At the point where the roads from Colombes and Chatou cross, they entered the shadow of the trees, removed the headgear that weighed so heavily on their heads, and wiped their brows.

On the Bezons bridge, they always stopped for a while to look at the Seine. They would remain there for two or three minutes, bent in two as they leaned on the parapet. Or else they'd gaze out over the vast river basin of Argenteuil, where white, slanting sails slid to and fro, perhaps reminding them of the sea in Brittany, of the port of Vannes from near which they came, and of the fishing boats coasting along the Morbihan peninsula toward the open sea.

As soon as they had crossed the Seine, they did their shopping at the local grocer's, baker's, and wine merchant's. A piece of blood sausage, four sous' worth of bread, and a liter of cheap red wine made up their provisions, which they carried in their neckerchiefs. But once they were out of the village, they walked very slowly and talked.

Before them, the flat fields with clumps of trees scattered here and there, led to the wood that reminded them of the woods of Kermarivan. Wheat and oats bordered the narrow path hidden in the young greenness of the crops; and each time Jean Kerderen would say to Luc le Ganidec:

"It's just like around Plounivon."

"Yes, just like it."

They walked side by side, full of vague recollections of their native countryside, of naïve scenes resembling the pictures in a child's penny coloring book. They felt they recognized a corner of a field, a hedge, a stretch of moorland, a crossroads, a granite cross.

Each time, too, they'd stop by a stone marking the boundary of a field because it had something of the dolmen of Locneuven about it.

Every Sunday, as they reached the first clump of trees, Luc le Ganidec would break off a hazel switch, and as he slowly peeled off the bark, he'd think of the folks back home.

Jean Kerderen carried the provisions.

From time to time, Luc would mention a name or recall some incident from their boyhood, using just a few words that were enough to set them dreaming for a long time. And home, their dear, remote native countryside, would take possession of them once again, overwhelm them, send them from afar its shapes, its sounds, its familiar vistas, and its smells—the fragrance of the green hills over which sea breezes glided.

They no longer noticed the stench of the Parisian dung fertilizing the fields surrounding the city, but instead smelt the aroma of furze in bloom picked up and carried by the briny winds from the open sea. And the sails of the pleasure craft they saw rising above the banks were to them the sails of trawlers at the edge of the broad field that stretched from their doorsteps to the sea.

And Luc le Ganidec and Jean Kerderen walked with short steps, melancholy and filled with a sweet sadness—the slow, penetrating sadness of the caged beast that remembers.

By the time Luc had finished peeling the thin bark from his switch, they had reached the edge of the wood where they ate their lunch every Sunday.

They found the two bricks they had hidden in the copse and they lit a small fire of dry wood on which to toast their blood sausage on the points of their knives.

And when they were through with their lunch—had eaten their bread down to the last crumb, drunk their wine to the last drop—they remained sitting side by side in the grass without talking, their eyes staring into the distance, their lids heavy, their fingers interlaced as at mass, their red-clad legs stretched out amid the poppies of the field, the leather of their *shakos* and the brass of their buttons gleaming in the bright sunlight and bringing the larks, singing as they hovered over their heads, to a stop.

~

Around twelve o'clock they gradually started to turn their eyes toward the village of Bezons, for the cowgirl would come from there.

She passed by them every Sunday on her way to milk her cow, the only cow in the neighborhood which was put out to graze, and to move it to a new grazing spot in a narrow meadow farther up along the edge of the wood.

Soon the soldiers caught sight of the farm girl, the only human being to be seen in the whole countryside, and the sight of the shiny reflections cast by her white tin bucket under the flame of the sun made them happy. They never mentioned her when they talked. They were simply happy to see her without even knowing why.

She was a big, strong redhead, burned by the ardor of those bright scorching days—a big, bold lass of the countryside around Paris.

Once, seeing them seated as always in the same spot, she said to them:

"Good morning, there. So you always come to this same spot?"

Luc le Ganidec, the bolder of the two, muttered:

"Yes, we come here when we're off."

That was all. But the following Sunday she laughed when she saw them—laughed with the protective friendliness of a woman of the world, very much aware of their shyness. She asked:

"What d'you do with yourselves all the time you're here? Maybe you're watching the grass grow?"

Luc, amused, smiled too and said: "Maybe that's just it."

She spoke again: "My, my! That don't go too fast!"

He replied, still laughing: "It sure don't."

She walked on. But when she passed by them on her way back with her pail full of milk, she stopped and said:

"Wouldn't you like a drop? It'll make you think of home."

Instinctively feeling that they were peasants like herself—she, too, perhaps being far from home—she had guessed how they felt and hit just the right note.

Both soldiers were greatly moved. She poured some milk into the neck of the wine bottle they had, which took quite a bit of effort, and Luc drank in little sips, stopping after each sip to see whether he hadn't taken more than his share. After that he handed the bottle to Jean.

She stood watching them, arms akimbo, the pail at her feet, and she seemed to enjoy the pleasure she was giving them.

As she walked off she called back to them:

"So long, then. See you next Sunday!"

And they followed her with their eyes for as long as they could see her tall figure which grew smaller and smaller and seemed to sink into the green of the land.

~

When they left the barracks the next Sunday, Jean said to Luc:

"Maybe we ought to buy something nice for her?"

And they were quite at a loss about what to get for the cowgirl.

Luc was for a piece of salami but Jean felt that candy would be much more suitable, for he himself had a sweet tooth. Finally he prevailed and they bought two sous' worth of red and white candies at the grocer's.

They went through their lunch faster than usual, agitated as they were by expectation.

Jean was the first to see her.

"Here she comes," he said.

"Yes, here she comes," Luc said.

They heard her laugh from afar when she caught sight of them, and she called out to them:

"Having yourselves a good time, fellows?"

Together they replied:

"And how are things with you?"

Then they chatted. She spoke of simple things that interested them, of the weather, of the crops, of her masters. They didn't dare to offer her their sweets, which were slowly melting in Jean's pocket.

Finally Luc gathered up enough courage and muttered:

"We've brought something for you."

She wanted to know: "What is it?"

So Jean, red to his ears, reached for the slender paper cone of candy and offered it to her.

She began to eat the small pieces of candy, rolling them from one cheek to the other so that they formed bulges in the skin. The two soldiers seated before her, watched her, moved and delighted.

Then she went to milk her cow and, on her way back, once again offered them some milk.

All week they thought of her, mentioning her several times a day. The following Sunday she sat down next to them to have a longer chat, and the three of them—sitting side by side, their eyes lost in the distance, their knees clasped in their crossed hands—told each other of minor incidents and of little peculiarities of the villages where they had been born; while the cow, seeing that the girl had stopped on the way, stretched her big head with its damp nostrils toward her and mooed protractedly to call her.

Soon she agreed to have a bite to eat with them and to wash it down with a drop of wine. Often she brought some plums for them in her pocket, for the plum season had arrived. Her presence brightened the two little soldiers from Brittany and they chattered like a couple of birds.

~

Then, one Tuesday, Luc le Ganidec put in a request for a leave of absence. He had never done so before. And he didn't come back until ten o'clock in the evening.

Jean was worried and racked his brains, trying to think of what could have made his friend act in such a way.

The following Friday, Luc, having borrowed half a franc

from the soldier who bunked next to him, requested and obtained permission to absent himself for a few hours.

And when, on Sunday, he and Jean set out for their usual walk, he looked quite strange, very agitated, and not at all his usual self.

Jean didn't understand. He vaguely suspected something but couldn't guess what it might be.

They didn't exchange a word until they had reached their usual spot, where the grass was worn thin in the place where they sat each time. They ate their lunch slowly, for neither of them was hungry.

Soon the milkmaid appeared. They watched her approaching as they did every Sunday. When she was quite close, Luc got up and took two steps toward her. She put down her pail and kissed him. She kissed him passionately, with her arms around his neck, without bothering about Jean—without a glance at him, as if he weren't even there.

And poor Jean felt lost. He felt so lost that he couldn't understand it himself—his soul had been turned inside out; his heart had burst, although he hadn't yet realized it.

Then the girl sat down next to Luc and they began to chat.

Jean didn't look at them. He had now guessed why his friend had gone out twice during the week and he felt a scorching pain inside him, a wound, the laceration that betrayal causes.

After a while Luc and the girl got up and went together to tether the cow in a fresh spot.

Jean followed them with his eyes. He saw their figures recede side by side. His friend's red breeches made a bright spot on the path. It was Luc who took the mallet and hammered in the stake to which the animal was tied.

The girl bent to milk the beast while he patted the cow's jagged spine with an absent-minded hand. Then, leaving the pail standing in the grass, the two of them disappeared among the trees.

Jean could see nothing but the wall of foliage through which they had vanished, and he was so shaky that if he had tried to get up he would certainly have fallen.

He remained there motionless, stunned by surprise and pain—a deep naïve pain. He wanted to cry, to run away, to hide, never to see anyone again.

Suddenly he caught sight of them as they emerged from the copse. They were coming back slowly, holding hands as betrothed people do in the villages. It was Luc who carried the pail.

They kissed again before taking leave, and the girl left after tossing a friendly "bye-bye" and an understanding smile at Jean. And it had never occurred to her to offer him any milk that day.

The two little soldiers remained behind, side by side, motionless, silent and impassive as usual, without any indication on their faces of what was going on in their hearts. The sunlight fell upon them. The cow looked at them from the distance, lowing from time to time.

At the usual time they got up to return to the barracks. Luc was peeling the bark from a switch. Jean carried the empty wine bottle. He returned it to the Bezons wine merchant. Then they walked onto the bridge and, as they did every Sunday, stopped in the middle of it to watch the water flowing under it for a few moments.

Jean was leaning over, leaning farther and farther over the iron railing, as though he had seen something that fascinated him in the current. Luc said to him:

"What are you trying to do—drink it or something?"

Just as he finished saying it, Jean's head carried the rest of him away; his legs were pulled up and described an arc in the air, and the little blue and red soldier fell in a mass into the water and disappeared.

Luc, his throat paralyzed by anguish, tried in vain to shout. He saw something stirring farther away, then his friend's head broke the surface of the river, only to vanish beneath it again.

Then, still farther off, he saw a hand—just one lonely hand—appear on the surface of the river and disappear again. And that was all.

The bargemen who came running were unable to find the soldier's body that day.

Luc returned to the barracks alone. He came in running, frantic, reported the accident with tears in his eyes and in his voice, blowing his nose again and again:

"He leaned . . . he . . . he leaned . . . he leaned so that his head pulled him . . . and the next thing, he was falling . . . falling. . . ."

Strangled by emotion, he couldn't say any more.

If he had only known!

[*Le Petit Soldat*, April 13, 1885]

V

LOVE

A Chairmender's Love

The dinner at the Marquis de Bertrans' marking the opening of the hunting season was coming to an end. Eleven hunters, eight ladies, and the village doctor sat at the large, brightly lit table which was covered with fruit and flowers.

They came to talk of love, and immediately the eternal debate started: could one love truly only once or several times? People who had known only one real love were mentioned by some, while others were cited who had loved often and each time violently. The men, on the whole, leaned toward the opinion that passion, like illness, can strike the same person several times and in some instances—if an insurmountable obstacle prevents such a passion from being assuaged—even cause death. Although this stand seems quite unassailable, the ladies, whose opinion was based on poetry rather than direct observation, maintained that love—truly great love—can descend only once upon a mortal; that it strikes like a thunderbolt and that a heart once struck by such a love is so drained, ravaged and burned out that no other strong feeling—no dream even—can possibly grow in it again.

The marquis, who had been in love many times, attacked this notion vehemently:

"I can tell you from personal experience that it is quite possible to love many times and each time with all the strength of passion. To prove the impossibility of loving twice, you have mentioned certain persons who have killed themselves for love. Well, let me answer that by saying that it was only because they had gotten the silly idea of killing themselves that convalescence was impossible. I'm sure that if they hadn't done so they would have recovered and then fallen in love again and again, continuing until they died a natural death. There are inveterate fallers-in-love, just as there are inveterate drunkards. A man who has once tasted liquor will drink, and one who has once known love will love. It's all a matter of temperament."

They asked the doctor—an old Parisian who had come to bury himself in the country—to decide. What was his opinion, they wanted to know.

It just so happened that the doctor didn't have one.

"It's just as the marquis said," the doctor remarked, "a matter of temperament. As for personal experience—well, I once came across a passionate love that continued for fifty-five years without abating for one single day and that only ended in death."

The wife of the marquis clapped her hands.

"Isn't that beautiful! What a wonderful thing it must be to be loved like that! What happiness to live for fifty-five years enveloped in such a passionate, all-encompassing love! The person so adored must have been really happy; he must have really relished his life, didn't he, Doctor?"

The doctor smiled.

"Well, you're right at least in one thing, madame—in referring to the object of that passionate love as *he*. In fact, you know him—he is Monsieur Chouquet, the owner of the village pharmacy. And she—I'm certain you knew her too. She was the old chairmender who used to come around every year to repair the straw bottoms of old chairs. Wait, let me explain. . . ."

But his audience was no longer enthusiastic; a disappointed "Pooh!" was written all over their faces. Apparently they felt that love was reserved to the distinguished and refined—or at least that only the passions of such persons were worthy of the interest of an elegant company.

But the doctor told his love story anyway.

❧

About three months ago, I was called to that old woman's bedside. She was dying. She had arrived the day before in the old wagon that also served as her house, drawn by a nag and accompanied by two big black dogs—her friends and guardians. The priest was already there and the old woman made us the executors of her will. And so that we should understand the meaning of her last wishes, she told us the story of her life. I suppose it is one of the strangest and most poignant things I've ever head.

Her father was a chairmender and so was her mother; and she had always lived on wheels, never in a home planted on the ground.

When she was a little girl, she would wander around, ragged and dirty, always scratching herself. The family would stop the wagon by a ditch just outside a village, unharness the nag, and let it graze. The dogs would go to sleep with their noses between their paws; the child would roll in the grass while her father and mother sat in the shade of the elms and attended to all the old chair seats in the vicinity that needed mending. They hardly ever spoke in that nomadic family, except for the few words needed to decide who would go around the community shouting "Chairmender, chairmender. . . ." They would set about weaving the straw in complete silence, sitting either face to face or side by side. When the little girl would stray too far afield or try to make the acquaintance of some village urchins, her father's angry voice would call out: "Come back here, you little slut!" And those were the only nice words she ever heard.

When she had grown a bit bigger, they sent her around from house to house to pick up the old chairs that needed mending. And on those rounds she was able to talk to some of the children she came across. But on these occasions, *their* parents would call back their young: "Come back here, you brat, and don't ever let me catch you chatting with tramps again!"

Often, village boys threw stones at her; but there were also some kind ladies who'd give her a few coppers for herself sometimes, and she hid the money with great care.

Once—she was eleven at the time—when her parents had stopped in this vicinity, she wandered behind the cemetery and met the little Chouquet boy, who was crying because some other boy had stolen a couple of coppers from him. The tears of a well-to-do little boy—one of those neat children who, in her simple have-not's head, she had imagined were always gay and happy—came as a shock to her. She went up to him and when she found out why he was crying, she pressed into his hand all her savings—seven sous—which he, wiping away his tears, took very naturally. Seeing this, in a burst of joy and audacity she kissed him. Since he was busy examining the coins, he didn't try to stop her; and she, finding that she was not rebuffed, tried again and ended up hugging and kissing him to her heart's content. Then she dashed off.

What was going on in her poor young head? Had she fallen for this urchin because she had given him all her miserable fortune or because she had given him her first tender kiss? The mystery is as impenetrable with children as with grown-ups.

For months she kept dreaming about that corner of the cemetery and the little boy. Hoping to see him again, she stole money from her parents—picking up a sou here, a sou there, or saving odd coppers on the shopping she did for the ambulant household.

When she saw him again, she had two francs in her pocket, but she had only been able to catch a glimpse of the little druggist's son in the window of the store, between a tapeworm in a jar and one of those large round flasks one finds in druggists' windows.

That only made her love him the more. She was completely conquered—overcome and subdued by the glamor of colored water and shining crystal.

That vision was etched so sharply in her memory that when, a year later, she saw him behind the school building playing marbles with his friends, she rushed up to him, flung her arms around his neck, and kissed him so violently that he screamed out in fear. Then, to calm him, she gave him all her money—three francs, twenty centimes—a real fortune that he admired with wide-open eyes.

He accepted it and allowed her to fondle him as much as she liked.

During the four years that followed, she handed all her savings over to him and he pocketed them, feeling that he had earned them by allowing her to kiss him. Once it was one franc, fifty centimes; once, two francs; on one occasion, only seventy centimes (that time she cried with sorrow and humiliation but it had been a very bad year); and the last time, she gave him five francs—a great, round coin that made him laugh contentedly.

He was all she thought of, and he too waited for her return quite impatiently and, when he caught sight of her, dashed to meet her—making the little girl's heart jump with joy.

Then he disappeared. They had sent him off to boarding school, as she managed to find out by skillful inquiry. She then used incredible cunning and diplomacy to change her parents' itinerary so that their stops at the village would coincide with his summer vacations. She succeeded, but only after a year of effort, so that two years had gone by without her seeing him. She hardly recognized him, so much had he changed and grown, and so handsome did he look in his school uniform with its shiny brass buttons. He pretended not to see her and swaggered haughtily by.

After that she cried for two days and from that time on remained infinitely unhappy.

She returned to the village every year, passed him without daring to greet him and without his ever condescending even to glance at her. She was desperately in love with him. "He is the only man I ever really saw in all my life, Doctor," she told me, "and I'm not even sure that any others exist."

Her parents died and she took over their trade. She replaced them by two huge, terrifying dogs that kept people away.

Once, returning to this village where her heart lived, she saw a young woman leaving the Chouquet drugstore arm-in-arm with her beloved. It was his wife. He was married.

That night she threw herself into the pond by the village square. Some drunkard out late fished her out and carried her to the pharmacy. Young Chouquet came down in his dressing gown and, apparently without recognizing her, undressed her, rubbed her with alcohol, and then said to her quite harshly:

"You must be insane! How could anyone be so stupid!"

That was enough to make her feel good. He had spoken to her! She was happy for a long time after that.

And, despite her insistence, he refused payment for his services.

So her entire life passed like that. She mended the bottoms of old chairs while dreaming of Chouquet. Every year she caught a glimpse of him through the shop window. She got into the habit of buying her little stock of medical supplies from him so that she could see him at close quarters, talk to him, and once again give him money.

As I mentioned at the beginning of my story, she died last spring. When she had told me this sad story, she asked me to hand over her entire life's savings to the man she had so patiently loved. She had worked for him alone, she told me, even grudging herself food in order to put more aside—to make sure he'd think of her, even if only after she was dead.

She then gave me 2,327 francs. When she had breathed her last, I handed the 27 francs to the priest to pay for her burial and kept the 2,300.

The next day I went to the Chouquets'. They were finishing their lunch. I saw them sitting at their table, both big and ruddy, smelling of pharmaceutical products, important and self-satisfied.

They invited me to sit down and offered me a drink of kirsch, which I accepted. Then I began to tell them my story, thinking they would dissolve into tears.

As soon as he gathered he had been loved by that ambulant chairmender, that ragged tramp, Chouquet well-nigh jumped out of his chair in his indignation; it was as if she had ruined his reputation, deprived him of the respect of honest people, stolen his self-esteem and his honor—things terribly important to him, indeed, more important than life itself.

His wife, just as outraged as he was, kept muttering: "Ah, the tramp, the miserable tramp!" unable to find any other words to express her feelings.

Chouquet got up and walked around the table in long strides; his pharmacist's white cap had slipped to one side and was almost resting on his ear; he kept mumbling:

"Can you imagine that, Doctor! What a horrible thing for a man! What can I do now? Ah, if I'd known it when she was still alive, I'd have had her arrested and clapped into jail for talking like that; and I assure you, she wouldn't have got out again so easily—I assure you!"

I was bewildered by the reaction evoked by my sentimental errand. I didn't know what to say or do. But I had to complete my mission.

"She asked me," I said, "to give you her savings. They amount to twenty-three hundred francs. Now, if you find what I've just told you so unpleasant, I suppose the best thing would be to turn it over to charity."

The man and woman stared at me, paralyzed by surprise. I pulled the money out of my pocket—wretched money gathered all over the country, money of all denominations, coppers and gold coins all mixed together. Then I asked:

"Well, what have you decided to do?"

Madame Chouquet was the first to speak:

"Well, since it was the woman's last wish . . . after all . . . it makes it rather awkward for us to refuse. . . ."

The husband, vaguely embarrassed, suggested:

"We could always buy something for our children with the money."

I said rather drily:

"Please yourselves."

"Well, I suppose you'd better give it to me since that's what she asked you to do. I'm sure we can find some good use for it."

I handed him the money and left.

The next day I received an unexpected visit from Chouquet.

"It occurred to me," he said abruptly, "that she must've left that wagon of hers behind, that woman. What do you intend to do with the wagon?"

"Me? Nothing. Take it if you wish."

"Good. I'll make a toolshed for my vegetable garden out of it."

As he was leaving, I called after him:

"She also left her old nag and her two dogs behind—perhaps you want them too?"

He stopped, surprised:

"Ah, no, certainly not! What do you want me to do with them? You may dispose of them as you wish." And he laughed.

Then he offered me his hand to shake and I shook it. Well, what can one do? It wouldn't be good for the druggist and the doctor in a town to become enemies.

So I kept the dogs and the priest, who has quite a large courtyard, took the horse. The wagon serves Monsieur Chouquet as a shed and he has bought himself five railroad bonds with the money.

And that is the only really deep love I have come across in my life.

~

The doctor was silent and the wife of the marquis, with tears in her eyes, sighed:

"Decidedly, only women know how to love. . . ."

[*La Rempailleuse,* September 17, 1882]

The Avenger

When Antoine Leuillet married the widowed Mathilde Souris, he had been in love with her for almost ten years.

Souris had been his friend, an old schoolmate. Leuillet had been rather fond of him, although he had thought him a bit dumb.

"Poor old Souris," he used to say. "He'll certainly never set the world on fire."

When Souris married Mademoiselle Mathilde Duvall, Leuillet was surprised and slightly vexed because he was a little sweet on her himself. She was the daughter of a local haberdasher who had put aside a tiny bit of capital and retired. She was pretty, well-mannered, and smart. She married Souris for his money.

After that Leuillet looked at her with different eyes and started pursuing his friend's wife with his attentions. He was a handsome man, not stupid, and also rather well off. He felt confident of success. He failed. So then he really fell in love and his love was made discreet, shy, and awkward because of his close friendship with her husband. For her part, Madame Souris, thinking that he had given up his ideas of seduction, relaxed and treated him with sincere fondness. And that went on for nine years.

Then one morning, Leuillet received a desperate note from

the poor woman: Souris had died suddenly of coronary thrombosis.

It was a frightful shock to him because he and Souris were exactly the same age. But the first shock was almost immediately followed by a deep joy and feeling of infinite relief that filled him body and soul. Madame Souris was free now.

Nevertheless, he managed to put on an appropriate air of grief to let the necessary time elapse, and in general, to observe all the conventional proprieties. Fifteen months later, he married the widow.

People considered his behavior natural, even noble: he had acted as a loyal friend and an honest man.

Now, at last, his happiness was complete.

They understood each other immediately and lived in a very close, warm intimacy. They had no secrets and shared their most private thoughts. Leuillet now loved his wife with a relaxed and trusting love and treated her like a loyal and tender companion, an equal and a confidante. However, there still lingered in his heart a strange and unaccountable resentment against the late Souris who had been the first to possess his wife—who had picked the flower of her youth and her girlish heart and had thus somewhat marred the poetic quality of it all. The memory of the dead husband spoiled the bliss of the living one, and gradually this jealousy came to torment Leuillet night and day.

He kept returning to the subject of Souris, questioning her on thousands of intimate and secret details, insisting on being told all the dead man's habits and then pursuing him into his grave with sarcasms and sneers, emphasizing his inadequacies.

At any moment he was likely to call his wife from the other end of the house:

"Hey, Mathilde!"

"Yes, dear, what is it?"

"Here, I'd like to tell you something. . . ."

And she'd come to him, always smiling, knowing very well that he was going to talk to her about Souris and quite willing to gratify her new husband's harmless mania.

"Say, do you remember the day when Souris tried to convince me that small guys are always loved more than big guys?"

And he'd launch into a series of remarks that were disparaging to the dead man, who had been small, and discreetly flattering to himself, Leuillet, who was big.

And Madame Leuillet would make him feel that he was right, absolutely right; and she would laugh wholeheartedly, quietly making fun of her former husband for the greater comfort of her present one, who always concluded thus:

"Well, never mind, he was a bit dumb, poor Souris!"

They were happy, extremely happy, and Leuillet continued to prove his unabated love to his wife by all the usual means.

Then one night, as they were prevented from sleeping by a renewal of youthful ardor, Leuillet, who was holding his wife tightly in his arms and kissing her with great zest on the mouth, suddenly asked her:

"Tell me something, darling."

"What?"

"Now, Souris. . . . This is rather an awkward question for me to ask. . . . Well, anyway, was he very amorous, Souris?"

She gave him a big, noisy kiss and murmured in his ear: "Not as much as you are, my sweet."

His male pride was flattered and he said:

"So he wasn't too good in these things, was he?"

She said nothing, only letting out a malicious little giggle and burying her face in her husband's neck. He insisted:

"He was a bit simple, I bet. Not too effective, if you see what I mean. Didn't have a very fine touch?"

She made a slight movement of the head that signified "No, no touch whatever."

"So I suppose he annoyed you at night, didn't he?"

This time, in an access of frankness, she said emphatically:

"Ah, he certainly did!"

He kissed her on hearing that and whispered:

"Ah, the awkward brute! You weren't happy with him, were you?"

"No," she said, "it certainly wasn't very gay. . . ."

Leuillet was delighted, setting up in his mind a very flattering comparison between the former state of affairs and the present one.

For some time he remained silent, then suddenly, shaking with merriment, he said:

"Tell me something."

"What?"

"Will you be absolutely frank with me?"

"Of course, darling."

"Well, tell me then, were you ever tempted to deceive . . . to cheat on that poor imbecile Souris?"

Madame Leuillet let out a coy "Oh!' and buried her face even deeper in her husband's chest. But he realized she was laughing. He insisted:

"No, really tell me. He had—well, the face of a husband whose wife cheats on him, the poor idiot! It would've been funny, really funny! Ah, poor Souris! Come, darling, you can tell me about it now! You can tell me, you know!"

He stressed the "me," certain that if she'd had any idea of being unfaithful to Souris, she'd have chosen him, Leuillet, for her accomplice. And he was fretting with gleeful impatience to hear her confess, fully confident that if she hadn't been the virtuous woman she was, she would've been his then too.

But she didn't say anything—just laughed as though she had remembered something that struck her as infinitely funny.

Leuillet laughed too then, at the thought that he could have cuckolded poor Souris all that time! Ah, wouldn't that have been funny! What a trick to have played on the fool! Ah, it would've been enough to make you really roll on the ground with laughter! And he stammered through his laughter:

"Ah, poor Souris sure would have looked the part! Ah, that's for sure."

Madame Leuillet was now twisting about under the sheets, laughing till she almost cried, almost screaming as Leuillet kept repeating:

"Come on, admit it, confess it, be frank with me! You must realize that it wouldn't be the least bit unpleasant for me now."

Finally, choking, she brought out: "Yes . . . yes. . . ."

Her husband insisted:

"Yes what? Come on, tell me everything."

Now she was only laughing a little. She brought her mouth close to his ear, and as he waited for the titillating admission, she said:

"Yes, I was unfaithful to him."

An icy shiver shook him to his bones. He stammered:

"You . . . you what? You actually . . . did it?"

She, still thinking that he was finding the thing infinitely titillating, went on:

"Yes . . . I did . . . I actually did."

He had to sit up, his breath cut short. He was almost as shocked as if someone had come and informed him that

Mathilde had been unfaithful to him, Leuillet. He was at a loss for words and it was only after a while that he said simply:

"Ah!"

She had stopped laughing, realizing her mistake when it was too late.

Finally Leuillet inquired:

"Who with?"

She remained silent, trying to think of some way out, but he said again:

"Who with?"

At last she murmured:

"With a young man."

He turned on her abruptly and said in a rasping voice: "I suspected it wasn't with a kitchenmaid. I want to know who the young man was."

She didn't answer. Then he tore away the sheet she had pulled over her head, repeating:

"I must know which young man, do you understand!"

She said painfully:

"I was only joking. . . ."

But he was trembling with rage.

"So you were joking, were you? You were just pulling my leg? Well, I want you to know you can't get around me like that! I want his name!"

She said nothing and lay motionless on her back. He seized her arm and squeezed it violently.

"Don't you hear me? I demand that you answer when I speak to you!"

She answered nervously:

"I think you've gone mad. Leave me alone!"

He was trembling in his fury; he shook her with all his might, repeating again and again:

"D'you hear! . . . d'you hear! . . ."

She made a sharp movement to free herself and her finger-tips grazed his nose. Then he, thinking she had intentionally struck him, flung himself upon her, held her down, and slapped her as hard as he could, shouting:

"Here, take that, take that, you whore! Here, that's for you, take that, you slut, take that, you whore, you whore!"

When he was out of breath and tired, he got up and went over to the cupboard to get himself a glass of orangeade because he was afraid he was going to faint.

And she, she was crying in the bed, sobbing loudly, and

feeling this was the end of her happiness and through her own fault.

Then, between her sobs, she mumbled:

"Listen, Antoine, come here. I lied to you. I'll explain. Listen. . . ."

Prepared to salvage whatever was left and armed with ready arguments and cunning, she raised her disheveled head in its nightcap that had slipped to one side.

He turned toward her, ashamed of himself for having struck her but aware that there was now an inexhaustible hatred in his husband's heart for this woman who had deceived her previous husband—Souris.

[*Le Vengeur,* November 6, 1883]

The Wreck

Yesterday, December 31st, I had lunch with my old friend Georges Garin. His butler came in and handed him a letter covered with seals and foreign stamps.

"Will you excuse me?"

"Of course."

And Georges proceeded to read the eight pages of the letter written in large, English handwriting slanted in all directions. He took his time, looking grave and intent. It was obvious that he was deeply touched.

When he was through, he put the letter on the mantelpiece and said:

"Well, here's a strange story that I've never told you before, a rather moving story in which I was involved myself. Ah, it was a strange New Year's Eve. . . . As a matter of fact, it must have been exactly twenty years ago, since I was thirty then and I'm fifty now."

And he told me the story.

⁂

At the time, I was an investigator for the maritime insurance company that I run today. I had intended to greet the New Year in Paris since it is a convention to make that day a holiday; but just as I was making the arrangements for my trip, I received a letter from my director informing me that I was to set out immediately for the Isle of Ré where a three-master out of Saint-Nazaire, which we had insured, had run aground. I received the letter at eight in the morning, at ten I was at the company offices where I received my instructions, and in the evening I boarded the night train to La Rochelle, where I arrived on the morning of December 31st.

I had two hours to kill before the sailing of the *Jean-Guiton,* the boat that made the daily run to the island. So I went for a stroll around La Rochelle, which is a strange town with a great deal of character. It has a maze of twisting streets with sidewalks roofed in to form glass arcades somewhat reminiscent of the Rue de Rivoli in Paris but much lower. Those low galleries and arcades have an air of mystery about them, as if they had been built specially as a setting for conspirators—an ancient and poignant background for the old wars, the savage and heroic wars of religion. La Rochelle is indeed an old Huguenot city, stern and austere, and lacking public monuments comparable to those that make Rouen, for instance, so beautiful. Nevertheless, it is striking in its very severity, which has, perhaps, a touch of cunning in it. This is a city of stubborn warriors, a breeding ground for all sorts of fanatical faiths, a city which witnessed the sprouting of Calvinism and gave birth to the Four Sergeants' Conspiracy in 1822.

After wandering for some time through those eerie streets, I boarded the little steamship, black and potbellied, that was to take me to the Isle of Ré. Puffing angrily, she steamed between the two ancient forts that guard the harbor, sailed through the roadstead, and passed beyond the mole built by Richelieu—its huge blocks of stone just awash and encircling the city like an immense neckpiece; then she veered off to starboard.

It was one of those sad days that oppress the mind and crush all thought, stifle the will and make one sluggish: a gray, raw day, begrimed by a heavy mist, damp as drizzle, like a cold jelly—as revolting to breathe as a whiff from a sewer.

Under the low ceiling of this sinister fog and bordered by endless stretches of sand, the shallow, yellow, turgid waters lay motionless, without a ripple, without a sign of life—a murky, motionless sea of stagnant water. The *Jean-Guiton* chugged along, rolling slightly as if by force of habit, cutting the smooth, heavy, solid oilcloth surface with her prow, and leaving a few splashes and wavelets in her wake that soon subsided.

I got into conversation with the captain—a short, almost limbless man, roly-poly like his boat, and rolling just like her. I wanted to obtain some information about the disaster I was going to investigate for my firm: on a stormy night a big three-masted square-rigger from Saint-Nazaire, the *Marie-Joseph,* had run aground on a sandbank off the Isle of Ré.

According to the owner, the storm had flung the *Marie-Joseph* so far onto the sandbank that it had been impossible to refloat her, and so he had been forced to have everything possible removed from the vessel. I had been sent to appraise the state of the wreck, to try to estimate what shape the ship had been in before she ran aground, and to satisfy myself that everything possible had been done to refloat her. I was to represent the interests of my company at the inquiry and, if it came to litigation, to testify on its behalf. It was my report to the director that would determine his decision about the next steps to be taken to safeguard our interests.

The ferry captain knew all about the *Marie-Joseph* shipwreck, having participated in the salvage operations with his boat, and he told me how the accident had happened—a very simple affair indeed.

The *Marie-Joseph,* running before a strong gale, was off course, and steering blindly in complete darkness through a foaming sea—"a frothy milk soup" as the captain put it—she ran onto one of those immense sandbars that, at low tide, turn the coasts of this area into a Sahara.

While we were talking, I looked around and ahead of us. Between the heavy sky and the ocean, there was a clear space where the eye could see for a great distance, and I realized we were sailing along a coast. I asked:

"Is that the Isle of Ré?"

"It is," the captain said, and suddenly stretching out his short arm and pointing straight in front of us at a faint object in the middle of the sea, he added: "And see, over there, that's your ship."

"You mean the *Marie-Joseph?"*

"Why, yes."

I was flabbergasted. That faint, black dot that I could very easily have mistaken for a reef looked at least two miles from land.

"But, Captain," I said, "it must be at least a hundred fathoms deep there."

"A hundred, you say?" the captain chuckled. "Well, I say there aren't even two fathoms of water there."

Speaking with his Bordeaux accent, the captain went on: "High tide is at twenty minutes to ten. So, when you've had your lunch at the Dauphin hotel, go down to the beach and start walking out. . . . Take your time, and I promise you, with your hands in your pockets, you'll reach the wreck without wetting your feet by ten to three, three at the latest. And then, my friend, you'll have between an hour and three-quarters and two hours at your disposal to spend there. But not more or you'll be caught, because the farther the sea retires, the faster it gallops back along this coast which is as flat as a bedbug. If you want my advice, be on your way back by ten minutes to five and then, by seven-thirty, you can be on board the *Jean-Guiton* again and we'll land you this very evening on the dock at La Rochelle."

I thanked the captain and went to sit in the bow of the boat and watch the small town of Saint-Martin that we were rapidly approaching.

Saint-Martin looked like any one of those miniature ports that are the chief towns of all the flimsy little islands strewn along the edge of the continent. Actually it was a large fishing village with one foot on land and one in the sea, living on fish and fowl, on vegetables and seafood, radishes and mussels. The rest of the island was flat and rather barren, and yet I had the impression that it was heavily populated, although I never went inland.

So I had my lunch, crossed the little promontory, and then, as the sea was rapidly receding, I set out across the sand toward something that looked like a distant black reef sticking out of the water.

I walked fast across the yellow plain, which was as resilient as living flesh and seemed to be sweating under my feet. The sea had been here a few moments before and now I could see it at a distance, slipping away, and soon I was no longer able to make out the dividing line between sand and water. It was like witnessing a supernatural transformation: one minute the Atlantic was before me and the next it was gone—like stage scenery swallowed up by a trap door—and replaced by a sandy expanse; and I found myself walking across a desert where only the salty breath of the ocean, the smell of seaweed, and the invigorating air of the seashore were still around me. I was walking fast and was no longer cold; I kept my eyes on the grounded wreck, which grew larger as I came closer to it and now resembled a huge, stranded whale.

As I came closer, the wreck seemed to rise up and loom formidably amidst the immense, pale-yellow plain. Finally, after an hour-long walk, I reached the ship. She lay over on her side and was gutted, like a beast with its breast split open and showing its broken ribs—tarred wooden ribs with many big nails sticking in them. The sand had already invaded it through every rent, clinging to it, claiming possession, determined never to let go of it. And the ship looked as if she had indeed taken root in the sand: her bow was deeply buried in the soft and treacherous ground. Only her raised stern seemed to be hurling at the sky a desperate, white-lettered appeal—*Marie-Joseph*—which stood out against the black bulwarks.

I climbed on top of the carcass by the side that lay on the sand; I reached the bridge and lowered myself inside. The daylight, coming in through the shattered hatches and the rents in the ship's side, dimly lighted long, narrow, cave-like gangways cluttered with broken woodwork. And even in the underground, boarded passage where I found myself, there was nothing underfoot but sand.

I began to make notes on the state of the wreck. I sat down on an empty, broken barrel and wrote by the light coming in at a large porthole through which I could see a vast stretch of the sandy plain. From time to time, a peculiar shudder, caused by the damp cold and by loneliness, would run down my spine; and I'd stop writing and listen to the vague and mysterious creakings of the wreck—the sounds of crabs scratching against the sides with their hooked claws, the sounds of the millions of tiny sea creatures which had already installed themselves in this carcass, and the sound of the gentle, regular, gimlet-like grinding of the teredo worm that gnaws relentlessly at all old hulks, undermining and destroying them.

Suddenly I heard human voices quite near me. I leapt to my feet, my first thought being of ghosts. For one second, I almost expected two drowned men to rise up and tell me of their death. It didn't take me long, I assure you, to hoist myself up through the hatch onto the bridge; and from there I saw standing below me on the sand a tall gentleman and three young ladies—as it turned out, an Englishman and his three English daughters. I'm sure that when they suddenly saw a man pop up from the entrails of the abandoned three-master, they were even more frightened than I had been. The youngest of the girls scampered away; the two others took hold of their father's arms, while he stood staring at me with gaping mouth. That, by the way, was the only sign of perturbation he displayed.

Recovering from his surprise, he said, speaking with a strong English accent:

"Oh, I say, sir, is this your ship?"

"Yes, monsieur."

"All right, we visit, sir?"

"Yes, monsieur."

Then he went into a stream of English in which I managed to catch the word "gracious" which recurred several times.

As he was looking around for the best place to climb on board, I pointed it out to him and extended a hand to help him. He clambered up and then we helped the three girls, who had now completely recovered from their fright, to climb up too. They were charming, the girls, particularly the oldest—an eighteen-year-old blonde with a complexion like a pink flower and very fine and lovely features. Pretty English girls have something about them that makes one think of the tender fruit of the sea; and this one looked as if she had just risen from the sand and that her hair had kept its reflection. Their exquisite freshness brings to mind the delicate hues of pink seashells, of rare and mysterious mother-of-pearl born in the unexplored depths of the oceans.

She spoke French a little better than her father and acted as interpreter. I had to tell them all the details of the shipwreck, and as I had to make them up, it sounded as if I had been there when it happened. After that, the whole family went down inside the hull. As soon as they reached the dim gallery, they let out exclamations of surprise and admiration; and the first thing I knew, all four of them—the father and the three daughters—produced sketchbooks that they must have been carrying under their loose raincoats, and proceeded to make pencil sketches of that strange and desolate place.

They sat side by side on a jutting beam and the four sketchbooks on eight knees were rapidly covered with black lines that doubtless were meant to convey the appearance of the *Marie-Joseph's* gutted hull.

Without pausing in her drawing, the oldest girl kept talking to me, while I myself continued to inspect the skeleton of the vessel.

I learned from her that they were spending the winter in Biarritz and that they had come to the Isle of Ré especially to have a look at this three-master stranded on the sand. These people had none of the stiffness one might expect to find in the English—they were nice, unpretentious eccentrics, examples of the eternal wanderers that England sends all over the world. The father—tall and lean, his ruddy face framed in white whiskers—made me think of a living sandwich, a human head carved out of a piece of ham between two pillows of white hair; the daughters—long-legged, adolescent wading birds, the two younger ones thin like their father—charming, all three of them, but especially the oldest.

She had such a funny way of talking, of laughing, of understanding and failing to understand, of questioningly raising eyes as blue as deep water, of interrupting her sketching to concentrate on guessing the meaning of French words she didn't understand, of resuming her work, and of saying *yes* and *no,* that I could have watched her and listened to her indefinitely.

Suddenly she announced:

"I heard something move inside this ship."

I listened and immediately detected a faint, peculiar, and continuous sound. What could it possibly be? I got up and looked out of the porthole and what I saw made me cry out in horror—the sea had reached our wreck and was about to surround us.

In seconds we were all on the bridge. It was too late. The water was all around us and it was speeding toward the shore at an incredible rate. Actually, the rush of the sea might better be described as a wild slide, a prodigious expansion; although a few inches of water still covered the sand, we could no longer see the fleeing edge of the spreading flood.

The Englishman wanted to try to make it to the shore but I dissuaded him; it was impossible because of the deep pools that we had been able to avoid coming out but that we would no longer be able to detect under the uniform surface of the water—we might very well wander into one of them.

We all went through a moment of unspeakable anguish, but then the young English girl smiled and said:

"I say, so it's we who are shipwrecked now!"

I wanted to laugh but was seized by a fear as cowardly, loathsome, and treacherous as the tide. All the dangers inherent in our situation presented themselves to me in a flash and I felt like screaming for help, hoping to reach I don't know whom.

The two younger girls pressed themselves against their father, who looked mournfully at the flooded expanse around us.

Night was falling, enveloping us just as rapidly as the rising tide; and it was a heavy, damp, and icy night at that. I said:

"We have no choice but to stay on the wreck."

The Englishman agreed:

"Yes, that's right."

And we remained there for a quarter of an hour—or was it half an hour?—I can't really say how long it was, staring at the yellow water thickening, turning, seething around us as if leaping with joy over its reconquered territory.

One of the smaller girls began to feel cold and we decided to go down below where we would be sheltered from the light but icy wind that was finding its way under our clothes and chilling our skins.

But I looked down the hatch and found that the ship was full of water; so we were forced to crouch against the after bulwark, which afforded us some small protection.

Darkness fell around us and we sat there pressed close together, surrounded now by the sea and the night. I felt the young English girl's shoulder tremble against my own and from time to time heard the chattering of her teeth; but I also felt the gentle warmth of her body through her clothes and that warmth was as sweet to me as a kiss. We didn't speak; we remained motionless and mute, crouching there like animals seeking refuge from a hurricane in a ditch. And then, despite everything—despite the night, despite the deadly and ever-increasing danger—I began to feel happy to be there; I welcomed the cold, the danger, the long dark hours of anguish I was condemned to spend on this narrow hulk, pressed against this sweet little girl. And I couldn't very well account for this strange sensation of well-being and joy that enveloped me.

Why? Who can tell? Was it because she was there, next to me? Who—that little English girl I didn't even know? I didn't love her. I didn't even know her. And yet I felt moved and tender. To save her, I would have given everything! I would have done the maddest things for her sake. Strange, that the mere presence of a woman can do so much to us! Is it the power of her charms that isolates us from the world? Is it a response to her prettiness and youth that goes to our heads like wine?

Or isn't it rather a fleeting touch of love, of that mysterious love which seeks constantly to unite beings—love that tries its power whenever man and woman meet—by penetrating them with a misty, deep, and mysterious emotion, just as one sprinkles the earth that it may bring forth flowers?

But the dark silence was becoming sinister—the silence of the sky, that is, because we kept hearing around us the quiet, relentless swishing, the hollow sound of the rising sea, the monotonous gurgling of the water against the side of our grounded wreck.

Suddenly I heard sobs; it was the smallest of the girls crying. Her father tried to comfort her and they began to talk in English. I couldn't follow what they said, but I gathered that he was reassuring her, and also that she was still afraid.

I asked my neighbor:

"You're not too cold, miss, I hope?"

"Oh yes, I am very cold."

I wanted to give her my overcoat. She refused. But I took it off and put it around her despite her protests. During the brief struggle that took place, our hands met and a delightful shudder ran through my whole body.

For some time, the air had been growing sharper and the water was slapping harder against the ship's side. I sat up straight and my face smarted in the biting wind. The wind was rising! The Englishman had noticed the change too and said simply:

"This is bad."

It was bad indeed; it was certain death if the waves—even waves of only moderate strength—came to bear directly on our wreck, for it was so shaky and disjointed by now that the first fair-sized billow could smash it to pieces and carry off what was left.

Our anguish increased with every second as the blasts of wind grew stronger and stronger. There were white caps on the waves now; I could see the light lines of foam appearing and disappearing in the darkness, while each impact sent a brief shudder through the *Marie-Joseph* and also tugged at our hearts.

The English girl was trembling. I felt her body shivering against my shoulder and a wild desire to fling my arms around her came over me.

Far away—ahead of us, on our left, on our right, behind us—there were the beams of lighthouses and beacons: white ones, yellow ones, red ones, revolving ones—huge eyes, the eyes of ogres, spying on us, waiting impatiently for us to vanish. One of them in particular got on my nerves. It went out every thirty seconds and then flashed on again; it was really too eye-like, that one, with its lid drooping regularly over its fiery glance.

Now and then the Englishman would strike a match to look at his watch. After one of these time-checks he suddenly turned my way and, speaking over his daughters' heads, said to me with great gravity:

"I wish you a happy New Year, sir!"

It was midnight. I stretched my hand out toward him and he shook it. Then he said something in English and the whole family proceeded to sing "God Save the Queen," the song rising into the silent air and dissolving in the dark emptiness.

I felt like laughing but then I was gripped by a strange and mighty emotion. There was something sinister and beautiful in the singing of these doomed and shipwrecked people; it was more than a prayer, it was comparable to the ancient and sublime *Ave, Caesar, morituri te salutant.*

When they had sung their national anthem, I asked my neighbor whether she wouldn't sing by herself some ballad or hymn for me—just to take our thoughts off our agony. She agreed and her clear young voice flew out into the night. She was apparently singing something sad, because the notes were long-drawn-out and dropped slowly from her lips, quivering in the air over the waves like wounded birds.

Now the waves were growing and beating violently against our wreck. But I thought only of the girl's voice and of mermaids. If a boat had sailed close by us at that moment, what would the seamen have imagined? My tormented thoughts were getting lost in the maze of these images. A mermaid. . . .Well, wasn't she really a mermaid, this siren out of the sea who had kept me on board this worm-eaten ship and who, any moment now, was going to plunge with me into the waves?

Then suddenly, all five of us were flung across the deck and the *Marie-Joseph* rolled heavily onto her right flank and settled there. The English girl fell on top of me; I seized her in my arms and madly—without knowing what I was doing, without understanding what was happening, thinking that I was living the last second of my life—I covered her face, her cheek, her temple, her hair, with passionate kisses.

The ship suddenly came to a stop. And so did we.

The Englishman said: "Kate!" And the girl whom I was holding in my arms answered: "Yes?" and made a movement to free herself. I am sure that at that moment I would have given anything to have the ship split in two and be swallowed by the sea while I held her in my arms.

"I say, that was a bit like a seesaw, wasn't it? And I still have my three daughters, I see."

At one point, apparently, not seeing his oldest daughter, he had thought her lost.

I stood up slowly and suddenly noticed a moving light on the sea quite close to us. I called out and they answered. A boat had come out to look for us—the owner of the Dauphin hotel had anticipated the possibility of our being caught by the sea.

We were rescued. But I was filled with sadness. They picked us off our wreck and took us to Saint-Martin. The Englishman kept rubbing his hands and repeating:

"Now for a good supper! Ah, what a nice supper we'll have!"

We did have that supper. It wasn't very gay. I wished we were back on board the *Marie-Joseph*.

Next day we had to part and we left each other after many embraces and promises to write. Then they went back to Biarritz, and at the last moment, I almost followed them.

I was crazy. I was on the point of asking the little girl to marry me. And I am quite certain that if we had spent a week together, she would have become my wife. Ah, man is so weak sometimes, so difficult to understand!

Two years went by without my hearing a word from them. Then I received a letter from New York. She was married, she wrote. And since that letter, we have written to each other every year on January 1st—she tells me about her life, about her children, her sisters, but never about her husband! Why? Yes, why? And I, I only write to her about the *Marie-Joseph*. . . .

Well, I think now that she is the only woman I have ever loved—no, I mean, I ever could have loved. But who can tell? Life flows on and then, before you realize it, everything's gone. She must be a middle-aged woman now and I suppose I wouldn't even recognize her. . . . But, the girl, the one who crouched next to me on that wreck—ah, what a divine creature she was! She wrote me that her hair was turning gray, and oh God, how it hurt me! Ah, the sandy blond of her hair! No, my English girl doesn't exist anymore. How sad it is . . . all that!

[*L'Épave,* January 1, 1886]

VI

THE SUPERNATURAL

The Horla

May 8.—What a lovely day! I spent the whole morning lying in the grass in front of my house under the huge plane tree that covers, shelters, and shades it.

I love this region; I love living here, because it is here that I have my roots—those deep and delicate roots that tie a man to the soil where his ancestors were born and where they died, attach him to the things the people around there eat and think, to the local customs and the local dishes, to the local way of saying things and the intonations of the peasants, to the smells of the earth, of the villages, and of the very air.

I love the house in which I grew up. Beneath my windows, I can see the Seine flowing past my garden on the other side of the road, almost on my grounds—the great, broad Seine between Rouen and Le Havre, dotted with passing ships.

To my left is Rouen, the vast city of blue roofs under a myriad of pointed Gothic belfries. They are innumerable—some big, others fragile, dominated by the spire of the cathedral and full of bells that send their chimes out into the blue morning air, so that the breeze carries their gentle, distant iron burr all the way to me, now quieter, now louder, depending on whether the breeze is dozing or wide awake.

Ah, what a lovely morning it was!

Toward eleven o'clock, a long file of ships towed by a tug the size of a fly—moaning and groaning in its efforts, vomiting a thick stream of smoke—passed before my garden gate.

After two British schooners whose red ensigns fluttered in the breeze, came a magnificent Brazilian three-master, all white, spotlessly clean and shiny. I waved to it, I don't know why—probably just out of the sheer pleasure the ship gave me looking at it.

May 12.—I've been slightly feverish for several days. I feel a bit sick, or rather, I feel sad.

From where do those secret influences which turn our happiness into despair and our confidence into distress come? One would think they come from the air, the invisible air filled with unknowable Powers whose mysterious proximity affects us. I wake up full of joy, with a desire to sing in my throat. Why? Then I go down to the river and after a brief walk I return home depressed, as though some disaster were awaiting me there. Why? Was it a breath of cold air brushing against my skin that shook my nerves and brought despondency to my heart? Is it the shape of clouds or the color of the day or the ever-changing color of things that, passing before my eyes, troubles my thought? Who knows? Everything around us—everything we see without looking, everything we brush past without knowing, everything we touch without feeling, everything we meet without discerning—has swift, amazing, and inexplicable effects upon our sense organs and thence upon our ideas and our hearts themselves.

The mystery of the invisible is so deep! We are incapable of penetrating it with our miserable senses; with our eyes that can perceive neither what is too small nor what is too large, neither what is too close nor what is too far off, neither the inhabitants of a star nor those of a drop of water; with our ears that deceive us because they can only convey the vibrations in the air to us in the form of sounds—they are the fairies that perform the miracle of transforming that movement into sound and thanks to that metamorphosis they give birth to the music that makes the silent rhythmical movements of nature sing; with our noses, weaker than a dog's; with our palates that can hardly tell the age of a wine!

Ah, if we had other sense organs that would perform other miracles for us, who can tell how many more things we would discover around us?

May 16.—I am ill—no doubt about it. And I felt so well

this past month! I am feverish, terribly feverish; or rather, it's a nervous exasperation that makes my spirit just as sick as my body. I have a constant sensation of danger threatening me, an apprehension of disaster or of approaching death, a presentiment that is doubtless the result of an unknown disease sprouting in my blood and in my flesh.

May 18.—I've consulted my doctor, for I could no longer sleep. He found that my pulse was accelerated, my pupils dilated, my nerves taut, but that there were no other alarming symptoms. He prescribed showers and said I should take bromide of potassium.

May 25.—No change. My condition is really quite strange. As the evening draws near, I am seized by an unaccountable anguish. It is as though the night carried some horrible threat for me. I eat my dinner hurriedly and then I try to read. But I can't make out the words. I can only just make out the letters. Then I pace up and down my drawing room in the throes of a vague and irresistible fear—fear of sleep, fear of my bed.

I go into my bedroom at about two o'clock. As soon as I am inside, I turn the key twice and shoot the bolts. I am afraid. What of? Until now, I feared nothing. I open my closets, I look under my bed, I listen and listen. . . . What am I listening for? Isn't it strange that a simple fever, perhaps a minor disorder of the circulatory system, some irritation of a knot of nerves, a slight congestion or some minute perturbation in the functioning—so imperfect—of our living mechanism can turn the most cheerful of men into a morbid depressive and the bravest of them into a coward? Then I lie down and wait for sleep to come. I wait for it like a condemned man waiting for the executioner. I wait for it with horror, with my heart pounding and my legs trembling. My whole body jerks between the hot sheets until the moment when I suddenly fall into rest—I fall into it like a man falling into an abyss filled with stagnant water, to drown himself. I don't feel sleep coming on as I used to—this perfidious sleep has been sneaking around me somewhere, waiting to seize my head suddenly, to shut my eyes, to annihilate me.

I sleep—I sleep for a long time, two or three hours perhaps—then I am plunged into a dream, or rather a nightmare.

I am fully aware that I am lying in bed and am asleep. I feel it, I see it; but at the same time I also feel that someone comes close to me, looks at me, touches me, climbs onto my bed, kneels on my chest, seizes me by the throat, squeezes it—squeezes it with all his strength, trying to strangle me. I—I try to tear myself loose, although I am tied down by the horrible paralysis of dreams. I want to shout but I cannot; I want to move but I am quite unable to budge. Panting and out of breath, I strive to turn onto my side, to throw off the creature who is strangling me . . . I cannot!

Then suddenly I wake up, completely beside myself, drenched in sweat. I light the candle. I am all alone.

After this nightly crisis, I am at last able to sleep calmly until dawn.

June 2.—My state has further deteriorated. What is the matter with me? The bromide has no effect. Neither have the showers. In the afternoon, to tire my body which is already so exhausted, I went for a walk in the Roumare forest. I hoped that the fresh air, so light and sweet and full of the fragrance of grass and leaves, would pour new blood into my veins and bring a new flow of energy to my heart. I followed the wide trail used by hunters and then turned off into a narrow path leading toward La Bouille, a path that runs between two rows of huge, tall trees whose branches formed a thick green—almost black—roof between my head and the sky.

Suddenly a shudder ran down my back—not a shudder of cold, but a strange shudder of anguish.

I hastened my step, feeling ill at ease at being alone in the forest and frightened stupidly, without any reason, by my complete solitude. Then suddenly I had the impression that someone was following me, that someone was walking at my heels, very close, close enough to touch me. . . .

Abruptly I turned around. I was alone. I saw nothing behind me but the straight, narrow alley—empty, high-roofed, and depressingly deserted. And in front of me there ran a similar frightening alley.

I shut my eyes. Why? I began to spin on my heels—very, very fast, like a top. I almost fell. I opened my eyes. The trees were dancing, the ground was swaying. I had to sit down. And then, ah, my God, I didn't know which direction I had come from! A strange feeling! A strange, uncanny feeling! I no longer had any idea. I went in the direction that happened to be to my right and rejoined the hunters' trail I had come by.

June 3.—It has been an atrocious night. I'll go away for a few weeks. I suppose a little trip will do me good.

July 2.—I am going back. I am cured. Besides, I've had a

delightful trip. I've been to Mont Saint-Michel, where I had never been before.

What a sight when one approaches Avranches, as I did, toward the end of the day! The town stands on a hill and I was taken to the public park at the edge of it. I exclaimed in surprise. A boundless bay stretched out before me as far as the eye could see, between the two far-flung shores that dissolved in mist in the distance. And in the middle of that immense yellow bay, under the gold and luminescent sky, there rose amid the sands that strange, pointed mountain. The sun had just vanished and on the horizon, which was still aflame, loomed the outline of that fantastic rock with the eerie structure at its summit.

In the morning, at dawn, I went toward it. It was low tide as on the evening before, and as I approached, the strange abbey seemed to grow. After several hours of walking, I reached the huge rocky mass that bears the small fortified town topped by the large church. After going up a steep, narrow street, I entered the most magnificent Gothic house of God on this earth: It is as vast as a town, full of low halls crushed under the vaults and tall galleries supported by slender colonnades. I entered that gigantic jewel of granite which is as light as lacework, covered with towers and fragile belfries that are reached by winding staircases and that thrust into the blue sky of day and the black sky of night their bizarre, disheveled heads of chimeras, devils, mythical beasts, and monstrous flowers linked together by fine, ornamented arches.

When I reached the top I said to the monk who accompanied me:

"You must be very happy here, Father."

"It is," he said, "very windy here, sir."

Then we began to chat, watching the sea come up, running toward us and covering the sand with a plate of steel.

And the monk told me stories: old stories about the place, old legends, and more old legends. One of them struck my imagination.

The local people claim that voices can be heard on the sands at night and that the bleating of two goats comes from there—one very loud and deep, the other weaker and shrill. The skeptics say that it's nothing but the cries of seagulls that sometimes sound like a goat's bleat and sometimes like human voices. But fishermen who have been caught out at night swear that they have seen, roving on the tidelands around the little town that has sprung up there away from the rest of the world, an old shepherd—whose head no one has ever seen as it is covered by his coat—leading two goats behind him: a he-goat with a man's head and a she-goat topped by the head of a woman. Both have long white hair and they keep up a constant, quarrelsome conversation in an unknown language that they suddenly interrupt to bleat at the top of their voices.

"Do you believe all that?" I asked the monk.

"I'm not sure," he muttered.

"If," I said, "there were other creatures in the world than us, how could we have failed to find out about them all this time? How could it be that neither you nor I have ever come across any of them?"

"But do we," he replied, "see even one hundred-thousandth of the things that exist? Take, for instance, the wind, which is the greatest force in nature—a force capable of throwing men down, of making edifices collapse, of uprooting trees and turning the sea into mountains of water, of destroying cliffs and reducing ships to splinters—a force that kills, that roars, that moans. . . . Well, have you ever seen the wind? Can you see it? On the other hand, it does exist, doesn't it?"

This simple reasoning reduced me to silence. The man was wise, unless he was a fool. I couldn't be sure of either so I remained silent. I had often thought of what he had just said myself.

July 3.—I didn't sleep well. It's certainly due to the effect of the fever that is in the air around here, for my coachman suffers from the same trouble as I do. When I came in yesterday, I noticed how unusually pale he was. I asked him:

"What's wrong with you, Jean?"

"The trouble is I can no longer rest, sir. My nights are eating up my days. Since you left, sir, it's been pestering me like a curse."

The other servants are all right but I am afraid the curse may come down on me again.

July 4.—There's no doubt about it; the curse is upon me again. The old nightmares have returned. Last night I felt someone bending over me, putting his mouth against mine and draining my life out through my open lips. Yes, he was sucking at it like a leech. Then, satiated, he stood up; and I woke up so battered, broken, annihilated that I couldn't move. If this goes on for a few more days, I shall certainly go off on another trip.

July 5.—Have I lost my mind? The things that happened last night are so strange that I am at a loss when I think of them.

As I do every night, I bolted my door. Then, feeling thirsty, I drank half a glass of water, noticing by chance that my decanter was full up to the crystal stopper.

Then I lay down and plunged into one of those frightful sleeps from which, a couple of hours later, I was awakened by an even more frightening shock.

Just imagine to yourself a man who is asleep, who is stabbed in his sleep and who then wakes up with a knife in his lung—in agony, covered with blood, unable to breathe—who is about to die, and who doesn't understand a thing. . . . So now you have it.

Having finally regained my senses, I felt thirsty once again. I lit a candle and went over to the table where the decanter was. I picked it up and tilted it over my glass but nothing came out. It was empty, absolutely empty! At first I couldn't understand. Then it came upon me so violently that I had to sit down, or rather let myself collapse into a chair! At once, I leaped up and looked around. Then I sat down once more, full of puzzlement and fear at the sight of the transparent decanter. I had my eyes fixed on it, trying to guess what had happened. My hands were trembling. Someone must have drunk the water. But who? Me? It could only be me, for who else? . . . So I was a sleep-walker then; I was leading that mysterious double life that makes one wonder if there are two creatures in us or if some unknown invisible stranger controls our body when our own soul is somnolent, making our body obey his orders as it obeys us—better than it obeys us.

Ah, who could ever understand my abominable anguish! Who could understand the feelings of a sane, fully conscious and reasonable human being who is filled with fright as he stares through the glass of a decanter because some water seems to have disappeared from it while he was asleep! I remained sitting there until dawn, without daring to look at my bed.

July 6.—I am going mad. Someone has once again drunk all the water from my decanter while I was asleep, or rather it was I who drank it!

But was it me? Who else could it be? Ah, my God, I'm really going insane! Who will save me?

July 10.—I've made a surprising experiment. There's no doubt—I'm crazy! However. . . .

Before getting into bed on July 6th, I placed some wine, some milk, some water, and some strawberries on the table in my room.

Someone drank up—I drank up—all the water and a bit of the milk. The wine and strawberries remained untouched.

On July 7th, I repeated the experiment with the same results.

On July 8th, I omitted the water and the milk and found that nothing had been touched.

Finally, on the 9th, I placed only milk and water on the table but with the containers wrapped in white muslin cloths and the crystal stoppers tied with string. Then I rubbed my lips, my beard, and my hands with black lead and lay down.

The irresistible sleep caught me at once, to be followed soon by an atrocious awakening. I hadn't budged. There were no lead marks on my sheets. The muslin cloths around the bottles were still immaculate. Trembling in my anguish, I untied the strings. All the water and all the milk had been drunk. Oh, my God! . . .

I am leaving for Paris this very day.

July 12.—I am in Paris. I really must have been out of my mind these last few days! I must have been the victim of my feverish imagination, unless I really happen to be a sleepwalker or am under one of those known but as yet unexplained influences that are called suggestions. In any case, my state was verging on insanity when I left, but twenty-four hours in Paris have been enough to restore my common sense.

Yesterday, after going around and visiting friends, which was like letting fresh air into my soul, I finished my evening by going to the Théâtre Français. They were giving a play by Alexander Dumas, the younger, and the sharp and powerful wit of that man was sufficient to cure me completely. No doubt about it: solitude is dangerous for people with active imaginations. We need to have people around us who can think and talk. When we are alone for a long time, we fill the emptiness with phantoms.

I walked along the boulevards on the way back to my hotel in a very happy frame of mind. Elbowing my way through the crowds, I thought rather scornfully of my terrors and superstitions of the past week when I had convinced myself —yes, convinced myself!—that some unknown creature was living under my roof. Ah, what a frail thing our head is and how easily it gets overwhelmed and lost when it is faced with something that is beyond its comprehension!

Instead of simply saying: "I don't understand because I cannot see what causes it," we immediately start imagining all sorts of fearful mysteries with sinister supernatural forces behind them.

July 14.—The national holiday of the French Republic. I went walking in the streets. Flags and firecrackers still delight me as much as they did when I was a boy. Of course, I realize that it is quite idiotic to be gay on certain dates fixed by government decrees. People are a stupid flock, now idiotically docile and submissive, now fierce and rebellious. When they are told: "Enjoy yourselves!"—they go and enjoy themselves. When told: "Go and fight the people next door!"—they go and fight. After that, they're told: "Vote for the Republic!"—and they go and vote for the Republic.

Those in charge are also a bunch of fools, like the rest. Only instead of obeying other men, they obey "principles" that can also only be inane, sterile, and false just *because* they are "principles"—which implies that they are well-established, safe, and immutable notions in a world in which nothing can be taken for granted since both light and sound are nothing but illusions.

July 16.—Yesterday I encountered certain things that troubled me no end.

I had dinner with my cousin, Madame Sablé, whose husband commands the Seventy-sixth Regiment of Fusiliers stationed in Limoges. At my cousin's house I met two young ladies. One of them was the wife of Doctor Parent, who specializes in nervous disorders and in the extraordinary phenomena discovered recently through experiments in hypnosis and suggestion.

He told us at length about the fantastic results obtained by the English scientists and by the doctors of the Nancy Medical School.

The things he told us struck me as too bizarre and I declared that my doubts on the subject remained.

The doctor said that we were just about to break one of nature's most important secrets on this earth—for, of course, there are other much more important ones up there in the stars, he remarked. Ever since man has been thinking, ever since he has been able to articulate and note down his thoughts, he has felt a mystery surrounding him that his crude and primitive senses could not possibly penetrate. And so he has tried to use his intelligence to make up for the limitations of his senses. But while his intelligence remained at a primitive level, that obsession with invisible phenomena took the vulgar form of fear. Thence came the popular beliefs in the supernatural, the legends about wandering spirits, about fairies and gnomes, about ghosts and, perhaps, even the legend about God—for the notion of God as the working creator of the universe, such as He is presented by any existing religion, shows a very mediocre imagination and is one of the most stupid and unacceptable inventions of men's terrorized brain. Nothing is truer than Voltaire's quip: "God made man in His image, but man has returned the favor."

"But for a little more than a century," Doctor Parent said, "men have been sensing something new. Mesmer and some others have opened up for us an unexpected path of exploration, and in the past four or five years, we have really obtained surprising results."

My cousin, skeptical like me, was smiling. Doctor Parent said to her:

"Would you like me to try to put you to sleep, madame?"

"All right, go ahead."

She installed herself in an armchair and he looked fixedly at her, trying to hypnotize her. I suddenly felt a bit ill at ease, my heart beat fast, my throat was quite tense. I saw Madame Sablé's lids grow heavy, her mouth contract, her bosom heave.

Ten minutes later, she was asleep.

"Would you sit down behind her?" the doctor asked me.

I sat behind her. He put a visiting card into her hand and said:

"This is a mirror. What do you see in it?"

She answered:

"I see my cousin."

"What is he doing?"

"He is twisting his moustache."

"And what is he doing now?"

"He is pulling a photograph out of his pocket."

"Who is in that photograph?"

"He himself."

It was correct. That picture of me had been handed to me that very evening in my hotel.

"What does he look like in the picture?"

"He is standing up, holding his hat in his hand."

So she could see what was going on behind her as though the white piece of cardboard were a mirror.

Rather frightened, the young women were saying: "Enough, enough, enough!!!"

But the doctor gave her an order:

"You'll get up tomorrow morning at eight, you'll go to the hotel where your cousin is staying, and you'll beg him to lend you five thousand francs to give to your husband when he comes back from his trip."

Then he awakened her.

Walking back to my hotel, I mused about the curious scene I had witnessed and some doubts assailed me—not about the absolute and unquestionable good faith of my cousin, whom I had known like a sister ever since she was a child, but about whether there hadn't been some trickery on the doctor's part. Had he concealed a mirror in his hand and held it before the sleeping lady along with the visiting card? Professional magicians, after all, carry off infinitely more perplexing tricks than that, I thought.

Thereupon I entered my hotel room and went to bed. At half past eight in the morning I was awakened by my valet.

"It is Madame Sablé, monsieur," he announced. "She asks whether you could see her right away."

I dressed hurriedly and received her.

She sat down looking very embarrassed and keeping her eyes lowered. Without raising her veil, she said:

"I must ask you for a very important favor, Cousin."

"What is it, Cousin?"

"It is terribly embarrassing to have to say this, but I have no choice. I must have, I absolutely must have five thousand francs."

"Are you serious? You need five thousand francs? You?"

"Yes, me. . . . Or rather my husband. He has asked me to raise that amount."

I was so stupefied that I could only stammer. I began to wonder seriously whether she wasn't in league with the doctor to play a practical joke on me, whether it wasn't all a well-planned and well-rehearsed comedy.

But looking closely at her, all my doubts vanished. She was

trembling with emotion and the step she had taken was obviously very painful to her. I realized that sobs were rising in her throat.

I knew that she was very well off and I said:

"How can your husband possibly be short of five thousand francs? Please, just think for a moment. Are you sure he requested you to ask me for that amount?"

She hesitated for a few seconds as if searching hard for something in her memory, after which she answered:

"Yes . . . I am quite sure."

"Did he write to you?"

Again she hesitated, stopping to think. I could guess the tortured labor of her thoughts. She didn't know. All she knew was that she had to borrow five thousand francs for her husband. So she decided to lie:

"Yes, he wrote to me."

"When? You never even mentioned it yesterday."

"I got the letter this morning."

"Could you show it to me?"

"Oh no, I couldn't. . . . There were personal things in it. . . . Much too personal. . . . I burnt it."

"Then your husband must have debts."

Again she hesitated.

"I don't know," she mumbled in the end.

Then I said quite drily:

"The thing is, my dear Cousin, I don't have five thousand francs available just now."

She let out a pained cry and said beseechingly:

"Oh, please, please, I beg you, try to raise it. . . ."

She even clasped her hands as though she were praying. Her very voice was changed. She sobbed and stammered, completely subdued and dominated by the irresistible order she had received.

"Oh! Couldn't you, please . . . If you knew how miserable I am! . . . I must get the money today!"

I felt sorry for her.

"You'll receive the sum in the afternoon," I said. "I give you my word."

"Oh, thank you!" she exclaimed; "you're so kind, so kind!"

"But tell me," I said, "do you remember what happened yesterday at your house?"

"Of course I do."

"Do you remember being put to sleep by Doctor Parent?"

"Yes, I do."

"Well, he ordered you to come to me this morning and ask me for five thousand francs. And now you are obeying that suggestion."

She thought for a few moments, then replied:

"But since it's my husband who needs the money?"

For an hour I kept trying to convince her of the truth, but to no avail.

When she had gone I rushed off to see the doctor. He was about to go out. He listened to me with a smile and said:

"Well, do you believe me now?"

"How could I help believing?"

"Then let's go to your relative's house."

She was dozing in a chaise longue, exhausted. The doctor felt her pulse and looked at her for a few moments with his hand raised to the level of her eyes, which gradually closed under the pressure of that magnetic power. When she was asleep, the doctor said:

"Your husband does not need the five thousand francs any longer. So you will forget that you asked your cousin to lend you that sum and even if he mentions it to you, you will not understand."

Then he woke her up. I drew my wallet from my pocket:

"Here is what you asked me for, my dear Cousin," I said.

She showed such surprise that I didn't dare say more. And although I tried hard to recall that morning's scene to her, she vigorously denied it all, thought that I was pulling her leg, and finally almost lost her temper.

So there you have it! When I got back to my hotel, I was unable to eat my lunch, so shaken was I by that experience.

July 19.—Many people to whom I have told the story have laughed in my face. I no longer know what to think. The wise man says: "Maybe."

July 21.—I had dinner at Bougival, then spent my evening at the oarsmen's party. Everything, decidedly, depends on place and environment. To believe in supernatural forces on La Grenouillère Island would be the height of madness. . . . But on Mont Saint-Michel? Or in India? We are enormously influenced by our environment.

Next week I am going home.

July 30.—I have been home since yesterday. Everything is fine.

August 2.—Nothing new. The weather is superb. I spend my days watching the Seine flow by.

August 4.—Quarrels have broken out among my servants. They claim that someone goes around breaking glasses in the pantry at night. The butler accuses the cook and she accuses the washerwoman, who accuses the other two. Who is the culprit? The person who finds out will need a very subtle nose.

August 6.—This time I know I am not insane. I saw . . . I saw . . . I saw! There is no longer any doubt left in my mind. I saw! I am still frozen from it right down to my nails. . . . I am still scared to the marrow of my bones. I saw! . . .

At two o'clock I was strolling in the sun, in my rose arbor, in the garden alley where the autumn roses are beginning to bloom.

As I stopped to look at a *géant des batailles* which bore three magnificent flowers, I saw—I saw very distinctly—the stalk of one of the roses bend, as if a hand had pulled it down, and then break, as if it had been picked by a hand! Then the flower rose, describing a curve such as it would have followed if a hand had brought it to a mouth; and it remained hanging in thin air, all by itself, immobile, horrifying, a red splotch three steps from my eyes.

I plunged forward madly, trying to get hold of it. It was no longer there. It had vanished. Then I was seized by an unbounded rage directed against myself. It was not permissible for a reasonable and self-respecting man to have such hallucinations!

But was it really a hallucination? I turned to look for the stalk. I saw it right away. It was there on the bush, freshly broken, between the other two roses which had remained where they were.

I returned to the house completely dejected, for now I was certain—just as I am certain that day succeeds night—that there exists in my vicinity an invisible creature who lives on milk and water; who can touch things, pick them up and move them; who therefore possesses a material substance, although he cannot be apprehended by our senses; and who is now living under my roof. . . .

August 7.—I had a quiet night of sleep. He drank all the water in the decanter but didn't trouble me.

I wonder if I am mad. Walking in full sunlight along the river bank in the afternoon, I began to doubt my sanity. And these were not the vague doubts I had experienced before, but precise, absolute doubts. I've seen madmen and I have known some who remained intelligent, lucid—even perspicacious—in all except one particular point. They talk about everything with clarity, with flexibility, with depth; then suddenly, their thought, stumbling on the reef of their madness, breaks into pieces that scatter and sink in that awesome ocean—full of furious, leaping waves, of fogs and squalls—that is called Madness.

Certainly I would have thought myself mad had I not been fully conscious of my state, had I not been constantly sounding and analyzing myself with the utmost lucidity. So maybe I was just a reasoning victim of hallucinations. Something must have gone wrong inside my brain, something of the sort that today's physiologists are trying to explore and define. The disorder must have caused a profound gap in my ability to think logically. A similar phenomenon occurs when we dream, sending us through the most incredible phantasmagorias without causing us the least surprise, because our checking mechanism—our sense of control—is asleep, whereas our imagination is awake and at work. Might it not be that one of those imperceptible keys in my mental keyboard is paralyzed? Following certain accidents, people forget names or verbs or figures or just simply dates. The fact that every scrap of thought is located in some particular spot in the brain is well established today. So why should it be so surprising if my ability to control certain hallucinations is impaired at the moment?

I was thinking of this while walking along the bank. Sunlight was spread over the river and made the countryside perfectly enchanting, filling me with a love for life, for the swallows whose grace is such a treat to my eye, for the grass along the bank whose rustling so pleases my ears.

Gradually, however, I became unaccountably ill at ease. Some force, some occult force, was making me numb, trying to prevent me from going any farther, pushing me back. I felt the sort of painful urge to return to the house that one feels when he has left someone who is sick behind and suddenly has a foreboding that the sickness has taken a turn for the worse.

So I retraced my steps despite myself, certain that some piece of bad news was waiting for me at home in the form of a letter or a cable. There was nothing and I was more surprised and worried than if I'd once again had one of those fantastic visions.

August 8.—I have spent a horrible evening. He doesn't manifest himself directly anymore; but I feel he is here, next to me, watching me, staring at me, getting inside me, dominating me. And the very fact that he conceals himself and makes his constant invisible presence known to me by supernatural phenomena is the most sinister part of it.

Nevertheless I slept.

August 9.—Nothing, but I am afraid.

August 10.—Nothing, but what will happen tomorrow?

August 11.—Still nothing, but I can't remain in my house in such fear and with the thoughts that have slipped into my soul. I will go away.

August 12.—It's ten o'clock in the evening. All day I wanted to go away, but I couldn't. I wanted to exercise my freedom in this easy, simple way: go out, get into my carriage, and drive off to Rouen. I coudn't do it. Why?

August 13.—Certain diseases seem to break the springs of our physical being, to make the muscles flabby, to make the bones as soft as flesh and the flesh as liquid as water. I am experiencing the same thing in my mental being in a strange and saddening way. I have no strength left, no courage, no control over myself; I am even unable to exercise my will. I can no longer want anything. Someone else wills for me and I obey.

August 14.—I am lost! Someone has got hold of my soul and is ruling it. Someone is commanding every one of my acts, all my movements, all my thoughts. I am nothing anymore, nothing but an enslaved spectator, terrified of my every act. I want to go out. I can't. He doesn't wish me to, so trembling, I remain seated in the armchair where he has made me sit. I would like to just get up, just rise from my chair, to prove to myself that I am still the master of my body. I cannot do it! I am riveted to my seat and my seat is riveted to the floor and nothing can raise me from it.

Then suddenly I must—I must, I must—go to the other end of my garden, pick some strawberries there and eat them. And off I go. I pick the strawberries and eat them. Ah, my God, my God! Is he a god? If he is, please rescue me from him, free me! Forgive me! Have pity on me! Save me! Ah, how I am suffering! What torture! It's all so horrible!

August 15.—There is no doubt that this is the way my poor cousin was dominated by someone outside her when she came to borrow those five thousand francs from me. She was made subject to an outsider's will that had broken in on her like a second soul, like a dominating, parasitic soul. Is it the end of the world?

But who is this creature ruling over me? Who is this invisible, unknowable invader belonging to a supernatural race?

So invisible beings do exist! But then, how is it that since the creation of the world, they have never before made their presence felt as fully and clearly as in my case? I have never read anything that has the remotest resemblance to what is going on in my house. Ah, if only I could get out of it now, run away and never come back! I would be saved. But I can't.

August 16.—Today I managed to escape for a couple of hours, like a prisoner who finds the door of his cell open. I suddenly felt I was free and that he was far away. I ordered the carriage harnessed in great haste and I drove to Rouen. Oh, what a joy it was for me to order a human being to "go to Rouen" and see him obey me.

I had the coachman stop at the library and I asked there for Doctor Hermann Herestauss' treatise on secret inhabitants of the ancient and modern world.

But when I climbed back into the carriage and started to give the order: "To the railway station!" I heard myself shout—yes, not just say, but shout loud enough to make the passers-by stop and turn their heads: "Home!" and in overwhelming anguish, I collapsed on the cushions of my seat.

He had found me and got his hands on me again.

August 17.—Ah, what a night, what a night! Yet it would seem that it should be an occasion for satisfaction for me. Until one o'clock, I read. Hermann Herestauss, Doctor of Philosophy and of Theogony, has written a history of the manifestations of all the invisible creatures that roam around man or appear in his dreams. He describes their origins, the places where they appear, and the power they wield. But none of them resembles the force pursuing me. It would seem that ever since man has existed, he has had a foreboding—has been in great fear of the appearance of a new creature, stronger than himself, that would succeed him in the domination of the world—and feeling the creature's coming imminent and unable to guess the nature of his future master, man in his terror has generated a whole race of fantastic occult creatures and ghosts in his frightened brain.

Having read the book until one in the morning, I went to

sit by the open window to let the fresh breeze coming from the quiet darkness cool my brow and my ideas.

The weather was nice, neither too hot nor too cold. Ah, how much I would have loved that night in the old days!

There was no moon. Far away in the sky, the stars twinkled faintly. Who inhabits those worlds? What forms of life? What animated beings? What sort of animals and plants? The thinking beings of those worlds—what do they know that we do not? What can they do that we cannot? What things imperceptible to us can they see? Some day, perhaps, one of them will cross space, land on our earth, and try to conquer it—just as the Normans of old crossed the water to conquer and subdue weaker peoples.

We are so impotent, so helpless, so ignorant, so small on this speck of mud floating in a drop of water.

Musing thus, I dozed off under the fresh night breeze.

I slept for forty minutes or so. I opened my eyes and remained motionless. I had been awakened by some strange, vague feeling. At first, I noticed nothing. Then suddenly I thought I saw the page of the book I had left open turn over by itself. Not a breath of air had come through the window at that moment. Surprised, I waited. Forty minutes or so later, I saw—yes, I saw—another page turn over in the air, as if flicked over by a finger. My armchair was empty but I understood that he had installed himself in my place and was reading. I leaped up like an enraged beast in revolt and bent on tearing its tamer to pieces; I crossed the room to reach him, to seize him by the throat, to kill him. . . . But before I reached my armchair, it tumbled over as though he had jumped up to evade me. . . . My table jerked, my lamp fell and went out, and my window closed as if a burglar, taken by surprise, had leapt through it into the night, grabbing the frame as he went.

So he had taken to his heels. He had been frightened. He was afraid of me!

If so, perhaps tomorrow, or at least some day, I will be able to get hold of him and pound him with my fists and smash him against the ground! Why, doesn't it happen now and then that dogs turn on their masters and tear their throats out?

August 18.—I've been thinking all day long. Yes, I will obey him, comply with his every whim, follow all his commands, be humble, submissive, and cowardly. He is the stronger. But the hour will come. . . .

August 19.—I know, I know, I know everything now! This is what I've just read in *The World's Scientific Review:*

> A rather curious report has reached us from Rio de Janeiro. An epidemic of madness comparable to the contagious epidemics of insanity that struck the peoples of Europe in the Middle Ages is raging at present in São Paolo Province. The panic-stricken inhabitants are deserting their homes and villages, claiming that they are being pursued, possessed, and controlled—as if they were human cattle—by invisible although tangible creatures: some sort of vampire which feeds on their lives when they are asleep and which, besides, drinks milk and water but touches no other food.
>
> Dr. Pedro Henriquez, accompanied by several other medical authorities, has left for São Paolo Province to study the origins and manifestations of this strange wave of madness on the spot and to suggest to the Emperor whatever measures he considers necessary to restore the sanity of the delirious population.

Ah, yes. I remember very well that beautiful Brazilian three-master that passed before my windows on May 8th! I found it so pretty, so white, so pleasing! It had the Creature on board. It came from the land where his race originates. He saw me. He saw my house, that was also white, and he jumped ashore from the ship! Ah, my God!

Now I know—I can see it: The rule of man has come to an end.

He has come, the being awaited in terror by primitive peoples! He is the being exorcised by worried priests, summoned by witches in the darkness of the night—although, even so, they never saw him; the being to whom the forebodings of the temporary masters of the earth have attributed all possible shapes, monstrous and graceful—the shapes of gnomes, of spirits, of genies, and what not. Then, after the crude notions of the primitives, the more perspicacious among men pictured him more accurately. Mesmer got an idea of him, and during the last ten years, the doctors have established the nature of his power quite reliably, even before he made use of it himself. They have played with the weapon of the new lord of the universe: the subjugation of the human soul to a mysterious willpower, thereby turning it into a slave. They have called it magnetism, hypnotism, suggestion, and what not. . . . I have seen them playing like irresponsible little children with that terrifying power! Woe to us, woe to man! He has come, the one . . . what is he called? . . . The . . . It seems to me that he is shouting his name to me but I can't hear him. . . . The . . . yes, he is shouting it. . . . I am listening. . . . I can't . . . repeat . . . the . . . Horla . . . I've got it—the Horla, that's it! The Horla has come!

Ah! The vulture ate the dove; the wolf ate the lamb; the lion devoured the buffalo, pointed horns and all. Man, using bow and arrows, sword and gunpowder, killed the lion. But now, the Horla will do to man what we have done to the horse and the ox: he will make a slave and a source of food out of man by using his superior will. Woe to us!

But then, sometimes it happens that the animal rebels and kills the man who has tamed it. I too, I want to, I'll be able to. . . .

But for that I must know him, touch him, have a look at him! Scientists say that an animal's eye is different from ours, that it does not see as ours does. . . . Yes, and in the same way, my eye cannot see the new oppressor.

Why? Oh, I remember so well now the words of the monk of Saint-Michel:

"Do we see even one hundred-thousandth of the things that exist? Take, for instance, the wind, which is the greatest force in nature, a force capable of throwing man down, of making edifices collapse, of uprooting trees and turning the sea into mountains of water, of destroying cliffs and reducing ships to splinters—a force that kills, that roars, that moans. . . . Well, have you ever seen the wind? Can you see it? On the other hand, it does exist, doesn't it?"

And I also thought: my eye is weak. It is so imperfect that it cannot even make out solids if they happen to be transparent, like glass. If a sheet of glass without a stain on it happened to be in my way, I might try to pass through it, just as a bird caught in a room ends by breaking its skull against the window pane. And there are thousands of other things that deceive and mislead the eye. So why be surprised if it cannot perceive an unfamiliar, transparent body?

A new creature! And why not? Surely he was bound to come, for why should man be the ultimate creature? Why can't we see him, as we see all the creatures that were created before us? Well, it's because he is more perfect than we are; his organism is of a finer essence than our weak, clumsily designed bodies encumbered by organs that are always tired, strained like taut springs, and much too complicated. Our bodies live like plants and beasts, feeding painfully on air, on grass, and on meat. Living mechanisms exposed to disease, deformation, and disintegration, they are nothing but the crude sketch of some being who could become intelligent and superb.

There are already quite a few of us in this world, from the oyster to man. Why not one more, once the time-span necessary for the appearance of a new species has elapsed?

Why not one more? Why shouldn't there appear new trees, too, with gigantic, dazzling flowers that would perfume whole regions? Why shouldn't there be other elements besides fire, air, earth, and water? There are four, only four, of them. Only four father-elements to feed all creatures! What a shame! Why aren't there forty, four hundred, four thousand? Isn't it all poor, petty, miserable, meanly dealt out, designed without inspiration, awkwardly put together? Ah, the elephant or the hippopotamus—what grace! The camel—how elegant!

But, you may say, the butterfly, the flower that flies! I have dreamed of one that would be the size of a hundred universes, with wings whose shape, beauty, color, and movements I would not even be able to apprehend. But I can see it. It flies from star to star, bringing them freshness and the fragrance of the light and harmonious breath it leaves in its wake. . . . And the inhabitants of those worlds up there watch it with delight! . . . What's the matter with me? It's he, the Horla, who is haunting me, who is making me think up all these crazy things! He is within me, he is taking over my soul. I will kill him!

August 19.—I will kill him! I have seen him. I sat down at my desk yesterday, pretending to be completely absorbed in what I was writing. I knew very well that he would come and hang around me, come very, very close. Perhaps he would come close enough for me to reach him, to grab him? And then! . . . Then with the strength of despair, I would use my hands, my knees, my chest, my forehead, my teeth—to strangle him, crush him, bite him, tear him to pieces.

And so all my overexcited sense organs were lying in wait for him.

I had lighted both my lamps and, on top of that, the eight candles on my mantelpiece, as if hoping to detect him somehow in all that light.

In front of me stood my old bed with its oak posts; the

mantelpiece was to my right; to my left was the tightly locked door that I had left open for a long while before in order to lure him in; behind my back was the tall mirrored wardrobe in front of which I usually shave and dress and into which I have the habit of looking every time I pass by.

I pretended to be writing in order to catch him off balance, for I knew he was observing me, too, when I suddenly felt—I was certain—that he was reading over my shoulder, that he was close by my ear.

I rose with my hands outstretched, turning so quickly that I almost lost my balance and fell. . . . Well, with all the lights on, I could see as clearly as in full daylight, yet I couldn't see my reflection in the mirror—it was empty, clear, deep, just filled with bright light. I was facing it, but my reflection wasn't there! I stared into the glass with bewildered eyes. I didn't dare to move, although I felt he was right there. I knew he would escape me again, he whose imperceptible body had devoured my reflection.

I was so frightened! Then suddenly I began to make out my reflection at the bottom of the mirror, as if through a thick layer of water which seemed to flow from left to right; and with every second, it became clearer and clearer. Finally I could see my image as perfectly as I see it every time I look into the mirror.

I saw him! The terror of it has remained with me, and the very thought of it makes me shudder.

August 20.—How can I kill him if I can't catch up with him? With poison? But he is sure to see me adding it to the water, and anyway, do our poisons have any effect upon imperceptible bodies? No, I suppose not. Well, what am I to do then?

August 21.—I have summoned an ironsmith from Rouen and ordered iron shutters for my room, like those which some private residences in Paris have on the ground-floor windows to keep out would-be burglars. I have also ordered a door of the same type from him. I revealed myself as a coward but I couldn't care less!

September 10.—Hotel Continental, Rouen. It's done. . . . But is he dead? My soul is inside out after what I have seen.

Yesterday, after the ironsmith had put up the shutters and the iron door, I left them all wide open until midnight, although by that time it had grown quite cold.

Suddenly I felt he was there and I was seized by a mad joy. I got up slowly and paced the room for a long time so as to hide my intentions from him. Then I removed my shoes and, looking as casual as I could, put on my slippers. Then I closed the iron shutters, and walking nonchalantly over to the iron door, I double-locked it. Then I returned to the window, fastened it with a padlock, and put the key in my pocket.

Suddenly I realized that he was by my side and in a state of great agitation, that it was now his turn to be scared and that he was ordering me to open the door for him. I almost complied. I didn't really obey him. I opened the door a crack, holding on to it. I opened it a bit more, just enough to back out through it; and since I am very tall, my head grazed against the door frame. I was sure he couldn't have escaped and I locked him in—all by himself. How wonderful! He was in my hands! Then I tore downstairs, took my two drawing room oil lamps, and poured the oil onto the carpet, the furniture, and all over the place. Then I lit it and ran away, after double-locking the heavy entrance door.

I hid myself in my garden behind a group of laurel bushes. Ah, it took so long! Everything was black, silent, motionless; not a breeze stirred, not a star shone—only mountains of cloud that I couldn't see but that weighed so heavily on my heart.

I looked at my house and I waited. What a terribly long wait it was! I was beginning to think that the fire had gone out or that he had succeeded in putting it out, when one of the ground-floor windows caved in under the pressure and a big red and yellow flame—long, soft, and caressing—climbed up the white wall, embracing it from the ground to the roof. A gleam passed over the trees, the branches, and the leaves—and along with it, a shudder of fear. Birds woke up, a dog howled. It was as though day was breaking! Two more windows caved in and I saw that the whole lower part of my house was one monstrous bonfire.

Then there was a cry—a horrible, shrill, heartrending cry—a woman's cry which flew through the night; and two attic windows burst open. I had completely forgotten about my servants! I saw their faces distorted by fear and their arms waving in the air.

Horrified, I began running toward the village, screaming: "Help! Help! Fire!" I met some people who were already on their way to the house and I returned with them to see what was happening.

My whole house was now nothing but a horrible, magnificent bonfire, a monstrous bonfire burning human beings but in which he too was burning—he, my prisoner, the New Creature, the New Master, the Horla!

Suddenly the whole roof sank between the walls and the flames shot skyward like the flames from the crater of a volcano.

Through the windows filled with the blaze, I looked into the fiery furnace, thinking that he was in there, dead now.

Dead? Maybe. Unless that body of his, that let light through it, could not be destroyed by means that would destroy our bodies.

If he wasn't dead, perhaps time was the only thing that could affect the terrible, invisible creature. Was that transparent, unknowable body—the body of a ghost—subject to pain, wounds, infirmities, and the premature destruction to which our bodies are subject?

Premature destruction? All human terror stems from that! After man, the Horla. After the creature who may die any day, any hour, any minute, through any accident, has come a creature who can die only on his day, at his minute, because he has reached the limit of his existence.

No, no, there is no doubt, not the slightest doubt. . . . He isn't dead. Then . . . then . . . then I shall have to kill myself.

[*Le Horla,* May 1887]

The Wolf

The old Marquis d'Arville told us this story after a dinner at Baron des Ravels' celebrating the feast of St. Hubert, the patron of hunters.

That day they had run down a stag. The marquis, who never hunted, was the only guest who had not taken part in the day's hunt.

During the whole of dinner, they spoke of nothing but the massacre of beasts. Even the ladies took an interest in the gory and often incredible tales told in thunderous voices with tremendous gesticulations.

D'Arville spoke well, and there was in what he said a good deal of poetry; it was perhaps a bit flowery but quite effective. He must have told the story often before because it flowed very smoothly and the words were skillfully chosen to give a strong picture of what had happened.

~

I have never hunted myself, nor did my father or my grandfather or my great-grandfather. But *his* father was a man who hunted more than any of you gentlemen. He died in 1764. Let me tell you how he died.

His name was Jean; he was married and had a son who was to become my great-grandfather; and he lived with his younger brother, Francis d'Arville, who loved hunting too much even to get married, in our château in Lorraine which stands in the middle of the forest.

The two brothers hunted from one end of the year to the other, without rest or letup. It was the only thing they loved and understood. They lived for it and never spoke of anything else. Hunting was an all-absorbing passion with them; it burned them, consumed them, leaving no room for any other interests.

No one was allowed to disturb them under any pretext while they were out hunting. My great-grandfather was born while his father and uncle were chasing a fox, and when informed, my forebear shouted, without halting his horse:

"Ah, damn him, the little beggar! He could at least have waited until we were through!"

Francis, his brother, seemed even more fanatical about hunting than he. As soon as he was up in the morning he would go to inspect the hounds and then the horses; then he would take a few shots at the birds around the château just to while away the time until they went out to follow some big game.

They called them, in our district, Monsieur le Marquis and Monsieur le Cadet. In those days the nobility made no attempt to establish a descending order of titles as do many of the makeshift aristocrats of today; for, in reality, the son of a marquis is no more a count, or the son of a viscount, a baron, than the son of a general is a colonel by birth. But then, the petty vanity of the present day finds advantage in this arrangement.

But let me get back to my great-grandfather and great-granduncle. They were, I gather, exceptionally tall, big-boned, hairy, violent, and strong. The younger, even bigger than his brother, had a voice so powerful that according to a legend in which he himself took pride all the leaves in the forest shook when he let out one of his big yells. And when the brothers rode out to hunt, it must have been a great sight to see the two giants astride their big horses.

Now it so happened that toward the middle of the winter of 1764 the weather turned exceptionally cold, which caused the wolves to become desperate and ferocious. At night they even attacked isolated peasants, and they roved around the houses between sunset and sunrise howling and wreaking havoc in the farmyards.

Soon a rumor spread. People spoke of a huge wolf with a light gray, almost-white coat who had devoured two children, ripped off a woman's arm, torn the throats of all the watch-dogs in the area, and who penetrated fearlessly into fenced-off farmyards and sniffed at the doors of the houses. All the local inhabitants claimed to have felt the beast's breath, a breath that made the light flicker. In no time panic spread throughout the whole province. No one dared go out after dark because the shadows seemed to be haunted by the shape of the beast.

The d'Arville brothers then resolved to find the beast and to kill it, and they invited all the neighboring nobility to a great hunting party.

It was in vain. They beat the forests and scoured the thickets without finding the beast. They killed wolves, but not that one.

And during the night following each such expedition, the beast, as if to avenge itself, would slay some farm animal—and always far from the place where they had been searching for it.

One night it broke into the pigsty of the Château d'Arville and killed two prize hogs.

The brothers were really angry now, viewing this attack as a provocation on the part of the monster, as an insult and a direct challenge. So they gathered their strongest hounds, which were well accustomed to pursuing large and dangerous game, and with fury in their hearts, they set out to run down the wolf. From dawn until the hour when the purplish sun descended behind the tall, bare trees, they beat the forest without finding a thing.

Then, as they were riding home at a walking pace along a brushwood-bordered path, furious in their frustration, they began to voice their stupefaction at the way the beast had managed to thwart all their hunting ruses, and a mysterious awe suddenly filled their hearts. The older brother said:

"That wolf is no ordinary beast. He seems to think rather like a man."

The younger brother suggested:

"Well, perhaps we ought to have a bullet blessed by our cousin the bishop or ask some priest to say whatever words are necessary."

They were silent for a while and then Jean spoke again:

"Look at the sun, Francis, see how red it is? The big wolf will cause some mischief tonight."

No sooner had he uttered these words than his horse reared, while Francis's started kicking wildly. A thick bush covered with dead leaves seemed to open up suddenly in front of them and a huge, light-gray beast leaped out and dashed off through the wood.

Letting out a sort of joyful growl, the brothers bent over the necks of their big, heavy horses and practically threw themselves forward, urging the animals on with shouts, gestures, and spurs; it looked as if the powerful riders had caught their heavy mounts between their thighs and were flying through the air with them.

Thus they rode at breathtaking speed, crashing through thickets, up and down ravines, climbing steep hills, hurtling down slopes, blowing their horns madly to summon their men and their dogs to join the hunt.

Suddenly, during this frantic pursuit, my great-grandfather struck his head against a huge branch. His skull was cracked and he fell dead, while his crazed horse vanished in the darkness among the trees.

The younger d'Arville stopped short, jumped down from his horse, and saw that his brother's brains were running out of the wound along with the blood.

He sat next to the body, placed the disfigured, red head on his knees, and waited there, staring at his brother's motionless features. And gradually, fear came over him, a strange fear such as he had never experienced before: fear of the darkness, fear of being alone, fear of the deserted forest, and also fear of the eerie wolf who had just killed his older brother to avenge itself on them.

The shadows thickened and a severe frost made the trees crack. Francis stood up, shuddering; he couldn't stay there any longer; he felt almost ready to faint. He could no longer hear either the baying of the hounds or the sounds of the hunting horns—everything was quiet in the invisible world around him. And this silence of the icy winter evening pressed upon him in a terrifying, uncanny way.

He picked the big body up in his giant's arms, laid it across the saddle, and set out slowly toward the château, his head unclear as if with too much to drink and full of horrible and weird visions.

Suddenly, down the path which was rapidly being erased by the night, there flitted a great shadow. It was the beast. A shudder of terror shook the hunter. Something cold, like a drop of water, slipped down his back, and like a monk besieged by the devil, he made a great sign of the cross, bewildered as he was by the sudden return of the horrible prowler. But then his eyes fell again on the dead body of his brother tied to the saddle in front of him, and shifting suddenly from fright to fury, he shook in uncontrolled rage.

He spurred his horse on and threw himself in pursuit of the wolf. He followed him through copses, across ravines, zigzagging among the ancient trees, crossing woods he had never been in before, his eyes glued on the whitish spot that was racing through the night, hugging the ground.

Francis's horse also seemed driven by an uncanny force and ardor: it galloped with its neck stretched out, straight ahead, so that the head and feet of the dead man thrown across the saddle banged against trees and rocks. The brambles tore the dead man's hair; his forehead, beating against the thick trunks, splattered them with blood; his spurs tore out great pieces of bark.

All of a sudden, just as the moon broke through a cloud, the horse and rider emerged from the forest and rushed down into a gorge. It was a stony gorge, blocked at one end by enormous rocks. There was no way out—the wolf was cornered and he turned around.

Francis then let out a howl of joy that the echoes caught up, making it sound like the rolling of thunder, and he jumped down from his horse.

The beast waited for him, its back arched, its coat bristling, its eyes gleaming like stars. But before joining in combat with it, the powerful huntsman grabbed his dead brother's body and sat it up on a rock, propping up with stones the head which was now no more than a bloody pulp and turning the face toward the wolf; then he hollered into the corpse's ear as one addresses a deaf man:

"Look, Jean, look!"

And he threw himself on the monster. Francis felt strong enough to topple a mountain, to crush stones with his bare hands. The wolf tried to sink its fangs into him, to tear his belly open, but Francis seized it by the throat and, without even using his knife, started strangling it—slowly, relentlessly, listening as the rattle in its throat weakened and its heartbeat dwindled. And he laughed madly, jubilantly, tightening his relentless grip harder and harder and shouting deliriously:

"Look, Jean, look!"

Then all resistance came to an end, the wolf's body went limp; it was dead.

Francis picked the wolf up in his arms, carried it over to

his brother's body, threw it down at his feet, and said in a gentle voice:

"Here, here, here, Jean, here it is, that animal."

After that, he placed the two corpses one on top of the other across his saddle and set out toward the château.

He arrived home laughing and crying like Gargantua when Pantagruel was born, yelling triumphantly and leaping about merrily as he told of the death of the beast, moaning and tearing his beard as he reported that of his brother.

And often, later, when he spoke of that night, he would say with his eyes full of tears:

"Ah, if only poor Jean had seen me strangle that beast, he'd have died happy, I'm sure."

My forebear's widow instilled in her orphaned son a horror of hunting, which since then has been transmitted from father to son, down to me.

The Marquis d'Arville fell silent. Then someone asked him:

"That's just a legend, isn't it?"

He answered:

"I swear that it all happened exactly as I've told you, from beginning to end."

Then a woman said in a soft little voice:

"Whatever it is, it is glorious to be so passionate."

[*Le Loup,* November 14, 1882]

SELECTED BIBLIOGRAPHY

OTHER WORKS BY MAUPASSANT

Une vie, 1883 Novel

Bel-Ami, 1885 Novel

Pierre et Jean, 1888 Novel

Fort comme la mort, 1889 Novel

Notre coeur, 1890 Novel

Contes de la bécasse, 1883 Stories

Contes et nouvelles, 1885 Stories

Contes du jour et de la nuit, 1885 Stories

Inutile beauté, 1890 Stories

SELECTED BIOGRAPHY AND CRITICISM

Artinian, A. *Maupassant Criticism in France* 1880-1940. New York: Kings Crown Press; London: Oxford University Press, 1941.

Boyd, E. A. *Guy de Maupassant.* Boston: Little, Brown & Co., 1926.

Jackson, S. *Guy de Maupassant.* London: Gerald Duckworth & Co., Ltd., 1938.

Kirkbride, R. de L. *The Private Life of Guy de Maupassant.* (rev. ed.) New York: Frederick Fell, Inc., 1947.

Lerner, Michel. *Maupassant.* New York: George Braziller, 1975.

Sherard, R. H. *Life, Work and Evil Fate of Guy de Maupassant.* New York: Brentano's, 1926; London: T. Werner Laurie, Ltd., 1929.

Steegmuller, Francis. *Maupassant: A Lion in the Path.* New York: Random House, Inc., 1949; London: William Collins Sons & Co., Ltd., 1950.

Sullivan, Edward D. *Maupassant the Novelist,* Princeton, New Jersey: Princeton University Press, 1954; London: Oxford University Press, 1955.

Wallace, Albert H. *Guy de Maupassant.* Twayne's Author Series Boston: Twayne Publishers, 1973.